Mark Bastable, the first son of a City copper and a home economist, was born in South London, just before Christmas 1958 – three months premature, according to the local Baptist minister's somewhat naïve calculations. He was educated at a local grammar school by teachers who couldn't figure out what it was about him that irritated them so.

Sometime in the mid-eighties, after an abortive sojourn in publishing, he discovered computer languages – and made a freelance career as a peripatetic nerd. Amsterdam, Boston, Barcelona, Stockholm – these are just some of the cities in the gutters of which Mark has woken up.

Back in Tooting now, Mark is the Director of a Management Consultancy, a contributor to *Esquire* magazine and also writes comedy for TV.

He has an eight-year-old son, Conor, who can't see why anyone would want to spend the afternoon writing a sleeve-note biography when they could be zapping aliens on the Playstation. Kid's got a point. Excuse me . . .

ICEBOX

Mark Bastable

HEADLINE

First published in 2000
by HEADLINE BOOK PUBLISHING

10 9 8 7 6 5 4 3 2 1

ISBN 0 7472 6839 8

Typeset by Palimpsest Book Production Limited,
Polmont, Stirlingshire
Printed and bound in Great Britain by
Mackays of Chatham plc, Chatham, Kent

HEADLINE BOOK PUBLISHING
A division of the Hodder Headline Group
338 Euston Road
LONDON NW1 3BH

www.headline.co.uk
www.hodderheadline.com

For my family

ACKNOWLEDGEMENTS

My thanks are due to Gerrie Van Noord, whose interest and enthusiasm sustained my own, even when I'd much rather have been out having a good time on the canals.

None of the science in this story is made up, I'm afraid. Most of it I found in *Great Mambo Chicken and the Transhuman Condition* by Ed Regis.

One dies only once, and it's for such a long time.
Molière

Merry and tragical! tedious and brief!
That is, hot ice and wondrous strange snow.
William Shakespeare

I would have waited all my life
For just a little death.
Declan MacManus

CHAPTER ONE

'. . . I WISH MY HEAD to be severed from my body at the earliest possible moment, ideally according to the instructions to be found in the plastic wallet worn around my neck – otherwise, by whatever method presents itself. THIS IS NO JOKE.'

The tattooist finished reading from the card in his hand and looked down at the man laid out on the table.

'You want this where, bud?'

The man tapped himself on the breastbone. 'Right here, in twelve-point Helvetica bold,' he said calmly.

The tattooist shrugged, and powered up his needle. 'You want a dotted line on the back of your neck, while I'm at it?'

CHAPTER TWO

THE CLEAVER FELL WITH a decisive thud and the fish's unblinking head was cleft from its body.

There was a shocked yelp.

'Oh, no. Don't do that!'

Unity strode over to Don and slapped the back of his wrist. She relieved him of both the cleaver and the chopping board, on which a doleful mackerel lay oozing.

'That's the *vegetable* board. The fish board is the *marble* one,' she said, pointing at it.

'The fish-shaped one,' Don observed. 'What diff?'

Unity slid the fish onto a paper towel, and began scrubbing the chopping board under running water. 'You never, *never* chop raw meat on the same board as vegetables. You might as well drink sewage.'

Don shrugged and went to the fridge for a beer. Unity took down the fish board and beheaded the second mackerel, wincing. She hated dead things. If she weren't so nervous of anaemia she'd become a veggie in a minute.

In the front room, Don slumped in front of a gameshow. On the bookshelf above the TV, a grotesque glove puppet of Margaret Thatcher lolled across a row of Virago paperbacks, and a Soviet poster showed sturdy representatives of the peasantry gazing steadfastly into a glorious future just above the Habitat paper lampshade. Unity had been a Brownie back when Jane Fonda was a Red, but the room attested that there was a small corner of W6 that would be forever Grosvenor Square.

After a few minutes, Don got to his feet and picked up three juggling balls from the windowsill. Every time he came here, he had a go at this. He tossed the balls in the air, and stepped back to catch the inevitable errant one. As he collided with a shelf, he felt something topple over his shoulder. He grasped for it as it clunked against the sideboard. It was a ten-inch porcelain Michelangelo's David. Or, now, a nine-inch porcelain headless David. Don froze, waiting for some reaction from the kitchen. When none came, he retrieved the head from under the sideboard and slotted the two pieces together. Then, very carefully, he put the whole thing back on its shelf, checking whether the join was apparent. It was almost invisible.

'Just here for the crack, Dave, huh?' he muttered, grinning. 'Makes two of us.'

When the meal was ready, Unity called Don through.

'Trays in front of the telly, or on the table like civilised human beings?' she asked, coaxing mangetouts onto the hexagonal plates.

'I'm easy.'

They sat at the pine table, and Don poured the white wine. 'Looks good,' he said, as she put the plate down. 'Sorry about the chopping board.'

'It's all right. How was work?' Unity asked.

'Well, you know what it was like Friday? It was like that. How 'bout you?'

'Casey's giving me grief. Budget restrictions. I don't mind the arguments – it's the aftershave that upsets me.'

'Uhuh. Did I leave a shirt here?'

'It's washed and ironed.'

'Cheers. You wearing stockings?'

'Could be.'

'Ah, the thrill of discovery . . . Oh, look. Eggs.' Don had cut open his headless mackerel to find it crammed to the truncated gills with roe.

Unity winced. 'Oh, Christ – sorry. Give it here. I'll ditch it. You can have mine – I'm not that hungry.'

Don poked the fish with his knife. 'It's okay. Isn't it supposed to be lucky? Or is it unlucky?'

Unity put a hand to her mouth as Don shovelled up a forkful. 'Don ... ugh ... oh, you couldn't – please.' He leered ghoulishly and raised the tumbling eggs to his lips. Unity pulled her brown fringe down over her eyes. 'I'm not watching this.'

'Ah, you may cover your eyes,' Don suggested, poking his tongue into the roe, 'but can you block out the screams of unborn mackerel grilled untimely in—'

Unity slammed a hand down on the table. 'Don! I mean it – shut up!' She picked up her wine glass and walked through to the lounge.

Don wrinkled his nose and looked up at the ceiling, shrugging.

'I've got to keep count of these weeks better.'

'Oh, Christ. Oh, Jesus. Oh, Mother of God.'

'How was that?' Unity smirked, sliding up the bed.

'A religious experience ...'

CHAPTER THREE

GABRIEL TODD LET OUT a slow breath as the tattooist straightened up and switched off the needle.

'There you go, bud. Should heal within a month.'

Gabriel nodded, peering down at his bloody chest. 'And finally,' he said, 'I'd like the name "Willie Rabblestack" tattooed on the inside of my lower lip.'

The tattooist snorted. *'Willie Rabblestack?'*

'Gotta problem there?' growled Willie Rabblestack from the corner.

It was twenty to twelve when the church clock by the roundabout, confident but mistaken, struck four. Casey Rushmore had been pontificating at the research team for a good half-hour and Unity's mind was wandering. She felt very over-addressed. She didn't have time for this. There was so much work to do. Research to be written up. Experiments to conduct. It was 6 September 1994. Jesus, she would be thirty-one next month. In actuarial terms, her life was – she did a quick sum on her notepad – forty-one point three per cent over, and she had achieved precisely damn all.

Out of the window, she could see the traffic coagulating on Hammersmith roundabout, like grease round the yolk of a sunnyside-up. A fug of bronchitis and asthma hung over the filthy griddle of the city. In LA, Unity had read, pedestrians wore protective masks in the street. What do you do – move to the country? Get radiation poisoning off the very rocks of Dartmoor? Suck lungsful of insecticides in Kent?

She shifted backwards in her chair to relieve the pain in her back, and glanced at her watch. She needed to be out of here by noon to make her doctor's appointment. Meanwhile, Casey was blatting on about annual expenditure again.

'. . . some of you on the research side seem to think that the corporation's funds are a bottomless pit. Well, I hate to be the bearer of bad tidings here, but that's not a practical reality in today's climate . . .'

Unity arched her spine and rotated her shoulders a little. Could be muscle strain. Could be some kind of tumour. She'd ask for a scan.

'However, it's worth remembering that in real terms the R&D budget of Splendid Corps has actually increased nine points across the last six fiscal quarters. I think that nixes any negative perception re the commitment to technological research in the European situation. Unity?'

Casey had mistaken Unity's lifted arm as an attempt to interrupt. She took advantage of the error.

'Casey, I'm no accountant, certainly. All I know is that I've produced a well-received paper, and I need money to experiment on the back of it. You're asking us for commercially-applicable results – and I'm offering you high-yield, giant-size root vegetables that do everything but rip off their skins and leap into the saucepan. If we don't develop this, someone else will.' She got to her feet and picked up her notebook. 'Now, you must all excuse me – I have an appointment.'

Hurrying out to the street, Unity tried not to inhale as she passed the little clutch of smokers gathered in the porch of Splendid Reach. She hailed a taxi on Hammersmith Bridge Road and asked for Harley Street. In the back of the cab, she rued her dismissive exit from the meeting. Casey was a pain but he wasn't the real problem. Nothing was *happening*. The entire corporation lacked vision – and vision was Unity's forte.

As a child of eight, she had fully expected that, before she left school, the human race would be living on foodstuffs cultivated in satellite gardens orbiting the Earth. When she'd joined Splendid Corps with an MA in biotechnology, she'd wanted to eradicate starvation by the end of the century. Ten years later, she was bickering over a measly three-million-pound research budget, and mankind had not raised so much as an extraterrestrial beansprout.

Not that it matters, she thought, flexing her shoulders as she walked up the steps to her doctor's office, when I've probably only got months to live.

It was a stock line of internal monologue – a morbid pessimism that had begun as a run-of-the-mill adolescent fantasy in which she was mourned by her guilt-sodden parents and peers. In adulthood, she tended to terrify herself not with the notion of dying, but of being dead. Of *not* being. The prospect of extinction would scuttle spiderlike into Unity's head, and she'd shriek, trap it under a glass, peer at it, magnified – in control of it, but unable either to squash it or to let it go. She had no comforting faith in any afterlife – she'd shucked all those homilies as a teenager. The nuns at the convent school, faced with this heresy, had misread Unity entirely. They'd assured her that God was calling, and that she must try hard to believe in Him.

But Unity had no trouble believing in God. On the contrary, she felt that human beings faced a terrible struggle *not* to. It would be so comforting to accept the existence of a caring, paternal Something – and if you wanted to construct an existence that encouraged such a hope, this fraught and fatal passage of days would be precisely what you came up with. But, Christ, what a waste of endeavour. What a frittering of creative vision. You had to work harder than that. You had to unwind the swaddling clothes of primitive superstition, coil by painstaking coil, until you stood naked in the cosmic gale – and then you could clothe yourself with the thin but honest hospital gown of science. And that meant, of course, that one day you would be quite dead.

On a holiday in Brighton, when she was ten, she had stepped on some broken glass on the beach and sliced the underside of her little toe. It wasn't serious, but it had made walking painful. When she complained, her mother had said, 'Try not to think about it, dear.' No doctor, no stitches, no antiseptic. Just a wipe with a tissue and *try not to think about it.*

Unity's mother had suffered dreadfully with haemorrhoids, but she wouldn't go to their GP. 'It's just one of those things – there's nothing they can do.' Varicose veins? 'Everybody has them.' Arthritis? 'You just learn to cope.'

Unity didn't accept this. *Why* should you learn to cope? The graveyards were stiff with the headstones of people who had learned to cope with a strange lump here, a flaky patch of skin there, an irritating little cough. What was science for, if not to save you?

'I'm Ms Siddorn,' she said to the receptionist. 'I have a twelve forty-five appointment with Dr Meddows.'

'If you'd just like to take a seat, the doctor will see you in a few minutes.'

She flicked through *The Lancet*, listening to the pitiless tick of the carriage clock on the mantel. It was ten to one, and the aches in each of her shoulders had joined up, lying now like a weight across her spine. In her mind's eye, she could see the tumour growing, exponentially, like rice on the squares of a chessboard. Three minutes to, and she could feel it protruding from her back – a malevolent quasi-Quasimodo hump.

She walked over to the desk. 'Look, excuse me. I'm on a very tight schedule here. I have to be back at work at half past.'

The door to the consulting room opened and a middle-aged man emerged, shrugging on his jacket. A box on the receptionist's desk buzzed and Unity was told to go through.

Dr Meddows was a cheerful, stockbrokerish man in a waistcoat. Unity had been going to him for three years.

'Hello, Unity. Take a seat. Lovely day, isn't it? Glad to see the back of all that rain.'

At seventy-five guineas a throw, Unity had no time for pleasantries.

She told him about the pain in her back. Not a pain on the surface, she explained precisely, but a deep pain, right inside her shoulders. Also, she'd noticed an increasing shortness of breath. It was keeping her awake at night.

The doctor prodded and tapped and listened, front and back. Having felt around her bristleless armpits and pressed his fingers into her Body-Shopped throat, he announced that she had lungs of Lutine clarity and a heart that could pump bilge from a Polaris.

'Still working at the same place?' he asked, taking his seat as she rebuttoned her blouse.

'Don't,' she told him curtly.

'I'm sorry?'

'I'm working hard, but not excessively. I'm getting regular sex and I have no problem with my boyfriend. My biological clock is keeping good but unobtrusive time. So don't tell me that I'm just suffering from stress.'

Dr Meddows laced his fingers under his chin and looked at her across the desk. 'Had a bit of a sniffle recently?' he asked.

Unity thought about it. 'Yes, actually. I've been sneezing a lot.'

Dr Meddows sighed and shook his head. 'Just as I thought,' he said. 'Can't rule out cancer . . .'

'Cricket's a ghastly game,' Don was saying to his colleague, as the phone rang. 'It manages to be simultaneously boring and dangerous – a combination you wouldn't have thought possible in a sport.' He put down his sandwich and picked up the receiver. 'Checkpoint. Oh, hi.'

'Well, he doesn't suspect cancer,' Unity said. 'Tension, he reckons.'

'That's a load off my mind. I was worried sick,' Don replied, deadpan.

'It's not funny, Don. Not since the cervical thing.'

Don nodded. 'Sorry. But you don't sound overjoyed.'

'I've *got* to get out of this job. I think I'll stay on for the America trip and then . . . I don't know.'

'We'll talk about it on the weekend. I'll come round Friday night, eh?'

'Yeah.' There was a pause, and then Unity brightened up suddenly. 'Hey, I've come up with a great one for the weekend. *Sea of Love.*'

'Uh?'

'*Sea of Love.* Al Pacino and—'

'Oh, yes!'

'I'll see you in the 7-Eleven on the corner at, what, eight thirty?'

'I'll be there,' Don grinned. 'See you . . .'

From his desk opposite, Don's colleague Spotty George had been listening to the phone conversation. As Don hung up, George said, 'That's the old lady, yeah?'

Don nodded, still smiling.

'Whass she like then, Donny – your bird?'

Don took another bite from his sandwich. 'I've *told* you about calling me Donny.'

'Sorry.' George leaned forward in his seat, the light playing psychedelically across his acne. 'Whass she look like an' that?'

Don leaned back. 'Five foot two. Eyes of blue. Wears little square glasses.' George was nodding eager encouragement. 'Size four feet,' Don revealed, helpfully.

'What I mean is,' George smirked, forming his hands into upturned claws at chest level, 'has she gotta lot of, er . . . ?'

'Just the standard-issue two, George,' Don said, getting to his feet. 'Do you want a coffee?'

He wandered through the open-plan to the coffee machine for a number eighteen. As it was spluttering into the cup, a girl came up and stood a little behind him, waiting her turn. Don glanced at her. He guessed her at twenty-one, maybe a little older. Her skin was white and clear as the truth, and her hair was thick and black as scandal. Her iced-jade eyes were staring blankly at the hatch where Don's cup was filling.

Don nodded and smiled. 'Don't touch the cola,' he suggested as he took his coffee. 'It's always flat.'

She looked at him expressionlessly, and then pressed the button for tea, turning her back.

'And welcome to the company,' he muttered as he walked away.

He went back to his desk and scanned the selection of books that occupied his time while he waited for the phone to ring. He picked up *The Dictionary of Troublesome Words* and opened it at random. He loved stuff like this – and, to his unceasing delight, he was paid to love it. After ten years drifting around, hauling hod loads of bricks and supplementing his income by winning pub quizzes, he'd found a job that actually required him to acquire arcane facts.

Don was Senior Information Consultant at Checkpoint, a bureau for the dissemination of trivia. The public would call a premium-rate number and ask any question they wished – to settle a pub bet, or prove their boyfriend wrong – and Don would quote chapter and verse from the relevant authority. He sat in front of a terminal that gave him access to a vast database of factual flotsam, but he considered it a small victory whenever he could resolve a query without opening a book or laying a finger on the keyboard. Indeed, as he logged the caller's query and his resolution of it, he also noted what source material he'd consulted, to review his performance and identify areas in need of improvement.

He was aware that there were subjects in which he was weak. Sport, for instance, tended to defeat him, which was why he had recruited Spotty George, whose supernatural charmlessness was balanced, in professional terms, by his obsessive interest in run totals and unlikely sending-offs. Don himself was second to none when it came to etymology, English pub names, popular music (post Bill Haley), and – his speciality – British Army regiments (their campaigns and uniforms).

Don would have considered it crass to suggest that he *loved* his job, but he certainly didn't mind getting up in the mornings. He considered himself the intellectual equivalent of a sex chat line, giving telephonic satisfaction to the desperate and intrigued. The only difference, as far as he could see, was that he got off on doing it – which was more than one could say, probably, for Sexy Susan and Moist Mandy. He assumed that the premium-rate line that he picked up every day made enough money to pay him, and George, and the others who worked at Checkpoint. In truth, he'd vastly over-estimated the revenue generated. Checkpoint cost its parent company about a million pounds a year.

And it was worth every penny.

In his office, an hour after his acrimonious meeting with the research staff, Casey Rushmore checked all the material he'd prepared for a presentation to his boss. He had overheads, a wallet of water-soluble markers, his pen that turned into a telescopic board-pointer and copious highlighted notes. Lastly, his own innovation, he had a stylised 'route map' of the presentation, which could tell him at a glance what milestones he should have reached at any time within his allotted half-hour.

Asked to describe himself in a phrase, Casey would have said *thoroughly thorough* – pronouncing the word, American style, to rhyme with 'morrow'.

Allowing ten minutes for the journey, he took the elevator three floors to the executive conference room, where he laid out his props. He switched on the overhead projector and adjusted the focus, using a slide of geometric patterns that he had prepared specifically for that purpose. He walked to the far end of the room and checked for visibility, then came back to the front and altered the ambient lighting. Satisfied, he took a seat near the top of the long table and checked his watch, tugging the crease of his trousers so that it ran directly over the crown of his knee. He looked at his watch again. He got up and walked over to the desk, unstrapped the watch, and laid it beside the coloured markers. He sat down in the chair behind the desk and waited.

A minute later, the door burst open and the room was suddenly crammed to the rafters with Robert Spleen, Chief Executive Officer of Splendid Corps. He looked like a lion in a Brook Brothers suit – a powerful, rippling creature with huge paws and a soft, dangerous mouth. Even the furniture seemed impressed. The chairs all straightened their backs and the table shuffled its feet into line. Spleen bore down on a chair, and it appeared to leap back in momentary panic, before sliding deferentially beneath the descending leonine behind.

'Casey – what have you got to say for yourself, old fellow?' rumbled the company's founder, with the warm briskness of a corporate Aslan.

Casey was standing to attention, quivering like an arrow that had just that second arrived. He flicked on his overhead.

'Good day, Mr Spleen,' he said.

'As far as I'm aware,' Spleen acknowledged, not unkindly. 'You bring me tidings of a "venture capital opportunity", so I understand.'

'I think it's the most exciting technological development of the decade, Mr Spleen,' Casey assured him.

'"Exciting" was indeed the adjective you over-used in your memo,' Spleen nodded. 'So – excite me, Mr Rushmore.'

Casey leaned forward and set the timer feature on his watch. It began to count down from 00:30:00.

'About three weeks ago, I came across a paper by an American research scientist – Dr Gabriel Todd. It is a proposed approach to the construction and use of microscopic robots. I must stress that Todd is no crackpot. He is well-respected in the area of, uh, forward-looking scientific applications. Over the next thirty minutes, I hope to convince you, sir, that Todd's ideas, and his practical plans for those ideas, represent a potential growth-and-investment area for the company in the coming . . .'

Spleen took a pack of M&Ms out of his inside pocket and tipped a couple into his hand. 'Get down to the bump and grind, Casey,' he said, palming the sweets into his mouth.

'Well, bear with me, sir,' the Senior Finance Controller coaxed. 'I have prepared some explanatory material here, which—'

'How many times have I told you, Casey?' Spleen interrupted. His tone was mellow but incontrovertible. 'It's the *idea*, the *idea* that matters. All the rest one can make up as one goes along. So, in words intelligible to a simple man such as myself, what's the big idea?'

Crestfallen but unsurprised, Casey looked down at his notes. 'You wouldn't just like to see the graphs?' he asked.

'I'm sure they would defeat me,' Spleen lied. 'I'll settle for verbal *son-et-lumière*.'

Casey sighed, flicked off the power on the projector, and raised his eyes to regard his boss. 'Okay, this is what Todd proposes.' He put his hands out and mimed the act of building. 'With your hands in a pair of computerised gloves, you make a half-scale pair of robot hands. The computer remembers how you did it, and gets the new little hands to make an even smaller set of hands. These make an even tinier pair, and so on. Then you go back to the full-size gloves and make a robot, and the computer teaches the tiny hands how to do *that* too! You could have tinier and tinier hands making teenier and teenier robots. Theoretically, you could end up manipulating matter *on a molecular scale*. You can construct any substance you want by building it out of *atoms*!' Casey paused, and looked eagerly towards his employer. 'Imagine that, Mr Spleen!' he said.

Robert Spleen imagined that. He laced his fingers and imagined that very clearly indeed.

'*Theoretically*,' he pointed out.

Casey Rushmore held up the research paper on which he had based his presentation. 'The way he talks about it in here, I think Todd's gone way beyond speculation. Even if he hasn't, the next developments are already forming in his head.'

Spleen thumped his fist down on the desk. 'In that case,' he roared, '*bring me the head of Gabriel Todd!*'

Casey jerked back in surprise, clattering into the projector.

'Dear me, take that look off your face, Casey,' Spleen tutted resignedly. 'It's a joke. Simply offer the chap a job.'

CHAPTER FOUR

GABRIEL TODD AND WILLIE Rabblestack lived in an unruly clapboard house off Prospect Avenue in Cambridge, Massachusetts. The large, dark rooms seemed to flow into one another. The kitchen opened out onto the lounge, which led through to the music room, whence the stairs led up to the study, from which you could walk straight through foldback doors to the main bedroom. The delineations of day-to-day life were blurred.

The decor was similarly inexact. Although the stairs were lined with Willie's gold discs, and the kitchen boasted several of Gabriel's entertaining little inventions, there was no theme to the place. One design of wallpaper would peter out and another gain dominance not at any natural break in the architecture, but apparently whenever the decorator had got bored. Mounted on the walls at irregular intervals were Bakelite household gadgets – a hairdryer, a phone handset – interspersed with shelves of cheap wind-up toys – an ugly little pugilist, a plastic King Kong, a hopping BigMac. If there was a leitmotif, it was the Buffalo Bills – pendants, football jerseys, photos of the team. Overhead in the stairwell, a mannequin in full kit was suspended from the ceiling, apparently diving over the upstairs banister with the ol' pigskin held at full stretch. From the upper landing, one could read the name on the back of the shirt – *Todd*.

Gabriel Todd had been the only member of his college football team who was not on a sports scholarship. In fact, he majored in applied physics, with a minor in twentieth-century poetry. Yet he was the most talented wide-receiver that ever graced BecTech, and for two seasons he played in

17

every game, barring those that clashed with rallies of the Pontiac Owners' Club. Gabriel qualified for the team by dint of a superb six-foot frame and a pair of hands as safe as bonds in the bank. But he also brought to the game, as he brought to all his interests, clear-eyed enthusiasm and a ravenous desire to learn. In order to improve as a wide-receiver, Gabriel read everything he could find on the subjects of: team psychology; aerodynamics; tribal ritual; the cultivation of grass; and the meteorological statistics of the Eastern seaboard. He soaked the stuff up.

Teachers had often accused Gabriel of lacking concentration, but they were wrong. What he lacked was discrimination – he concentrated on whatever was in front of his nose.

'Nothing,' he would tell his students in later life, 'is really boring. It's like a fractal image – you just have to keep zooming in to the picture until you reach a level where your vision is filled with something beautiful and fascinating.'

He was drafted to the Buffalo Bills when he graduated, but quit within a year to take a job in robotics research at MIT. After a hard day designing pancake-tossing automata, he would relax by teaching himself to play pedal-steel guitar. It was this interest that led him to meet Willie Rabblestack, at a roadhouse in Billerica, Mass.

At that time, Willie was a no-account wheat-whites singer from Del Harta, Texas. He was twenty-four, and he'd been on the road, one way or another, for nearly a decade. He was sharp, wry and totally without pretension. Gabe clocked him singing 'One Look in Your Eyes (And the South Gonna Rise)', and fell brilliant head over Cuban heels in love. Willie, for his part, was totally smitten by this broad, grinning Yankee who used words longer than regular folks' conversations – plus, he could play pedal-steel like an eagle swooping across the Dakota Hills. That very night, from a phone booth at the gas station, Willie broke off his engagement with MayBelle while Gabriel was paying for the gas that would take them directly to Niagara Falls.

Nearly thirty years later, they still travelled together, co-ordinating Willie's concert commitments with Gabe's lecture tours. After each annual trip, they returned to the modest Cambridge house, where Willie wrote songs and cooked soul food, while Gabriel worked on a scheme to ensure that this lifestyle carried on forever.

'These guys just don't know when to quit,' Gabe remarked as he walked into the kitchen with the morning mail. He shoved the letter back into its envelope and opened the fridge. 'Juice?'

'Thanks. What guys?' Willie asked, sitting at the table. He poured a bowl of Cheerios.

'These Brits – they've been calling me on and off all month, want to give me a job.'

'Good bread?' Willie asked, smearing CowFree on his wheat toast.

'Highly leavened. But who'd want to live in Britain?'

'Fine place, Britain,' Willie nodded. 'Could be you should think it through. I'm fixin' t'go home to Texas pretty soon now anyways.'

Gabriel smiled as he sat down. Willie had been doing this for decades, practically since they got back from Niagara. Any day now he was going to pack his bags and return to the South. Probably come the fall. Or after Christmas at the latest.

'No, I don't think so. I'll go see them when we're in Europe next month, tell them I'm not in the market.'

'A lotta towns there are kinda like Boston,' Willie mused. 'How's your chest this mornin'?'

Gabriel pulled down the neck of his T-shirt. 'Scabs are healing fine. Damn itchy where the hair's growing back though.'

'Tellin' *me*,' Willie said.

After breakfast, Gabriel climbed into his ice-blue T-Bird and set off towards MIT. The sun was bright as a flash of insight, and in the air Gabe could taste the crisp tang of a New England fall. With time to spare, he parked the car by the bridge, and sat awhile, simply looking across the Charles River. He wound down a window and breathed in through his nose.

He was forty-seven years old. He had three doctorates, an IQ of 183 and an extensive collection of antique clockwork models of the solar system. His prominent curved nose, his fidgety, dark eyes and his swept-back collar-length hair made him look like a good-natured eagle. He was balding evenly from the brow, at the rate of four-tenths of an inch per year, by his own calculation. He figured he'd be totally bald by the age of seventy-five. Gabriel was a little vain, as one might have guessed from his closely-considered outfit of informal denim and supple cowboy boots, so his insouciance about baldness in old age was surprising – particularly as he planned to live well past seventy-five. Indeed, he planned to live longer than anyone had ever lived before.

Grinning broadly at the gleaming September skyline of Boston, he leaned out of the window of the car and filled his lungs.

'Incredible!' he yelled. 'What a glorious morning in a glorious, glorious world!'

The world, shiny and new-pressed, appeared to accept this assessment with equanimity.

Gabriel, still beaming at the sheer goddamned terrificness of it all, made his way to MIT. He went along to the lab to pick up his props and carried them to the lecture hall. He set up a table in front of the dais, three feet from the front row of seats, and placed a steaming styrofoam bucket on it.

Eventually, his audience filed in, filling the hall to capacity. Gabriel was talking this morning not to students, but to delegates of the Tomorrow Today Conference. Each of them had paid a hefty whack to get clued up on the latest creative developments in Humanistically-Oriented Technology. When they had settled, Gabriel Todd began.

'I want to talk to you about death. Whatever your religious or spiritual beliefs, it's a fair bet you figure the long, cold slumber in the college dorms of extinction is inevitable. Well, today I'm going to tell you it's not. Death is as dated as the Black Bottom, the beehive and the beach movie.'

This was billed as a Keynote Lecture, but Gabriel considered it missionary work – and he sure enjoyed evangelising. He strode to and fro at the front of the hall, gesticulating dramatically and delivering his sentences with theatrical pauses and changes in pace. He managed to give the impression that, although he obviously knew his stuff every which way, it was almost as recent a revelation for him as it was for his transfixed listeners. And who could *fail* to be transfixed? Who could be so blasé as to glance surreptitiously at the Swatch when being offered dominion over Death?

Gabriel told his audience about experiments in which frog spawn had been frozen and then thawed out after several days to produce perfectly healthy tadpoles. The success rate with gerbils was fairly good, he said, and in Paris they had managed to re-animate a deep-frosted kitten, who had looked pretty much okay for *several minutes* before expiring with a stiff-tongued mew.

He pointed out that the fatal diseases that have claimed human lives for aeons were themselves dying out. How stupid, then, to die of a disease that would be curable in a few years' time. In fact, how stupid to hang on to a body that was already past its best – the lungs sooty with pollution, the arteries brittle as breadsticks, the muscles exhausted with pulling the entire assembly round and about.

Gabriel picked up a two-foot length of rubber hose from the table. As he spoke, he thwacked it idly into the palm of his hand in slow, curved strokes. In front of him, vapour curled in slo-mo down the sides of the styrofoam bucket, and crept across the tabletop.

'I don't know about you, ladies and gentlemen, but *I'm* not going gentle into that good night. When this body gives up on me, I'm going to make damn sure that the *important* part of me – the part of me that *is* me – will be preserved, waiting for a time when I can rise again, and feel the cool

21

New England breezes on my face. This—' he indicated the steaming bucket in front of him ' – is liquid nitrogen. Let me show you what it can do.'

Nonchalantly, he immersed the length of rubber, keeping his hand clear of the rim. After four or five seconds, he pulled the tube out and slammed it against the edge of the table. It shattered into a million tiny shards, which skittered across the floor. The audience gasped and then began to chatter excitedly.

'Quick freeze,' Gabe smiled, raising his voice above the general conversation. 'That's where Gabriel Todd's head is going when the old pump finally blows – straight into a bucket of this stuff. Everything I've learned, everything I've seen and heard, everything that makes me Gabriel Todd will be held on file, up here in the synapses of the brain, until they can find a new body to slot all that information into. What a prospect! What bliss in that dawn to be alive again! And all it really takes, ladies and gentlemen, apart from a few technical niceties I won't bore you with, *all it really takes* is some foresight and a couple of gallons of *this stuff*!'

And with an unhesitating, fluid movement he plunged his hands into the bucket, and scooped out a great splash of clear nitrogen, throwing it wide into the front row of the audience. There were screams, and panicked backward scrambling. Those behind were on their feet, horrified – but as the steam and the shock subsided, there stood Gabriel, hands raised and fingers wiggling.

'Evaporates real fast in air,' he grinned.

As the audience filed out of the hall, a thirtysomething couple in matching jogging suits approached Gabriel at the podium. He glanced up and registered their excited, glowing faces, their tan skin, their glinting gold jewellery.

'Pardon me, Dr Todd,' the woman said, offering a hand, 'I'm Sammy Petz, and this is my husband Mikey. We came all the way from Sacramento to hear you speak this afternoon.'

'Glad you could make it,' Gabriel nodded, smiling.

'Hey, no problem,' Mikey declared. 'We consider you a true visionary, sir. It's a real honour, a *real* honour.'

'Dr Todd,' Sammy continued, 'we want to state up front that we are pretty comfortable right now, capital-wise. Life's been good to us, y'know? We kinda had plans for our future, but your lecture has totally turned us around. Totally.' She paused and glanced at her husband, and then back to Gabriel. 'Bottom line – we want in.'

Clinch that sale, Gabriel thought.

'This is a major financial commitment you're considering here,' he warned. 'Maybe in six figures. That's a serious—'

Sammy leapt in to reassure him. 'Money is not an issue in this scenario. I mean, hey, how much would a person be prepared to pay for eternal life, right?'

Gabriel winced inwardly. Sammy and Mikey had been drawn to him not by curiosity and delight, but by greed and self-regard. These were not the people he would have chosen to wake up next to in the twenty-third century. What's more, they seemed to believe that they needed his blessing, when all that was required was a Gold Amex.

He reached into his back pocket and took out a business card. Handing it to Sammy, he said, 'Call this guy – Jeff Epstein. He handles the legal and financial side.'

Sammy squealed with delight as she took the card, and Mikey punched the air. 'Yes!' He turned to Gabriel. 'Thanks, man. Really.' As they walked away, Mikey said to Sammy, 'We're making the right decision, babe. I mean, nothing could be more important than this, right?'

'Sure, honey,' Sammy replied, putting the palm of her hand to Mikey's cheek. 'I'll go back on the pill tonight, okay?'

Gabriel made a mental note to call Jeff and have him raise the rent on this couple – they were good for more than a bunsen burner or two.

* * *

Unity lay with her head on Don's chest, and listened to his heart. He had the most infuriating heartbeat. It rattled on like a stick dragged along railings. Diggerdy-diggerdy-diggerdy-diggerdy. It wasn't just the sex – it was always like that. He was using them up too fast. Since childhood, Unity had held a superstitious belief that everyone was born with an exact allocation of heartbeats, and that you had to spend them slowly. Unless Don had won some pre-natal lottery, he was going to be out of beats before he was forty. She shifted her shoulder and brought her left hand up to her ear, being careful not to wake him. She pressed hard and listened to her own pulse. *Kerdumf. Kerdumf.* Slow – that was good. *Kerdumf. Kerdumf.* Plenty of time, surely? *Kerdumf. Kerdumf. Ker-*

. . . *Kerdumf.*

She stiffened at the aortal hiccup. Why did it *do* that so often? For God's sake, it had a stupidly simple job. Why did it screw up like that?

She closed her eyes.

Because it's all so *unlikely*, she thought. That's why. That this fistful of muscle should squeeze and relax, squeeze and relax in just the right rhythm for a straight seventy years. That the two spongy bags in one's chest should inflate and contract in precisely the correct way for month after month after month. She'd seen a sports programme once where some rugby player got his neck broken in a tackle. Snap – a nanosecond. Paralysed forever.

It didn't make sense. *It didn't make sense.*

Unity hiked herself up onto one elbow, and ran a finger across Don's lips. In his sleep, he tried to push her hand away. She did it again.

'Don?' she whispered.

He rolled his head to one side and frowned, nearly awake.

'Don? Don. Fuck me senseless.'

CHAPTER FIVE

JOHNNY O'CASEY HAD BEEN the white sheep of his family. In a Dublin dynasty of wastrels, layabouts and fiddle-players, John had determined, at the age of nine, to become a corporate accountant.

It was all his father's fault. Eoin O'Casey was an architect by profession and a talented improviser of inebriate songs by inclination. Johnny was the first of Eoin's seven children – and the only one to inherit none of his father's creative bent. But if Johnny was devoid of that, he also lacked Eoin O'Casey's gift for avoiding real success.

Whenever Eoin was offered some lucrative opening by one of the entrepreneurs or businessmen within his vast circle of drinking pals, he would find a way to blow it. He'd fail to make the clinching phone call. He'd forget the vital appointment. On one memorable occasion, as he was walking to some office to sign a contract, he contrived to get his head kicked by the milkman's horse. And after each of these debacles, as they all sat round for their dinner, Eoin would address the family with a broad grin.

'It was obviously not meant to be. Sure, I'da hated the job anyways – and I'da hardly ever been home. I tell you,' and he'd slap his plastered thigh, 'I'm *glad* I fell down the fokkin manhole.'

It was apparent to Johnny, during his childhood, that all his siblings, like his father, were in on something that he'd missed. They knew some secret that enabled them to be perfectly happy swanning through school picking up straight Cs and detentions. Johnny, on the other hand, couldn't bear to hand in a piece of work unless he'd done the research thoroughly, planned the composition and checked the spelling. He rarely got worse than a B, and he agonised over every A that might have been an A+.

And it seemed that every evening when he got home with a satchel full of homework, there was yet another new baby at the table, glugging from a bottle of milk with one hand and playing the harp, effortlessly, with the other. Johnny really tried to learn an instrument. He attempted piano, guitar, fiddle, drums, saxophone and bagpipes – but it wasn't in him. When the other kids started up a band in their teens, John became their manager. He hassled the pub landlords, divvied up the money and got the hired Hammond back to the shop on time the following morning.

'We're all good at what we're good at,' Eoin said, 'as long as you're good at *something*.'

But it was obvious to Johnny that, in Da's eyes at least, being a good organist was better than being a good organiser.

Having read about the Harvard Business School in a magazine he'd found whilst waiting for his father in outpatients, seventeen-year-old Johnny O'Casey tried for a scholarship. To absolutely no one's surprise, and therefore to very little congratulation, he got it. He kissed his mammy goodbye, shook his dadda's unbandaged left hand, and boarded the plane to Boston, Mass.

After Dublin, the place was a revelation. The students were serious, hard-working and dedicated. They called themselves the Leaders of Tomorrow. They also called themselves Sterling Grover or Robinson Winberg or Randall Baxter.

Johnny decided that his name, like his accent, had to go.

As everyone's first name seemed to be a surname, he beheaded O'Casey and moved it forward. Then, having rejected Kennedy, Lincoln and Wayne, he picked a family name which, he hoped, would be associated in the American subconscious with reliability, permanence and power. It was the name by which he was known in his first job, as a graduate trainee for Splendid Corps in Tallahassee, Florida. And over the ensuing fifteen years, it was inscribed on a series of increasingly forbidding office doors in Fort Worth, Tucson, Hong Kong and, most recently, London.

One clear fall morning, the telephone rang in the clapboard house in Cambridge, Massachusetts. Willie Rabblestack answered it, and then shouted through to Gabriel.

'Got a Casey Rushmore on the phone, Gabe. 'Pears he's flown into Boston partickly to visit with you.'

The bar of the Providence Hotel on the Hill typified everything Casey loved about America. His move to London had been a career decision – and London was okay, but it was too feckless and shabby really. And too damn close to Dublin. But here, in his adopted home of Boston, amongst the efficient, deferential waiters and the perfect, crisp tablecloths, Casey felt at ease.

He caught sight of himself in the mirror and grinned with satisfaction. Was that a strong jaw? It made Rock Hudson look like a tortoise. And the teeth! The natural, God-given teeth! Americans didn't end up with teeth like that without several thousand dollars' worth of orthodontistry. Were those eyes a clear, trustworthy blue? You bet, brother – and never seen the inside of a tinted contact lens, either. Did Casey look like a boy from the Emerald Isle? No – he looked like the *great-grandson* of a boy from the Emerald Isle. He looked like an American. A Bostonian.

What he especially liked about Bean Town was that it generated such streamlined, glass-fronted prosperity despite being the second largest Irish city in the world. Yup, this was the biggest concentration of his erstwhile countrymen outside of Dublin. Jesus, the guy who owned this hotel chain was called Flynn, for God's sake.

Casey clenched his fist against his chin. The Irish could do it, you see, if they wanted to – and if they were in America.

Gabriel Todd came back from the washroom and took his seat at the table.

'Where were we?' he said, as he poured the rest of his beer.

'I was telling you about your research budget,' Casey reminded him. 'In fact, I was asking you how much you'd need.'

Gabe leaned back in his chair and stretched his long legs out. 'It's not *my* budget, Casey. I'm not going to take the job. I'm flattered that you've come all this way to speak to me, and it would have been churlish to have stood you up, but I only showed this evening so we could get this straight. I don't want to work for you. I'm not *gonna* work for you. I'm happy where I am.'

Casey nodded. 'Uhuh. Okay, Gabriel, I'm taking that on board. I hear you, okay? But let's say I find someone else for this position – how about if I tell you what kind of package Splendid would be offering to that individual?'

'Sure,' Todd grinned. 'As my friend Willie would say, if you got beers, I got ears.' He lifted the empty bottle and waggled it in the air. 'Run another of these onto your expense claim, huh?'

'Sure thing,' Casey said, signalling the order to a distant but apparently telepathic waiter. 'So, let's break down this package. We're offering a salary in six figures – and I'm talking basic, no-frills salary, before we roll in bonuses, share options, health care and non-contributory pension scheme. Vacation – as much as you want, within reason. We appreciate that creative individuals such as yourself need ample r'n'r to re-charge those batteries. Research budget – listen, this is a no-ceiling venture for us. That's a measure of our commitment to this area of cutting-edge technology, huh? Plus, if you don't want to work in our British facility – which is a state-of-the-art installation, by the way – we have major centres in Tucson, 'Frisco and Tallahassee.'

'But not dear ole Cambridge, Mass,' Gabriel pointed out, smiling.

Casey looked back at him, silent for a moment, and sipped his beer.

'Okay,' he said, hunching forward, 'Scope this. If I could rent space at MIT and install all the necessary equipment there, would we have a deal? Hey, I'm not saying I could swing this – but if I *could*, huh?'

Gabriel looked at his watch. 'I'd certainly give it some thought – let's leave it at that. Listen, there's a country band playing at a bar down on Kenmore Square in a little while. You wanna finish these drinks and come along? Do you like music?'

Reaching for the bill, Casey loosened his tie.

'Well, you may not believe it, looking at me in my dark suit and polished shoes, Gabriel, but I was brought up in a family of musicians. Yessir, music's just there in the Rushmore blood, I guess . . .'

Casey and Gabriel met up with Willie at the gig, and watched a country-grunge band who enthusiastically beat up 'Jolene', mugged 'Ruby' and blacked 'Bette Davis Eyes'. Gabriel invited Casey back for a nightcap, and the three of them, all pretty drunk, piled into a cab that took them across the river. Back home they sat around drinking bourbon, while Gabriel mused on the nature of his profession.

'The job of science,' he said, 'is to make imagination viable. In fact, it's the job *art* used to do, when patronage was a *sine qua non* of being an artist. There was a time when you didn't paint just whatever you liked. You were *commissioned* to paint, I dunno, an altarpiece. And there's rules to that – it's got to have a religious subject; it's got to be yea wide by yea high; it's got to have lots of bright colours so that it can be seen from the back of the church. And it's the *tension* between specification and imagination that makes *art*.

'Same with science. I'm boiling over with ideas, but I have to work within the constraints of the market. And, just as Michelangelo would have pushed for the best price for a chapel ceiling, I have to screw as much money out of you guys as I possibly can, to do what I want to do anyway.'

Casey leaned forward excitedly, and a little clumsily. His bourbon sloshed unnoticed over the rim of his glass. 'Exactly, Gabriel! You're talking my language. That's why I'm batting so hard on this one. I'm willing to have you screw Splendid Corps for all you can get.'

Willie, who was lounging with his hand-tooled boots on a low table and a glass resting on his belt buckle, grinned across at Casey. 'Just makin' a note here, boy, to mail you an invite next time we play poker.'

'The thing is,' Gabe went on, 'I have a life outside of science. I have other things to do. So I publish my papers, release the ideas into the ether – maybe someone else can pick up on the ones I don't have time for. Which is what you're doing, right? Picking up on my microbots.' He shrugged. 'Find someone else to develop them – there's a whole lot of talented, ambitious people out there.'

Casey knew that he was more than a little fuzzy. He wanted to say that Gabriel was throwing away a terrific opportunity. He wanted to convince this infuriatingly talented man that he, Casey Rushmore, could arrange things so that all this genius benefited not only Splendid Corps and Gabriel Todd but very probably mankind to boot. He wanted to guide Gabriel round the manholes and away from the milkman's horse.

Sighing, he shook his head sadly and poured another drink.

Willie swung his feet onto the floor. 'I got some hay to hit. You gonna sleep over, Case?' he asked as he made his way to the door.

Concentrating on pouring bourbon into his glass, Casey was momentarily and drunkenly flustered. 'I . . . er . . . do you, er, have a spare room?'

Gabriel snorted with laughter and Willie leaned nonchalantly in the doorway. 'Well, you sure ain't about to snuggle up with me, son. I don't like your loafers.'

Casey felt his face flush. 'No – sorry,' he blurted. 'I didn't mean I thought . . . I mean, I didn't assume you were trying to . . . Well, obviously I was aware that you're . . . ummm . . .'

'. . . queer as a candy-coated Corvette?' Willie suggested, gravely. 'Catch you at breakfast.' And he left.

Casey winced and turned back to Gabe. 'Look, I didn't mean to offend anyone . . .'

'Forget it. Willie was kidding around.' They sat in silence for a while and then Gabriel said, 'Listen, come upstairs – I'll show you what I've been working on.'

Somewhat unsteadily, and still willing away the glow of embarrassment and drunkenness, Casey followed Gabe up the stairs. The doors to the main bedroom were closed. Gabe indicated a workbench. 'What do you see?' he asked as he turned on the light.

Casey looked. The bench was old wood, with large cupboards under-neath. There was a sink at one end, and a clutter of electronic paraphernalia – coils of wire, pliers, a soldering iron. He shrugged.

Gabe picked up a small box, like a TV remote control, and held it out towards the bench. 'Look closer – right there on the edge.' Casey peered. He noticed what appeared to be two perfect circles of splashed solder, like silver contact lenses.

'These?' he said, pointing.

'Don't touch them,' Gabe warned. 'Abracadabra!' He pressed a button on the box in his hand, and the two shiny discs moved, with a slight judder, to the right. 'And stop,' he grinned, lifting his finger.

Casey gasped. 'Did you do that?'

'Remotely,' Gabe admitted. 'They're not real intelligent. All they can do is . . . go left,' he pressed a button, and the discs moved left, 'and right . . .' and again the discs obeyed the instruction of Gabe's fingers. 'And, stop.' The discs stopped.

Casey was amazed. 'What are they?'

'Robots. Very simple, but extremely tiny robots. Built by a tiny pair of hands that were themselves built by a scaled-up pair of hands, which also taught them how to build the robots. It's a practical demonstration of the paper you're so fired up about. Pretty fine, huh?'

'They're incredible. Where are the hands?'

31

'Took 'em to bits. I needed the parts for something else. And anyhow, these are just toys. I reckon you'd need about three hundred thousand dollars to take the next little step – which is to make a microbot that could do something useful.'

'Then *why*, for Christ's sake,' Casey almost screeched, 'won't you come and work for Splendid?'

'Hey, keep your voice down. Willie's trying to sleep. Come downstairs – I'll show you to your room.'

At the door of the spare room, Gabe said, 'You need to understand this – I don't trust corporations. You – you're a reasonable enough guy, but I don't want what you represent. In short, I'll do most anything necessary to screw money out of you and your bosses – but I won't sell you my soul. Hell, I plan to be using it several hundred years from now. You'll find a hanger on the back of the door for your suit. Goodnight.'

'Goodnight,' Casey gulped. He was almost in tears.

CHAPTER SIX

'DON, CAN YOU GET up, please?'

'Hang on a minute. I haven't even got my breath back.'

'Come on – get off. I've got to clean this mess up. There's flour all over the place.'

Don nuzzled his face into her shoulder. 'It'll wait.'

'Don . . .'

'Jesus, all right.' He levered himself off the kitchen table and began buttoning and zipping himself up. 'You don't get to see this bit in the movie, do you?' he tutted. 'Jessica Lange doesn't get straight in to nagging Jack Nicholson to shift his arse so she can sweep the floor. You want a coffee or something?'

'No, I've given up caffeine. I'll have a mineral water.'

Don paused with one hand on the kettle. 'What?'

'Have you any idea what caffeine does to the nervous system? The stuff's lethal.' She was opening the cupboard to find the dustpan. 'I just decided not to do that to my body any more.'

'That's the third one this month,' Don said incredulously. 'You gave up beef last week because of mad cow disease, and tap water went on the blacklist because of, I dunno, adders in the reservoirs or something.'

'Additives. And what difference does it make to you?'

Don watched the back of her head as she knelt down and started brushing up the flour. Could he be bothered to have a row? You couldn't, could you? You couldn't screw someone over the kitchen table in a cloud of Homepride and then launch into a major criticism of their neuroses. It wasn't gentlemanly.

'I'm going out for a smoke,' he muttered, as if it made his point.

He slid back the door, and walked out onto the terrace. Unity's flat was at the top of a small block on the river in Fulham. It was a crisp autumn night, and Don stood blowing smoke into it. The river was low down the bank and calm. In the clear air, he watched as an airliner's lights approached from the east. By the time it was overhead, he could see the next one coming in behind it, and maybe even the one after that. Just in the few minutes he'd been standing there, seven or eight hundred people had zipped over his head into Heathrow. If they were anything like him, every single soul of them would be craning at the window, gazing at the sparkle of the city, grinning with excitement. They'd be looking forward to restaurants and theatres, to conversation and jokes, to walking the streets or hailing cabs, to seeing their kids and their lovers. Hundreds of them in the jumbo that was going overhead right now – and not a single one, he would bet on it, thinking about mad fucking cow disease.

Don didn't understand what Unity was so afraid of. When he first met her – what? a year ago? – he'd thought she was a bit faddy, a bit obsessive about her health. But, well, she'd just got over a cervical cancer scare, and she was a bit insecure anyway, so he could see her point. He'd reckoned that with a little time and a lot of reassurance, she'd lighten up. But it wasn't happening. To be honest, it was getting worse.

'You want to go to a sushi bar, Unity?'

'*Raw fish?* Are you *insane?*'

'Let's wander down to the fair on the common.'

'They're death traps, those rides. Held together with rusty bolts.'

'We'll get a minicab back.'

'We will *not!* No one regulates safety standards for those things, you know.'

He glanced back through the French doors. She'd more or less finished clearing up. It was very nearly time to go in and offer to help.

The sex was terrific, no two ways. A little desperate on her part, perhaps. A panicky proof of something, rather than an unalloyed pleasure. But – well – kitchens, car parks and party bathrooms; stockings, masks, silk ropes and long boots; sprints, marathons and high jumps. It was pure Henry Miller. Don had never had a relationship in which he'd got laid so often. Or laughed so rarely.

He fizzed his cigarette in a little puddle on the terrace wall and walked back into the kitchen with the damp stub. He flicked it into the swing-top, and bumped into Unity as she turned to empty the last dustpan of flour. She looked up at him through a fine white film on her glasses.

'I'd kiss you,' he said, 'but I've still got a mouthful of cancer.'

'Not funny.'

'Not intended to be. Do you want to send out for a pizza? Or have they recently discovered a hitherto unsuspected link between mozzarella and multiple sclerosis?'

'God, you can be a snide bastard, can't you?'

She was right, of course, but he was on a roll.

'Hey, there could be something in it. Those vulnerable little motor neurons quake at the very thought of being napalmed with soft cheese. "Look out!" they squeak. "Incoming Camembert!"'

Unity put the pan and brush back in the cupboard, not looking at him. 'I've got to go and pack. Why don't you sod off outside and smoke yourself to death?'

'Good idea. I'll take a beer with me – make it a suicide pact between my liver and lungs.'

Back out on the terrace he lit a cigarette and checked the sky for traffic. He guessed it at about four planes before the exhilaration of being obnoxious wore off and he'd feel the need to go in and apologise.

*　　*　　*

35

At seven the following evening, Unity unwrapped her complimentary boiled sweet, unfolded her complimentary copy of the *Independent*, and threw up in her complimentary sick bag.

The woman in the next seat smiled reassuringly as Unity came up for air. She tapped the newspaper headline – '316 Perish in Milan Air Disaster' – and said, 'It's a million to one, you know.'

'Urghh,' Unity countered.

The small boy in the aisle seat regarded Unity with frank concern. 'That lady sicked up,' he observed.

'She did, didn't she?' his mother agreed.

'What colour she sicked up?' the kid inquired.

A stewardess came to ask whether Unity was all right. Would she like some water?

'That lady sicked up,' the kid explained. And then, taking a shot in the dark, he added, 'Yellow.'

The stewardess suggested that tea might help. Unity shook her head and held up a hand.

'I want Coke,' the kid put in. 'And fries and vinegar.'

'Oh, *please*,' Unity moaned.

'Please,' the kid amended.

They were well out over the Atlantic before Unity felt confident enough to relinquish her grip on the supply of sick bags. She was aware of a certain irony. Here she was, the child who'd envisaged living on the moon, and the very hiss of airport doors made her clammy with fear. Every time she boarded a plane, she determined that this would be the flight where she'd keep control – and today, she had really believed she might make it. The pilot's voice had thrummed with those middle-class cello tones that inspire confidence. He was called Captain Simmons – a clean-jawed, Windsor-knot kind of name, of which Unity approved strongly. During the safety routine, she had made a note of the nearest emergency exit, and worked out who she would have to trample to get to it. She had checked the wing on her side for hairline fractures and found none – reminding herself that the visible vibration was not only normal but necessary, if the wing was not to be torn clean off the fuselage. As Heathrow dropped away to the east, she had massaged the fingernail dents out of the palms of her hands and confidently accepted the offer of a booby-trapped newspaper.

She knew she ought to eat. It was a long way to Boston and, at the very worst, she ought to have something solid inside her to throw up. Picking up her bag, she squeezed past mother and child, casually raking a stiletto along the kid's shin on the way, and tottered to the toilet at the back of the plane. Once inside, she checked the cubicle for smouldering cigarettes and suspect parcels, and then retrieved some toothpaste and a brush from her bag. She was simultaneously cleaning her teeth and having a pee when the captain announced, 'Ladies and gentlemen, we're told there's a little turbulence ahead, so may I ask you to return to your seats and . . .'

'Oh, *Chr-rist*,' Unity wailed.

She was back in her seat before the toilet finished flushing.

At about the time that Unity was yelping verdantly into a series of British Airways paper bags, Don was already onto his second bowl of guacamole in a Mexican joint just off the Charing Cross Road. It was an office night out – somebody's birthday or leaving do or something. He'd certainly signed some card that was doing the rounds disguised as a purchase order, and bunged a quid into a brown paper envelope.

Thirty of them had met up in the Dutch Courage on the edge of Chinatown. One of the more acceptable blokes from Comms had just got a round in when Come-Along Cathy announced that it was time to go to the restaurant.

'Come along, you people. We shall lose our table. Come along, Sheryl – let's be getting along, shall we? Come along, you lads there.'

'We'll see you there, Cath,' Don told her – though she obviously suspected that they would slip off to Wong Kei's and have a splinter-group party.

But for being cajoled, Don was all for downing his pint and sprinting to the restaurant ahead of the crowd. The trouble with turning up insouciantly late was that you had to sit wherever there was a spare seat. You might end up next to – well, the girl he'd encountered by the coffee machine, for instance. She was retarded, apparently, and had been given the job as part of a Community Care Scheme. Don didn't fancy having to make dinner conversation with her. You'd spend all your time resisting the impulse to cut up her food.

As it turned out, the Scheme girl was way down the other end of the table. Don found himself with Flirty Brenda, who was always good for a few chortling indiscretions concerning her husband's inadequacies, and Spotty George, whose naked wish to be Don's pal made him a willing victim of any crack that sprang to mind. As Brenda calculated aloud the fortune she'd spent on unappreciated underwear, Don glanced along at the pale, black-haired girl. She still wore that impassive expression as she gazed at the menu. Jesus, you'd think someone would help her.

'Waste, innit?' George suggested, noticing Don's interest.

It had been George who had given Don the inside track on the girl. Don had mentioned his coffee-machine meeting with her, and George, who scoped any female that fell within what he regarded as his catchment area, had tapped the table knowingly.

'Loony, that one. Lovely little body on 'er, granted – but tuppence ha'penny short. So you *can't*, can yer? in all fairness.'

'Loony?'

'Well, not loony *bonkers*. Loony *stupid*. Slow – y'know.'

'She has learning difficulties,' Don suggested primly.

'Whatever. They got her doing filing and stuff. She's going back to special school in November. Name's Ellen.'

'How come you always know this stuff, George?'

George shrugged and leered. 'Here and there, Donny my son. Here and there . . .'

'George,' Don said pleasantly, 'have you seen those Tom and Jerry cartoons where the cat gets punched by the dog and slowly shatters into teeny fragments? Well, that's what'll happen to you if you ever refer to me as Donny again.'

Throughout the evening, Don's eyes flicked towards Ellen from time to time. She seemed simply to be following the conversation around her – he never saw her speak. But he saw her smile on one occasion and she had the most enchanting smile. Totally guileless, he thought. Beautiful. As he got drunker, he realised that she needed someone to – well – look after her interests. Make her feel involved and part of the team. Someone who wouldn't patronise her on the one hand, or dismiss her out of hand on the . . . er . . . other hand. In fact, what he should do – he should wander along right now and adopt just such a role.

He was getting to his feet when Flirty Brenda said something quite unbelievable about her Dave's attitude towards 'down there', and Don decided to hear this anecdote out before moving seats.

Next time he looked, just after the coffee arrived, Ellen was gone.

At Leicester Square tube, Don glanced at his watch. A little past eleven.

'Listen,' he said to George and Flirty Brenda as they began to walk down the stairs, 'I think I'm going to get a cab – I can't face the train. I'll see you tomorrow.'

Striding off along the street before anyone could suggest a taxi-share, he cut up through Chinatown and across Shaftesbury Avenue into Soho. On St Anne's Court, he ducked through an ill-lit doorway and up a flight of stairs. The bouffanted and uniformed woman on the front desk didn't know him, although he'd become quite a regular over the preceding few weeks.

'Member?' she asked, opening the book in front of her.

'Yeah,' Don replied. 'But my card hasn't arrived yet.'

'Name?'

Don groaned. His life had been, on the whole, unblighted by misfortune. In fact, the worst thing that had ever happened to him had been at the age of six months in St Michael's Church, Rye, where he'd been christened. He looked the woman squarely in the chest, bracing himself for the inevitable wisecrack, and mumbled his name.

'Don Osman.'

She laughed. 'Oh, wow. I really liked "Puppy Love". It was the first record I bought.'

'No,' he sighed. 'Not Donny – Don. Not Osmond – Osman.'

'Right – well, say hi to Little Jimmy for me.' Still tittering, the woman verified Don's membership and waved him past. He thanked her with a vinegar smile, and walked through the beaded curtain into the only club in the capital that catered to his particular vice.

Unity arrived at Boston Logan Airport at about the same time as Casey Rushmore. Indeed, the cab that had brought him out from the city was the one that took her in. Unity didn't like American cabs. She didn't like the way they were fortified against the world, and she hated how the driver was protected behind a grille. It merely emphasised how threatening a place America was.

She opened her briefcase and took out the itinerary of her trip. Tomorrow she was booked to attend a conference at MIT concerning the husbandry of high-protein fungi in low-gravity environments. The following day there was a series of lectures on genetic engineering in agriculture – MegaMaize and TurboCarrot. After that she had three free days in which she planned to drive out to the Berkshires to see an old college friend, then back to Massachusetts for a 'brainstorming forum'.

She checked into the Peerless, took a shower and ordered a tuna sandwich from room service. She scrupulously specified dolphin-friendly tuna, agar-free tomato, non-irradiated cucumber and black pepper from any developing Third World democracy with a clean record on human rights. Whilst awaiting the arrival of this caring comestible, she set up the laptop and put the final touches to her paper proposing the manipulation of vegetable genes to produce radishes like beach balls.

CHAPTER SEVEN

MARMADUKE RANSOME MALVERN SPLEEN, the last Lord Rincer, had an eventful 1938.

In March he married Ruth Sara Middletort and lost five hundred pounds at blackjack to a Fabian he'd met at the Dorchester. In April he impregnated his wife and wrote a strongly-worded letter to *The Times* concerning the parasitic degeneracy of the British royal family. In June he renounced his peerage and, accompanied by a butler to carry his golf clubs, went to Spain to fight the Fascists. In October he became a member of the Communist Party and his butler deserted to the other side in disgust. In December he was shot dead by a Spanish sniper called Albert Willougby and was posthumously awarded a son.

Despite entreaties from his noble and respected family, the Crown would not reinstate the hereditary peerage that Lord Rincer had, in so principled a fashion, thrust aside, and so the squalling infant who inherited the Great House at Hegley-Rincer was announced in *The Times* as plain Robert Percy Malvern Middletort Spleen.

The boy Robert Spleen may have been denied his title, but one would never have mistaken him for a commoner. Even as a toddler, Robert displayed an open, gracious charm that marked him out as (to quote the upstairs maid) *a real little gent.* When, at the age of five, Robert was considered grown-up enough to be sent to boarding school, this same maid spoke for all the household staff as she declared, 'Seeing him standing there on the porch, bless 'im, with his trunk and his cricket bat – he looked ready to take on the world.'

It would be inaccurate to suggest that, by virtue of his family's wealth and position, the young Spleen was untouched by the rigours of the Second World War and the austerity that followed it. He may have been shielded from the discomforts of rationing and shortage, but he was not unaware of them. Indeed, Robert's time at Eton would have been much less agreeable had he not so readily perceived his housemaster's dismay at the post-war scarcity of silk lingerie and, further, had he not worked so assiduously to assuage that dismay. The early fifties created many demands – often of a covert nature – that might profitably be fulfilled by a helpful chap of discreet and trustworthy mien.

The dawning of the sixties found Robert Spleen in Soho, having just come down from Oxford with a degree in philosophy and economics. What interested Robert was *ideas*. Take his father, for instance. The last Lord Rincer had completely revised his life – *lost* his life, in fact – in support of an idea. At the time, Robert supposed, it must have seemed an enormous, undeniable thing, this idea that his father had. But in 1961, a quarter of a century later, Lord Rincer's grand gesture appeared laughable. Did that make Robert's father a deluded fool? Robert didn't think so, because ideas were fashion items, like brothel creepers or chrome tail-fins. They came and went.

In building the Splendid empire, Spleen *employed* ideas, and he insisted that an idea, like any employee, had to pull its weight. He wasn't going to sink time and resources into some notion that pottered about the place with its thumb in its fundament and its head in the clouds. An idea was no damn good unless it earned its keep.

Had Casey Rushmore been aware of his employer's guiding principle, he may not have asked for a meeting with Mr Spleen the day after he returned from his encounter with Gabriel Todd in Cambridge, Massachusetts.

Here is Casey, in bed, jet-lagged and Valiumed. Though quite asleep, he hurls himself from side to side, clutching at the duvet, kicking out at nocturnal fancies.

His dreams are haunted by swarms of little silver discs, like splashes of solder. They slide silently from beneath the bedroom door and in through the closed windows. They scoot in shoals around the polished floorboards. Swarming over the furniture, they sprout minuscule arms with three-fingered hands, and thousands of them crowd onto the dresser, where they perform a silent, mocking Mexican wave.

Casey leaps to his feet and tries to grab them, but they're quicksilver. He spins around, naked in the middle of the bedroom, to see them lined up along the shelves and windowsills, derisively applauding his deflating erection.

'Please,' he moans. 'Please, please.'

They're marching in ranks across the floor towards him, a wave of shimmering scales, goose-stepping in their tiny silver jackboots. Casey retreats, but one of them sticks out a microscopic foot, and he sprawls onto his back. On the ceiling, they've arranged themselves to form a message in sequins:—

Paddy Go Home.

'Casey, come in,' said Robert Spleen. 'How was your trip?'

Casey sat in the offered chair. 'A, er, qualified success, sir. Illuminating.'

Spleen opened up an Edwardian cigarette box and offered it to his employee. The head honcho of Splendid Corps had long ago given up cigarettes, but he was fond of chocolates. 'Montelimar to the left,' he explained, 'ginger slings to the right.'

Casey declined.

'So,' Spleen said, chewing, 'how did your recruitment exercise go? Can R&D pencil in another real American for their softball team?'

Casey told Spleen about his encounter with Gabriel Todd. He attempted to conjure a man of vision, a seer. A maverick, certainly, but one who could be relied upon for innovation and creative nous. He quoted verbatim Gabriel's philosophy that science must be of service. He explained about the analogous altarpiece and described, in awed tones, the little silver robots.

'Dr Todd sounds our sort of chap with a cherry on top,' Spleen agreed when Casey reached the breathless end of a paragraph. 'So it grieves me that your facial aspect presages a "but".'

Casey sighed. 'He has this *fixation* about large corporations. It's – I don't know – he doesn't trust them, or something. Obviously, it's a *completely* irrational attitude . . .'

'Completely,' smiled the man who'd first introduced Mike Oldfield to Richard Branson.

'But, believe me, sir,' Casey rushed on, 'he is absolutely the resource we're after. These microbots – oh, they were beautiful. If we could just win Todd over, we'd be looking at a potential research arena that would stagger the competition. We simply need to win his trust, that's all.' He paused. 'And I have a proposal to achieve that, sir.'

Spleen raised one eyebrow and Casey took it as permission to continue.

'We make him a no-strings grant of two hundred k to develop the microbots. A gift. Just to convince him of our good intentions, our willingness to allow him his freedom.'

Spleen tossed a ginger sling into his mouth. 'Certainly not,' he said straightforwardly.

'Sir,' Casey pleaded, 'it's *peanuts* on our research budget. And the potential comeback is vast. It's an investment.'

Robert Spleen shook his head. His voice was smooth and enfolding, like a boa. 'My father was addicted to *vingt-et-un*. He used to say he was investing in the turn of a card, but he was just a gambler. My *grand*father owned a casino in Nice. *He* was an investor.'

Casey opened his mouth to make a point, but Spleen held up one silencing finger.

'We only play,' he said quietly, 'if we own the deck. Now, I agree with you that this chap would be an asset to us, and I will sanction all attempts to secure his services. But we do *not* give money away on the off chance.' Spleen paused to study Rushmore's disconsolate face. 'Ideas are like buses, Casey—'

'Yeah, I know,' Casey interrupted, unconvinced. 'There'll be another one along in a minute.'

'Actually,' Spleen grinned, 'I was going to say "better privatised than subsidised".'

CHAPTER EIGHT

DON WAS OUT OF contact lens fluid again. In the bathroom, he licked a lens and deftly slapped it onto his eyeball. It stung like hell for thirty seconds and then settled down. He repeated the operation with the other lens and then looked into the mirror. His eyes were watering, but that would pass.

Wearing contact lenses was one of the things that Don liked about himself. He wasn't a closet squinter, an ashamed myopic, pretending he had the eyesight of a magpie. He was proud of his eighteen-year association with the contact lens, and constructed complex dinner-party anecdotes about his adventures with them. As a gangling fourteen-year-old, Don had worn glasses. A teenager in the seventies was given a narrow choice of spectacle frames on the National Health. There were the thick, black Michael Caines, as worn only by members of the School Chess Club. And there were the little round wire ones which, once you'd ripped the tortoiseshell plastic off them, were known as John Lennons. The implied endorsement of a rock star, however passé, encouraged most teenagers to feel comfortable with these frames. But those teenagers, unlike Don, didn't have a dad who had been wearing just such frames since the fifties – and who had at no point looked cool in them.

When pushed, young Don had settled for the John Lennons, but he was far from happy. He saved up the wages from his Saturday job and bought his first pair of contacts. The day he collected them, he ceremoniously stamped his glasses into the pavement outside the optician's surgery. As he collected the pieces into a brown envelope he'd brought along for the purpose, Don told himself solemnly that this ritual signified his passage from childhood to manhood.

When he got home, his dad said, 'Where are your spectacles, Donald?'

'Smashed.'

'Oh, Lord. Not another pair. How did *that* happen?'

Don told him. It was the first that Donald Osman Senior had heard of his son's investment, but he was too fair-minded a man to find fault with the scheme. If the boy wished to spend his money on contact lenses, well, he'd worked hard and saved, so it was up to him. But Mr Osman, too, recognised that the decision represented some kind of moving away by his son. As the adolescent decanted the debris of his spectacles into the kitchen bin, Osman Senior remarked, 'Still, I shall miss seeing you in glasses. I think they made you look a little like me at your age.'

Osman Junior agreed that this was very probably the case.

When, as an adult, Don looked in a mirror, he was checking what he could *not* see, rather than what he could. It had begun in adolescence, and it was now an unconscious habit. He liked to ascertain, for instance, that his hair was not sandy and wavy but dead straight and trodden-blond. Before she'd gone grey, his mother had had straight blondish hair.

His dad, on the other hand, had the kind of hair that they stopped making after the Battle of Britain – rippled and ochre-brown, like the sand when the sea goes out. Such hair was fixed somehow into a single piece that couldn't be disturbed even by the whirring prop of a Lancaster bomber. Douglas Bader had that kind of hair. And all those chocks-away actors had it. Don's dad, a toddler himself when the Few were entering the field of human conflict, had it in spades.

Having verified the fact on a daily basis for twenty years, Don was confident that he *didn't* have squadron leader hair. Other features he was pretty sure he lacked included: freckles; hazel eyes; narrow, slightly-rounded shoulders; brown shoes; corduroy trousers; and a pipe. He'd studied this phenomenon dispassionately, and he was certain that, by a superb fluke, he had inherited not a single dominant gene from his father.

Quite often, Don would find himself humming a song for no apparent reason, and when this happened, he couldn't relax until he'd figured out how that particular tune had got into his head. As he emerged from Euston tube, he was singing 'Marrakesh Express', a song he didn't even like. By the time he walked into the annexe and pressed the button for the lift, Crosby, Stills and Nash were bugging the hell out of him.

Spotty George was hunched over his terminal in the attitude of one who has recently installed some pirated software displaying animations of fit young Americans enjoying sexual congress. It was impossible to tell whether this was actually the case because lip-smacking shiftiness was George's default expression. He could just as easily have been downloading news from alt.fan.pratchett.

'Morning, George,' Don said as he sat down.

'What's good about it?' George parried, scowling, but evidently pleased with his rejoinder.

Despite the aggression, Don could not believe that George was in a mood – he wasn't sufficiently evolved to inhabit an emotional landscape. It was more likely that he'd picked up the gag from a sitcom last night and wanted to use it.

'I didn't say it was,' Don pointed out, accurately.

'Was what?'

'Good,' Don said.

'Too right!' George nodded, humphing.

Don looked down at his feet for a couple of seconds and considered a response. 'Do you want a coffee?' he asked eventually.

'Just 'ad one.'

On the way to the coffee machine, Don hummed about blowing smoke rings from the corner of his mou-mou-mou-m'mouth. As his number eighteen gurgled into a plastic cup, he melodiously exhorted the general public to get on board that tray-ain. The bloody song was driving him up the wall. He went back to his desk, trying to remember whether it was CS&N or CSN&Y. He asked George, who shrugged and claimed never to have heard of the song.

'Before my time.' He nodded towards Don's terminal. 'Search on "hippy-fuckin-dippy".'

'Before my time, too,' Don protested. 'I must have been all of six.' He snapped his Zippo open and shut. 'I'm going down to the smoking room.'

The mirror on the back wall of the lift was painted with a map of the world, and Don turned to look at it. He was pleased to remark that his hair was all over the place.

Behind him, reflected in the middle of the Atlantic, the lift doors opened, and Don saw Ellen the simpleton get in. She came and stood beside him, and also gazed at the map. Don watched her out of the corner of his eye as she leaned in towards him, her attention fixed solidly and uncomprehendingly on the Andes. The poor woman obviously had no concept whatsoever of the sanctity of personal space. Don shifted a little and pointed at the map.

'Mountains,' he explained, uncomfortably.

Ellen looked up at him expressionlessly.

'Formed by, uh, landmasses colliding,' he continued.

He found her stare quite disconcerting. He knew he should shut up, but his automatic mouth had kicked in.

'See, the continents are in constant motion. Uh, you'll notice that the, umm, western profile of Africa . . .'

Ellen was holding her head slightly to one side, her unblinking eyes steady and green.

'. . . fits, like a jigsaw, into the eastern profile of South America . . .'

The lift stopped at the first floor and the doors slid open.

'. . . suggesting, umm . . . well . . .'

'Plate tectonics,' Ellen said matter-of-factly. She stepped nimbly between the closing doors and was gone.

Don was momentarily stunned – and then embarrassment hit him in a hot, damp burst, like a bucket of custard. He leaned forward and pressed his brow against Milwaukee.

'I'm going to kill George,' he muttered, 'and then myself.'

At lunchtime, as Don was leaving the office to go to the sandwich shop, he saw Ellen coming into the building, and despite a sheepish instinct to hide, he approached her. He noticed that she was still wearing that unfathomable expression – and he gave a self-critical tut. When she was a retard, it was 'blank'. Now it's 'unfathomable', he thought.

He stepped in front of her as she made for the elevator. 'Look, excuse me, hello. It's Ellen, right? Uh, I just wanted to apologise.'

'For what?' she asked.

'For, uh . . .' For thinking that you were simple. For pitying you from afar. For finding a disabled person attractive. 'For making a bit of a prat of myself in the lift.'

'What's your usual venue?' Ellen inquired.

'Well, it's not so much the venue as the timing. Generally I don't patronise on a first date. Have you got time for a beer?'

'Okay,' she replied, without the slightest hesitation. 'I'm completely broke though.'

They walked down towards King's Cross and ducked into the Rocking Sierra, a tiny backstreet pub unfrequented by commuters or Norwegian tourists. It was populated mainly by hookers and policemen taking lunch. Don was reminded of the cartoon wolf and sheepdog – 'Night, Wally' 'Night, Ralph' – clocking off after a hard day's thwarting.

It turned out that Ellen had recently graduated from Durham and was working for a year before taking up a postgraduate course at University College. This, presumably, was George's reported 'special school'. Don told her what he'd been led to believe about her, and she shrugged, unconcerned.

'Be fair, though,' Don said, 'you do walk around with a look of total vacancy on. I suppose you're simply bored stiff.'

'No, not at all. It's the perfect interim job. I just go from floor to floor putting mail in the basket marked "In" and picking up mail from the basket marked "Out". It uses about one per cent of my concentration. I suppose my face in repose is just particularly dull.'

Don was tempted to say something nauseatingly gallant. Instead, he mentioned his problem with 'Marrakesh Express' which was back to torment him, like indigestion. Ellen knew the song, which surprised him as she wasn't even born when it was released.

'Well,' she said, 'I suppose I'm – what's the musical equivalent of well-read? Well-listened. Try this – close your eyes and run through your journey to work. Re-live it, from the moment you left the house.'

Don shut his eyes, and envisaged the street outside his flat. 'I'm crossing at the lights,' he told Ellen.

'Are you humming "Marrakesh Express"?'

'No. I'm buying a paper from the stand outside the station. I can't find my tube pass. Ah – there's a guy I vaguely know just going through the barrier. I'm hanging back so that I don't have to talk to him. I'm standing by a blackboard that has a message apologising for disruption to services.'

'What does it say?'

'Umm . . . yesterday's date and . . .' He burst into song. '*Re Delays and Cancellations Going South. Da-da-da-d'dah!*' He opened his eyes. 'That's the tune! God – thanks. That was really bugging me.'

'You're welcome,' Ellen said.

As they walked back to the office, Don inquired about the subject of Ellen's postgrad course.

'I'm going to be researching the behaviour under stress of strata at the periphery of continental plates,' she told him offhandedly.

Don was convulsed by an embarrassed wince, but fought to retain some cool

'Oh, right,' he nodded, with a cynical sneer, 'you say that *now* – now you've wheedled all my best ideas out of me.'

When Robert Spleen uncompromisingly rejected the proposal for buttering up Gabriel Todd, Casey Rushmore marched to the elevator with a furious sense of disappointment and injustice. For once in his life he had conceived and proposed a bold, untried, speculative course of action – and he'd been told off like a schoolboy. As he hurried past his secretary into his office, his ears were crimson and his bottom lip jutted out. He threw himself into his chair, crossed his arms and frowned fixedly at his knees.

It was just *so* goddamn frustrating. On one side, he had Gabriel Todd, an innovative genius with a pragmatic view of the interaction between science and commerce. On the other side, he had Robert Spleen, a corporate visionary with an unparalleled talent for marketing innovation. And in between, Casey Rushmore, the arch-enabler, offering each of them a fitting and worthy match. And yet Todd smilingly rejected any overture. And Spleen good-naturedly accepted rejection.

Casey couldn't understand what was *wrong* with these people.

He was not going to let this slide. It *had* to happen; it was just too right *not* to happen. He told his secretary to book the earliest available seat to Boston, and then he left the office and headed for the shops on King Street. He went to Halford's and paid cash for a rubberised torch and a sucker-fixed rearview mirror. At Boots, he bought a contact lens case.

He doubted whether he had the guts to do what he was planning – but even playing out a fantasy, Casey was never less than thorough.

The day following his lunchtime beer with Ellen, Don joined some people from his department for an after-work drink at the Duke of Earl. Ellen and some of her colleagues were standing at the bar.

'What a coincidence,' Don remarked.

'Spooky,' Ellen agreed with her unedged smile. 'What can be the chances of two people who work in the same building meeting at twenty-five to six in a pub right next door to the office? Makes you think.'

'Oh, sod off,' Don told her pleasantly.

The two groups merged and Come-Along Cathy organised a kitty. At nine thirty all those who had insisted that they had to be gone by seven fifteen agreed that it was already too late for the five to ten train and that a swift curry would leave them good time to get the twenty past eleven. Ellen made noises about not being able to afford to eat out and Don insisted on paying her share. 'Listen,' he explained tipsily, 'one day you'll be rich and someone you work with will be poor and then *you* can buy *them* a curry. It all comes around on the karma wheel.'

'I'm a geologist,' Ellen shrugged. 'Could be a big wheel.'

After the meal, as Don ordered a third Irish coffee, someone offered Ellen a lift home. She thanked him for picking up her share of the bill, and went. The rest of the group began to thin out, leaving a pile of tenners in a poppadom basket on the table. As usual, Don, George and Flirty Brenda were the last ones left.

'Well, smoothin' in there,' George leered, 'with that Ellen bird.'

'*That Ellen bird?* Oh, you mean the loony?'

George grimaced. 'Yeah, all right. Give it a rest. Still, yer in there, eh?'

Flirty Brenda nodded enthusiastically. 'He's right, Don. Looking for a proper going-over, that one is.'

Don sighed. 'Look, she's an amusing, attractive, clever woman. I like her loads but I'm not after her bod, okay?' It was his stock response in such a situation; but when he heard himself trot it out, he was surprised – and strangely proud – to realise that it was quite true.

'Look, Donny – I mean, Don,' George explained, putting a matey arm round Don's shoulders, 'basically, you're definitely in with a chance there, big-time right? Green light, no worries. And if you don't poke it, I for one will atch'ly be very disappointed, yeah?'

'Not half as disappointed as her!' Flirty Brenda screeched, and she and George yelped with drunken laughter.

Don caught a cab on Euston Road. He toyed with the idea of going to the club, but decided that he was too drunk to concentrate or enjoy it. He gave the driver his home address. When he got in, the phone was ringing and he picked it up before the machine could cut in.

'Hi, it's me,' Unity said. 'Did I wake you up?'

'No, it's okay. I just got in.'

'Oh, right. Where've you been?'

'Just out with the usual crowd from work. Nothing exciting. So how are you?'

Unity talked about her flight, and gave sketchy accounts of her two days at the convention. She said that she'd hired a car and was driving out to see Sally in the Berkshires the following day. Don made listening noises – he was beginning to feel very tired. He stretched out on the sofa and kicked his shoes off.

'Are you missing me?' Unity asked.

'Of course,' Don told her drowsily. He wasn't. He rarely started to miss her before day four.

'*I'm* missing *you*,' she assured him.

Don doubted that this was true. When she was in England, she could quite easily go a whole working week without even calling him – unless it was for hypochondria support.

'Well, I should hope so,' he said. He was no more than a blink from falling asleep. There was a pause on the line, and what sounded like rustling. Don stifled a yawn.

Then Unity said, 'Guess what I'm wearing.'

Immediately, Don sat bolt upright. Grinning, he reached for his cigarettes.

'I don't know,' he admitted, snapping open his Zippo. 'Why don't you *tell* me what you're wearing?'

CHAPTER NINE

'GOOD MORNING,' SAID A recorded voice. 'The time is. Eight. Fifteen. Press any key for another call in ten minutes.'

Unity hung up and slumped back onto the bed. Outside, along the street, she could see the digital clock on the top of some banking building. 08:14. It blinked. 08:15.

She reached for the remote and zapped on the TV, bringing a breakfast show to life. In the corner of the screen, the figures appeared again: 08:15. Reflexively, Unity glanced at her watch. All the evidence pointed to it being a quarter past eight.

Four hundred and ninety-five minutes into the 11302nd day of my life, she thought, sighing. This observation required no maths. Ever since she could remember, Unity had known how many days she'd lived. She'd become desperately depressed in the month leading up to breaking five figures.

It was God's fault that she was plummeting helplessly down the fun-park flume that led from womb to worms. The Old Testament deity, with his patronising tease about Chosen Peoples, had given Time a goal – and so life had become linear, directed. Other cultures didn't see it that way. If Unity had been born an Ancient Egyptian, she would have seen existence as cyclical, flood-driven. As a Buddhist, she would have thought life indivisible. If she'd been born in the rainforests of Africa, the past and the future would have been no more than bookends that bracketed a perpetual now.

But she was a child of the Catholic Church, brought up on stories of corruptible flesh, judgement and inevitable decay. Forward and down – whatever curves and doglegs, everything moved forward and down. Somewhere in the world, right now, the marble that would be her headstone was lying in a quarry. The plot that would be her grave was being pollinated by dandelions. The ancestors of the virus that would kill her were being exhaled from a hopeless lung.

She rubbed her eyes and reached for her glasses, and put them on. Then she picked up the phone and called room service.

'Could I order some English breakfast tea, please, and a bowl of bran cereal?'

'Sure thing,' said the voice brightly. 'What kinda milk with your cereal? You want full-cream? You want skimmed? Or you want longlife?'

Unity frowned and then grinned a crumpled grin. She put one hand over the mouthpiece of the phone and lifted her eyes to heaven.

'You're doing this on purpose, aren't you?' she asked.

Unity was surprised at how quickly she became used to driving an automatic car on the wrong side of the road.

She had been spiky with anxiety driving in Boston – the road signs were unfamiliar, the pedestrians were suicidal and people had honked her at junctions. As she was waiting jumpily for the lights on one intersection, a truck driver queuing behind her had descended from his vehicle and tapped on her window. She refused to wind it down, so he explained, using loud, simple words and easily comprehended mime, that one was permitted to turn right on a red in this country. Unity knew this, but years of conditioning made it impossible for her to do it; so she feigned incomprehension until the lights changed, and then she sped off with a screech. The truck driver was moved to perform a more inventive but equally understandable mime.

Now she was out on the twisting blacktop, and the sun was at her shoulder. She'd taken the MassPike west as far as Worcester, and then cut across country to look at the scenery.

On either side of the road, the trees were modelling the Fall Collection. Orange was big this year, with russet and gold to tone. Accessories came in many shades of yellow, from jazzy lemon to understated ochre. Massachusetts was doing autumn like only America can do anything – large-scale, big-budget, seamlessly organised and oddly unreal. At home, Unity realised, autumn was that damp week before it got really cold. But this was autumn as England envisaged it, designed it – but had never seen it.

She'd been in the Black Forest once, a little before Christmas. The snow lay over the hills, deep and crisp and even, and in the town square of Freiburg, children wearing mufflers ran from stall to stall in the Christmas market, buying twisted sticks of candy and golden toffee apples. There was a merry-go-round and jugglers and a crusty old cathedral to tower over it all. It was the perfect English Christmas scene – and Unity had never seen anything like it north of Calais.

'The Germans have got our winters; the Americans have got our autumns,' Unity mused. 'Practically everyone has our summers. I suppose our springs are more or less our own.'

She was smiling as she thumbed a tape into the machine – Brahms' Concerto in A Minor, the cartoon-chase third movement. She put her foot down. It was the worst kind of day for driving. Clear, dry, bright. On such days, people drive as if they were immortal, and prove they're not. But – a glance in the rearview – the nearest car was half a mile back and there was no one in sight ahead. The music was leaping gleefully around the upholstery, and Unity imagined the scene as the opening of a movie. First the beeping and bleating city sounds; she'd be shot long-range as she sat at the lights in Boston. The soundtrack would be of passing cars, snatches of street talk, a dial running down the wavelengths of the FM band. Then, silence; an aerial shot of the empty road; far away, the burr of an engine. Cut to the centre of the westbound lane. The camera is low, flush to the tarmac, looking back at a bend. Suddenly, the car rounds the curve, roars over the camera and Johannes's strings skitter in, accelerating with the station wagon through the incendiary forestscape.

Unity laughed aloud. How happy she was! Why on earth was she so happy?

She abstracted, as was her habit.

Why was she happy? Well, to be frank, why not? She was clever, good-looking, well-paid and thirty-not-much. The weather was fine, the scenery astonishing, the tank three-quarters full and the whole thing was on Splendid's tab. Back home, she had a boyfriend who tolerated her less lovable traits, the sex was no worse than usual, and he didn't belch at the dinner table. In fifty years she would be a smear of ash, it was true. But – dammit – all the more reason to keep your sunnyside up, up.

Swinging easily through the serpentine curves, Unity decided that she was going to change her outlook. She was going to think positive and live each day for its own sake. She was, in short, going to the press the pedal to the metal and meet life head on.

With this optimistic resolve ringing in her head, Unity drove the car into a full-grown deer, spun off the road and ploughed into a clump of saplings.

Looking back, Unity would realise that she had caught sight of the stag when it dashed from the trees and came towards her at an angle across Route 9. It moved with great bounds, oblivious, apparently, of the imminent collision. Unity watched it as if it were an irrelevance, like an aeroplane passing overhead, or lightning cracking on the horizon. Almost at the last second, it occurred to her that the car was about to crash into a large, solid animal. She braked, twisted the wheel. There was a thud of the deer smacking hard against the side of the station wagon. As the vehicle spun, antlers shattered the windscreen. Unity watched the eastbound lane slide past her, then the brown, muscled flank of the animal filled her vision and was gone. Suddenly, with a screeching of rubber and a snapping of wood, she was surrounded by leaves, and the forest gathered her in. The engine died and everything was quiet.

Forever, Unity stared at her hands in her lap. '*Oh God, oh God, oh God, oh God . . .*' Her voice was low and breathless. Her hands just lay there, miles away. '*Oh God, oh God, oh God . . .*' She willed herself to shut up – but there was no stopping. Her sweater was sparkling. Her jeans glinted. She was covered in little diamonds of glass. How fast had she been going? Fifty? Sixty? What was that in kilometres? '*Oh God, oh God, oh God . . .*' She used to know the formula for miles to kilometres. Five over something. '*Oh God . . .*'

A face appeared at the window beside her. 'You okay, lady? Wow, you hit that big buck dead centre!' Big bucks. This was going to cost big bucks. 'You want to get outta there?' Still staring at her knees, Unity opened the door. A red-headed boy in a Patriots sweatshirt took her arm. She stood shakily, and looked back at the road.

The stag was lying with its feet towards her, maybe fifty feet away. 'Hey, hold still – you got pieces of windshield in your hair there.' The animal lifted its head, weakly. One antler was splintered and trailing on the ground. The deer looked at Unity for five or six seconds, for hours and hours, looked at her with brown, live eyes. And then it slumped back onto the road, dead.

Unity's legs folded. She sat down in the bracken and burst into tears.

The red-headed lad, Carl, had seen the accident as he approached eastbound. Boy, he thought she was dead for sure. Could she use a ride back to Boston? Hey, no sweat! Man, he saw her whale into that buck, he just figured she was dead meat. Jesus, he was scared to run over and look in her car, man. Thought she just about had the radish there. Listen, they better stop and call the cops, get them to move that deer. One hell of a road kill – used to go to the state prison, back in the old days. Probably wind up in some trooper's freezer tonight. That was a rental car, right? So it could be worse, right? But, hey, you sure were lucky. Shit. You feeling okay now? You English? Hey, right! Listen, you know *A Tale of Two Cities* by Charles Dickens? You read that? Dickens was English. All those old guys – all English . . .

And every mile to Boston, Unity stared out of the window of Carl's pickup, deaf to everything but the echo of a phrase from a poem she'd read at school about death. Death and dread and hope and a dying animal . . .

Unity stared dry-eyed at the ceiling.

What's the difference between dead and alive? This ghost we give up – what function does it perform that, when the ghost leaves, ceases?

She was stretched on the bed in her hotel room, wrapped in an enormous fluffy bathrobe, resting a glass of orange juice on her stomach. The lights were off, but she could still make out the cupboard, the minibar, the dark TV. When she had stepped from the shower and lain down, it had been full day. The orange juice she was holding had been ice-cold. Now it was as warm as her hands.

The Victorians weighed the soul. They contrived to have some pauper expire on a set of scales – and after death, six ounces had gone missing. In every other respect, the corpse was indistinguishable from the living, breathing human being that he'd been minutes before.

Was that possible? That some insubstantial part of a human being just got up and walked out, taking the secret of ignition with it? All right, if something is irreparably damaged, if the heart blows or the brain is pulped, obviously the machine conks out. But, Jesus, what about 'natural causes'? Why do people slip peacefully away at six o'clock? Why not seven fifteen, or just after lunch? What happened at six o'clock to make them dead?

Unity shifted her shoulders against the pillow and crossed her legs at the ankle.

People die under torture. They hold out for weeks and months, until one day they stop living. They're not significantly more damaged than they were yesterday. Given the gradual healing process, they might even be a little *healthier* than they were yesterday. A little healthier and completely dead.

'Completely dead,' Unity said aloud.

Perhaps alive-or-dead was not that binary. Perhaps one became *less and less alive*. And yet, the brain carries on sparking, the heart keeps beating right up until the moment of death. Does all that activity stop because you're *too* dead?

Unity screwed her eyes shut, concentrating.

No. *Dead* and *alive* are not useful notches on an analogue scale, like *wet* and *dry*. There's no life-and-death equivalent of *damp* or *moist*. You're dead or you're not – and life-support machines don't count. Unity had pinned out and jerked about enough A-level frogs to know that dead could be made to look lively.

She put the orange juice on the bedside table and swung her legs to the floor. She still felt a little unsteady. She walked to the window and looked out across the Charles River. 'I am looking at the Charles River,' she told herself in a quavering voice. 'I am alive, not dead. I'm a thinking, breathing human being – not a corpse.'

She turned back into the hotel room, switched on the bedside light and pointed the remote at the TV. Channel thirty-eight was running *The Honeymooners*, as ever. With one eye on the screen, Unity picked up the phone to call room service. She wanted a cheeseburger and fries. Maybe some pecan pie.

You had to just *live* it. It was all you could do – just *live* it.

On the television, the skinny one was telling the fat one a gag about the optimist who fell off the Empire State Building. So this guy's falling past the hundredth floor, the ninetieth, the eightieth, the seventieth, and he's yelling, 'So far, so good! So far, so good!'

Sitting down on the bed, Unity calmly hung up the phone before room service answered. She clutched herself around the waist and, rocking gently to and fro, she sobbed and sobbed.

CHAPTER TEN

THE NEXT DAY, WITH nothing on her itinerary, Unity was fidgety and lost. She called Sally in the Berkshires and explained about the encounter with the deer. Sally off-handedly agreed that it was a real pain but why didn't Unity just rent another car and come down anyway? Unity declined.

She decided to go to MIT and see whether she could find anyone to have lunch with. She walked from Boston across the river to the Cambridge side, and made her way to the building in which her first seminar had taken place. Outside the lecture hall was a board announcing the day's programme. In fifteen minutes, Dr Gabriel Todd would give a talk entitled 'The Grave Is Not Its Goal – Life Beyond Man's Traditional Span'. Unity stared at the title for a few moments and then, with a shrug, she walked into the auditorium and took an unobtrusive seat high up in the shadows at the back. An hour later, her life had been transformed.

For a woman of Unity's appetites, Gabriel Todd was a freebased narcotic. She wasn't completely convinced, but she was intellectually hooked, which was ten times more compulsive than conviction would have been. She watched Gabriel's pantomime with the liquid nitrogen and immediately realised that there would be freeze damage to human cells. This didn't strike her as an obstacle but as a problem – and therefore soluble. She wondered how one could be sure that the revived brain would retain the data that made one oneself. How might one construct an experiment on the persistence of memory with, say, frogs? By the time the lecture concluded, she was already planning a procedure for such work.

People were applauding. Dr Todd was walking out of the door. Unity pushed her way along the row of bench seats to the aisle, and clattered down the steps of the banked auditorium. Pausing to kick off her high heels and pick them up, she sprinted through the doors of the hall in time to see Gabriel leaving the building. She sped after him, taking the steps at the front of the college two at a time.

'Dr Todd! Dr Todd!'

Gabriel turned and saw a short, slim, dark woman in a print skirt and cream blouse, carrying navy shoes. She was wearing small blue-frame glasses and vermilion lipstick. She screeched to a halt beside him and began speaking very fast indeed.

'My name is Unity Siddorn. I'm well above average intelligence and I have a Masters in biotechnology. I thought your lecture was fascinating, and I have loads of questions I want to ask you. The first one is: do you have a vacancy for me? I'm not usually this forward, and I'm *never* this impulsive, but it's been a very trying twenty-four hours, and I shall probably never again be in the correct state of mind to make this approach.'

She paused, gulping, and looked up at Gabriel's puzzled face.

'Well?' she demanded.

Gabriel needed to go into Boston, and he offered to drive Unity over so that they could talk in the car. In the few minutes it took to reach Gabriel's destination, Unity explained about her work with Splendid Corps and her frustration with that work. Gabriel in turn told her that, flattered as he was by her wish to work for him, he had no job to offer. He was an academic, and had no team outside of his postgrads. He also mentioned that he'd had some exchanges with her employers and asked if she knew Casey Rushmore.

'Casey? He's my paymaster,' Unity exclaimed, as they got out of the car near the Christian Science Headquarters. 'He's the one who's cutting back my budget and making us sign for every bloody pipette we take out of stores.'

Gabriel raised his eyebrows. Then he motioned Unity to follow him. 'Come this way – I'll show you something wonderful.'

He walked up the steps towards the entrance of the Christian Science complex. Unity hesitated and then tagged along, frowning slightly. She would be both astonished and disappointed if this Dr Todd turned out to be some kind of religious type. They walked briskly into the building, and followed signs that indicated 'The Mapparium'.

Suddenly Gabriel took hold of Unity's hand and pulled her through a doorway into a chamber of blue-green light. Looking around, Unity saw she was standing at one end of a narrow bridge that spanned the interior of a vast glass sphere. She walked forward eight or nine feet to the centre of the bridge, and looked at the curving, translucent walls around her.

It was an enormous map of the earth.

Directly above Unity's head was the North Pole. The doorway she had come through was in the middle of the Pacific Ocean, and ahead of her, in the Atlantic, was another door, flanked by Europe and the Eastern Seaboard of North America. Peering over the edge of the bridge, Unity could see the Antipodes and, if she leaned out a little, Antarctica. She revolved slowly on the spot, gazing first at the tiny British Isles, and then at Russia, Kazakhstan, Mongolia, the Far East. Then came the vast expanse of the ocean, with Gabriel Todd lounging easily in its doorway, and on to California, the deserts, the plains, the mountains, and eventually the ocean again.

And just there at the brink of the American continent, there, it seemed, *she* was – a microscopic speck on the cusp between the unfathomable darkness of the water and the inconceivable forever of the land.

Unity raised her face to the North Pole again. There was a strange silence in this chamber – a thick silence that seemed crammed with many different kinds of quiet. A muted rushing came from every direction at once, without ever quite resolving into a noise. Unity held her breath to listen better – and the rushing diminished. She cocked her head to one side and raised her hand to her mouth – and from all around there was a brief sussuration. She realised it was the sound of her arm brushing against her silk blouse.

'It's an acoustic effect caused by standing inside a sphere,' Gabriel breathed in her ear – in both her ears. She turned. He was still ten feet away, by the door. He chuckled. 'Disconcerting, isn't it?'

Unity snapped her fingers experimentally. The click came soft and immediate from everywhere and nowhere, like the smell of the sea. She frowned, and listened to her badly dubbed footsteps as she walked to the far end of the bridge. Facing the blue wall of the ocean, she looked up and to her right, at the British Isles.

'So,' came a whisper from the air, 'is your interest in my work merely academic, or do you have immortal longings in you?'

Unity spun slowly to look through the submarine gloom at Gabriel Todd, still slouching in the mouth of the Pacific. His voice was a musical, atmospheric thrum that seemed disconnected from the man himself. In the murk, she couldn't make out the movement of his lips.

'There's an awful lot of it to take in,' Gabriel murmured, indicating the world with a casual sweep of his arm. 'I recommend the extended tour. Though it's expensive, immortality. If I am honest, the current roll call of our recruits leans more toward moneyed vanity than adventurous intelligence. It would be a pleasure to have you along.'

'I've already done the sums,' Unity began – but was startled by the volume of her normal voice. She continued at a mutter. 'I couldn't afford it.'

'There's so much that needs to be done,' came Gabriel's sighing tones. 'And by someone with access to good equipment, research funds, state-of-the-art technology. You know, the down payment is only a guarantee. A personal recommendation from an associate director, such as myself, would be enough to secure a place in the suspension halls. I guess you've played with DNA at super-low temperatures?'

'Yes. I've written a paper on it.'

'Really? I'd love to see it. I wonder how far they'll have advanced in that field in two, three hundred years. I hear Splendid's London sites are pretty much cutting-edge. Do you know what I'd do, if I had access to that equipment?'

'I can't work for you while I'm getting paid by Splendid. It's unethical.'

'Ol' Casey's a tricky one. So he's squeezing your budget, huh? Do you know what he offered me to go to Splendid? Shall I tell you?' The air filled with numbers, sizzling around Unity's head like locusts. 'See? You wouldn't be doing anything that they wouldn't pay ten times as much for.'

'That slimy bastard.'

'And anyway, knowledge belongs to no man or corporation. The hell with such petty scruples – life's too long.'

Unity considered, looking down at her feet, and then her gaze followed the bridge that spanned the core of the planet and ended where Gabriel leant, cross-legged, in the doorway that led beyond.

'Actually,' she conceded in a cautious whisper, 'this is more or less the area of research that I was planning anyway.'

Dr Todd straightened up, became a silhouette in the frame of the door. 'Precisely, precisely.'

He took a few steps along the catwalk, and stood at the centre of the globe, the light of the world illuminating his easy grin.

'Listen, you think it over. In the meantime, do you want to come with me to the music store? I have to pick up my fiddle.'

As they parted company after taking lunch, Gabriel asked Unity to dine at the house in Cambridge the following evening. Unity watched him lope off down MassAve towards his car and then turned to stroll back to the Peerless. Had she turned the other way, she would have seen Casey Rushmore emerging from a jewellery store across the street.

71

In his suite at the Providence, Casey laid out his tools on the bed. He surveyed them, appalled at his own intention.

There was a red jewellery box containing a diamond engagement ring, of which the stone was small but acutely cut. There was the rear-view mirror he had brought from England and, beside it, the torch. From his sponge bag, Casey produced the contact lens case and put it on the bed.

Then he took off his business clothes, hung them in the wardrobe and donned a black jogging suit, woollen gloves and Nikes. He distributed the implements from the bed amongst the pockets of the jogging suit, and looked at himself in the mirror. He raised one foot to the level of his waist. Plenty of room for movement. He touched his toes and the contact lens case dropped onto the floor. He picked it up, replaced it in a pocket with a zip, and bent again. He switched the torch on, to check the batteries.

Satisfied, he took off the jogging suit and hung it in the wardrobe. Having put on a bathrobe, he sat at the desk and opened *Scientific American* at the bookmarked page. It was twenty past two in the afternoon. Casey was waiting for midnight.

Earlier that day, at around noon London time, a call had come through on Don's internal line. He'd been in the middle of a conversation with a client, and was frantically signalling at George to pick up. George was engrossed with something on his terminal and didn't notice Don's arm-waving.

'No, it's a language thing' Don was saying into the phone. 'An American biscuit is an English scone, and an English biscuit is an American cookie. An American muffin is an overweight fairy cake, and God knows what the thing the Americans call an English muffin is. Excuse me . . .' He covered the mouthpiece. *'George, will you please get my fucking phone?'*

Having answered the call, George appeared to be indicating, by use of his right hand and left bicep, that someone with cramp of the upper arm was waiting to speak to Don.

'Hope that helps,' Don offered. 'No – you're welcome. That's what we're here for. 'Bye.'

As he hung up, George put the internal call through.

'Hello?' Don said, shaking his head resignedly at the leering George.

'Hiya,' said Ellen. 'I just phoned to thank you for the Indian again. That was nice of you. I was wondering if I can buy you a drink sometime, to even things up a bit. We could go and see a band or something.'

'Sure. Certainly.'

'Fine. I'll look through *Time Out*. By the way, I got a most macabre call from a friend of mine this morning. We have this mate from college called Mick who was always on for a bet. And apparently he got into a conversation at a party the other day which ended up with someone betting him he couldn't eat a whole tub of curry powder.'

'Oh, God!' Don grimaced.

'So he got out a teaspoon and did it. I mean, I think he was allowed a beer or something to wash it down, but he ate the whole tub. Won a tidy sum.'

'That is *disgusting*.'

'Well, a couple of hours later, he collapsed. He was rushed to hospital in an ambulance. They're keeping him in.'

'Christ, I'm not surprised,' Don replied, revoltedly intrigued.

'Yeah,' Ellen said, deadpan. 'Apparently, he's in a deep korma.'

As she hung up, sniggering, Don erupted in cathedral peals of laughter. Five minutes later, wiping tears from his eyes, he reached for his cigarettes and Zippo, and took the lift to the smoking room. He grinned as he slumped in a low chair – it was a long time since he'd heard a new joke. And it was even longer since a woman had made him laugh out loud. He lipped a cigarette, and chuckled again.

'A chap could seriously get to like that female,' he warned himself, firing up the flame.

* * *

The last upstairs light had gone out at twenty to one.

Casey waited an hour and then, emerging from the shadows, he approached Gabriel and Willie's darkened house. He was so nervous he could scarcely breathe. Gulping back the indigestion that spouted in his chest, he made his way to the side of the building.

He inspected each window with a growing sense of pointlessness. They were all grilled and deadlocked. You'd need more than an improvised glass-cutter to get through there. Casey followed the wall to the back yard. The kitchen door had two small panes and no grille but, pressing the side of his face to the glass, Casey could see two mortice locks and a bolt. He tiptoed, silent and discouraged, to the back of the building. The windows of the den were secure. The whole project was hopeless.

And then he came to a window of which the glass had been painted black. At least, most of it had. At eye level, an oval about the size of a man's head was still transparent. Casey peered in, to see tiny red and green lights, like the indicators on electrical equipment. A quick scan with the torch revealed that this was exactly what they were. He was looking into a small room – more a closet, really – that contained a photocopier, a fax machine, shelves full of stationery and, hard by the window, a large printer. There was no grille barring entry, and a simple handle catch could be seen to the right of the clear oval.

From his pocket, Casey produced the rearview mirror. He gently pressed the sucker to the window pane, and turned the little lever that created a vacuum to hold it there. Then he removed the jewellery box from another pocket, and from it he took the engagement ring. He pushed the ring onto the first joint of his right index finger and then, pinching it firm with his thumb and holding his right wrist with his left hand, he slowly traced the black outline of the oval with the cutting edge of the diamond. Then he took hold of the rearview mirror, and gently tapped around the perimeter of the oval with the heel of the rubberised torch. With the faintest musical *tink*, the glass came away attached to the sucker.

Still holding the glass and rearview, Casey turned and slid down the wall. He felt weird and dizzy. For a moment, he thought he was going to faint, but instinct kicked in. He exhaled and then sucked a huge lungful of air. It was the first breath he'd taken in nearly two minutes.

Okay, he thought, when his ears stopped thumping. That's the difficult part. Now for the dangerous part.

He stood and looked through the window at the door of the closet. He wasn't quite sure where he would emerge in relation to the stairs. He envisaged the staircase. Eleven or twelve feet from the top of the flight, and a little to the right, was the workbench. With luck, the microbots would be right there where he'd last seen them. Gabriel's casual attitude led Casey to doubt that the little machines would have been put away somewhere safe. In the best case, he'd find the control box too, but the microbots on their own would be enough to convince Mr Spleen that Dr Todd's services were worth any compromise, any exceptional arrangement. And, of course, he'd make sure that Gabriel got the robots back. He wasn't a thief, after all.

He reached through the hole in the glass, and turned the window catch. The window swung silently towards him. Casey picked the torch up and pocketed it. Then he raised a foot to the window ledge. This was it.

He stood there, frozen for a moment, and then put his foot back on the ground. He leant against the windowsill and asked himself why on earth he was doing this.

Why? Because history would judge that, just as the twentieth century was kick-started in 1908 by Henry Ford, the twentieth-first century began, for all practical purposes, with the partnership forged in the mid-nineteen nineties between Robert Spleen and Gabriel Todd. And when the documentaries and schoolbooks related this fact, Casey Rushmore would be able to dandle his grandson on his knee and, with a modest grin, say, 'Dad . . .'

No, hang on.

. . . say, 'Kid, if it weren't for me . . .'

That, he knew, was why he was doing it.

He slid his leg through the window and pulled himself up to straddle the sill. Taking the torch from his pocket and turning it on, he checked that there was nothing on the floor to trip over. Reassured, he lowered one foot to the carpet and took yet another deep breath.

Suddenly, the laser printer whirred.

Casey let out a little yelp, and slapped a hand to his mouth. The printer made a grinding noise as paper was fed from some hopper deep within and the digital display flashed PRINTING. With one leg outside the window, Casey leaned forward with his torch to see what emerged.

A piece of A4 began to roll slowly from the slot. The orientation of the letters showed that it was printing tail out, so that the bottom of the page would be the first to be seen. Slowly, the final line became visible. The block black letters read 'DO YOU HAVE THE STOMACH FOR IT?' Then came a pair of naked feet, one pointing bottom left and the other bottom right. Then the shins and knees emerged, streaked red. The thighs, as they became apparent, were strewn with what appeared to be lengths of thick, glistening rope. These also covered the naked crotch and . . .

Oh, Christ, Casey realised. *They're his bowels.*

The entrails slithered from a long, yawning gash that ran from the base of the abdomen to the cleft of the now visible rib-cage, which was splattered with thick gobbets of blood. On either side of the torso, the hands were curled in pain, the wrists nailed brutally to the board on which the victim was splayed.

The reproduction was of near-photographic quality. Had the printer's manufacturers required an endorsement, they could have done worse than approach Casey – though perhaps not at this moment, as his hand was clamped firmly over his mouth, and his greenish cheeks were puffing like synchronised toads.

Finally, as the amateur Raffles stared transfixed, the sorry victim's face came into view. The expression, surprisingly, was not one of unbearable agony, but of pale nervousness and anticipation. The eyes were glancing querulously to one side of the picture – as if, beyond the edge of the page, there might lurk something more ghastly yet.

Casey's hand dropped from his mouth.

'Oh, Jesus and Mary!' he gasped softly.

He teetered for a second, and then tumbled out of the window onto the grass. He scrambled to his feet and sprinted, gagging, onto the sidewalk and away towards Boston.

Back in the house, the printer stopped whirring and its display winked to WAITING. The disembowelled man on the picture in the print tray wore the face of Casey Rushmore.

CHAPTER ELEVEN

UNITY SHOWED UP AT Gabriel and Willie's around seven thirty the following evening. There was a huge old oak table in the kitchen and Unity sat at one end of it, as the boffin and the country singer opened wine, chopped onions and floured pork fillets.

'See anythin' here you don't like to eat?' Willie asked as he ground pepper into some emulsifying butter. 'It's not too late to scare up a carrot pot roast.'

Unity took in the butter, the lumps of pig, the sour cream, the puff pastry – and shrugged cheerfully. 'You only go round once,' she said.

'Yeah, but it's better to take the long way round,' Gabriel grinned. 'You wanna pass me the cinnamon, Willie?'

Unity relaxed into the high-backed chair and sipped her Chablis. Though she'd been in the house no more than fifteen minutes, she felt comfortable here, watching the two men working together. As Willie moved from the breakfast bar to the stove, Gabriel, without looking, would lean forward to let him pass. As Gabriel reached for an onion and the cutting board, Willie would hand him a knife unasked. Simultaneously, they raised their wine glasses in a gesture that was directed at each other but that encompassed Unity as a household member for the evening.

At the front door, Gabriel had introduced Willie as 'my partner', and Unity had assumed they had some kind of professional relationship. But the gold records she'd seen as she'd walked through the family room, and

Willie's evident familiarity with the kitchen, made it plain that he lived here. Unity speculated idly for the first few minutes, but as she watched them cook and chat and put on a bit of a show for her, she ceased to care what their sleeping arrangements were. She was simply flattered to be part of their intimacy.

'Chives,' Gabriel said suddenly, standing in the middle of the kitchen and scratching his forehead. 'Chives, chives, goddamn chives. I forgot 'em. I'll take a walk down to Bread'n'Circus.' He brushed his floury hands on his Levis, and headed for the door. 'I'll be ten minutes, no more. You wanna come, Unity?'

'I'm happy here with the wine,' Unity told him. 'Too comfy to move.' She waggled her fingers goodbye.

'Well, that'll about do it fer now,' Willie remarked, as the front door slammed. He opened the fridge and put a bowl of salad inside, and then picked up his wine glass and came round to sit with Unity at the table.

'So Gabe wants your head in a bucket, huh?' he asked pleasantly as he took a seat. 'What y'planning to do 'bout that?'

'I don't know. I'm – haha – blowing hot and cold,' Unity admitted. 'Are *you* going to . . . umm?'

'Don't be shy about sayin' it, ma'am. There's no shame in tryin' to beat that mean bastard with the cloak and the grinning skull.' He shrugged. 'And though I believe that the Good Lord has a place for me, I trust Him to keep it open for a while yet.'

Unity was surprised at the allusion. She had always felt that religion and science were mutually exclusive passions, like Scalextric and *haute couture*.

'So . . . er . . . do you think Heaven can wait, then?'

Willie grinned. 'That sounds like one o' them thar philosophical conundrums, ma'am,' he drawled, in a parody of his own accent. 'Don't seem fittin' fer a pure ol' country boy t'speak o' such thangs.'

Unity smiled back. In a lifetime of being told to mind her own business, she'd never been quite so gently diverted.

'So, you're a singer,' she said brightly, nodding at the guitar mounted on the far wall. 'I'm afraid I don't know much about country music.'

'Sure you do,' Willie said. 'It's all broken hearts an' lonely times an' getting drunk an' fighting back. Most folk know about that. What you're sayin' is you don't *listen* to country music – most likely 'cause it's sentimental an' melodramatic an' all sounds the same. That's okay. I don't listen to opera for the same reasons.'

'Shouldn't you be living in Nashville or Memphis or somewhere?' Unity inquired, emboldened by his candour. 'Boston's hardly renowned for its downhomeness, is it?'

'Well, you got that right. Boston, Mass, sure ain't Hayseed Central. Still, I can write an' record anywheres, I guess. But Gabe needs to be where the ideas are.'

Unity nodded. 'That's true. You need people to bounce off when you're doing research. You need the co-operation and the competition.'

'Well, maybe that's true fer you, ma'am,' Willie replied, pouring Unity another glass of wine, 'but it's not what I meant. Gabe needs to be where *his* ideas are – and they're here. There's something about Massachusetts that purely fires him up. I don't believe he could work anyplace else. He's just solid-gone Yankee, I guess.' He ran the tips of his fingers through his beard. 'Me, I can see broken hearts and betrayed love everywhere I go. In my line o' work, the research is easy.'

He got up and walked through to the main room, and slid a CD into the player.

'This is Patsy Cline,' he said as he came back to the table. 'My country, right or wrong.'

William Ezekiel Rabblestack was born in late November 1946, on the back seat of a cab in Tamataccatanna, Florida. In line with tradition, he was named after the cab driver who delivered him, one William (originally Vladislav) Witoszinski. This was a doubly traditional name-giving because William Witoszinski, though he didn't know it, was the infant's father.

Whilst cruising the three hundred yards of First Street that townsfolk laughingly referred to as 'The Strip', Witoszinski had been whistled up by the bouncer of the Honest Injun, a burlesque joint that represented the town's entire contribution to American post-war decadence. As William's cab swerved across the traffic to the sidewalk, the bouncer rushed across and pulled open the door.

'Hospital!' he yelled. 'It's Judy. She's havin' the fuckin' baby!'

This information threw Witoszinski into a flat spin. It was only in the last few weeks that he had begun to feel in control of his passion for Judith Rabblestack. They had enjoyed an encounter or two some time back, but William had realised that the sparkling, irreverent showgirl could never be serious about an impoverished, immigrant drifter such as himself. Though neither of them had ever explicity finished it, their fling had quietly ceased.

William didn't go to the Honest Injun for a while but when he did return, after a six-month absence, he was astonished to see Judith dealing blackjack, rather than kicking and pouting up on the stage. When he saw the bump that had made her too ungainly to strut her stuff, he was plunged into a treacly depression, in which his sticky resentment of *some other guy* was complemented by saccharine reflections concerning Judy's *little bundle of joy*. William Witoszinski's expressions of emotional extremis were supplied exclusively by the manufacturers of Sunlight Soap, who sponsored his favourite radio show.

So, that late November midnight, as the bouncer jigged nervously up and down on the sidewalk, Judy Rabblestack was arm-chaired out of the club and shovelled into the back of Willie's cab. A couple of the girls offered to come with her, but Judith wasn't having it.

'Go back and work,' she told them grittily, as the cab pulled away. 'You think I'd quit a night's money for you?'

Three blocks and twenty-five minutes later, William Witoszinski was wiping Judy's baby down with the chamois he kept for the windshield.

These things bring people together. Over the next few weeks, William spent a lot of time with Judith and little Willie. Without prompting, he gave up the cab and opened a tailor's shop on Peachtree and Fourth. Brought up in the family business, he'd fled Europe as much to escape sewing machines as Cossacks, but now he wanted to show Judy that he could offer a steady kind of life. He loved her and he was prepared – willing even – to bring up another man's child.

Judy, for her part, was flattered by William's uncynical devotion. She decided to settle down – to make pancakes in the mornings, to call 'Well, hullo!' to the lady from the drugstore. And she would certainly tell William that little Willie was his own boy.

Two years later, Judith was sitting in the caboose of a freight train headed for Texas. Little Willie was asleep in her arms, and Tamataccatanna was lost in the darkness behind them. In her purse was four hundred dollars won in a poker game on Thanksgiving Night; and in her heart was the guilty excitement that comes from deciding on a new course.

She had never found the right moment to tell the tailor that Willie was his son.

Over coffee, Gabriel prompted Willie to relate the story of his early life.

'I was raised in Del Harta, Texas,' he said, helping himself to thin-mints. 'Ma made a little money waiting tables, dancing in the chorus line at the Silver Rig, but mostly she put food in our mouths by playin' poker. Started off as a once-in-a-while thing but kinda became her trade. Still is. She moved to Vegas when I got out from under her skirts, and she's been there ever since.

'When I was twelve, thirteen – so this'd be the late fifties – she took up with a bass player called Tucker Orlando. In between stints on the road, he helped me learn guitar, piano and a little drums. One day in 1963, I went down to the railroad station to see him and the boys in the band leavin' fer some gigs on the West Coast, and I just climbed on the train. Didn't see Ma fer six months. After that, it was ten years of hotels and railroad cars, until I fetched up one night in a roadhouse just a spit an' a kick from here, where I ran into Gabe.'

'Of course,' Gabriel put in, 'Willie's still a Southern boy at heart. Come the spring, he's going back to Texas. To set up a mink ranch.'

'I may just do that,' Willie told him, wagging an admonitory mint. 'Born in the South, die in the South – that's what Ma says.'

Unity leaned over to pour Willie some white wine. 'Except you don't intend to die at all,' she pointed out. 'Neither of you do.'

Gabriel laughed aloud.

'Well, we're not so unusual in that. Very few people *intend* to die . . .'

CHAPTER TWELVE

CASEY HAD SPENT THE previous night in a fever of restless terror. Why, in God's name, was Todd constructing pictures of him being drawn and quartered? What kind of psychopathic lunatic would do such a thing?

He hadn't slept when he'd got back to the hotel after his house-breaking attempt. The image of disembowelment hung in front of him as he stared at the ceiling. It didn't fade when he closed his eyes. On the contrary, it became animated; it gained a soundtrack; it played in Sensurround. By dawn, Casey was convinced that he would never sleep again.

He began a desperate and deliberate assault on the minibar, starting with the beers and working through the wines to the spirits. As he finished each bottle, he lined it up along the escritoire and reached for the next, punctiliously ticking the new one off on the list provided. He expected, momentarily, a sharp rap on the door. It would be the police. Or – oh God – it would be Gabriel Todd, dressed in S&M leather and twisting a wicked scalpel in his rubber-gloved hand . . .

He placed an empty vodka miniature at the end of the rank of dead bottles and took a brandy from the fridge. He put a tick against 'Courvoisier' and sat back in the armchair.

But wait, he urged himself. Time out. Let's not confuse guilt and fear.

Obviously Gabriel was perverted, warped, but he didn't know that Casey knew so. That Casey had discovered this twisted freakery was merely fortuitous. Neither was Gabriel aware of the attempted burglary.

Therefore, Casey reasoned, he was ahead. He hadn't got his hands on the robots, but he had gained an advantageous insight to Dr Todd's appalling mind.

There was going to be no police raid. And no over-educated torturer would be paying a visit. Casey could relax, get some sleep and take his scheduled flight that evening. He could go back to London and plan his next move.

Just to be on the safe side, he jammed the back of a chair beneath the door handle before crawling into bed. He slept until late afternoon, then called a cab to take him to the airport. About the time that Unity was sipping Chablis in the kitchen, Casey boarded his plane. From Heathrow, he went directly to the office, in order to instigate a new plan for recruiting Gabriel Todd.

After dinner, Willie went upstairs 'to wrassle with a lyric', while Unity and Gabriel slouched on the big sofa, swapping catty gossip about the scientific community. Unity was aware that her host had not so much as mentioned his proposal of the previous day, and wondered whether he had thought better of it.

They had been chatting for only a few minutes when Gabriel suddenly jumped to his feet.

'Come upstairs,' he suggested. 'I'd like to show you something.'

He took her to the work area and pointed out to her the little silver discs lying on the polished wooden benchtop. He walked over and picked up the remote control, pushing shut a slightly open cupboard door as he did so. He explained to Unity that the little robots had been built by robot hands, and that those hands were scaled down from two or three generations of larger ancestors. Unity admitted that she was aware of the theory but she had never seen it in practice.

'Well, here it is,' Gabriel announced. He pointed the remote at the robots. 'Abracadabra! They move left ... and stop. And right ... and stop. It's pretty basic, but it's a start, huh? And move left again. And stop. What do you think?'

Unity moved towards the discs.

'Don't touch them,' Gabriel warned.

She bent down, frowning, trying to see beneath the little teardrops of silver.

'So, do they run on wheels? Air? Electromagnets? I can't believe you've got room for a braking mechanism in there. Why make them such a hard-to-produce shape? And that's an infrared remote – but these things aren't translucent, so how do they pick it up? Surely ultrasound would make more sense.' She straightened up to look at Gabriel. 'And you wish me to believe that these were built by robot hands that you subsequently cannibalised for parts? No, that'd be a marketable prototype. You're too practical to break up that kind of investment.'

Gabriel was grinning like Satchmo watching Dizzy do his thing.

'That metal casing worries me,' Unity continued, shaking her head. 'It's so difficult to make – and so pointless.' She turned and looked back at the bench and the discs lying on top of it. 'It must be a trick. They really look like little splashes of metal. So . . .' She turned back to Gabriel. 'My guess is magnetism.'

Gabriel was beaming like a lighthouse. 'She's very good,' he chuckled. 'She's really very good.'

'Sure is,' came the familiar Texan drawl.

Unity spun round and saw Willie clambering out of the huge cupboard beneath the workbench. He had a large ACME-style magnet in his hand. 'Sharp as a treadle needle and twice as fast.'

'Good brain,' Gabriel conceded. 'Damn fine brain.'

Unity frowned, annoyed now. 'What's this – a test of intelligence? I could have just brought my graduation photograph.'

Gabriel put an arm round her shoulders and led her back towards the stairs. 'No, it's just friendly mischief. It's not what I wanted to show you

– just the warm-up. Let me tell you something about your colleague, Casey Rushmore . . .'

He let her go ahead and then followed her back down to the lounge.

The previous evening, when Casey had peered through the painted pane in the closet window, he had broken a sensor beam, causing an infra-red photograph to be taken of his face framed precisely in the dark oval. This was the first stage of Gabriel Todd's intricate anti-burglar trap – a trap that had put the fear of God into less sensitive house-breakers than Casey Rushmore. Whilst the Senior Finance Director had been cutting the glass from the window, Gabriel's computer was digitising the photograph of Casey's wide-eyed visage and merging it with a horrific graphic chosen at random from a collection of similarly repulsive images. As Casey climbed through the window, the weight of his foot on a pad under the carpet had triggered the printer.

Discovering the picture in the morning, Gabriel had decided against transmitting it to the local precinct. He did, however, show it to Unity.

'He broke in here for two splashes of *solder*?' she asked, incredulous.

Gabriel shrugged an affirmative.

Unity was aghast. 'That is just *so* immoral.'

Gabriel poured her another glass of wine. 'Oh, I don't think so. He was just doing what he thought was the best thing to advance the cause of science.'

Taking the drink, Unity gasped. 'You're *joking*! He tried to steal your invention – or what he thought was your invention, which comes to about the same.'

'I *thought* of the little robots, sure,' Gabriel admitted. 'But that doesn't make the idea mine. Ideas, like cats, have an independent existence, regardless of where they snuggle up at night. Casey just wanted to give this little kitty a boost out of my back yard.'

'I can't believe you're being so generous about it,' Unity said, shaking her head. 'I'd throttle the slimy little bastard.'

'All that matters, in the end, is the work. How the work gets done doesn't matter. Where the money comes from doesn't matter. All that matters is the work – and the microbots would never have worked.'

Gabriel sat back on the sofa, and grinned.

'But have I told you yet about The Entrecote Engine?'

Gabriel had often wondered how pigs make bacon. How lambs get their chops together. How chickens knock out nuggets.

He understood the farmyard miracle by which two crazy lovestruck kids bring about a new and perfect little kid with no tiny fingers and eight tiny toes. But he wanted to know how that baby goat, with nothing to work on but half an acre of scrub and the occasional rambler's hat, managed to turn itself into a full-grown, bad-tempered billy. Gabriel found that a fascinating alchemy. Give a goat grass, he observed, and a goat makes more goat. Give the same stuff to a cow or a pig, and what do *they* do? Turn out beef and pork respectively. An incredibly neat trick!

At an atomic level, practically everything is made of the same stuff – it's just a matter of how you put it together. That was precisely the principle behind the microbots. Mother Nature, against whom Gabriel felt he was pretty evenly pitted, had beaten him to the punch on this one. But that didn't mean she hadn't left room for improvement.

Normally, Gabriel had noticed, the enzymes that make beefsteak will do so only within the confines of a cow. On the other hand, of course, they rarely get to work anywhere *except* within the confines of a cow. Gabriel Todd felt it was time to give those enzymes a taste of freedom. Fiddle with their genes a little and he couldn't see any reason why, given a bale of grass and a sunny day, they wouldn't be able to manufacture prime sirloin in, say, a cucumber frame.

CHAPTER THIRTEEN

DON WAS CLEANING HIS teeth when he was surprised by a snigger. It caught him unawares with a mouthful of toothpaste, and he snorted some up the back of his nose. This kind of thing had been happening a lot over the last couple of days. He'd tittered out loud on the tube as the train was sitting becalmed in a tunnel. Catching the alarmed glares of his fellow commuters, he'd tried to turn it into a coughing fit. Yesterday evening, without warning, he'd spluttered with laughter whilst waiting for his takeaway in the temple-like hush of the Heer Ranjha. The head waiter looked at him as if a jihad might not be out of the question.

He couldn't help it. He'd reached an age at which it is rare to hear a new joke, and there was something about Ellen's deep-korma gag that tickled his soul. He'd phoned a few pals and, fighting hard to keep a straight face, repeated the set-up. It had unfailingly gone down a storm. Admittedly, no one thought it *quite* as life-threateningly hilarious as Don did but everyone confessed, when pressed, that it was more or less the best gag they'd heard this month.

Don was pulling on his jacket ready to leave when the phone rang. It was Unity.

'Hiya. I was hoping I'd catch you before you left for work,' she said.

'It must be the middle of the night where you are,' Don calculated, looking at his watch.

'Yeah, I've just got in. I've been out to dinner with the most amazingly brilliant man. His name's Gabriel Todd. But he's gay, so don't worry.'

'Okay,' Don consented, unconcerned. 'Hey, listen, you know Dave's friend Ben?'

'Uh . . . no . . .'

'Well, I heard this strange story about him. Apparently, Dave and he were at a party and Dave bet him some large amount of money that he couldn't eat a whole jar of curry powder.'

'Oh, God,' Unity sighed. 'Why do men have to do these things?'

'Sad, I agree. Anyway, with the aid of a pint of water, he actually did it. Scoffed the lot.'

'As they say here, *gross*.'

'Two hours later,' Don continued, hopping from foot to foot in silent glee, 'he collapses and is rushed to hospital. Ambulance, the lot. They're keeping him in for observation.'

'Serves him right,' Unity remarked. 'Listen—'

'Yeah, he's in a deep korma!'

Unity tutted. 'Well, if people will abuse their bodies, then . . . Oh, I see. Very funny. A little contrived, but funny.'

Don cracked up. 'Isn't it though? Isn't that a killer gag? A woman at work told me it. It's made my week.'

'Yeah, all right – I laughed, didn't I? Listen, I really want to talk to you about this guy I met. He's got some ideas that – well, they might just change my career. Will you be in tonight?'

'Yup, I'll be here. Everybody else I've told it to fell off their seats.'

'Oh, for God's sake, *all right*. It's the funniest joke I've ever heard, okay? I'll call you tonight. Jesus!' She hung up.

Don put the phone back on the table. He was deeply disappointed.

'Absolutely no sense of humour, that woman,' he muttered with a shake of the head. 'None whatsoever.'

He reached for his Zippo and put it in his pocket.

'What's the bloody point?'

*　　*　　*

92

At the age of nine, Unity had applied to NASA for a job as an astronaut. She had eventually received a reply from the Agency explaining that if she were to gain a few qualifications and a few inches, there was no reason to suppose that she would not be colonising the stars before the end of the century. Not since the day she received that letter had Unity felt so excited, so optimistic, so sure of her calling as she did now.

Gabriel's theoretical Entrecote Engine – a machine for producing endless, cheap, cruelty-free beef (or pork, or pineapple, or cotton, or *anything*) – would have been an astounding enough project on its own. But, as Dr Todd explained it, the miraculous engine was simply part of a considered global plan to eradicate disease, hunger, death and eventually taxes. Gabriel wanted to be sure that the universe in which he would be revived hundreds of years hence would be the kind of place he'd be happy to hang out. As he put it himself, 'If Mr AD2400 is crowded, choked, starving and sick, he's going to think twice about bringing *me* back into the world. No, I want that guy to have the time and space and intellectual resources to be curious about his frozen ancestors. I want to be *irresistible* to him.'

Even the confessed self-interest of Gabriel's vision appealed to Unity. She found it refreshing not to have to ascribe her dreams of scientific panaceas to some spurious desire to serve humanity. It gave her permission to admit that she wanted a better world, primarily, for Unity Siddorn.

She did not allow herself to be upset by her phone conversation with Don. After all, he'd just got up, and could hardly be expected, without any prior warning, to fall in with her new, bright mood. She'd explain it all to him, when the time was right.

She pulled shut her curtains to block out the dawn, kicked off her skirt and heels and dragged the duvet over her head. As she fell asleep, her thoughts were full of the harnessed powers of enzymes. In a hallowed hut in every African village, a steel box rolled carpets of good, red meat out into the cooking pots.

And if you could design enzymes to build beef, why not human flesh and bone? Genetically-programmed single-cell workers could restore limbs abbreviated by leprosy. They could repair damaged organs at a cellular level. No more cancer, Alzheimer's, MS. No more congenital defects. How could any scientist – hell, how could any *human being* – turn down the opportunity to build such a future and live in it? As a child, Unity had believed that she would be seduced and swept away by a life like that. But life had turned out to be less impetuous and much more steady than she'd hoped. Now, after years of mundane living-together, her romance with life was on again.

'That's the kind of place I need to thrive in,' Unity murmured tipsily, rediscovering the idealistic and cinematic terminology of her adolescence. 'That's the New Frontier I belong to,' she told the pillow, as she fell asleep. 'That's the Tomorrow that belongs to me.'

CHAPTER FOURTEEN

DON WAS LEAVING WORK, about to head for the tube and home, when Ellen tapped him on the shoulder.

'I owe you a drink,' she said. 'How about now? Do you like the blues?'

They caught a bus up to Kentish Town and grabbed a quick and cheap pizza at Dough-Boy's. They chatted easily about people at work, their respective school careers, their favourite TV shows. Given that Ellen was little more than twenty – more than ten years his junior – Don was surprised at the breadth of her cultural references. She knew all the words to the H.R. Pufnstuff theme; she'd heard of The Buzzcocks; she claimed to remember *Department S*. On the other hand, part of the pleasure of her company was discovering unexpected cavities in her knowledge, into which Don was happy to pour the quick-setting cement of his own prejudice. He dusted off rehearsed aphorisms, and paraded opinions of outrageous subjectivity.

'Have you read Mervyn Peake? Passable cartoonist, lousy writer. Les Dawson? Seminal feminist, strangely. Tower of London? Terrific in February, crap in August.'

Throughout, Ellen maintained an expression of easy amusement which Don took to be unjudgemental if not uncritical. He was showing off, he knew. His personality was on maximum dazzle. He'd read enough *Cosmo* articles to believe that what women prefer in men is a sense of humour – a trait that always topped the polls above a trim bum and friendly eyes. He honestly didn't intend to get Ellen into bed. He merely wanted her to become a little smitten with him. He was after an intellectual fling, a flirty little frisson in his life. When the subject arose, as it would soon, he'd admit that he was powerfully attracted, but that any consummation of their bubbling desire would spoil a very special friendship. She was – what? – twenty-three. A child, practically. In future years, she would look back on her association with him and shake her head, a sad smile playing on her lips, and realise that he'd been right. Perhaps they would both regret their failure to grasp the moment but, hell, life is full of such regrets.

Don not only thought all this through, but related it to Ellen. It got the biggest laugh of the night.

It was eight o'clock when Ellen suggested that they might make their way to the Harvest, a chapel converted into a gig on the road up towards Archway. By the time they'd reached the place, elbowed to the bar and ordered a beer, the band were going on for their first set. Don was hardly paying attention. Instead, he was looking up at the vaulted roof of the deconsecrated church.

The beams had been painted in red and yellow candystripe, and ten-foot plaster cornucopias hung there, each spilling a frozen outfall of luscious wax fruit into the air above the audience. There were halloween pumpkins and nursery rhyme cherries and fairytale apples, all caught in the act of dropping like a wish into the laps of those below. It was an impressive trompe l'oeil, and Don found himself salivating slightly. He was about to make a comment to Ellen when the church was filled with the sound of a terrible, desperate sorrow.

It was a single blue tone, dipping at first and then rising through an octave. It was pure, and yet there was a fuzzed edge to it, like a sob snagged on the twist of a sentence. For a moment, Don couldn't identify what instrument might make such a sound. The climb through the semi-tones was too smooth for a guitar. The timbre of the voice was too feminine for a saxophone. Don arched his back to see over the heads between him and the stage. At that moment, the band kicked in behind the banshee wail, and the note resolved into a tearful minor lick. The player stepped back from the mike. He was the only blues flautist Don had ever heard or heard of

The band, it turned out, were no more than competent. They knocked out some perfectly acceptable standards and a couple of wittily ersatz originals, but whenever the flautist played, the sound was transfixing. There was an ungainsayable bluesy feeling in there, and an almost lateral approach to the instrument. The musician himself was just as extraordinary. His suit was pure '75. The trousers had v-knees allowing an extravagant pleated flare, and the jacket sported chunky, curvaceous lapels like the thighs of a lady rugby player. This creation was worn with red brothel creepers and an orange mohair jumper. None of these clothes was anything like big enough for the flautist, who was well over six feet and skeletal with it. His age was difficult to estimate because of the fly's-eye shades that covered a large proportion of his face, which was topped by a skull that was completely and uncompromisingly bald.

At the wringing end of a solo on 'Nobody's Child', Don tapped Ellen on the shoulder. She turned and fixed her unplumbable jade gaze on him, and he nodded towards the stage.

'That guy is quite something.'

Ellen nodded, smiling. 'I thought you'd like him. He's very special.'

The band left the stage to deserved applause, and the PA kicked in to discourage an encore. The bald flautist was making his way through the crowd to the bar, grinning in reply to compliments and handshakes. He squeezed between Ellen and Don, and signalled to the barman for a beer.

'Wotcher fink nen, doll?' he asked, out of the blue, glancing sideways at Ellen through his shades.

Close up, Don could tell that he was no chicken – mid-forties, probably. Certainly too old for her.

'Be honest,' the musician coaxed. 'Can this old geezer toot that flute, or whass goin' on, eh?'

Ellen appeared unconcerned. 'Triffic,' she agreed, adopting the flautist's accent.

Don frowned, waiting for the man's next move.

'Triffic?' the flautist repeated, aggrieved, 'It was *blindin'*, that woz.'

'Yeah, go on then,' Ellen agreed, pure Bow Belle. 'It *woz* blindin', granted.'

The flautist slid a casual arm round Ellen's waist. 'Blindin' enough to get me a cooked breakfast, princess?'

Instantly, Don grabbed the flautist's shoulder. 'Okay, pal, that's enough. Jesus, you're old enough to be her father.'

Ellen reached gently for Don's wrist. 'Don, allow me to introduce my father,' she said.

With his unrestricted hand, the flautist slid his shades down his nose, and peered at Don with bright green eyes.

'My word,' he said, with no trace of his former Cockney accent, 'you're on the keen side, aren't you, young man?'

Don and Ellen installed themselves at a table in the back of a bistro in Crouch End.

'I'm really, really sorry,' Don was saying as he accepted a wine list from the waitress. 'Honest to God, I've never been so embarrassed in my life. I'm . . . oh, Christ . . .' He put his elbows on the table and covered his face with his hands. 'Oh, God,' he mumbled.

'We'll have a bottle of the house white,' Ellen told the waitress. 'Don, leave it be. You've been making craven apologies for fifteen minutes straight, all the way from Archway. The cab driver was speculating that you had some kind of ejaculatory problem.'

Don dragged his palms into his cheeks, pulling down his lower eyelids like a bloodhound's. 'Terrific. Thanks.' He reached for his cigarettes, and hung one in the corner of his mouth. 'I can't believe I did that, though. Ten years from now, I'm going to wake up in the night, cold with sweat . . .'

Ellen laughed. 'Yeah, well, we've all got a few of those. Threatening my dad can't possibly be your worst.' She leaned across the table, eagerly. 'Hey, that's an idea. What *is* your worst? What's the thing that you're most ashamed of?'

Don lit his Marlboro. 'Nuh-uh,' he said, inhaling. 'We're not going to do *that* conversation.'

'Oh, go on,' Ellen coaxed, wrinkling her nose and grinning. 'You know you want to.'

There's no rationale to a feeling of shame. The chap next to you might be cripplingly ashamed of his ears, incapable of believing that no one else in the world has even noticed them. The woman over there might be paralysed with embarrassment because of her personal odour, unaware that she could easily evade a pack of tracker dogs for a week. Here's a man appalled at being called Nobbs, standing next to another who's mortified by his working-class parents, beside someone cringing at the thought of having to buy toilet paper.

Faced with the challenge, Don had instantly identified a clutch of faintly embarrassing habits that he'd be prepared to trot out. But these anecdotal confessions were, by definition, dispensable; like Presidential bodyguards, they flung themselves into the path of the bullet in order to protect Don's primary unspeakable secret.

Two or three times a month, Don's vice carried him up those narrow Soho stairs. He had to be slightly drunk to contain the shame that made him feel tweedy and leather-patched and Old-Spiced. The compulsion smacked of childhood Bank Holidays in the Master's Lodge, his mother's three o'clock delivery of crumpets and his father's chummy and awkward encouragement to enjoy himself, to do his best. The teenage Osman's merciless application of adolescent petulance had eventually put a stop to these sessions, and a couple of years later he'd wound up in a squat in Kennington. It was 1978, and he was a crypto-anarchist regular down the

Roxy and the Marquee – spiked blue hair and a lip so curled you could get a pin through it twice. He'd left small-town Sussex to the moles and the commuters, the Latin teachers and local magistrates. At eighteen, Don's contempt had been comprehensive and egalitarian. He loathed absolutely everything outside of Siouxsie Sioux.

But as he'd matured, he'd honed his feelings. These days, his scorn was pinpointed incisively at people who referred to the publican as 'Mine Host'; who caught 'the up-train' to the Varsity match; who bought educational partworks for their children Edmund and Rosie; who lived in a house with a name; who spotted inconsistencies in *The Archers*. Don despised, to be brief, the county-cosy English middle-class.

And yet, in his thirties now, he indulged in the most middle-class and English and cosy of pastimes. In an unlicensed room above a strip club on a Soho back street, Don played board games.

He played all the traditional wet-afternoon games – Monopoly, Cluedo, Yahtzee, Risk. He played the gimmicky TV-advertised ones – Operation, Hungry Hippos, Buckin' Bronco. To his depthless embarrassment, he even liked the role-playing games in which he got to be an axe-wielding troll by the name of Qrth. He couldn't justify it, and he hated the thought of it. Every time he went to the club, he could feel his hair becoming sandier and wavier. And he listened to himself as he played these games with acquaintances and strangers. 'Oh, good move!' he'd hear himself say. 'Well, that's a stroke of luck. My go, I believe.' And when he won, which he usually did, 'Oh, hard cheese. Still, there's always next time.'

They were, of course, his father's words. It was unmistakably his father's voice.

In the end, Don's unspeakable secret was not his game-playing. It was that he was becoming his dad.

CHAPTER FIFTEEN

ROBERT SPLEEN´S THIRTIES HAD coincided, more or less, with the nineteen seventies. The decade had seemed to him tawdry and uninventive – a time of second-hand music, third-rate fashion and fourth-form philosophies. An era of re-hashes and cold cuts. The kids were passive consumers of recipe-book fads, and each latest craze was identifiably a warmed-over version of something that had gone before.

It was true even of people. Everyone that Spleen met reminded him of someone else. After five minutes' chatter, he could tell precisely what this woman would think about Wagner, what that fellow would object to in fox hunting, why this chap would never eat seafood. Spleen felt that his experience encompassed every possible conversation with all the available personality types under the full panoply of social conditions. It was a melancholy observation.

Was this it, then, once you hit thirty? Was the carnival over? You'd been on all the rides, played all the slot machines, eaten your candyfloss and it was still only twenty to eight. Would you be forced to go on the roller-coaster again and again, becoming ever more blasé and diluting even the memory of the first heart-stopping thrill? Or would it be preferable to hang around by the dodgems and sneer at the teenagers as they hurtled past, screeching and laughing and knowing no better?

Faced with this dilemma in 1974, Robert Spleen became deeply depressed. For want of anything better to do, he spent day after day in the British Library, reading books at random, disinterestedly. Deprived of his constant attention, the stock of Splendid began to dip slightly on the market. The words 'troubled' and 'burned out' began to be used in conjunction with Spleen's name.

Spleen's practice at the British Library was to ask for a book at the desk by inventing an ISBN. One day, this technique turned up a dissertation in neurology entitled *Preferred Paths – A Study of Reduced Electrical Resistance between Frequently-Activated Synapses*. The theory presented in this paper was very straightforward. Electrical impulses, it stated, travel along the line of least electrical resistance. In the brain, there is a lower resistance between synapses that are often fired than between those that are triggered more rarely. This means that the way one tends to think will be dictated by the way one has thought in the past. A very slight difference in resistance in the young, untrained brain will be exaggerated with use. Come maturity, 'preferred paths' will be set up. The brain will be set in its ways.

This, it seemed to Spleen, was the cause of his recent disaffection. His thoughts were in a rut. It was not the world that was repeating itself, but his brain. Frankly, he was ashamed of it.

However, he saw no reason to surrender to this process. He would not tolerate such laziness in his primary organ. If there were synapses in there that thought they had a job for life, that sat around with their feet on the desk desultorily processing the occasional pro-forma thought, then they'd better get ready for a serious shake-up. And if there were others moping in cul-de-sacs, feeling that intellectual life was passing them by, then they'd get their chance to shine.

Spleen embarked on a furious round of intellectual stimulation. He visited art galleries, sponsored undergrad exhibitions, read scientific papers and pursued odd and offbeat people. It was difficult, at first, to overcome the habit of jadedness; but whenever he heard his inner voice carping that such and such a painter was derivative of Pollock, or that some aspiring playwright was re-frying Wesker, he slammed the thought down. He trained himself to look for what was new, different, original in any endeavour. He was not uncritical – often he had to conclude that there was nothing there to commend – but he developed an attitude that was, by default, optimistically inquisitive rather than wearily dismissive.

When it became apparent that Splendid Corps was sympathetic to new talent, Spleen was besieged by designers, inventors, crackpots and visionaries. He didn't mind. He made a lot of friends that way. And an enormous amount of money.

One could not, of course, sustain the manic pursuit of innovation that Spleen at first demanded of himself. He wryly observed that he was developing *techniques* for open-mindedness. His very avoidance of habit was becoming a habit. Still, he resolved to continue putting himself in the way of new experience.

For instance, he received a request for the renewal of the lease on a building he owned in St Anne's Court. He hadn't been there for years, and had almost forgotten that he was the freeholder. According to the letter, the ground floor housed an establishment called the Mount of Venus, which was referred to as 'a venue for exotic cabaret'. The first floor, however, was sub-let, and was run as a club called Movers and Shakers. The upstairs premises had neither liquor licence nor music licence, which made Spleen curious as to what kind of entertainment might be on offer there. And so he found himself, one evening, queuing for entry behind a dishevelled young man with slept-in blond hair, and a girl with paint-white skin and ice-green eyes.

The decor of Movers and Shakers affirmed that the proprietors were attuned to precisely the nostalgia they catered for. The walls were hung with posters from sixties TV shows – *Mission Impossible, Thunderbirds, The Clangers* – and the theme from *The Great Escape* was playing in the background. Robert Spleen took a stool at the bar, which served Nesquik, cream soda and a variety of half-forgotten breakfast cereals. The barman, who was dolled up in a turquoise Pepperesque uniform, handed him a menu of games.

'Are you expecting company,' he asked, 'or would you like me to match you with some competitors?'

Spleen ran his eye across the menu. 'Good Lord,' he said. 'You play Twister here? I haven't thought of Twister in twenty years.'

'Very popular later in the evening, when things warm up. But we do insist on our guests sticking to the clothed version. Can I offer you a drink?'

Open-mindedly, Spleen asked for cherryade, which he loathed.

'U or X?' the barman inquired.

It took Spleen a few moments to place the allusion – they were outmoded film ratings. He opted for X, and was given a crimson concoction which, by the taste of it, flouted the club's unlicensed status.

'Don't tell matron,' the barman advised as Spleen took a sip. He indicated the couple that had come into the club just ahead of Spleen. 'I have a pair looking for someone to play Mousetrap. Perhaps you'd care to indulge?'

Spleen followed the barman to the table. It was topped with yellow Formica patterned with tiny black flecks. The chairs were spindly and plastic and had padded oval backs. He'd had just such a set in the kitchen of his King's Road flat in '64.

'One more for Mousetrap,' the barman announced. And as he walked away, 'Play nicely together.'

'Ellen,' said the green-eyed girl. 'Pleased to meet you.'

'Don,' said the blond young man. 'Take a seat, why don't you?'

'I'm Robert,' Spleen told them, shucking his tattered denim jacket and hanging it on the back of his chair. 'Thanks for letting me play.'

A woman in a kaftan and headband delivered the huge Mousetrap box to the table. As they took the board out and decided who was to be which coloured mouse, the rush of memories was – Spleen couldn't help but use the word – trippy. The pieces were summer blue and sunburst red.

There was a disconcerting familiarity to the cranky staircase, the serpentine drainpipe, the boot-on-a-stick. For a moment, Spleen caught a whiff of joss sticks and an unidentified taste beneath his tongue – couscous. It was an illusory rush of yesterdays. He'd played this game, one long Frascatied summer evening, years back, with Quant and Syd Barrett and whichever mad, lissom sculptress he'd been subsidising at the time.

'Your throw, old man,' Don said.

Spleen was astonished at how the characteristic flaws of the game haemorrhaged from his memory. The contraption was completely unreliable – but that, he remembered, was the fun of it. The bloody ball bearing would get stuck halfway down the stairs. The cage would wobble down the pole and leave the mouse's tail untrapped.

'No, that doesn't count,' he heard himself insist. 'The mouse, the whole mouse and nothing but the mouse must be within the cage.'

The girl Ellen checked the rules. 'He's not wrong,' she admitted. 'Let him out.'

'Fair enough,' Don conceded, resetting the trap. 'A rule's a rule.'

As they played, Spleen sized up his companions.

The blond young man, Don, was concentrating completely on the game – scrutinising every roll of the die, precisely fitting each new piece of the contraption with watchmaker's care, as if this simplistic child's play merited consideration and respect. But there was something edgy in the lad, something overkeen and anxious. It was obvious that, from Don's perspective, Spleen was a tolerated supernumerary at a first date. Don's agenda was to impress Ellen.

Ellen. Spleen was fascinated by Ellen. She was assured, beautiful, intelligent, young – *God*, she was young. How did people get to be that young? When the third millennium began, she would be, at a guess, twenty-eight. Spleen would be sixty-two – and lucky to see the century into its teens. It seemed so arbitrary that the timely coincidence of sperm and egg should give one a passport to the twenty-first century. What would he give, he wondered, to see what she would see, to learn what she might learn? He'd give flower power, Woodstock, the summer of love. He'd give the lissom sculptresses, the innumerable homes, the franchised computer outlets. He'd give *everything so far* just to *be* her. Or, better yet, to be her child.

Don won the game. He sportingly protested his luck and ordered a round of X-rated sodas as consolation to the others, but you could tell that he was inordinately pleased. They packed up the game, reverentially laying the pieces back in the box, and called for the menu to see what they might play next.

'Frustration!' Ellen suggested, scanning the options. 'The game with the famous Pop-O-Matic.'

'With the what?' Spleen asked.

'It's a plastic dome with a die in it,' Don explained. 'You press it and it rolls the die for you.'

'A marketing gimmick *par excellence*,' suggested Ellen offhandedly, passing the Mousetrap box back to the attendant waitress. She looked towards Spleen. 'You know the kinda thing, Robert.'

Don rather resented those commercial games that were merely McGuffined re-packagings of traditional pastimes. He'd once seen noughts and crosses, with pre-printed grids, knocking out at twelve and a half quid a throw. Frustration was simply Ludo with a dumb-tech die, but this was not to say that he was loath to play it. Don considered his approach to Frustration a breakthrough in the strategic appreciation of brainless board games. Were it not for some appalling luck on the roll, he'd have been creaming the opposition.

But as the game went on, he realised that it wasn't just bad luck that kept returning his exploratory tokens to the loading bay. He was being ganged up on. Given the choice of any two moves, both Ellen and this smooth, self-satisfied Robert character would always elect to land on Don's man

– when they might, for example, go for the finish, or knock back one of each other's counters. And they weren't even subtle about this confederacy. Ellen would gleefully mark out the steps – *one, two, three* – and giggle like an airhead as she took Don's piece out. And Robert would laugh and exclaim, 'Right on the button!' before popping the die and leapfrogging Ellen's token.

Don wondered why he'd told Ellen about this place. He'd never told anyone else, not even Unity – if his relationship with Unity qualified as a test of such things. He supposed it was to flatter Ellen by letting her in on his secret. And he wanted to reveal that unexpected, whimsical bent that so endeared one to a girl. But the evening that Don had envisaged, in which he admitted her to his frivolous, esoteric sanctum, was being spoiled by the smug git across the table.

He reeked of money, this Robert. Don wasn't fooled by the faded jeans or the battered trainers. The man smelled of unlimited credit and chilled Clicquot; Kensington panoramas and slim hi-fi systems. He wore exactly that scent which might, for instance, turn a young girl's head.

'So,' Don said, as he pulled yet another red counter back to the starting grid, 'what's your line then, Robert?'

'Oh, I don't do lines any more,' Spleen smiled. 'I prefer sweeties these days.' He produced a cellophane bag from his jacket pocket. 'Would you like a sherbet lemon?'

'I'd love one,' Ellen interjected, reaching into the bag. 'Though my daddy told me not to take sweets from strange men.'

'Ha! I've *met* your dad,' Don remarked, pointedly. He turned back to Spleen. 'No, I'm seriously interested. You're an unusual type of bloke to find in this place. I've not seen you here before. I was just wondering what you do for a living.'

Spleen helped himself to a sweet. 'I market inspiration.'

'Ah, you're a PR man,' Don nodded, knowingly satisfied. 'Figures.'

Spleen shrugged unconcernedly. 'No, not really. But would that be so bad? Why does it irritate you so?'

Don bridled, realising he was being upstaged. 'Hey, just making conversation. I'm not irritated. Don't flatter yourself, mate.'

'Okay, okay,' Spleen agreed, holding up his hands. 'I'm sorry.'

Ellen popped the die. 'You detected, perhaps, something *splenetic* in my colleague's attitude?' she suggested, and counted her green token four spaces along. 'Your move, I believe, Robert . . .'

Eventually, on the back of a hot streak of sixes, Don won the game.

'Oh, yes, he strokes it in!' he exclaimed as he counted his last man home. 'What would you like me to humiliate you all at next?'

Spleen declined, saying it was time he was pushing along. He thanked them for their company, and left. As he disappeared through the door, Ellen asked where the loo was, and Don told her that it was out by the top of the stairs. She excused herself, and followed Spleen. Don tapped out a cigarette and watched her go.

She could make it down to the street, give him her phone number. She could even give the bastard a peck on the cheek, a squeeze of the arm. She could decide not to come back at all.

He fired up his smoke. 'None of my business,' he thought, shrugging.

But he smiled broadly when she reappeared through the door, and a straight sets win at Flounders, plus a couple of spiked Sprites, cheered him up considerably. Later, he saw her to the tube, and then set off south, wanting to walk the streets awhile. Heading down Shaftesbury Avenue, he allowed himself a cinematic strut, humming about staying alive, staying alive.

He flicked a guilt-assuaging pound at a dosser on Piccadilly Circus, and turned towards Green Park, feeling at home, feeling a long way from Sussex. With the air of one who owns the place, he ducked into a doorway opposite the Savoy for a pee. He was in mid-flow when a voice from the pavement said, 'Caught short, were we, sir?'

It was half past twelve and beginning to rain. Don knew that there was a copper standing behind him who wanted nothing more than to be back at the station with a cup of tea and a charge sheet to fill out.

Tucking it back in, he turned with an expression of contrite sheepishness on his face.

'I'm sorry, officer. You know how it is sometimes.'

'What's your name, son?' the policeman asked, getting his notebook out.

Don groaned. 'Son' was bad, and the question was worse. A truthful response would sound facetious – and facetious is a policeman's least favourite tone.

'Don Osman,' he mumbled.

The policeman's expression hardened.

'Pleased to meet you,' he said flatly. 'I'm David Cassidy.'

'No, not *Donny*,' Don sighed resignedly. 'Don. Not *Osmond*, Osman.' He pulled his Visa card from his pocket and handed it over.

The officer turned halfway to the light, and tilted the Visa, studying it.

'Fuck, you think *that's* bad,' he remarked, giving it back.

He produced his warrant card, and held it up in the orange glow of the streetlamp. Don peered, and then burst out laughing. He was indeed about to be arrested by PC David Cassidy.

'Sod off home, mate,' the copper advised, grinning. 'I get enough grief down the nick, without pulling *you* in.'

When he got home, Don found a message from Unity on his machine. Where was he? He'd promised he'd be in. She was flying home tomorrow and she'd call him.

He played the message twice. She sounded remarkably cheerful, but Don sensed trouble. He was already constructing excuses, and he hadn't even done anything yet.

CHAPTER SIXTEEN

UNITY WAS WATCHING THE ocean, amazed at herself. She was God knows how many feet up, gazing down at the Atlantic. Usually, at this point in a flight, she'd be cursing her own reluctance to take any kind of drug. She'd be desperate for mandies or Dramamine or anything that would put her out cold. She'd be breathing regular and deep, trying to slow her heart down, repressing the scream that she wanted to be let out, to be put down, to be home.

But on this trip, it was all all right. She wasn't going to die. Gabriel had shown her that she could live forever. Because she was brilliant and could serve the plan and was worthy of immortality, she would be spared. There was work to do – work with a point and a future.

Unity mused that you can't tell how high you are, over the sea. You can see white, frozen breakers; but surely they can't be actual waves. They must be vast swirls of current, or huge tidal peaks. It's impossible to tell, having nothing to scale by. The ocean looks big, but it doesn't look *vast*. It looks like a manageable thing, negotiable.

There was a time when people stood on the dock at Plymouth and looked out at the impossible green, and dared it. They set off on laughable splinters of wood, with the prospect of endless months of peril ahead. They clung to slivers of oak and ate balsa biscuits and dropped mahogany stools over the side into the salt. They died like leaves. But these days the journey of a million miles began with one step through the sighing doors of the departure lounge. Humanity progressed.

And by what power had this miracle of safety and speed and warm bread rolls been wrought? By the limitless ingenuity and the rigorous application of the human brain. Faced with the problem of travelling through space, humanity had turned to its scientists and demanded that something be done. Scientists had done something. Eight hours, comfy seats and all the Chateauneuf du Pape one can glug. What would Veluspucci have thought of that?

Unity did not believe that she had been born into an era that represented the apex of human achievement. On the contrary, she suspected that future generations would look back and sneer at the cherished achievements of her age. If she found it hard to imagine the pilgrims accepting that it would take endless weeks to make it to the colonies, she supposed that her descendants would find it quaint, pathetic even, that she was prepared to spend eight hours of her life plodding from Boston to London. She wanted to leave them a note saying, 'I know! I know it was risible – but it was all we had. It was as far as we'd got.'

For Unity, scientific progress was an endless continuum; a relay race, in which you tried to outrun death. You ran as fast as you could, and then, even as you collapsed in a fatal heap, you passed the baton on. You mustn't despise the baggy-shorted runner who'd given the baton to you, any more than you would want to be despised by the silver-sprayed sprinter to whom you handed it. But, over the last few days, the rules had changed. Suddenly, like a camera trick, she would be able to pick up the baton *herself* from the muscular specimen to whom she passed it. She would be beamed down just ahead of him – a bit stiff maybe, but hitting the ground running. She'd blow a kiss over her shoulder and stride out into whatever came next. And all this because of what was in her brain. Because her brain, thanks to Gabriel Todd, could be made to leapfrog into forever.

Unity looked down at the silver-green water thousands of feet below her. One day she'd walk on it.

* * *

In the warm light of day, Don thought that perhaps he had been a little overwrought the previous evening, allowing that flash of jealousy to surface. He must have had a Seven-Up over the eight.

Towelling himself from the bath and munching a piece of toast, he wandered into the front room and looked at his stereo. He had bought it with the wages from the same Saturday job that had paid for his contact lenses. It was a monument, all teak finish and Stonehenge speakers. When you hit the eject button, the cassette player presented the cassette with a slow grace that one didn't see in modern systems. These days they simply slapped the tape into your palm with a curt 'Here you go then'. It just wasn't polite.

And the turntable – oh, the cranky old turntable was wonderful. You had to weight the tracking arm with small coins, but on receipt of a mere couple of pence, it would be infinitely forgiving of scratches and beer stains and warps like poppadoms. Don loved that turntable. It was an honest thing without a hint of brushed black steel about it. It had never even heard of CDs.

But the turntable was sick. It kept slowing down and speeding up. Don was afraid that it might really be losing track. He had taken it to several repair shops, but the unfeeling bastards had all suggested that it was not worth repairing. 'Upgrade,' they'd said. 'Can't get the parts,' they'd shrugged. 'Take it to the Victoria and Albert,' the sods had quipped. There was one ray of hope. A friend at work had mentioned a bloke in Tooting who could repair *anything*. He had a shop in the market somewhere – not sure where exactly, but somewhere near the entrance by the bus stand.

Don dressed and didn't comb his hair and cradled the turntable out to the car. He laid it on the back seat and contrived to strap it in.

'You're going to be fine,' he told it over his shoulder as he swung out onto the Camberwell New Road.

It was a bright autumn Saturday in South London. The sun was bounding gleefully from windshield to windshield, and the traffic was hanging about at each red light as if it had all the time in the world. As Don's unremarkable blue Fiat sauntered along the edge of Clapham Common, he glanced at the dads and sons fishing in the Round Pond, and marvelled at their imperturbable perseverance. Maybe there really was a fish in there somewhere but they weren't going to catch it. They had more chance of reeling in the *Lusitania*, love 'em.

On the Balham stretch he cheerily waved out every motorist who nosed from a side street, and from Tooting Bec onwards he amused himself in the clotted gridlocks by peering into Asian supermarkets to spot vegetables that he didn't know the names of. With his indicator winking chummily at a stalled coupé, he selected an arbitrary turning off the Broadway and was rewarded with a parking space that had just that minute been vacated by a crack dealer's Merc. He lifted the turntable from the car and carried it in both arms, like an injured animal, to the indoor market.

By the entrance there was a fruit and veg stall, hemmed in by a cackle of housewives feeling the toms and inspecting the runners. Opposite that, a Mr Minit heel bar – *All standerd key's while you 'shop'* – and a Hong Kong supermarket, frequented by young white couples buying Eastern spices that would lie untouched in the back of the larder until the lovers saved up the deposit on a mews house in Chiswick.

Don wandered deep into the throng. He pushed past the Dub Exchange, from which a heavy, physical on-beat emerged, shouldering its way into the mêlée like a skanking giant. He lifted his ailing turntable above the heads of kids gathered around the rabbit cages outside the pet shop, and squeezed by fag-ash old women who grouped by the fish stall, exchanging horror stories about the price of cod. He did a round tour of the market and found no hi-fi repair shop.

Back at the fruit and veg stall, he queued by the bananas.

'Oo's next?' asked the stallholder brightly. 'Yes, son?'

Don gauged the accent and adjusted his accordingly.

''Scuse me, mate. D'you know if there's a bloke in the market who repairs stereos?' He lifted his turntable a few inches, to clarify the inquiry. 'I was told there was a geezer round here somewhere.'

'Aah, you're after old Mr Mount. 'E chucked it in, well, musta bin two years gone. 'Ang on a sec.' He turned and called to a woman who was in the act of tipping some Grannies from the weighing pan into a brown bag. 'Where'd old Mounty move out to, Lil?'

She grabbed the bag by its open corners and, with a deft flick of both wrists, made it back-somersault to form a mouse-eared fastening.

'Out in the sticks somewhere,' she said, handing the bag to a small boy clutching a shopping list. 'West Byfleet. 'Is daughter lives out there.' She took the list from the boy. 'Whass that say, love? Spuds?'

The man turned back to Don. ''Sright, West Byfleet. 'E got hisself a little shop out there, fie remember. In Surrey.'

'Shit,' Don sighed. 'Oh, well, cheers. Give us a pound of Victorias, will yer?'

As Don turned to leave, with the plums balanced atop the turntable, the stallholder advised, 'Be lucky. Mind 'ow yer go.'

Don grinned. 'I will,' he promised under his breath. 'I'll be lucky and I'll mind how I go.'

Back at the car, he turned the radio on, and caught the traffic report. Everything everywhere was apparently flowing smoothly. People all over the South-East were setting off to go places and getting there in precisely the time they'd allowed. The internal combustion engine was having a field day.

'Sod it,' Don told the turntable. 'Let's go to West Byfleet.'

The route out of South London to Surrey is an A-road that's got rather above itself. It's no more than a narrow-lane three-strip, but it thinks it's an autobahn. In his little Fiat, Don pootled along in the slow lane and watched the BMWs and Cosworths torrent past as if he were a line of cones. These people, Don observed, were not minding how they were going. He took the exit signposted for his destination, and eventually pulled up in a template commuter village. Confident of the bourgeois honesty rife in the pink-gin belt, he left the turntable on the back seat of the car and wandered along the High Street. There was a chain supermarket, a music shop with a window full of Spanish guitars, a Montessori nursery and a newsagent's that drew the line at *Playboy*. There was no sign of old Mr Mount.

Don went into the newsagent's.

'Can I help you?' asked the blue-smocked matron at the counter from within a cloud of Anaïs Anaïs.

'I certainly hope so,' said Don, adopting his what-a-nice-young-man tone. 'I'm looking for a shop run by one Mr Mount, who's apparently a whizz with hi-fi equipment.'

'You mean Stanley,' the woman told him, with an unhesitating smile. 'But he doesn't have a shop as such; just a card in our window. He lives round the corner.' She gave directions – scarcely a three-minute stroll, she said. 'Tell him Dorothy says hello.'

You can't beat the human race, Don thought as he went and collected his turntable from the car. They're by far my favourite species.

Mr Mount's house was a nineteen thirties job, with curved corners and windows like an ocean-going liner. Hoiking the turntable onto one arm, Don pressed the bell, and it ding-donged as one simply knew it must. He stepped back an unthreatening two paces, as the door was opened by an elderly, dapper little man in a claret cardigan. His trousers were of the drip dry type that come with a built-in plastic belt, and he wore – of course he wore – half-glasses, over which he peered at his unexpected visitor.

'Hello?'

'I very much hope that you are Mr Mount,' Don beamed, offering his turntable.

'A BS five fifty-one!' the old gentleman exclaimed, laying a delicate hand on its lid. 'They don't make them like this any more. Come through to the workshop.'

There was a polished bench, and ledges stacked with labelled coffee jars full of screws and fuses and intricate little electrical whatnots. There was an immaculately clean soldering iron in an equally immaculate holder One wall bore wide shelves, on which sat an assortment of speakers and turntables and cassette decks, a luggage tag hanging from every one, identifying its owner.

'Bellman Sonic,' Mr Mount marvelled, gently lifting the arm of Don's turntable with one finger. 'Went bust a few years back. Tragic, because it's beautifully manufactured equipment. And this would be the, what, seventy-three model? Seventy-six, you say? No, it was old stock when you bought it, Mr Osman. A hundred and forty pounds for the whole system, eh? Well, that was a lot of money in those days. And never had to spend a penny on it since, I'll be bound.'

Don explained the problem with the motor. Could it, by any chance, be made better?

'Well, I shall have to have it to bits, of course. Clean it up, find out what's what. If, as I fear, the motor is simply old and tired, then I'll have to see if I can dig out a substitute. They don't make them any more. It could be a rather pricey operation, I'm afraid.'

Silently, Don decided that anything over sixty quid wasn't worth it. Well, seventy, tops. 'How much, do you think?'

'Put it this way,' Mr Mount said, running his finger through the dust on the imitation teak surround. 'Give me your telephone number, and if it looks like being more than fifteen pounds, I'll call you to get the go-ahead.'

Don tried to stifle a laugh. 'No, it's okay. Just do whatever needs to be done.'

'Oh, no, no,' Mr Mount frowned. 'I don't like to give people nasty surprises. I guarantee it'll be no more than fifteen unless something unexpected comes up, in which case I'll phone.' He closed the lid and patted it wistfully.

'Old school, you see,' he smiled. 'Designed to last.'

*   *   *

'Hiya,' said Unity, kissing Don at the door. 'How are you? You look cheerful.'

Don walked through to the kitchen and made for the fridge.

'I have had,' he said, 'the most fantastically pleasant day. A real glad-to-be-alive day. It's been brilliant. How about yourself?'

'Fine. The flight was smooth – I think I've cracked this fear of flying thing – and I slept all afternoon. I feel great.'

'Terrific. Get your knickers off.'

'I'm ahead of you.'

At an Italian restaurant on the Fulham Palace Road, they ordered a bottle of Cava. They chinked their glasses together, and held each other's gaze as they knocked it back.

This is okay, Don thought. I can live like this, no trouble. I can bear someone who orders Parma ham and melon without the ham, as long as she'll put up with me ordering it without the melon. Come to think of it, it's a perfect match.

Over the main course, she told him about the accident with the deer. He was concerned and shocked. Part of his astonishment was at the tone she employed to tell the story – she seemed almost amused by it. Where was her self-obsessive angst, her capitulating conviction that imminent death was no more than you could expect from life?

'Blimey,' he said. 'You seem to be taking it very well.'

'Oh, believe me, I didn't at the time. I was more of a write-off than the car. But then – well, wait until we've finished eating. I've got loads to tell you.'

They were starting on their third bottle of wine as the dessert plates were taken away.

'And a cappuccino,' Don told the waiter.

'Make it two,' said Unity.

Don raised his eyebrows. 'You went to Boston, right? Not Damascus.' He was feeling tired and mellow. Though intrigued by the prospect of

Unity's news, he was hoping that it would be brief, so that they could get back to her place for an unenergetic round of duvet-rumpling and eight hours' kip. He lit a cigarette.

'Go on then,' he cued her. 'Get it off your beautifully-formed chest.'

Unity described her desperate mood after the car crash, and her long night of sobbing.

'I was in shock, I suppose. I would be, really.' She told how she'd happened upon Gabriel Todd's lecture and how she'd pursued him. Over twenty minutes, the story came out in a tumbling rush, but the progression of the argument was characteristically exact.

'So, given that your brain is just an organic database – a way of storing information – it follows that if you can preserve the brain, then you can preserve all that it holds. It's much too expensive to store a whole corpse, obviously. Anyway, Gabriel believes – and there's no reason to argue with him – that we will soon be able to transplant a brain to a different body. Maybe not in our lifetimes but – well, when I say our lifetimes, I mean within the useful shelf life of our current bodies. And this, of course, is the point—'

'Hang on, hang on,' Don interrupted. 'Has this bloke asked you to do work in this field? Are you going to move to America?'

Unity laughed. 'No, I can work here. You see, we need to start developing genetically-engineered enzymes that can repair potential damage to suspended brain cells. You wouldn't want to wake up a drooling idiot – or even with great holes in your personality.'

'Jesus,' Don shrugged. 'I wouldn't think you'd want to wake up *at all*, would you? I mean, who wants to be stranded in some unknowable, friendless future? You'd be a freak. You'd be Kasper Hauser.'

Unity bridled. 'No, I wouldn't,' she protested.

'Er, actually, I didn't mean you *personally*,' Don pointed out, as he flicked his lighter. He paused in the act of lighting his cigarette, and looked across at her. 'Fuck – *you* don't mean *you*, do you?'

'Why not?' Unity exclaimed, a zealot's flush on her cheeks. 'Why on earth not? It'd be amazing!'

'It'd be horrible!' Don sucked hard on his cigarette and leaned forward with his elbows on the table. 'Think about it. We're all children of our time. Everything we are is connected to everything around us. Take – I dunno – Shakespeare, Newton, Socrates. How do you think they'd fare in downtown LA? It's ludicrous.'

'You'd *adjust*,' Unity insisted. 'Certainly there'd be a culture shock – *let me finish!* – but you'd learn new ways, you'd get used to the new environment. God, when I went on my trip to the Arctic—'

'Oh, come *on*. It's not the same thing.'

'It's *exactly* the same bloody thing. I'll tell you what *your* problem is – you're just scared of being a tourist, of not being *streetwise*. You managed to get all the way across France without getting out of the car in case you committed some embarrassing *faux pas*. Me, I'd learn. I'd revel in it. I *will* revel in it. And I'm not the only one, either. A lot of people are very serious about this. There's a network right across the US, planning the best way to ensure a better world for a second life. They're not crackpots. They're just ordinary people – some of them are scrimping and saving to get the money to secure a place for themselves and their families.'

Don pushed away from the table and spread his arms, as if in an appeal for sanity. 'Christ, Unity, that's half my point! There are poor, deluded sods spending their whole and only lives investing in the chance of a second run at it. And they don't even know that it'll *work*! What a fucking obscene waste of three score and ten!' He gestured with his cigarette, taking in the restaurant, the street outside, and everything beyond it. 'Look around. This is *it*, baby! This is the only one you get! And no Maharishi or Billy Graham or Gabriel Whatsisname can give you another one.'

Unity shook her head. 'Superstitious fear and lack of imagination,' she declared. 'The bugbear of progress since the discovery of fire. You might think differently when you're diagnosed with a tumour on your lung.'

Don dragged hard on his cigarette and blew out a stream of smoke.

'Yeah, well,' he shrugged dismissively, 'don't you go worrying your severed little head about it.'

They didn't agree to differ precisely, but their silence over coffee acted as a mutual concession that there was, for the present, no further to go. As they walked back to the flat, Don waited for Unity to suggest that perhaps it'd be better if he didn't stay over – but they were at her gate now, and the suggestion hadn't come. For his part, Don didn't reckon the argument was severe enough to warrant postponing a perfectly good leg-over. Actually, he couldn't imagine ever having an argument *that* severe.

Unity was angry though, he could tell. As she lay in the dark, asleep in a knotted ball, he moved his back gingerly against the sheets. The scratches were going to take days to heal.

CHAPTER SEVENTEEN

SPLEEN PALMED THE REMOTE, and pushed up the volume of Mozart's *Requiem Mass*. He was listening to a lot of requiems recently. For weeks he had endeavoured to find something more than hackneyed in his overwhelming intimations of mortality, yet he could not but conclude that he was in the thrall of a cliché. He was fifty-eight years old, wealthy beyond calculation and his innards were going insane.

A couple of years ago, his gall bladder had gone barmy – squabbling with itself, the cells dividing and re-dividing, getting ideas above their station. He'd had it whipped out. Into the hospital incinerator it went, and so perish all traitors to the corporate ideal.

Five years, the consultant had said. *If nothing else goes haywire within five years, then you're in the clear.*

He'd ticked off the days. One, two . . . thirty, a month. An equinox, a test, a solstice, the first anniversary of his puckered little scar. Another anniversary and an annual return. Two whole years.

And then, *Robert, it's Gerard here. Something's come up on your last test. Probably nothing, but could you drop by? Well, this week, if you can find the time.*

The prostate, that mischievous little life-giver.

We'll just have a poke around, see what's afoot. Even in the worst case, it's immensely treatable.

Something was indeed afoot. Cheerio, prostate. Another second-division organ consigned to the flames. Dammit, he was being serially cremated.

One, two . . . Thirty. An equinox . . .

He got up from the sofa and walked to the kitchen, past Warhol's litho of him with the infant Patti Hearst on his knee, past the photo of Frank Zappa handing him a Marlboro, past the framed napkin on which he and Lennon had scribbled drunken nonsense about walruses, past a yellowing snap of his father holding a Lee Enfield in one hand and a glass of sangria in the other.

Spleen opened the freezer and took out a bottle of vodka.

He glanced around the kitchen as if he'd misplaced something – and then grinned hollowly as he realised what he was looking for. How strange, after all this time, that he should crave a cigarette when he was in this mood. How odd that he should believe a deep drag would solve something. He took the frosted bottle and a shot glass back to the drawing room. The Mass was in full swing and he couldn't bear it. He switched it off and sat down, resting the vodka bottle in his lap.

The image of the green-eyed girl, Ellen, swam into his mind, as it had several times over the last few days. He closed his eyes and pondered this recurring phenomenon.

She was, unarguably, beautiful, but his life had been filled with such beauty, more or less on demand. She seemed intelligent, but no more than those women who inspired no particular interest in him. She was young, and he had no history of attraction to very young women. Indeed, he regarded as pitiable those of his contemporaries who were sustained by the flesh of barely-adult companions. And yet – Ellen's youth seemed so much less gaudy and fizzy a thing than that of the Cindys and Arabellas who greeted him at house-warmings as their smug, bald new husbands helloed from the gleaming open-plan bar. There was a stillness around Ellen, a serenity that the shifty Zen gurus of the sixties had tried to embody, package and sell on, and that their eager, snake-oil smirks had so demonstrably lacked.

. . . There it was then. This preoccupation was no more than another

124

hackneyed hunger. He was an ageing, troubled businessman transfixed by what he could never have – youth and inner peace.

His grandmother, who had lorded it – *ladied* it – over large swathes of the twilight Raj, had lived to be eighty-one. In the latter years of her life, her hands had become wooden, like mandrake roots. Her eyes, which reportedly had once stared down a tiger, paled. The stately body – a body that Millais, spurned, had been moved to paint from imagination alone – became a genteel slum in which she lived.

'I look at myself in the mirror, you know, Robbie,' she'd told her grandson, 'and I cannot believe that it's me.' He was about to go up to university. She was about to die. 'I expect daily some inner transformation that will cause me to feel as I imagine an old lady should, and yet I continue to feel exactly as I felt when I was nineteen.'

Oh, surely not, Robert had thought. You can't. You're *old.*

At twenty, thirty, forty even, it had seemed to Spleen that there was plenty of time left. Assuming he made it to sixty-odd – well, twenty years plus in hand. Hardly an immediate problem. And there was always the much-vaunted and comforting notion that old people became friendly with death. *Oh, I don't mind going now. I've had a good life.*

To hell with that. Grandmamma was spot on. Robert was as bright, as keen, as interested as he'd ever been. He felt exactly as he'd felt when he was nineteen, except that he had a wider understanding. He'd worked at it. He had earned more right *now* to be a part of the seething mass of humanity than he could ever have claimed as a self-righteous, self-serving, testosterone-driven youth.

Christ Almighty, at the very moment you get good at it, you're taken out of the game. Where was the sense in *that*?

There was a pencil lying on the low Thai-imported table beside the sofa. Spleen picked it up and lodged it in the corner of his mouth. He took a deep pull on it and emitted a silent laugh that was just as nearly a sob. He downed a shot of vodka and poured another, then reached out for the pile of magazines and newspapers stacked on the Berber rug in front of him. Flicking through the tabloids, he read about twenty-two-year-old soap stars dumping eighteen-year-old models, and seventeen-year-old footballers with Europe at their feet. The quality rags feted bum-fluffed novelists dribbling on about their newborn babies, and profiled pasty, callow politicians with multimillion-pound defence budgets but no idea who Khrushchev was.

Christ.

He switched to an unread Sunday supplement. Central Europeans were obligingly dying in colour; American celebrities were contracting AIDS in monochrome. And in a box headed 'In Next Week's Magazine', there was a head and shoulders shot of an aquiline, dark-eyed fellow, resting his chin on a chainsaw. The caption read, 'This man plans to live forever. For £20,000 down, you can too.'

Gabriel was at the workbench in the laboratory, tossing the planet earth from hand to hand. He'd been restoring a sixteenth-century orrery – a clockwork model of the solar system – and three months' work was about to reach fruition. He screwed the little sphere onto its rod, and then wound the contraption up. The toothed wheels began their regular, jerky movement, and the system moved smoothly into life. Gabriel chuckled with delight, watching the escapement mechanism click, the planets rotate. He leaned forward and blew dust from the rings of Saturn, and then sat back and relaxed, sipping his coffee, as a year went by.

The unreclaimable passage of the days caused no anxiety in Gabriel Todd. His endless tinkering with clockwork sprang from a fascination with elegant engineering rather than with time-keeping. 'You can't keep time,' he told his students. 'You can only choose how to spend it.'

In the room to his left, on the bedside table, stood a timepiece that Gabriel had made himself – one which woke him and Willie every day. Gabe had hand-tooled each brass wheel of the movement, and tenderly

126

crafted the wooden case. In all, it was the perfect reproduction of an early nineteenth-century Massachusetts Shelf — except that it had no hands, and there were no numbers on its face. Instead, at each hour position, in careful Gothic script, was the word *Whenever*.

Don and Ellen had fallen into the habit of sharing a drink after work. By some tacit proportional mathematic, they had agreed that Don would buy three times out of four. The price that Ellen paid for Don's generosity was allowing him to make a big deal of her round.

'Now that's something you don't see every day,' he beamed as she came back to the table with two pints. 'And so gracefully delivered as well.'

It was nearly two weeks since Unity had returned from the States. She'd been to a friend's wedding in Yorkshire on the first weekend back, so she and Don had an excuse for not meeting. Their phone calls had been guarded, undemonstrative.

'So, on your own again tonight, huh?' Ellen asked, ladling back her long black hair with a sweeping snowdrop hand. The gesture always caught Don full in the solar plexus. She lit a cigarette. 'Still broken up about Unity?'

This was a new one on Don. He talked to Ellen as if she were a bloke. He'd told her about the row with Unity, and about what that row represented. He'd laid bare all his doubts about the relationship, its trials and its mismatches. Also, its pleasures and its compulsions. The very act of doing this had convinced him that he wasn't attempting to seduce Ellen, because, he reasoned, you don't blat on about Girl A to Girl B if you're trying to get Girl B horizontal.

Then again, his candour with Ellen, his *ability* for candour with her, made her pillow-huggingly attractive.

'Shit,' he sighed, 'I dunno. I really think she wants to have her head preserved in aspic or whatever. I mean, *that's* no kind of ambition. It's an arrogant rejection, isn't it? A way of saying that this world isn't good enough for you. Okay, I'm pretty cynical, on a day-to-day level, but I like it here. I think the world's pretty good. Unity wants a better world – but she's giving up on improving this one. She's running away.'

'Is she?' Ellen asked, lifting her glass. 'Cheers, by the way.'

'Of course she is. She thinks that she's going to wake up in a world free of disease, poverty, gender prejudice and cars that collide with the local fauna. All her problems'll be solved.'

Ellen wrinkled her nose and rubbed it. 'But it would be bloody amazing if you *could* get to the future, wouldn't it?'

'No.' Don tapped out a cigarette. 'I'm happy with the life I've been given. If I achieve immortality, it'll be through writing the definitive history of the Boer War, or by passing on my genes to my children.'

'Oh, right,' Ellen nodded. 'So where's the manuscript?' She made a show of scanning the area around the table. 'Where are the golden-haired toddlers?'

Don laughed. 'There's time yet.' He lit his coffin-nail. 'Hey, I saw something on the news today about Splendid Corps. You know that guy we met at Movers and Shakers? It was—'

'Robert Spleen,' Ellen nodded.

Don blinked. 'Uh . . . yeah. I *knew* there was something I didn't like about him.'

'What have you got against him?' Ellen asked. 'Your girlfriend works for him, ultimately.'

'Yeah, and pretty hypocritical it is of her too, being the committed socialist she is. It'd be difficult to think of a more exploitative, money-oriented, paternalistic example of an overblown, self-perpetuating multinational enterprise than Splendid – as I've pointed out to her on many an occasion.'

'And I'm sure she appreciates you sharing,' Ellen suggested.

'No, seriously. She tells herself that she's playing the system, getting the free market to finance her highly ethical humanitarian research – but, of course, whatever she develops is immediately packaged and sold, like any other Splendid product.'

'What exactly does she develop?' inquired Ellen. 'You always refer to her, rather dismissively, as a "whitecoat".'

'Well, umm . . .' Don hesitated. 'It's, er, quite difficult to explain. You know DNA and genetic engineering and all that sort of thing?'

'Yes,' Ellen confirmed, encouragingly.

'Do you?' Don nodded. 'Ah. Well, so does she.'

Sitting by the window in her corner of the laboratory on the third floor of Splendid Reach, Unity watched the evening descend on West London. The dusk stroked each building and illuminated it. The flat, glassy faces of the office blocks were suddenly three-dimensional, lived-in, alive. The church clock by the roundabout offered the confident opinion that it was twenty-five to two.

Away to the right, Unity could see the river, black and insoluble, hooping beneath the bridge. It shouldered past land that had once been flood meadow and marshland, where woad-clad hunters had pursued duck and elk. Over the millennia, mankind had boxed the Thames in, made it serve as a gutter stream.

Unity had grown up close to the river's source. Out near Oxford, when she was a child, the water had been clear and clean. She had come to London and seen it writhing in froth, scummy with the city's bathwater. Now she wondered what humanity would do to it next. What would the river be like in three hundred years? Buried underground, maybe – a subterranean sewer, a slurried Styx of ordure. Or perhaps an Elysian waterway, alive with carp and pleasure boats and splashing children. To her surprise, Unity didn't give a damn. She was no longer specifically interested in the river's fate, as long as she was there to see it.

She turned back to her terminal and saved a progress report. The project she was working on had eighteen months to run, but she wanted out. She had to sell Casey the idea of enzyme research.

She considered simply walking into his office and saying, 'Casey, you're a corrupt lowlife who would stoop even to theft to further your slimeball career, but I will keep my mouth shut in exchange for a million pound start-up budget and a completely free rein.' But that would mean divulging her links with Gabriel, and it would make her Casey's open enemy. She didn't have the time.

There was only one real course. She'd have to tell the creep what she wanted to do without telling him why she wanted to do it. She'd have to be damn near honest – which was what she was best at.

Casey was thinking over the Todd problem, trying to lay his hand on a lever. The man was candidly though unobtrusively queer, so that was no use, but it was unlikely MIT knew he was into this heavy S&M thing. If one could get some documentary evidence of that, then maybe . . .

There was a polite knock at the door of the office.

Casey swung his feet off the desk and called, 'Come!'

Unity Siddorn slipped deferentially into the room, smiling an open, charming smile. Casey knew that look from his childhood. He knew what it heralded. *Johnny, would you help me with my geography homework? I'll give you a lend of my leather jacket Saturday . . .*

'Unity – take a seat. To what do I owe this?'

She sat opposite him, casually draping herself back in the chair. Ah, for pity's sake – the top button of her blouse was undone. How dumb did she think he was? Was it a secondment to some sunnier clime she was after? A hike in her budget? Sweet Jesus, she was crossing her legs so that her dress rode up. It must be a paid sabbatical.

'I haven't seen you since you got back, Casey,' she said. 'How was your trip to the States?'

'Informative,' Casey admitted breezily. 'How about yours?'

'Tedious. You know scientists. Isn't New England beautiful though?'

'Oh, I didn't get out of Boston. Meetings, business – like that.' He could soak this sort of stuff up all night.

'Shame. Look, Casey, the reason I dropped by – I wanted to have a chat about my personal resourcing over the next few months.'

Aha. Casey turned to a chart on the wall beside him and ran a finger down the left-hand side. When it reached Unity's name, the finger slid horizontally along the red bar beside it. 'Uh, it seems you're inked in on Project Tuber until at least last quarter next year.' He turned back to her and smiled. 'Producing impressive results, that project, as you've strenuously pointed out.'

The muscles in her neck tightened momentarily, as if she were biting hard. Then she gave a martyred sigh and made an exposed-wrists gesture of theatrical candour.

'Well, this is it, Casey. I really feel I've contributed all I can there.'

Oh, Johnny, I've been thumping away at those drums for hours. Could you not just carry them out to the van for me?

'You need a holiday, Unity – is that what you're saying?' Give her a cue, why not? Encourage the charade a little. 'Perhaps you're right.'

She raised her hands, pushing away the suggestion. 'Oh, no. Quite the opposite, Casey. No, I'm looking for a challenge, something to stretch me a bit more. And I've come up with something that you'll be crazy for.'

She idly brushed an invisible something from her knee, causing her skirt to fall back along her thigh. Casey had to admit that she was hamming her little heart out – getting it right, without it ever quite coming off. It was like watching an actor sing.

'Well,' Casey admitted easily, 'employee input is what the company's all about.' He jerked a thumb at the corporate slogan framed on the wall behind him. 'What's the Big Idea?' he quoted.

'Doctor cells,' she said eagerly.

Picking up a dry-marker, she stood and scribbled the words on Casey's whiteboard. As she explained the notion of genetically-engineered enzymes coursing around the human body, repairing damage at a cellular level, her specious bonhomie evaporated. She extemporised diagrams and busked budgets. She glowed with honest enthusiasm, as researchers always did. Casey had had boffins in here trying to raise funds for perpetual motion, cold fire, time machines and nuclear-powered baby buggies. But, despite the company slogan, Casey had not, in fifteen years, seen a good idea simply waltz in from the corridor. Life wasn't that easy.

'. . . it's a whole new area of research, Casey. It's green-field at the moment. We can steal a march on the industry here.'

Casey puffed out a long breath – a punctuating technique he'd picked up from Mr Spleen. 'Well, there's your problem, you see,' he explained. 'No precedent. On whose supportable theorem would you be basing this research?'

That stopped her in her tracks. She'd been about to speak, but she hesitated. Obviously the whole thing was pie in the sky.

Casey laced his fingers and went on. 'As it happens, I do have some background knowledge in this area of interest. And it's my belief that the best way forward here will be in the arena of micro robotics. There's been some very impressive work done in the field already.'

He thought that might surprise her, and it did. She stared at him wordlessly for a moment and then cast a pained look at the heavens. Her temper broke and she slammed an exasperated hand on the desk.

'Jesus *Christ*, Casey! Don't tell *me* what the best way forward is! *I'm* the bloody scientist here – you're an *administrator*!'

Jaysus, Johnny, would you stop making that racket with me guitar and go talk the landlord out of a few beers for us?

Casey held it a moment, staring at her. Then he said calmly, 'You're right. I'm an administrator.' She'd made it a synonym for *pimp*. 'And at the present time, Unity, I'd suggest that you knuckle down and fulfil your professional commitment to the current project.'

He paused, and put an open palm to his cheek.

'Well, how about that?' he observed, his tone heavy with wonderment. 'There I go *administrating* again.'

CHAPTER EIGHTEEN

ELLEN ASKED DON BACK home for beans on toast and a bottle of wine. Though perfectly pleasant, her tone made it plain that beans on toast and wine comprised the entire offer. The basement apartment of 2 Eldritch Place was no more than twenty minutes' walk from Don's own flat. He was surprised that he'd never before come across this crumbling Georgian square.

The front door of the flat opened directly onto a most singular room. The bookshelves that ran round two walls were home to psychedelic shoals of glass fish, streaked in blues and greens, dappled with congealing crimson and oozing yellow. A fishing net was suspended loosely across the width of the low ceiling, weighed down with a catch of rubber lizards and decoy ducks. The furniture was threadbare and sagging. Each component of the three-piece suite had evidently started life with two completely different companions, but had more recently come together to form this battered mongrel set. In the centre of the room, on a Big Bird rug, there was a coffee table in the form of a statuesque blonde on her hands and knees in her underwear, supporting a sheet of glass on her shoulders and buttocks.

Dusk was falling, and Ellen switched on the side lights – they were plastic babies mounted around the walls. Their translucent tummies diffused a pink-yellow glow.

'I'll get some drinks,' Ellen said, walking through to the kitchen. 'White okay?'

Don flopped down on the sofa. 'Sure.'

As glasses chinked in the kitchen, he gazed around the remarkable room – and decided that he had to put real effort into exploring the personality of the woman who had conceived it. This was not the type of mind you come across every day.

'Here you go,' Ellen said, handing him a glazed pottery chalice. She leant behind the sofa and pulled out a Pink Floyd album, which she put on a battered Dansette that made Don's system look state-of-the-art. 'What's the problem?' she asked, catching the distaste on Don's face.

Don snorted. 'I seem to remember that drugs are necessary to appreciate the finer points of the Floyd,' he said.

'If you insist,' she shrugged. She went to an antiquated shop till in one corner, and rang up a sale. The drawer chinged open and she took out a small plastic bag of grass and some jumbo Rizlas, which she handed to him. 'I'm just going to get changed.'

Don rolled a joint, and was just lighting it when Ellen came back. She was wearing bell-bottom loons, an embroidered cheesecloth blouse and black clogs. As she picked up her wine from the coffee table, Don was jolted by a twinge in his stomach. It was adolescent lust.

The nineties revival of seventies fashion was a source of frequent emotional ambivalence to Don. Young women these days were dressing exactly as they had during the years that his interest in the opposite sex had first burgeoned – usually on the bus, behind a satchel. He used to ferret magazines away beneath his bed, illicit and exciting insurance against the boredom of algebra and *The Mayor of Casterbridge*. In those magazines, Stacey and Zoe and Brighton Pia had always started out (*first page, take your time, no rush*) clad in velvet hotpants, knee-high patent boots, skinny-rib sweaters that should have required a licence. By page three of the photo shoot only the boots remained, and they were scarcely the focus of attention. But twenty years later, the conditioning was kicking in and Don's reaction to girls in blouses with long minstrel sleeves was incorrigibly Pavlovian. He caught himself, in sandwich bars and parks, gazing guppie-like at young women and thinking *Go on, talk to her. Say hello.* He'd make an estimate and do the maths. *Jesus, I'm probably old enough to be her father.*

How the hell had that happened? He'd stared a hole in his bedroom ceiling thinking about this, and come to the conclusion that it just wasn't on. If you're over thirty, you can't sleep with people who are still interested in what's top of the charts. You can't take them back to your place (and it has to be your place, because nineteen-year-olds these days still live with their parents) and impress them with the Chablis in your fridge and your only Nirvana LP, whilst trying to avoid mentioning that you remember the last Labour government. One had a responsibility – oh God, the voice of Donald Osman Senior – to the young and trusting and easily led.

So the alternative was, say, Unity. Someone stiff with history, set like the accumulated wax on a wine bar candle. You take on a life that you haven't lived.

'Let's go to El Greco.'

'No! I once . . . no, not El Greco.'

Places that were out of bounds; records you couldn't play; turns of phrase that prompted violent and unexpected reactions. The problem with getting old – you have to spend your life with people who are getting old too.

Dark Side of the Moon was chugging along nicely when Ellen said, 'This song, "Time", is the first song I ever remember hearing. Dad and I were living outside Glastonbury, in a tiny house with crooked stairs.'

Don, lounging with the joint in his mouth, murmured, 'Why doesn't that surprise me?'

'From my bedroom, you could see the Tor. What was I – three? four? The winter sun was slanting in through the window, and the little fan heater was pumping out. I can still see its red on-light. I had this cheap little plastic doll – a Made-in-Taiwan thing. I'd dropped it by the fan heater, and it melted. Its head and arms kind of drooped and flowed.

'What I remember is the smell. The smell of melting plastic. And the scorched streaks of black on her pink arms. Her face was blurred. Scary. The sun was low and golden, the rays coming through the window – solid rays, with the dust defining them. It must have been nearly Christmas.'

Don offered her the joint and she refused it, caught up in a focused memory.

'And I remember snatching the doll away from the heat. It was still hot and malleable. I think I tried to mould it back into recognisable features, but I couldn't, obviously. The sun was falling on my knees – I was wearing a black print dress with sunflowers on it – and I was twisting and kneading this setting plastic. And from downstairs I could hear this song. The line that stays with me is the one about running to catch up with the sinking sun.' She smiled, distantly. 'I think that's my earliest memory.'

Something shifted inside Don. He was overwhelmed with the inappropriate desire to hug her. He'd been a lanky adolescent when Ellen was four. In a fit of punk-inspired self-reinvention, he'd traded his once-cherished copy of *Dark Side of the Moon* for some trash by the New York Dolls, and a poster of Tom Verlaine. It was a good deal at the time, long-hair albums being something of a drug on the swap mart since the advent of the Pistols. Hearing the music again, he remembered how much he'd loved it, before he'd despised it so passionately.

And here was Ellen – a woman whose view was uncoloured by fashion or embarrassment or anything but her experience of the music itself; who simply loved it as part of the weave of her life – like the house she was raised in, or summers on the beach.

She'd been brought up on this stuff *and* she wore loons.

Don lit a cigarette, and swigged his beer.

Then again, one had to acknowledge the moral technicality that he was still going out with Unity. The relationship may not be firing on all four at the moment, but neither had it been scrapped – and Don wasn't at all sure that he wanted to write it off. Although Unity's flaking, flinty fearfulness irritated him, he felt he was pretty good at shoring her up. He liked feeling his way through the dark, dripping tunnels of her personality, emerging every so often into some unexpected, crystalline chamber that would entrance him. He admired her vision, loopy though it was, and her commitment to it. His own enthusiasms, he knew, were mundane and diurnal. He had a talent for small-scale passions and petty hatreds. While Unity railed against pan-continental starvation, he directed the same kind of bright outrage at undisciplined apostrophes.

Then there was the sex. Don was prepared to swallow any amount of tofu for a woman who trawled the shelves of Blockbuster Videos in search of movies with re-enactable sex scenes. It would be difficult to chuck the inexhaustible surprises of Unity's erotic imagination for the company of a twentysomething who knew all the words to the first Paul McCartney album. Certainly, one couldn't run a relationship on lumbar-wrenching sex alone – but a shared affection for Sergeant Bilko was no guarantee of marital harmony either.

Don didn't suppose for an instant that it was possible to get both.

'That's enough mind expansion,' Ellen suggested as the album came to a close. 'Time for some heart-searching.' She pulled an LP from behind the sofa and slid the record out, frisbeeing the sleeve to Don as she turned to the Dansette.

Don picked up the cover and looked at it. It showed a beat-up Ford truck, parked beside a chain-link fence. Beyond the fence was some kind of modern, low-rise, blue-glass installation that might have been a microchip plant or a weather research station; and way beyond that stretched a flat, heat-blurred desert. Reclining on the hood of the pick-up, a guitar flat on his lap, was a figure wearing a sleeveless T-shirt and cowboy hat. On the back of the album was a close-up of the artist's face, the windshield of the pick-up behind him. He was middle-aged and dark-featured, eyes close-set and brown, with shoulder-length, greying hair and a cropped beard. In the dim interior of the truck, behind the steering wheel, a coal-eyed snowman was melting pathetically. The album was called *Jack Frost's Talkin' Blues* and it was the work of Willie Rabblestack.

'Oh, no,' Don complained. 'This is country music, right? I'm sorry, you have to draw the line at bloody awful country music.'

'I have so much to learn from you,' Ellen deadpanned, as she lifted the Floyd off the deck.

Don ran a sceptical eye down the list of songs. Some of them, he had to admit, were not your garden variety C&W titles. 'To Heaven in a Helium Balloon'. 'The Secret Loves of Buffalo Bill'. 'Going Down in Massachusetts'. But then there were tracks at the sight of which Don cringed. 'All the Girls I Never Kissed'. 'Homerun to Texas'. 'Lord, Lift Me Up on Gabriel's Wings'. You didn't need to hear songs with titles like that. Not if you wanted to hold on to your lunch.

'Last track side one,' Ellen said, taking the reefer from Don. '"What the Hell". Give it a chance.'

'What the hell,' Don agreed dismissively, not realising, until he looked again at the cover, that it was the title of the song.

Willie Rabblestack had a growling, warm voice, pitched in a low register that brought it close to the ear. The words were carefully phrased, and sat on top of the arrangement without fighting the finger-picking electric guitar or the breezy drums.

> *Well, hello. I guess you got the kind of face I like,*
> *Though I do feel sorta threatened by your smile.*
> *You're smart enough to know*
> *that I don't want to hear about your life.*
> *'Coz I don't care for content – just for style.*
> *And if you take me home tonight, I'll hate myself,*
> *And I'll do my best to hate you as well,*
> *'Coz you believe I'm thinking 'bout another girl . . .*
> *But what the hell – let's give it a whirl.*

The tune was a mid-paced, jaunty affair, full of country sevenths that belied the ironic weariness of the lyric. Don had always considered that such two-tiered sentiments were the preserve of the blues and Motown. From country, he expected only knee-jerk sentimentality and family values.

> *I oughta say my recent past inspires no confidence*
> *But I reckon you can read that in my eyes.*
> *So lean across the table and I'll organise an accident.*
> *Fake anything you want, except surprise.*
> *You're not the one who rescues me, we both can tell.*
> *I'm not the one who's gonna make you well.*
> *And you believe I'm thinking 'bout another girl . . .*
> *But what the hell – let's give it a whirl.*

> *Your skin is cool; your breath is hot;*
> *But all I feel is what you're not.*
> *You're different to someone who's not the same.*
> *And so I couldn't blame you*
> *When you called out your own angel's name.*
> *If I should fall short, it's not your fault.*
> *It's no one's fault.*

Don found something uncomfortably apposite in the lyric. He glanced at Ellen, but she was leaning back with the joint in her mouth and her eyes closed.

> *It's such a shame we both prefer the same side of the bed,*
> *Otherwise we could have something going here.*
> *A moment there the noise we made*
>   *drowned out the voice inside my head,*
> *But my heart's still coming through, loud and clear.*

I don't suppose we'll meet again. Why should we, dear?
There's lotsa lonely people in the world.
But you believe I'm thinking 'bout another girl . . .
So what the hell – let's give it a whirl.

The song finished with a descending flurry of twanging, down-home licks, and faded in a cavernous wash of reverb.

Don nodded, and grinned. 'Yeah, all right. It's a cut above the usual gingham dross.'

'It gives the lyric an extra twist,' Ellen said, 'when you know he's gay.'

Don frowned with surprise and looked again at the photo on the back of the sleeve. 'No – really? Country singers aren't allowed to be, are they? It's written into the American Constitution somewhere. *Deeply* attached to their mothers, certainly, but straight as a corn-belt interstate.'

'He's playing in London next week. You want to come?'

'No thanks,' Don replied. 'It was a pretty good song, but I don't want to listen to an hour and a half of it. I've got to this advanced stage in life without ever liking country music, and I think it's too late even for Willie Rabblestack to get to me now.'

CHAPTER NINETEEN

UNITY RAGED OUT OF Casey's office and went home. As she stomped furiously up the stairs to the door of her flat, the heel snapped from her left stiletto.

'*Shit!*' she yelled, stumbling forward onto her hands. '*Fuck and shit!*'

She took off both shoes, and carried them the rest of the way. She was trembling with such anger, she couldn't get the key into the lock.

'Get *in*, you bastard,' she hissed. '*Thank* you!'

She slammed the door behind her, and strode into the front room. Reaching to turn on the table lamp, she stubbed her toe on the leg of the occasional table.

'*Jee*-sus!' she shrieked, and in a flash of rage she flung both her shoes across the room. One bounced off the wall and fell to the floor; the other swept Michelangelo's David over the end of the shelf, and it toppled behind an armchair out of sight. Unity clenched and unclenched her fists, and made another attempt to turn the light on. Then she went to retrieve the fallen David.

'Perfect,' she groaned, on discovering that she had neatly decapitated it. She put the abbreviated body back on the shelf, and placed its head at its feet.

The phone rang and she grabbed it.

'*What?*' she snapped.

'That Old World charm,' came a Texan drawl. 'Kinda gets you right here.'

'Willie! Sorry – let's start again. Hello, Unity Siddorn speaking.'

'Afternoon, ma'am. Or, good evenin', I guess. How's Britain?'

'Stinking. You caught me in a foul temper. How are you?'

It was a balm to hear Willie Rabblestack's easy tones. They exchanged weather reports and thanked each other for an evening shared in Cambridge. Willie said that he'd phoned to call in a debt. 'Gabe an' me are comin' to England next week. It says right here in Gabe's little computer diary that you owe us dinner. Nuthin' fancy – we'll be happy t'accept plain ol' roast beef an' all the fixin's.'

Unity laughed. 'Not if you want to hang on to your brain.' She gave a brief explanation of mad cow disease, and Willie suggested that he'd never met a cow that he considered sane. They arranged a date.

'Is Gabriel there?' Unity asked. 'Can I have a word?'

Gabriel came on the line. 'Unity! I'm sitting here looking at the fall frost on the window – it's a lesson in the beauty of crystal geometry. The sun's throwing lace onto the desk in front of me. I've skipped class. How's things?'

Unity sighed, and told him about her unsatisfactory encounter with Casey. 'I don't know how to work the situation. Either I resign, or I blackmail him. Or kill him, of course.'

'A short-term pleasure. Life is long – there's plenty of time.'

'You don't know that's true. There might be a bus out there with my name on it. We've got do the work right now. We've got to get on with it.'

There was a silence on the line. Unity looked around the room.

Her graduation photo stood on the shelf above the TV. Her mother had given it to her, much to her protested embarrassment. But still, she'd transported the silver-framed photo carefully from flat to flat throughout her twenties. Each time she'd unpacked her crates of gewgaws and bric-a-brac, she'd placed it in a prominent spot in her new front room, making a mental note to move it somewhere less showy as soon as she'd got herself sorted out. Against the backdrop of King's Chapel, she was pictured with her mortarboard slipping sideways from her rad-fem crop, clasping the rolled parchment that proclaimed a distinction. She was happy with nerves and excitement like a ten-year-old in the queue for Santa's grotto, bursting with Christmas wishes. A decade later, she had longer hair, stronger glasses and the know-how to make spinach pump iron like Schwarzenegger. It wasn't enough, really.

'You'll figure out what to do,' Gabriel said reassuringly. 'Though if you resign, it'll be difficult to do *anything*.'

'I know.'

There was another brief silence, then Gabriel said, 'Can we put you on the guest list for Willie's gig? He's opening the tour in London at the – Willie, where are you playing? Some place called the Sunrise.'

Unity accepted and, after some inconsequential chat, she hung up.

Blackmail. How could she justify it?

She went to the kitchen and opened the fridge. There was soft cheese, which was a calculated risk, given listeria and all that. Mushrooms – know how they grow mushrooms? Celery – good fibre-wise, but think of the work the digestive tract had to do breaking it down – like hitting the motorway in second, it must strip the gears of your gut.

Just *eating* kills you. Breathing destroys your lungs. Moving grinds your joints down. The body, like any machine, decays, goes clunky, fails.

If there's work to be done, Unity told herself, *now* is when to do it. There was no time for prissy morality – who wanted to be a moral corpse? At some point in the far future, when she was resurrected in a new, perfect, replaceable body, no one was going to say. But hang on, didn't you fuck over that nice Casey Rushmore?

Unity poured herself a glass of mineral water. 'I'm sure I'll feel just terrible,' she thought. 'But not forever.'

The following day, at the Checkpoint office, Spotty George answered a call.

'Uhuh. Yeah – I'll 'and you over to our music specialist.' He covered the mouthpiece. 'Don, this one's for you. I'll put it froo.'

'Hi,' Don said. 'How can I help?'

'Yeah, uh, I don't know if you'll be able to answer this but – I've got this album by Willie Rabblestack called *Jack Frost's Talkin' Blues* . . .'

Don chuckled and shook his head. He loved it when life set up these little gags. 'Yeah, I know it,' he confirmed.

'Well, I was wondering – for no good reason, like – what's the building on the cover?'

'Good question. Absolutely no idea. Let me have your number, and I'll get back to you.'

Don called a contact at the Virgin Megastore, who read the photo credit from the sleeve of the album. Then he worked his way through the *Media Yearbook* until he found the agency that represented the photographer. They put him on to their New York office, who were eventually persuaded to give out the photographer's number. The photographer was flattered to be asked about the shoot and told Don what he wanted to know. Within an hour of the original query, Don called the inquirer.

As he spoke, he logged the call on the computer.

'It's the Nevada Cryonic Research Institute,' he told the caller. 'Also known locally as the Icebox. It's a repository for bodies held in suspended animation against the time that they can be revived, and cured of whatever ails them.'

'Wow. Thanks.'

'My pleasure,' Don said. And then, as a mischievous afterthought, he added. 'For further information, please call Unity Siddorn, who is an expert in this field.'

He gave Unity's work number, and hung up, giggling to himself.

As well as burning in neon on the roof of the building in Hammersmith,

Splendid's corporate logo – the word *Splendid* rendered as if rubber-stamped in blue ink could be seen on CD sleeves, intercity coaches, electrical office equipment and a popular line of children's confectionery. Robert Spleen's marketing department assured him that the corporation enjoyed a high-impact feel-good recognition rating across the complete range of targeted consumer profiles.

But the multinational was only the most visible of the companies in which Robert Spleen had an interest. He also had a controlling share in two estate agencies, a kit-car company, a worldwide chemical concern and many other less obviously lucrative endeavours. One of these last was a loss-maker to the tune of about one million sterling per annum, and it was a source of constant irritation to the corporate accountants who drew up the annual returns of the Splendid conglomerate. In financial terms, it was a wastrel second cousin of the extended family, and the accountants simply couldn't understand why Mr Spleen indulged it so cheerfully. Every year they advised him to throw it out on the street, and every year he would shrug and say, 'I'm rather fond it of it. Write it off against something.'

The company in question was Checkpoint, the organisation for which Don worked, and of which he, too, was so fond; the organisation which he considered the antithesis of profit-orientated capitalist endeavour.

Although Spleen was sincere when he protested his affection for Checkpoint, he had a completely practical justification for ensuring its continued existence. He regularly dipped into the database on which Checkpoint's operators logged all the questions they'd been asked. Over the years, this catalogue of semi-informed curiosity had thrown up some solid commercial ideas, which Spleen had been happy to exploit. Sometimes, these notions would be blindingly simple – for instance, why are door keys all the same shape? Within a year of that one, Splendid was manufacturing key blanks with a variety of different-shaped heads for easy identification. Two years later, the facetiously-named Harvard Key Company was sold for a sum that effectively funded Checkpoint over the next thirty-six months.

On other occasions, the database would merely point up a growing area of interest in the general population. A number of questions concerning post-war Chicago blues, prompted by a throwaway remark from a new young guitar hero, encouraged Spleen to obtain, for a pittance, the rights to hours of forgotten recordings, which he then marketed on CD at an irresistibly low price. The return on the investment would keep Don and his colleagues in a job for four years.

Spleen had divulged to no one the profit-making potential of Checkpoint. But every so often, from his office in Hammersmith, he would log on to the mainframe in Tottenham Court Road and browse. He'd flick dismissively through the queries about Elvis's burger of choice and the personnel of Top Cat's gang, looking for the million-making idea that some unwitting housewife or bank clerk had pondered, phoned in and forgotten. The database recorded some seven hundred calls per week. Spleen reckoned he needed one money-spinner every eighteen months.

It was Thursday morning, early November. Spleen had cycled to work, feeling the new, sharp teeth of winter nipping his cheeks. Leaving his bike with the doorman, he took the lift to the eighth floor, and walked into his office at eight twenty. He strode across the polished wood boards, past the Georgian desk and through the door that led to his work apartment. He put the nautilus through its paces, shucked his tracksuit and showered. Wearing a bathrobe stolen from the New Delhi Hilton (Ginsberg had smuggled out a canework armchair), he scrambled some eggs with shredded salmon and a little dill, and made cinnamon tea. He selected a linen shirt, one of a dozen unpatterned ties, and plumped for a jet-black suit by some designer to whom he'd once lost a girlfriend. He went back to the office and sat behind his desk at nine five, and switched on his computer.

He was paging through the Checkpoint database, making notes in a school exercise book from time to time.

Who was the composer who was jealous of Mozart?

'Salieri,' Spleen muttered, before looking at the next zone. This was a part of the fun of Checkpoint for him. He liked to respond to the questions before looking at the answer that the operator had given.

When curtains fade, where does the colour go?

Might be something there, Spleen thought. Must get one of the chemists onto it. He made a note, in his looping, Eton-trained style. *Chem; ctns pigment. Fix?* The idiosyncratic encryption was all he needed to keep track. He continued flicking through the data, but found nothing to pique his interest.

The phone rang. 'Dr Hunter for you, Mr Spleen.' A call from the short-order chef, looking for another cut to griddle. Spleen told his secretary to put it through.

'Robert, it's Gerard. Just calling to tell you that your last test was clear. Still waiting for the X-rays, but no news is good news, and all that.'

'The good news is there's no bad news,' Spleen murmured, 'and the bad news is that's all the good news there is.'

Dr Hunter gave the chuckling cough of a man who can't tell whether he's expected to laugh. 'Yes, well, thought you'd want to hear the, umm, good news. See you in six months then.'

'I'm impressed by your optimism,' Spleen told him. 'Goodbye.'

He stared blankly across the office for a few moments, registering and suppressing the momentary desire for a cigarette. Then he snapped his focus back to the computer screen and paged through a few entries. Suddenly, he stopped. He was looking at an entry made only the previous day.

Category: Popular Music. Sub-Category: C&W. Cross Reference: Science. Consultant: DO.

He re-read the screen carefully and reached for his pen. In the exercise book he wrote, *Dp frz, Nvda. WHO??* Looking at what he'd written, he allowed himself a self-mocking half-smile.

'What a straw,' he said out loud. 'And what a clutch reflex.'

*   *   *

At the very moment that Robert Spleen was sitting in his eighth floor office reading Don's recent entry in the Checkpoint database, Unity Siddorn was five storeys below him planning the first unethical move of her career. She sat with her chin in her hands, scarcely believing what she was about to do. For several minutes she gazed sightlessly out of the window, rehearsing her approach. Eventually, she picked up the phone, and dialled Casey's number.

'Rushmore.'

'Casey, it's Unity,' she said, her voice steady. 'Listen, can we get together? I'd like to follow up on our meeting of the other evening.'

'Sure. Mr Spleen's with me right now – he's just dropped by for an unscheduled conference . . .'

Unity held the phone away from her ear and made a gagging face.

'. . . but I have a window at twelve, if that coincides with your own day-plan.'

'Noon. See you then.'

How she was looking forward to seeing the meltdown of that smug, supercilious smile.

Casey put the phone down, and re-directed all calls to his voice-mail.

'Sorry, Mr Spleen. To what do I owe this pleasure?'

Spleen hesitated. He'd walked out of his office for no reason other than to take his mind off the ridiculous hope of having himself frozen until they found a cure for cancer. He'd got into the lift because it was there, and got out on Casey's floor because that's where the doors had opened.

Spleen had never considered himself a lonely man. Private, certainly. Solitary. But not friendless. And yet, in recent years, he'd found it more and more difficult to connect. The pals of his early adulthood had all checked out with needles in their arms, or had redefined themselves by sticking with the wife of the moment and raising spiky offspring. Spleen had never been in danger of succumbing to either fate. Each of his seven houses on three continents had been designed with a view to being home to two. Yet, despite the empty walk in closets, despite the attics that might accommodate a studio, music room or study, Spleen couldn't find space for any further sculptresses, cellists or *Cosmo* editors.

Casey had asked him what he wanted, and the answer was that he wanted to talk – about his mortality, about the subsonic rumble of terror that had become the soundtrack of his waking hours. He wanted to say that the magnolia ceiling of his spartan bedroom pressed against his face in the small hours; and that sleep, when it came, was no escape, because his dreams were a loop of bleak and surreal horror, in which he was stabbed in the kidneys by captain's chairs, and throttled by Italian ties.

But he knew he couldn't say any of it. There was no short-circuiting the synaptic connection that connected his brain to his upper lip, and stiffened it at times such as these. No human being would ever exert upon him the magnetic force required to destabilise those basic electronics.

'Just taking a walk around the grounds,' Spleen told Casey, with a patrician smile. 'How are things going, by and large?'

Rushmore launched into an impromptu but comprehensive rundown of current projects and their expected returns. Spleen watched his mouth move, but didn't listen. As Casey progressed to the medium-term plan for the half-year, Spleen glanced around the room. On the white board mounted to his left, he read the words *Doctor cells.* There were some diagrams that resembled frogspawn, and a list of figures, totalled to half a million. Spleen turned back to Casey, and indicated the board.

'What's that?' he asked casually.

Casey halted mid-flow, and glanced at Unity's scribble. 'Oh, I had one of the researchers in here with a typically impractical scheme. I nixed it.'

'What scheme?'

'Pure fantasy.' He gave Spleen a brief and dismissive account of Unity's pitch. 'It's a warped version of Dr Todd's robotics idea – which, as I told her, is where the future lies.' Casey paused. 'Speaking of which . . .' he resumed, hopefully.

'Give her a budget of a million,' Spleen interrupted. 'All the equipment she needs, and whatever staff. I'll sponsor this one personally. Please ask her to send the monthly reviews direct to my office.'

Casey gaped. 'Mr Spleen, *please*. I'm not unacquainted with this field of research, and I can assure you—'

'Unity Siddorn,' Spleen said thoughtfully. 'Is she the small, bespectacled girl who unfailingly wears high heels?'

Casey assessed his boss's tone and then subsided into his chair. 'The myopic midget, yeah,' he confirmed with sullen recklessness.

'I thought so. She's always seemed particularly bright, as I remember.'

Defeated, Casey rubbed his eyes with the tips of his fingers.

Johnny O'Casey? Would you be the brother of Kelly O'Casey who sings at the Plough on a Friday night?

'She's a highly-valued member of the team,' he said wearily. 'We're very proud of her.'

As Unity stepped out of the lift a calculated ten minutes late, the thrilled tightness in her stomach felt like the precursor to sex. *Christ*, she thought, as she approached the door of Casey's office. *I do believe I'm turned on.*

She strode in without knocking, and saw Casey look up from the document he was reading.

'Unity!' he almost yelled, tossing the papers onto his desk and jumping to his feet. 'Great to see you.'

He hurried round to her, and pulled out the chair for her to sit on. Smarmy bastard, patronising git. He was so sure he had her flat that he was allowing himself to be pleasant. She'd go for the balls, no question.

'Casey,' she said, 'I'm going to make a deal with you.'

He sat back in his chair. 'No need for a deal,' he beamed. 'I'm not a man for compromises. Listen, I've had to go to the plate on this one, and it's not been easy, I can tell you, but I've gotten you the finance. A million start-up, okay?' He leaned forward and grinned at her. 'Surprised, yeah? Ol' Casey pulls one out of the bag under pressure.'

She was floundering. 'I'm sorry?'

He'd put her idea to Spleen – hard sell. Not an easy project to make fly, but he'd given it wings. In fact, he'd done such a good job that Mr Spleen had agreed to sponsor it *personally*. It was going to play hell with the budget projections but, shoot, sometimes you just had to go with the creative conviction of the people on the payroll. Hey, he had severe doubts about the concept – he was big enough to admit that – but Unity's vision was enough for him. That's the kind of manager he was.

Unity was stunned. 'I'll . . . umm . . . I'll need . . .'

'Whatever, whatever. Just get it up and running. I want *results* here, Unity. I've put my balls on the line for this.'

Shaking her head, containing her confusion, Unity got to her feet. 'Well, Jesus, thanks, Casey. I mean . . .'

Casey led her to the door. 'No problem – none at all.' He pointed a loaded-gun finger at her as she stopped by the lift. 'Leave the admin to me, yeah? You just get yourself back to work, little lady.'

CHAPTER TWENTY

THEY MET IN THE driving rain on Friday night outside the Odeon, Leicester Square. Don had been apprehensive, dreading a continuation of their argument, or even the tacit denial of it. Spit or sulk – another relationship come to this. But Unity had been in a buoyant, frivolous mood; and, with Unity, buoyant and frivolous meant horny. She fondled and squeezed him all the way through the movie – somewhat inappropriate for *The Lion King*, he felt – and afterwards dragged him into an alley in Chinatown for a re-run of the downpour scene from *Nine and a Half Weeks*. In the taxi back to Fulham, he shifted uncomfortably in his seat.

'I've got rain in my underpants,' he told her.

'Now you know how women feel,' she remarked cheerfully.

As if it were an act of gratitude, Don cooked a Spanish omelette when they got back to her place. They shared a bottle of wine and, contrary to Unity's advice, Don ate a chocolate mousse that was three days past its best-by.

Lying in bed, curled together, in no hurry, Don said, 'Okay, then?'

It didn't mean anything much. It was just a noise.

'Fine,' she replied. 'Great.'

Don stared at the ceiling.

'Yeah,' he said. 'Me too.'

Dr Gabriel Todd had nothing to declare. He pushed his trolley through, chatting to Lori McCormick who was the sound engineer for Willie's

155

band. Willie and the other musicians were still dragging guitar cases off the carousel.

The lone customs officer in the green channel stepped in front of Gabriel.

'Excuse me, sir, madam. May I ask where you've come from?'

Gabriel smiled. 'Sure, go ahead.'

Lori McCormick, a tie-dyed, frizz-haired Californian who'd been stopped by customs officials in countries that didn't even exist any more, winced slightly. Smart, she knew, did not play well in these situations.

'Outa Boston, sir,' she put in. 'We're here on business.'

This was a calculated risk, because the next question might well concern the nature of the business. Any mention of music got you halfway to the rubber glove. But Gabriel would be able to say academic business – which was a solid-gone passport to the cab rank outside.

The customs guy's moustache gave a little jink to the left.

'Are you travelling together?'

Lori recognised this as a trap. If the response was anything but an uncompromising yes, you laid yourself open to queries about your relationship. Customs officers loved to ask such questions. They were all frustrated cops.

'Sure,' Lori stated unequivocally.

'Yup,' Gabriel agreed. 'Just me, Lori here and a bunch of long-hair musicians who'll be slouching through at any moment with their patched jeans and their satanic instruments of pleasure.'

Lori's shoulders sagged. She'd seen Gabe in this mood before. He wanted to make a point and he was looking for a fight in which to do it. The customs officer's moustache jigged to the right.

'If I could ask you to wheel your luggage over here to the bench . . .'

Every time this happened, Lori was impressed by how wanton her underwear looked. In the drawer at home, her lingerie seemed real conservative, but when it was rummaged and tossed aside under the fluorescent strips of a customs hall, she had to admit that she was nothing but a shameless tramp. The same could not be said, she noted, of Gabriel. Though his shirts were stylish and his jeans cool, his undergarments were pure New England professor. If they'd seen better days, they can't have been *very* much better.

As the cases were unpacked, the moustache ticked to and fro like a pendulum. Willie and the musicians trooped past, glancing sidelong at the customs man unzipping Gabe and Lori's washbags. Pots of hand cream and tubes of KY were unscrewed and raised to the official nose, and the moustache leapt forward like something erectile. Lori knew the guy didn't expect to find drugs in the lip balm or explosives in the Mentadent; he was simply giving Gabriel time to say whatever was needed to escalate the argument. He was squaring up for the fight.

The official laid a palm on an oblong silver flight case – it might have contained a violin, for instance.

'Open it, please,' he said.

Gabriel flicked the catches, and the lid popped. The customs officer pulled back a little in surprise.

'What in God's name is it?' he asked.

'It's a battery-powered surgical saw,' Gabriel told him, nonchalantly. 'It'll take your arm off in approximately twenty seconds. *That*,' he added, nodding towards a white canister about the size of a small beer keg, 'is a vacuum flask of liquid nitrogen. And right here is an electric pump with a hypodermic needle on one end.'

The lively moustache was about ready to leap off the guy's face. 'God's teeth! What's it all for?'

'In the event of my death, or that of my loved one, the saw will be used to decapitate the warm corpse and the canister will serve to preserve the severed head.' Gabriel paused, and smiled his guileless smile. 'In the small case to your left, you'll find chemicals which must be pumped into the deceased's jugular before this operation is carried out. Naturally, I have the required papers to permit the import of this equipment to your fine country.'

The customs officer looked at the saw, the canister and lastly at Gabriel. Then he began to throw the strewn clothes back into the open suitcases.

'I can think of a dozen good reasons to pull you in, sunshine,' he grimaced, 'but, frankly, I want you out of my sight.'

'Thank you, officer,' Gabriel nodded, closing the lid on the saw. And then, picking his words carefully, he added, 'I'll tell my loved one of your broad-mindedness. He'll be touched.'

As they wheeled their trolley away, Lori hissed furiously, 'Friggin' *great*, Gabe. I *really* needed that. I hope you're pleased with yourself.'

Gabriel nodded. 'Yup, I am, to tell you the truth. Willie just walked through with two ounces of grass in his guitar case.'

Unity took a day's leave to prepare dinner for Gabriel and Willie. She went to the shops and bought ingredients for carrot soup, paella and baked Alaska. At twelve thirty, a case of assorted wine was delivered, and she put the white in the fridge.

She hoovered things, polished stuff and washed the kitchen floor. She was worried about the framed posters in the hall – a Carlos Clarke blonde in stockings, and a still of Kate Hepburn kissing Spencer Tracey. Afraid they might be too aggressively heterosexual, she swapped them with the Mondrians from the bedroom. At half past four, while the carrots were sweating gently in a pan on the stove, she went to the hall to call Don.

'You won't be late, will you?'

'I won't be late, no.'

'And you'll remember to pick up the truffles from Van Noord's?'

'Certainly,' Don told her testily.

'It's on Greek Street. They close at five thirty.'

'You told me. Also, you wrote it down on a note that I am looking at even as we speak.'

'I've bought you a linen shirt – a white one – so you don't need to go home to change. Which jeans are you wearing?'

Don growled. 'Black 501s. And my baseball boots. Give me a break.'

'Oh, and I've only got wholemeal bread, so could you pick up—'

'Jesus, Unity!' Don snapped. 'You're not making dinner for the Pope! It's only some over-educated Yank conman with a neat line of patter.'

Unity smacked the ball of her hand against the wall, and shrieked into the phone. 'How dare you speak of my friends like that! Christ, you're ill-mannered. You'd better improve *that* attitude before you turn up here.'

'I'd better do *what*?' Don squawked back. 'Who are you – my mother? Don't tell *me* what fucking attitude I'm allowed.'

'Look,' Unity hissed. 'I'm not going to have you screw up this evening with your snide bloody comments. Unless you can conduct yourself like a civilised human being—'

'See? *See?* There you go again! What are you going to do? Send me to bed with no supper?'

'Oh, grow up, Don,' Unity said bitterly. 'It's pathetic.'

'*Sweetie*,' Don said, caustically, 'if you're so worried about my *attitude*, why did you invite me along to this act of abject hero worship?'

Unity shrugged, scowling. 'God knows. I wish I hadn't.'

'Well, your *wish* is my command,' Don told her. 'Go and get your own fucking truffles.'

He hung up.

Unity waited a moment, listening to the blank line.

'Don? Don, you sod!' Her voice rose to a yell. '*How am I going to get to Greek Street, you selfish bastard?*'

She slammed the phone down on the table, and let out a scream of rage. That was it – that was *definitely* it. She reached for the Yellow Pages and began to flick through it. If the self-centred, petty sonofabitch thought he was going to talk her into any more quickies in alleyways, he had another think coming. She ran her finger down the section headed Confectioners.

It was some kind of jealousy thing, she reckoned. In some warped way, Don felt threatened by her admiration for Gabriel. She dialled Van Noord's number.

'Come on, come on.'

And, of course, he was in denial. He smoked twenty cigarettes a day, drank like a fish – so the idea of someone else challenging the fact of their own mortality got him right where it hurt.

'Ah, hello. My name's Uni . . . what? Yes, I'll hold.'

He completely lacked vision. He grubbed around all day with his useless and pathetic trivia about pop music and situation comedies – and he couldn't see further than the end of his stupid nose. To put it bluntly, she and Don were just on utterly different intellectual planes.

'Oh, there you are. Yes, this is Ms Siddorn here. I ordered a dozen truffles to be picked up this afternoon. Well, there's been a bit of a hitch, so I was wondering whether you could put them in a cab and . . . *Oh, no!*'

She flung down the phone and rushed back to the kitchen. The carrots were caramelised – stuck to the bottom of the saucepan.

'Oh, no, *please,*' she wailed, running cold water into the sticky pot. 'Oh, please be salvageable, please, please . . .'

The carrots were not salvageable – they were a write-off. Unity dropped the entire mess into the sink and slumped into a kitchen chair. With her elbows on the table, she grabbed two fistfuls of her hair, and stared down at the woodgrain. It would be inexcusably girly to cry, so she merely breathed in and out through clenched teeth, and sniffed. After a couple of minutes, she swallowed hard, cleaned her glasses and assessed the situation.

Quarter to five. She wouldn't have time to go out for more carrots and start all over again but she did have an emergency jar of M&S lobster bisque that she could stretch to four portions. *Three* portions. Okay. The truffles might still . . . oh, God, the phone was off the hook.

Van Noord's, not surprisingly, had hung up. She was about to re-dial, when the phone rang, making her jump back in surprise.

'If that's you, you bastard . . .' she muttered as she picked it up. 'Yes?' she demanded. 'Who is it?'

'There y'go again, you sweet-talkin' rosebud,' observed Willie Rabblestack cheerfully. 'I jus' cain't get enough o' those sugar lips.'

Unity gave an embarrassed laugh. 'Oops. Sorry. How are you?'

'Just fine. But Gabriel's sicker than a honeybee with hay fever. He's gotten some kind o' stomach ailment. You can likely hear him hooting in the bathroom there right now. You started into cookin' yet?'

Unity felt simultaneous relief and annoyance at the prospect of the dinner being cancelled. 'Not so's you'd notice. Is he okay?'

'He'll be fine. Just smoked some bad weed – it happens. So how's about you and me slippin' out somewhere for a bite?'

Relief blossomed and annoyance wilted.

'That'd be great,' Unity said.

It was going to be tricky, Don knew, to talk himself back from this one. Unity was *really* pissed off this time.

Grow up, she'd said. So which kind of grown-up was he supposed to be? The kind who was polite and acquiescent when faced with unreasonableness and idiocy? The unconfrontational, civilised kind of grown-up that his father would have approved of? Or the kind that was assertive, that refused to be treated like a child, that had the self-confidence to draw the line? That was honest maturity, wasn't it?

He pushed the phone across the desk, out of his reach. His problems with Unity had damn all to do with growing up, of course. They were about growing away. She was an increasingly obsessive, self-righteous, screwed-up brat. To hell with her.

'Here, George,' he said. 'Do you fancy a drink?'

George raised his head to peer over the top of the terminal. He looked like Chad. *Wot – no Clearasil?*

'Swift half or two, eh?' the spotty one asked. 'Lads' night out?'

Put like that, it didn't seem quite such an attractive notion. 'Er, well, I was thinking more of phoning round to see if we can get a few people together. It's nearly five.' He was already regretting his impulse.

'Triffic! Unscheduled office sesh! Throw some down our necks and then up the Red Fort for a ruby! Good call, my son.'

Cringing slightly, Don opened the internal phone directory. He hoped to God he could drum up some support for this.

Eight of them gathered in the local, but within an hour they were down to three – George, Don and Ellen. It was a crowd, in Don's opinion.

Ellen was quiet, reserved, while Don's comparative silence seemed, even to himself, little more than petulant. George, on the other hand, appeared to be having the time of his life. With much hooting laughter, he was relating a tale that involved himself and the Palace Posse trashing a blameless Chinky cafe in Leeds. He evidently believed that this would come over to Don as comedy of recognition.

'So we done a runner – like you do, yeah?'

'Do I?' Don asked sourly.

'Come on, son. I bet you've bin a bit naughty in yer day, eh? Course you 'ave.'

'Your shout, George,' Don said, indicating his empty glass. 'This pint's dead.'

The gears in George's brain clicked through a few notches. 'This pint is dead,' he announced nasally, his acne lit up by a great, thick smile. 'It is deceased. It 'as shuffled off this mortal coil, rung down the curtain and joined the Choir Invisible. It is,' he finished with an adenoidal flourish, 'no more!'

Don sighed and bit his bottom lip. Comedy by rote – the wit of the witless.

'Just get 'em in, pillock,' he advised leadenly.

Whilst George was at the bar, Don said to Ellen, 'Sorry about this. He's in one of his aggressively chummy moods.'

'Oh, right,' she nodded solemnly. 'I hadn't realised it was your fault.'

It proved impossible to scrape George off on the way to the trattoria. Don found himself translating the menu as George wrinkled his nose and looked dubious.

'Chrissake, George, it's only fucking prawns. What do you want? Cockles?'

'How's Unity?' Ellen asked out of the blue, as the wine arrived. 'Unity is Don's girlfriend,' she told George, and winked at him.

Winked at him – Don couldn't believe it.

'Yeah, sorted,' George replied. At the mention of girlfriends he seemed suddenly subdued.

Don explained that Unity was entertaining Gabriel tonight. Not only Gabriel but also – get this – *Willie Rabblestack.* Ellen had been right about him being gay. Apparently the supersensitive writer of 'What the Hell' was an item with this medicine-show charlatan who was about to dupe Unity out of her life savings. Don offered the theory that it was all up for Unity and himself. She was absolutely impossible, not worth the effort, a waste of space.

'That's bad, that,' George agreed soberly. 'When it gets like that, that's bad.'

Don pulled his attention away from Ellen, and regarded George from beneath his eyebrows. 'Thank you, Leonard bloody Cohen,' he said. He glanced swiftly at Ellen, checking for a laugh. A small smile – good enough.

'No, straight up,' George continued, brooding into his Barolo. 'When I split up with Julie – I mean, that really brought me down big time. I was major-league sick.'

'As a parrot?' Don inquired innocently. The evening, he felt, was looking up.

'Really,' George confirmed, with a heavy sigh. 'Then again, she was well out of order. Right offside. It even affected me – you know – *physically.*'

'She was offside and you were flagging, eh?' Don asked. George really ought to be invoicing him for straight lines like this.

George looked across and gave a mirthless little chuckle. 'Nah, nothin' like that,' he murmured. 'She was havin' it away with my mate Gerry. He was my partner in the snooker doubles.'

'Ah, Gerry was potting a few behind your back,' Don suggested gravely. He glanced at Ellen again. She was biting both her lips.

'Could say that.' George drained his glass, and put it back on the table. He grinned unconvincingly at Ellen. 'I dunno – what do you do? It's a fuckin' game, innit?' He scratched his eyebrow and loosened his tie. He stroked his hair forward over his balding forehead and rubbed his mouth with his open palm. 'Look,' he sighed, 'I'm feeling a bit iffy. Think I'll call it a day. We'll settle up for the wine tomorrer, Don, yeah?'

'Well, er, okay,' Don conceded, smirking, as George stood up. 'You all right?'

'Yeah, I'll ... you know ...'

'Look after yourself, George,' Ellen said. 'You'll be okay.'

After George had left the restaurant, Don turned to Ellen and gave a hands-spread shrug.

'A jerk,' he opined, 'but essentially harmless.'

Ellen stared across at him for a few moments.

'Yes,' she agreed, with a tiny twitch of one eyebrow. 'Precisely what I was thinking.'

The trattoria was about a hundred yards along Goodge Street from the station, one of many restaurants in that stretch. Next door was a TexMex joint called Wetbacks, in which, at the moment that George was leaving the trattoria, Willie and Unity were being led to their seats. The booth they occupied was on the other side of the wall from Don and Ellen's table. Don was actually sitting closer to Unity than to Ellen.

'Are you certain that this is what you want?' Unity asked, scanning the menu. 'I'm sure you're going to be disappointed.'

'Just curious to find out what the Brits make of it,' Willie explained. 'An' I've a hankering for a margarita.'

A waitress appeared, dressed in faded jeans and a baggy black T-shirt, and put a jug of iced water on the table.

'Howdy,' she drawled brightly. 'What kin I get you folks t'drink tonight?' She scribbled down their order, saying, 'On top o' what y'kin read on the card, we got ourselves a special this evenin'. That's the HogDog; a foot-long hotdog smothered in mega-spicy pork'n'bean chilli with a side o'fries. You take y'sweet time now.'

Willie watched her walk away and chuckled. 'Hell of an accent. Must be from Lubbock,' he suggested.

The trattoria and Wetbacks shared a kitchen. Megan Davies, Willie and Unity's waitress, dropped their drinks order off at the bar of Wetbacks, descended the stairs and walked through the kitchen to the flight that led up to the trattoria. She sauntered over to Don and Ellen's table.

'Ciao,' she said, 'Is ready to make-a you order, si?'

Both Don and the waitress were a little taken aback when Ellen ordered in fluent Italian.

'Blimey,' Don said. 'What was all that?'

Ellen gave him an English précis of what she'd asked for, and Megan, somewhat relieved, wrote it down. Don went for the gazpacho and, as a completely futile act of spite towards Unity, the veal.

'I've been thinking about this frozen head thing,' Ellen remarked as Megan Davies disappeared down the stairs. 'How do they know that they'll wake up with their memories intact?'

'Because it's not like saving data to a hard disk, is it?' Unity was saying to Willie at the same moment. 'We're not really sure how memory is constructed at all.'

'Sure, we figure that there may be blank spots,' Willie explained. 'Which is why I have this . . .' He pulled forward his bottom lip, to reveal a tattoo that read 'Gabriel Todd'.

'Well, exactly,' Don scoffed. 'If you wake up with a blank brain, you're not *you*, are you? To all intents and purposes that twentieth-century individual *is* dead.'

'Gabriel may mean nothing to you,' Unity pointed out. 'You wouldn't even know why his name was on your lip.'

'Maybe. But I'd sure be intrigued. You can bet I'd make damn certain that he got thawed. Then I'd get to meet him all over again . . . Well, hi, ma'am,' Willie said to the waitress. 'Guess I'll get the special.'

'And you might not only be blank,' Ellen mused, 'but also stupid, with the IQ of . . . I don't know . . .'

'A vegetarian enchilada,' Unity said. 'A small portion.'

'And how do you form relationships when you have eternity to play with?' Don asked. 'Jesus, I can barely keep one going for a fortnight.'

Unity dabbed a finger on the salt of her margarita. 'Are you sure you want to spend forever with one person? With Gabriel?' she asked Willie. 'It's hard to imagine.'

'Have him talk to you about the Buffalo Bills. It helps the imagination along a whole lot.'

Megan Davies retreated to the kitchen. She honestly didn't mind table work. After all, you had to make a living somehow whilst waiting for the RSC to offer you Ophelia. The schizophrenic accents had been her own idea – it helped her regard the job as a kind of improv-thing. To sustain the appropriate voice in each restaurant, she had developed the habit of reciting apposite, anchoring phrases under her breath as she ascended the stairs. 'Hey, Benito Mussolini, shaddapa y'face,' she'd mutter as she carried two plates of spaghetti to the trattoria. 'Well, heck, ma'am, that's real hospitable o'yew,' she'd murmur, backing through Wetbacks' saloon doors with an armful of ribs. It sounded like madness, but it was Method.

'Table six,' the chef called, dumping a soup and some garlic mushrooms on the bottom ledge, 'and twenty-five.' He slid a HogDog and a veggie enchilada onto the next shelf up. Megan pinched out her cigarette and put it back in the pack. She grabbed the TexMex order, failing to notice a french fry that dropped off the plate and plopped into the gazpacho, and made her way up the stairs.

'Ah jest cain't take it no more, JR!' she insisted, as she approached the table.

'What if cloning turns out to be impossible?' Unity asked, inspecting her meal.

'Half the attraction's getting a brand-new body, of course,' Don shrugged. 'Eternal life, resurrected flesh – start to sound like a familiar scam?'

'And if the Christian scam's correct,' Ellen went on, 'where does that leave a sort-of-dead person in regard to God? Does He take your soul unto His bosom for a couple of hundred years and then decant it back when they wake you up?'

'We just plan on sleepin' in the bucket until they figure something out. Folk are curious. They'll try t'reanimate us one fine day fer sure. An' I ain't too concerned about the body I get. This one's gettin' kinda run down anyhow.'

'I can think of a few improvements I wouldn't mind myself,' Unity suggested, looking down at herself.

'If I was going to design a body,' Ellen continued, 'I'd certainly come up with something better than this.'

'Ah, bullshit,' Willie and Don said in unison, 'you're damn near perfect already.'

The remark took Unity by surprise. From a hetero man – from Don, for instance – it would be a standard first-stage seduction move; but what did it mean from Willie? It'd really help if he were a bit more camp, if he'd give a nod to the queer stereotype. What with the easy chat and the margaritas and the throwaway flattery, the whole evening was beginning to feel like a date. Maybe it was her own failing that she made such a connection, but she simply never went out to dinner with a man unless it was a courtship ritual.

Don wondered if he'd pushed his luck. From most women, the self-deprecating comment about some supposed physical imperfection would have been a deliberate permission to direct the conversation towards the carnal. Unity gave that kind of cue all the time. *Do you think my tits are sagging? Have I put on a bit of weight?* But Ellen was far too self-possessed to use such tactics, surely.

Megan Davies arrived with Don and Ellen's starters, and laid them on the table.

'Is a leetle wooden boy,' she announced, absent-mindedly. 'I willa coll him Pinocchio.'

Ellen gave an incredulous laugh. 'I'm *sorry*?' she asked.

The waitress froze in an attitude of open-mouthed embarrassment.

'Ummm ... gazpacho! Mushrooms! Shit! Scusi!' she blurted, and rushed away.

Don and Ellen watched her go and then looked at each other and collapsed into a heap of giggles.

'What on *earth* was that about?' Don wondered aloud, dipping a spoon into his gazpacho. He fished out an item that quite obviously didn't belong there and inspected it. Ellen was buckled with laughter as he called Megan Davies back to their table. He held up his spoon to show her what he'd found.

'You're going to hate me for this,' he said, straight-faced, 'but – waitress, there's a fry in my soup.'

Casey Rushmore had phoned eighteen hotels before one of them admitted to having a Dr Todd in the place.

'Could you tell me his room number, please?'

'Just putting you through,' the operator said.

'No!' yelped Casey, 'I . . .'

'Gabe Todd,' came a feeble voice as the phone was answered on the first ring.

'Is that room, umm, 304?' Casey asked, attempting to sound like anyone other than Casey Rushmore. He'd picked the room number at random, hoping that Todd would correct him by giving the correct one. He could then claim he'd been misrouted and come away with the information required. Pretty goddamn fiendish, Casey thought. Pretty goddamn fiendish for a spur-of-the-moment plan.

'Yeah, 304,' Gabriel croaked. 'Who is this?'

Casey gave a burp of astonishment. '*What?* Damn! Forget it. Wrong number.' He hurriedly hung up the payphone and slumped back against the side of the booth, exhaling.

Absolutely frigging typical, he thought bitterly.

Still, he had the hotel and the room number. Gabriel was bound to go to Willie's gig the following night, which only left the small matter of how to get into the room.

That, and the fact that he had no idea what he intended to do when he got there.

Willie and Unity were on to their second pitcher of margaritas. Just the other side of the wall, Ellen and Don were into their third bottle of wine. All four of them were somewhat drunk. As Unity got back from the Ladies, Willie was crooning softly to himself.

'*I crossed the river to the Promised Land,*' he gospelled, his voice like gravel in syrup, '*when I took that pale angel's hand . . .*'

'Is that an old spiritual?' Unity asked, sitting down.

'Nope, just written to sound like one,' Willie told her. 'It's the first song I wrote after I met Gabe.'

'You want my opinion,' Don remarked, 'old Willie paddles both sides of the canoe.'

'Not necessarily,' Ellen said. 'Lots of gay writers make their work ambiguous.'

'I like to sneak in some personal references,' Willie admitted, 'but there's no point alienatin' folk. I wanna sell records, and the country music audience can be a little conservative if they've a mind. I guess they know I'm gay, but so long as I don't wear any more sequins than Dolly . . .'

Unity laughed. It was only since meeting him and becoming his friend that she'd realised how famous Willie was. The posters for his album and tour were on the tube, flyposted on empty shops. His media coverage had even been remarked upon by the late-show comedians – which, in terms of environmental trickle-down, was like finding mercury in plankton. Whilst Willie and Unity had been sitting in Wetbacks, they'd twice been politely interrupted by autograph hunters. If Willie's sexuality was common knowledge, it obviously didn't bother the smitten women who read his scribbled messages on Wetbacks' napkins, and then, eyes gleaming, backed away with the autographs hugged to their breasts.

'My point is,' Don said, 'that "What the Hell" isn't in the *least* ambiguous. It's quite definitely addressed to a woman, and the only confusion is in what *she* believes. And, as you said, it has a more intriguing twist if you know he's gay. But I'd say he *isn't*, totally – and that's the point of the song.'

'I suppose that fame is sexy,' Unity mused, indicating the women at the next table who were still glancing across at Willie from time to time and smiling fondly, 'even if you know the object of your attention isn't interested.'

Willie shrugged. 'No one's one hunnerd per cent pink or blue.'

'You think we're all somewhere in the middle – different shades of purple,' Unity suggested.

'Nope, more like ice cream. Mainly one colour, but kinduva a raspberry-ripple effect goin' right through it.'

'We should *in* him,' Don exclaimed. 'There's all these sorry bastards being *outed* all over the shop – we should expose Rabblestack as a latent straight.'

'If that's true, then you could live your life anything up to fifty per cent unfulfilled,' Unity pointed out, ever the statistician.

'He'd thank us in the end,' Ellen agreed, laughing. 'Think of all the straight male pleasures he's denied.'

'Exactly,' Don nodded. 'Using his cafetiere to drain the vinegar off gherkins during *Match of the Day*; farting on the way to the fridge at half-time; blowing his nose on the antimacassars. Ah, the fun-filled life of the hetero philistine. Does he know what he's missing?'

'Depends how you arrange your life,' Willie said, cryptically.

He and Unity shared a taxi; it would drop Willie off at the Kensington WestPark before taking Unity on to Fulham. As they passed Marble Arch, Willie gave Unity a hug.

Unity had been on the sharp end of sufficient hugs to distinguish the types. This one gave a fraternal first impression (his hands clasped to her shoulders, the kiss planted on the trailing edge of the cheekbone), despite an unassumingly seductive bouquet (lemon, liquor, old leather), yet the bloom was subtly, unmistakably insistent (the trail of the kiss straying to the earlobe, the withdrawing fingers butterflying at the edge of the breasts). She was taken aback. Though she hadn't officially given Don the bad news, there was nothing really to stop her responding to Willie's overture – except, perhaps, her fondness for Gabriel. But then, behaviour such as Willie's might be covered by the terms of his relationship with Gabe. Could be they both swung like metronomes.

She attempted a noncommittal, time-buying gambit.

'What happens if it turns out that they can't revive you at all?' she asked. 'It'll all have been a terrible waste of time and money, won't it?'

Willie sat back in the cab seat and frowned. 'You mean, what if a thousand years pass, the fourth millennium's right there at the door and my head's still lyin' in the deep-freeze, frosted like a popsicle and with no prospect of ever bein' raised to a blessed, eternal life?'

Unity nodded. 'Exactly. *Exactly*.'

Willie appeared to consider the notion for a few seconds.

'Well,' he finally drawled, scratching his beard, 'I guess I'll begin to feel pretty damn foolish right about then . . .'

Gabriel was in bed reading a collection of twentieth-century verse. He heard the door of the hotel room open, and Willie's whistling, as he came to the bedroom.

'Good time?' he asked as Willie sat on the end of the bed to pull off his boots.

'Yeah – she's a cute kid. How you feelin'?'

'I feel like failing the physics major who sold me that grass, the bastard. So – you gonna break Unity's heart?'

The singer paused in the act of tugging at his boot, and looked at Gabe sidelong, an expression of facetious innocence on his face. 'Well, now – you think I could?'

These flirtations of Willie's, Gabe knew, were as necessary to the singer's health and his work as Boston was to Gabe himself. He could live with that – didn't have to like it, but he could live with it. As far as he knew, Willie had never gone any further than the wry innuendo and the fond embrace. Well, maybe he had. On the road, far from home – yeah, maybe he had. Whatever. The point was, he always came back – punctual, unchanged and guiltless.

Gabe closed his book and put it on the nightstand. 'I like her, and I need her work. Don't fuck her up, Willie.'

Willie grinned, hefting his boots into a corner and heading for the bathroom. 'Y'know, it's like a drug with me, Gabe,' he said, turning on the tap. 'I don't inhale the stuff. I just like bein' around the smoke.'

CHAPTER TWENTY-ONE

THE FOLLOWING DAY, SATURDAY, Unity went into the office. She felt guilty about having taken a day off, and she was excited at the prospect of putting together a project charter for her new endeavour. She got in around two, having cured her hangover with freshly-squeezed orange juice and a jog through Bishop's Park. She sat at her desk, turned on the PC and typed furiously for two straight hours. A little after four, she went to the kitchen and got an iced Spa from the fridge.

Wandering back through the open-plan, she grinned, soaking up the hush, the computers, the whirr of the laser printer as it produced her draft. She loved being at work on her own. It made her feel that she was doing something important, that progress was being made.

She took the paper from the printer, went back to her desk and read through it, marking it in pencil as she went. She had taught herself correct proof-reader's notation, and was always slightly thrilled when she found a transposition that allowed her to flourish the standard squiggle, or a missed space that demanded a very specific hieroglyph in the margin. From the mark-up, she corrected the computer file. She saved it, backed it up to the network and then copied it to floppy. She labelled the floppy and filed it in her Work-In-Progress drawer. She put the hard copy in the recycling bin.

That was another thing about Don – he had absolutely no sense of order. She'd seen the trestle table in his flat that he referred to as his 'study'. There were Babel towers of books; disks strewn about in collapsing black heaps, like the aftermath of *moules marinières*; bits of print-out with completely unrelated notes scribbled on the back. No wonder he never achieved anything. She'd seen him once, trying to find some short story that he'd written. He'd pushed disk after unlabelled disk into the drive. *Er, that's a letter to the bank. Hang on – no, more pornography. Wait a minute – what the fuck's that? Oh, I dunno – it'll turn up.*

It had turned into a row, of course – but he had so much *potential*. If he would only get himself together and stop wasting his time on ephemera.

'Still,' she muttered, 'not my problem any more.'

What would she miss? The sex? Sex was easy to get – but one of the intriguing things about Don was how imaginative you had to be to impress him. Jesus, she'd spent a fortune on props, clothes, make-up. Maybe it'd be a relief to go back to someone who panted at the thought of a black bra. And anyway, if she had to go through all those charades to keep him fascinated, what kind of respect must he have for her?

Dismissing the thought, Unity gave a satisfied sigh, and opened up a new window on her screen. The sun was shining; she had a project to bring in; and this evening she was going to be the companion of a world-famous scientist who wanted her brain, at a concert by a world-famous musician who wanted her body.

Don sat and looked at the phone, which was made to resemble a hamburger. The top of the bun unfolded to reveal a keypad, set in the lettuce, and when the phone rang, the meat patty flashed. The time was five past five and the patty had not flashed all day.

He could call Ellen. He really should call Ellen. If you've rounded off an enjoyable evening with the suggestion, *Come back to mine for coffee, just coffee, no funny business, really,* then you should probably call that person and apologise for forcing them to tell you that you're drunk. Even at the risk of making things worse, you should call them.

Or he could call Unity. He really ought to call Unity. If you've been going out with someone for better than a year, and you duck out of their dinner party in a petulant spat, you really ought to call them to apologise. Or at least to make sure that you won.

Or you can wait. You can light a cigarette and wait for the patty to flash.

Don lit a cigarette.

At seven thirty, Unity glanced out of the window. The church clock by the roundabout was of the opinion that it was just before three.

Flexing her stiff shoulders, she went through the careful process of storing the two-year project plan to several disks. She then picked up her jacket and handbag and walked to the ladies' toilets. She combed her hair and put on some deep red lipstick, black eyeliner and a kiss of blusher. She cleaned her glasses. Standing on tiptoe, she tried to get a full-length view of herself in the mirror above the sink. Concerned that she should look right for a country music concert, she had on a calf-length claret skirt, lace-up ankle boots and an embroidered white shirt. She pulled on her denim jacket and tilted her head to one side.

It would do. Nobody would feel embarrassed to be seen with her.

The Sunrise was no more than a minute's walk away, on the other side of the flyover. She was due to meet Gabriel there at eight fifteen, so she decided to take a stroll along the river. She crossed Hammersmith Bridge Road and cut down the side of the bridge, following the path past a couple of pubs, to the floodlit patch of green beyond.

A group of people were flinging an American football about on the grass. Unity didn't recognise them at first, but then the ball was thrown high in a vertiginous arc towards the path, and a voice called, 'I got it, I got it!' It was Gabriel, galloping across the park in her direction, but looking over his shoulder as the ball spun high through the air.

There was no way he could catch it, in Unity's estimation. The ball had reached the apex of its curve and would drop fifteen yards beyond him – but he kicked forward into a smooth sprint, judging the trajectory and adjusting his line with each long stride. He moved with such predatory speed and accuracy, it seemed as if the ball, knowing he'd fail, was hanging still, taunting him. He was almost there as it dropped, and he lunged forward, scooping with one hand, catching it just as it bent the blades of grass. Still running, he clutched the ball to his chest and straightened up. He slowed to a jog, curving behind Unity onto the path, and slammed the ball into the paving stones.

'Go Bills!' he yelled, and swivelled through three-sixty on the toes of one foot, a clenched fist held above his head.

As the group on the grass whistled and cheered, Unity said, 'Not bad, for a boffin.'

Gabriel turned and noticed her. 'Hey, Unity! Good to see you. You a gridiron fan?'

'I don't even understand the question,' she told him.

Willie waved from the other side of the park as Gabriel and Unity walked over to join them. She was introduced to the band and to Lori, and allowed herself to be included in the impromptu game. Gabriel tried to teach her how to throw the football.

'No, pull your arm back – way back. You have to aim it in front of him. Ha! No – push through the ball. Try again.'

The bass player good-naturedly ran up and down the edge of the park as Unity attempted to direct the ball into his path. Eventually she got it right, and Gabriel suggested that she try it for real.

'For real?' she asked. 'He caught it, didn't he?'

'Yeah, but no one was trying to stop you,' Gabriel told her. 'Joe, Willie, Lori – you're the defense. Jay, Tom – run wide when I snap it to Unity.'

As the defense took up crouching positions facing her, Unity realised what was about to happen. As soon as Gabe threw her the ball, they were going to leap on her and stamp her into the turf. Gabriel leaned forward on the knuckles of one hand, the ball at his feet. He glanced over his shoulder at her and winked.

'Now, wait a minute . . .' she began.

'HIKE!' Gabriel yelled, and the ball came at her like a bullet.

She was so surprised to have caught it that she simply stared at it for a moment. Then, looking up, she saw Willie bounding towards her. She fell back a pace and flung the ball hard, hoping that if she wasn't holding it, he wouldn't knock her over. He caught her round the waist, and swung her, quite gently, in a circle; then he lowered her feet to the ground. Gabriel was hooting with laughter, holding the ball that he'd plucked easily from the air.

'Not bad,' he chuckled. 'Not bad for a girl.' He turned and pitched the ball out to the bass player.

Unity looked up at Willie, whose arms were still round her waist. He squeezed her slightly, and let go.

'Not bad, for a girl,' he murmured.

As they made their way back to the venue, Gabriel gave Unity a clip-on badge that bore her name and the words 'Willie Rabblestack/Access All Areas'. They cut up a cul-de-sac that ran behind the concert hall, leading to a door marked Pass Holders Only. As the musicians trooped inside, Gabriel put a hand on Unity's shoulder.

'Come look at this,' he said.

Just beyond the door, parked against a wall, was a stretch-limousine. The paintwork was dove-white and the windows were silvered mirrors. Gabriel pointed a sonic key at it, and there was a *beep* as the doors unlocked. Gabriel opened the driver's door and invited Unity to get in.

'Isn't this a fine machine?' he asked, as she slid into the seat. 'Look at this styling. Check those instruments. It comes complete with a chauffeur, but I gave him a week's vacation. For a car like this, I'm prepared to be a rock star's driver.'

'You rented this?' Unity asked, leaning back in the seat and grasping the wheel.

Gabriel laughed. 'You're kidding! The record company pick up the tab. We just get to play with it. I drove it across town from the hotel this afternoon. Tomorrow I'm going to drive it to Nottingham.'

'You drove from the hotel? It's only a ten-minute walk.'

'Whatever. Isn't it beautiful?'

'It's amazing,' Unity agreed.

'Want to try it, drive it a couple of blocks?'

Unity let go of the wheel. 'God, no. I'd be terrified.'

They went inside and made their way to the dressing room. Upstairs, the support band were on and the thud of the music was quite audible. Unity sat silently, feeling like an intruder as the musicians chatted, tuned their instruments, drank mineral water. The pounding from upstairs ceased, and Lori left 'to ride the desk'.

'Time?' asked Tom, the drummer, tapping his sticks on his thigh.

'Fifteen minutes,' Willie said.

The conversation idled, and eventually ceased. A quiet tension hung in the air, and Unity felt even more an outsider. Willie took a biro from the table and wrote 'London' on the palm of his left hand. He caught Unity's quizzical look.

'Habit,' he grinned. 'Just so's I don't say "Good evening, Liverpool" by mistake.' He took a deep breath and addressed the others. 'Okay? Let's go.'

The band got to their feet, the drummer lit a cigarette, and they filed out to the corridor. Unity and Gabriel were left alone in the dressing room. Gabriel opened a beer.

'We'll give them time to get on, and then go up to watch from the wings.'

'I know it's ridiculous,' Unity said, 'but I'm really nervous for them – well, for Willie really. He's just so reserved and unshowy.'

'Yeah, he's about the same with an audience. He can project self-effacement right to the back of the hall.'

178

From upstairs there was a huge roar and an eruption of applause. A country-rock guitar intro cut through the noise, and the drums leapt in behind it. Gabriel stood up, holding his can of beer.

'Coming?'

'Yeah. Hey, I meant to tell you – I got the budget! The project starts Monday!'

Gabriel turned in the doorway, and smiled broadly. 'Never doubted you for a second, kid.' He raised his beer to her. 'Congratulations. We'll talk about it after the gig.'

They squeezed to the side of the stage, slightly back from the lead mike. They could see Willie full face only when he turned towards the left-hand section of the crowd. Though they were not by most standards a loud act, the Willie Rabblestack Band packed sufficient wattage to make conversation impossible where Gabriel and Unity stood.

Between numbers, Willie chatted amiably to the crowd, not in the hectoring tone Unity expected at concerts, but in an offhand, unhurried way. Gabriel had been right about his onstage persona. In a hall holding eight hundred people, he managed to create precisely the same relaxed informality that Unity had first enjoyed in the kitchen of the house off Prospect Avenue. He gave the impression that, seeing as how a few folks had dropped by out of the blue, he might just play them a song or two, if they didn't mind.

Unity also discovered the confusing mix of pride and embarrassment that comes from watching someone you know perform his own songs. When Willie sang the gospelly 'Lord, Lift Me Up On Gabriel's Wings', she turned to look at Gabe Todd, almost wanting to apologise for being privy to the hidden lyric. Gabriel's eyes were fixed on the stage, and he was mouthing the words along with Willie.

> . . . *I know that fiery sword of peace*
> *Will give my troubled soul release.*

As the song ended, Gabriel glanced at Unity and gave a sheepish, bashful shrug, as if to say, What can I do? I'm crazy about the guy.

Whatever the terms of Willie and Gabe's relationship, Unity realised, she wouldn't get involved with the singer. Blackmail, apparently, she could stomach, but betrayal of affection was beyond her.

The band ended the set with a rousing twelve-bar. As the guitarist was soloing, Willie, still strumming, strolled towards the side of the stage and, looking at Gabriel, took his hand from the fretboard to mime the action of drinking. Gabriel stepped back into the corridor and retrieved a bottle of mineral water. The song ended with a drag-out-knock-down chord, and the band unplugged their instruments and strode offstage.

Willie came directly to Gabriel and took the bottle from him. He was sweating heavily and panting; he glugged from the bottle and then splashed some over his face.

'Reckon I'm getting too old for this shit,' he yelled breathlessly over the whooping and clapping crowd. 'I feel kinda dizzy.'

'You look bushed,' the drummer shouted in his ear. 'You wanna skip the encore?'

Willie shook his head, droplets of water scattering from his beard. 'No, I'm just outta practice. C'mon.'

Turning to go, he smiled at Gabriel as he handed him the bottle. Gabe squeezed his arm and smiled back.

The rest of the band took their places as the stage lights came up, and then Willie strolled into view. The volume of the applause doubled as he waved to the crowd and bent to pick up his guitar lead.

As he walked to the back of the stage to adjust the tone of his amp, he seemed to stumble. He fell against the amplifier, one elbow resting on top of it, and his knees sagged. There was a banshee screech of feedback as his body pressed the guitar to the speaker. It was a leaping, lipless, uncoiled sound – sudden pain. Then Willie toppled sideways, twisting as he went down.

The head of the Telecaster smacked against the floor, and a leaden, funereal open chord hung in the air like nightfall.

Casey had simply walked up to the desk and said, 'Room 304, please.' Almost distractedly, the receptionist handed him the keycard.

Number 304 turned out to be rather more than a room. There was a large main area with two sofas, an enormous television and a 'conference facility' – a reproduction Queen Anne table and chairs, with a notepad and pen in each place. To one side was a double bedroom with a walk-in wardrobe and an en-suite bathroom, housing a whirlpool bath and a shower.

Casey tiptoed, as if it made any difference, from the main room to the bedroom to the bathroom and back again. He carefully flicked through the papers on the table. There were notes for Gabriel's lecture; an invitation for Willie to a Loretta Lynn Convention in Sheffield; a tour itinerary. Nothing incriminating. No polaroids of hotel-room bondage; no Post-Its reading *Must buy manacles, leather mask.*

In one corner of the bedroom was a neat pile of small silver flight cases, presumably for musical instruments and effects pedals or whatnot. Casey ignored them, and went to the wardrobe. He rather hoped he'd find a latex jumpsuit hanging between the shirts and jackets, or a pair of size-eleven patent stilettos jumbled amongst the sneakers on the floor. But there was not the slightest hint of the occupants' sexual preferences.

Nothing, Casey noted bitterly. Not even a knotted chiffon scarf. As raving pain-queens go, he felt, Gabriel and Willie were simply not pulling their weight. He went back to the bedroom but a quick riffle through the bedside drawers turned up damn all of interest, and the bathroom offered little solace either.

Casey sat disconsolately on the bed. Another complete waste of time, then. He checked his watch. He had a good half-hour before the concert ended, but where else was there to look? He scanned the room, and his gaze fell on the flight cases. Musical instruments. Concert currently underway. *What were they doing here in the hotel room then?*

He dived off the bed and skidded on his knees to the pile of cases. He flicked open the catches of the top one and lifted the lid.

'Bingo,' he breathed.

It was some kind of electric saw – a vicious, black-and-silver job nestling in red velvet. God alone knew what it was for. Casey put it carefully to one side and opened the next case. Laid out, like a junkie's birthday, were shrink-wrapped needles, a row of brown, medical-looking bottles and a sterilising kit. The next case – Casey couldn't believe his luck – contained several pairs of rubber gloves and a surgeon's plastic apron.

Casey sat back on his haunches and put his hands on his hips, trying to imagine what foul and unnatural practices required such monstrous props. He scrabbled in his pocket for a small, expensive camera and excitedly clicked through three or four shots, breathing rapidly and almost giggling with delight.

Then he stopped, and told himself to calm down. He took the lens cap off and started again.

As the audience's cheers dropped to a thrum of concerned muttering, Gabriel ran onto the stage and knelt beside Willie. The singer's eyes and mouth were wide open and he was making a dry *kuk-kuk-kuk* deep in his throat. He didn't seem to be aware. Gabriel undid the guitar strap and lifted Willie's head and shoulders.

'Help me!' he yelled at the stagehands who were hanging back, uncertain what to do. The concert promoter rushed onstage and told the band to play something, *any fucking thing*, as Willie was cradled off.

In the wings, someone with a mobile phone said, 'I'll call an ambulance, yeah?'

Gabriel pushed through, shouting, 'The car! Get him to the car!'

With the roadies supporting Willie's back and legs and Gabriel cradling his head and shoulders, they scurried crabwise along the corridor and down the stairs that led to the stage door. Unity ran behind, one of a group of horrified and useless people trying to think of some way to help.

There was fine rain falling in the alley. When they reached the limo, a record company man reached ahead of the stricken singer to open the door. It was locked. Unity elbowed him aside and squeezed between Gabriel and the car, reaching into the pocket of Gabe's jeans for the key.

'Willie, hang on,' Gabriel was saying. 'Hang on in there, Willie.'

Unity beeped the doors open and Gabriel told the roadies to help him get the singer onto the back seat. He turned to Unity as he backed into the limo. 'Where's the hospital?'

'Er . . . Fulham Palace Road – two minutes away.'

'Drive.' He pulled the door shut, disappearing behind the mirrored glass.

Unity stood stone still, clutching the car key. 'Christ,' she whimpered, and yanked open the door. She fumbled the key into the ignition and turned it. She found reverse and stalled the engine.

'Fuck! I'm sorry! I'm sorry!'

Twisting the key again, she glanced over her shoulder into the huge, dim interior of the limo. Willie was full stretch on the sheepskin-covered seat, Gabriel kneeling beside him, clutching his hand and speaking low and desperate into his ear. Unity eased her foot down and the car slid backwards. The limo was so long that there was no hope of her being able to see oncoming traffic as she backed onto the road, so she simply pressed the heel of her hand onto the horn and cruised out. She straightened it up and headed towards Hammersmith roundabout. The lights had just changed against her, and she could see a line of traffic starting to move from her right. She gunned the motor and the limo accelerated with smooth grace. She cut across to the inside lane and scanned the dash for the headlight switch.

The sliding window that separated the driver from the passengers hummed open, and Gabriel's head poked through. She glanced sidelong at him. His face was pale. Even his eyes seemed to have lost their chestnut shine. 'Hurry! Where's this hospital?'

Unity pointed to her right. 'We've got to go all the way round the roundabout.'

'Fuck's sake!' Gabriel said, his eyes brimming. He withdrew to the back of the car.

Unity ran another red and cut through the bus-stands on the east side of the roundabout. Pedestrians leapt from her path, screaming abuse.

'Get out of the way! Sorry! Jesus, sorry!' she shouted, checking in the wing mirrors before veering back across the traffic, and cutting through to the top of the Fulham Palace Road.

She turned the corner to find herself stuck behind a bus. Holding her breath, she leaned on the horn and pulled to the wrong side of the street, swerving back just in time to miss a truck coming the other way. They were no more than a minute from Charing Cross Hospital, but the Saturday night traffic was building up, and there was a crawling line of it a hundred yards ahead.

In the back she could hear Gabriel sobbing. She glanced over her shoulder, and saw that he had laid his head on Willie's chest, looking up at the bearded face. His hand was against Willie's cheek, stroking it gently. Unity pulled the limo out to straddle the white line, planning to force her way between the rows of traffic. If she had to crunch the nose of the limo to get through, then she would. She smacked her hand on the horn as she approached the jam.

'Get out of the way!' she screamed. 'Get out of the fucking way, you bastards!'

Suddenly, Gabriel's arm appeared over her shoulder, and took her wrist, lifting it from the horn. His face was wet with tears.

'Stop the car,' he said, quietly. 'We haven't got much time. I'll drive.'

'No,' she told him. 'You look after Willie.'

'I plan to. We're going back to the hotel.'

CHAPTER TWENTY-TWO

ATTEMPTING TO KEEP HER expression normal, Unity collected the second keycard to Room 304 from the desk, as Gabriel lifted Willie from the back of the car. The doorman took one arm.

'A little the worse for wear, sir?' he asked Gabriel.

'Right. Right,' Gabriel told him.

Unity joined them as they chair-lifted Willie into the lift.

'We'll be fine from here,' Gabe told the doorman.

As the lift ascended, he turned to Unity. His face was pale, and all depth was gone from it. 'Once we get him to the room, you're to go away. I don't want you there.'

Unity protested briefly and without conviction, relieved to be excused the red-clawed science that was to follow. As Gabriel had sped the car towards Kensington, she'd glanced over her shoulder at the corpse in the back. It was the first time that she'd considered the violence that must inevitably occur between animation and suspension. Until that moment, her vision of cryonic hiatus had been of a misty, antiseptic cocoon in which the personality might slumber, like a mythical king. There had been nothing of bone and blood in the image – no severed jugulars or oozing marrow.

Nothing that looked quite so much like death.

As he closed the lid on the surgical saw, Casey heard the hallway door of the hotel room open. He stifled a shriek of surprise, and dived across the bed and into the closet. Wrapping his fingers round the top of the door, he pulled it nearly closed. He shrank back amongst the clothes as he heard stumbling, hurried footsteps come into the bedroom.

'The bathtub,' came Gabriel's voice. It was hoarse and a little breathless.

There was panting – two people panting, one sounded female – and a released sigh, as if some load had been laid down.

'Will you . . . ?' came the female voice, but it was cut off by Dr Todd, speaking in a flat, clipped tone.

'I'll be in touch. Please go away now.'

The woman left – Casey heard the main door closing behind her – and Dr Todd came back into the bedroom.

Not the closet, Casey prayed. Don't come to the closet. Take a nap or something.

Things were being moved. The flight cases – he was taking them into the bathroom. Casey buried his face in a lumberjack shirt, and held his breath. That female voice – though it had spoken barely two words, it was familiar. He knew it from somewhere.

There came a snap of rubber gloves being pulled on. Perhaps Todd would stay in there, in the bathroom, and do whatever it was he did with all that macabre equipment. Maybe – Casey suddenly thrilled with daring – *maybe he could get a photo*. He put his hand to the pocket of his jacket to check the camera – and failed to contain a high-pitched squeak of terror. *Jesus Christ, I've left it out there!*

He edged forward towards the crack of light, only to freeze instantly at the soft chink of two coat hangers banging together. Pushing back a shirt with trembling slowness, he peered through the gap. He could see the corner of the bed, and the door of the bathroom. Dr Todd was filling the doorway, turning, coming back into the room. Casey didn't dare move as Gabriel strode to the corner, out of sight, and then reappeared carrying two more cases – the one with the needles and bottles, and the one that contained some kind of pump.

Casey saw Gabriel check his watch as he went back to the bathroom, muttering, 'Eight minutes – nearly nine. Nearly nine goddamn minutes.' He pushed the door of the bathroom fully open, and rested the case on the sink. Whilst taking out the hypodermic, attaching it to the pump and filling it with liquid from one of the bottles, he kept glancing into the deep tub.

If Casey twisted his head and peered sideways, he could just see the camera beyond the bed, on the nightstand. He cursed himself. How long before Todd came out and noticed it? He shifted again and looked towards the bathroom. Gabriel was leaning over the whirlpool bath now, the spiked pump in one hand, the other reaching out of sight and moving something – supporting something. His elbow flexed and the needle went in. There was a low electric hum – the pump.

What did he have in there? Some kind of animal? A dog or a goat or what? Maybe he was experimenting on stolen animals. That would do – that would be a lever.

Once the injection had been administered, Gabriel appeared to relax. He moved the case from which he'd taken the needle and chemicals, and leaned back against the sink, looking at his watch again. Still he stared into the tub. He was quarter-face to Casey, and it seemed that – yes, it was really so – tears were coursing down his face. Gabriel was slouched in an attitude of deep contemplation, hands clasped in his lap, feet crossed at the ankle, but he was weeping, silently and without a tremor. Tears were dripping from his chin onto his rubber-gloved hands.

Tentatively, Casey glanced down at his own watch.

The seconds passed, and Dr Todd stayed still, his gaze fixed on the bath. Casey moved his head a little to look again at the camera. Ten feet maybe. If only Todd would shut the door, it would be worth the risk to slip from the closet. He could grab the camera, barge into the bathroom and take a blind shot before hightailing it out of there. But with the bathroom door wide open like that, Todd could easily be on top of him before he got across the bed.

Suddenly, Gabriel pushed himself forward from the basin and bent down to a flight case on the floor at his feet. He opened it and took out the surgical saw. He laid it carefully on the rim of the tub, and turned to his right, his back to Casey. He clicked open another case, just within Casey's range of vision. It was the size of a small beer keg, and as Gabriel laid back the lid, white vapour tumbled over the rim and down its sides.

Again, Dr Todd straightened up, taking the surgical saw in his hand. He breathed in a deep breath, and wiped his nose and mouth across the shoulder of his white T-shirt.

'This was the deal, sweet boy,' he said tremulously. 'You'd do the same for me . . .'

His thumb pressed a button on the hilt of the saw and it began to buzz.

Casey almost whimpered. *Sweet boy? Did he have a* person *in there? Jesus fucking Christ – what kind of sick freak was Todd turning out to be?*

Casey clamped a hand across his mouth as Gabriel Todd stepped into the tub, his legs far apart, straddling whatever lay there. He leaned forward and grasped something with his left hand, and brought the singing saw down. There was a moment's hesitation – some fathomless anguish flitted across Gabriel's face – and then he bit his lip and the note of the saw changed. It dropped an octave and stuttered. There was the sound of splashing on the porcelain of the bath, and below that organic trickle, the insistent, electric whine of the saw.

Casey stomach churned, and he swallowed hard. All he wanted now was to escape, to dash for the door, to dive through the window.

But the camera . . . Whatever came of this appalling situation, Casey didn't want to leave the camera behind, covered with his fingerprints.

He heard his own breath coming in short, squeaky sobs. He wanted to be back in his office with its wall charts and its ball-bearing toys. He wanted to plot little office coups and go up a storey every year or two. He wanted – oh, God – he wanted the dull sizzle of the saw to stop.

With a curdled retch of terror, he burst out of the closet and launched himself across the bed. He grabbed the camera on the move and rolled across the floor, smacking against the wall and almost dislocating his shoulder. Painless, he scrambled to his feet, and was making for the door as Gabriel stood upright in the tub and stepped out onto the rug. In mid-flight, with the camera upside down in his curled hand, Casey turned to face the bathroom, and a spasm of unalloyed horror twitched every muscle in his body.

The camera clicked, capturing the image of Gabriel Todd – eyes blind, mouth grief-buckled, hands dark with fresh blood – cradling the severed head of Willie Rabblestack tenderly, in folded arms, like a newborn.

CHAPTER TWENTY-THREE

UNITY HAD NOT BEEN able to leave. She'd got as far as the street and then turned round and walked back into the hotel. She'd sat in the bar for a while, drinking coffee, then returned to the lobby and flicked blindly through a magazine. She had no real idea of what she was waiting for, but she couldn't bring herself to go home, sit by the phone, gaze at the ceiling all night.

She decided to give it an hour. Then she would call his room, just to let him know that she was here if he wanted her.

She stood up and was walking across the foyer back towards the bar, when the door to the stairway burst open and a figure hurtled through, buffeting her against a potted palm. She staggered and fell back. In the tangle of legs, the running man stumbled, going down on one knee, a hand pressed to the carpet by Unity's hip. She looked up and saw Casey's face, white and panicked, and heard him saying, '*Oh Christ, oh Christ, oh Christ . . .*' At the same moment, he recognised her. Momentarily, a frown replaced the expression of jangled alarm, as if he couldn't place her. Then, in a hoarse whisper, he exclaimed, 'It was you!'

Unity broke away from his stare, glancing down to see a camera clutched to his chest. He caught the look, and guiltily shoved the camera inside his jacket. It wasn't until she saw the gesture that Unity made a connection. Pushing herself up from the floor, she grabbed Casey's wrist.

'What have you done?' she demanded, in a low, angry hiss. 'What have you done, you creep?'

Casey yanked his hand free. 'What have *I* done?' he replied, his voice shaky with fright and incredulity. 'Jesus!'

He leapt to his feet and ran for the street, leaving Unity sprawling in the split soil of the potted palm.

Half an hour earlier, police constables Gilzean and Chivers had been sitting in their squad car, four vehicles back in a queue at the drive-in Burger King. They were debating the relative merits of truncheons and batons when a white stretch limo screeched round the corner, side-swiped a parked Fiat and burned past them, accelerating to sixty in the direction of Kensington. Chivers turned on the siren, but by the time they'd got out of the fast-food line and onto the street, the limo was gone. They called in the registration, and the car was identified as a rental, currently hired out to a record company. Further calls turned up the name of Willie Rabblestack, and the address of the Kensington WestPark.

Cheered at the prospect of a dull evening being enlivened by charges of reckless driving and, almost certainly, possession of illegal substances, Chivers and Gilzean made their way to the hotel.

Unity got to her feet and went over to the courtesy phone by the check-in desk. She dialled Gabriel's room number. As it rang, she wondered what Casey had been up to, the lowlife scumbag, dreading to think what he might have on that camera. The phone rang and rang. *Come on, Gabriel, pick it up. Please pick it up.* She'd give it three more rings, and then . . .

'Todd.' His voice was high, sob-ridden.

'Gabe, it's Unity. I'm downstairs. Did you just see Casey Rushmore?'

'He dropped by, yeah,' Gabriel replied, and almost seemed to chuckle – but it was a frightening, fleshless sound.

'Gabe, are you okay?'

There was a silence, then a shivering intake of breath, the gulping echo of swallowed tears.

'Gabe? Gabe, please, speak to me.'

'What if I'm wrong, Unity? I've just done the most terrible thing. What if I'm wrong?'

Unity bit her lip and closed her eyes, answerless.

Suddenly, a voice beside her asked, 'Excuse me, miss. Can you tell us what room Mr Rabblestack is in?'

Unity snapped her head to the left and saw a policeman talking not to her but to the woman on reception. The woman checked her computer screen and gave the number. The policeman nodded, asking her not to call the room, and then he and a second policeman made their leisurely way to the lifts.

With one eye on the cops, Unity whispered urgently into the phone.

'Gabriel, the police are here! Gabriel? Are you still there?'

'Yeah . . .' came the flat reply.

'Listen, there are two policemen getting into the lift. They've got your room number. Gabriel? *Gabriel?*'

But the purr on the line told her that Gabriel had hung up.

Five minutes passed, and Unity paced up and down the lobby of the WestPark. She couldn't help but picture the scene that would greet the two PCs in Room 304. She tried to shake it, but always came back to the image conjured by Gabriel's quavering voice – *I've just done the most terrible thing . . .*

Eventually, the elevator doors opened and one of the policemen came back to the desk. His face was ashen, and he seemed a little unsteady on his feet. The receptionist greeted him with a bright, corporate smile.

'Did you find Mr Rabblestack?' she asked cheerfully.

The copper licked his lips, and nodded.

'Most of him, yeah.'

The rain, having dawdled half-heartedly for a while, hit its stride. The noise of water on concrete competed with the slushy hum of the traffic, and the flooded sidewalk was alive underfoot, as if fish were feeding frenziedly just below the surface.

Gabriel had walked blindly for half an hour, clutching the canister to his chest, the rain soaking through the clean T-shirt and jeans he had dragged on after hanging up on Unity. Unaware, uncaring, he'd trudged through Kensington towards the West End. He strode oblivious across Hyde Park Corner, cars swerving around him, and made his way past Green Park to Piccadilly Circus. Now, sodden and lost, he was huddled in a shop doorway on Regent Street, watching the buses go past.

He knew that he had to make a decision; he had to do something positive. Somehow, in his pain-stoned detachment, he told himself that when he saw a bus number that was a prime, he'd figure out the next move. Until then, he'd just stand and grieve.

A bus hissed past in the wet. 12.

The essence of a human being, Gabriel knew, was intellectual. The body was just a mineral machine that carried the brain around. And so what he had done was no more than lift the engine out of the chassis of Willie. But . . . what was a Pontiac? More than merely the engine. It was the styling, the chrome, the hubcaps. You didn't just take a chainsaw to that. Here, in this vacuum flask, he held everything that made Willie who he was – and yet, Gabriel had lived with Willie's body for thirty years. He'd stroked it, hugged it, kissed it and loved it. He'd charted the terrain of its muscle and skin; cherished its scars and its rogue hairs; tasted its sweat in the hush of the night and sucked in the sharp morning-breath of its lungs.

Did he really, deeply, have so much faith in science that he could imagine Willie's body being resurrected from a single cell of a lip? Or was he raging against an inevitability, and committing horrendous sacrilege in his rage, and ultimately destroying a sacred memory by pursuing a hubristic hope?

Another bus. 159.

If he was wrong, if there was going to be no resurrection, then he had no excuse. He would be damned by whatever cosmic authority judged these things. Damned by the reality of his own survival, in fact – because what he'd done to Willie's vacated machine was horrifying enough, but what he'd done to himself was also unforgivable. For the rest of his life – for the rest of all his lives – he'd wake up in the night from carnal dreams; the skin of Willie's neck twisting around the blade the instant before the saw bit; the jolt in his own wrist as the blade met bone.

And yet, what cowardice it would have been to have shirked that responsibility. One day, please God, someone would have to remove the head from *his* corpse; and later, if God remained pleased, he would be awoken in a new body for a new life. How could he live, then, if it was with the knowledge that he'd shrunk squeamishly back, denying that second chance to the only person he loved?

A number 15 bus slooshed past.

The police – the police, so quickly. And, presumably, coroners and lawyers and all the bureaucratic power of the establishment. Eventually, he would have to face the suits – that was inescapable. But not yet. He needed time to get things straight in his mind. The confrontation with the authorities would require delicate care, painstaking negotiation. He'd have to do some research and bring in some serious legal firepower; and he wasn't ready for that yet.

Soon, they'd be out looking for him. In a tiny little country like this, it wouldn't be long before they found him, and then . . .

An awful realisation hit Gabriel Todd, and he slid down the door to a crouch, hugging the canister that contained Willie's head to his chest.

. . . and *when* they found him, the first thing they'd do is open the canister. They'd consider it evidence. They'd take Willie's head out and do an autopsy on it. It wouldn't even matter if he fought them and won, because it'd be too late. Willie would be gone forever.

The rain had quietened to a sullen patter, and there was a roar of diesel as a bus revved along the avenue, spraying a puddle across the pavement short of Gabriel's feet. He looked up. Bus number 13. It was time to make a decision.

He had to find a safe place for Willie.

Gabriel knew very few people in London – a couple of academics, a publisher. None of them was close enough to trust. There was only Unity, really – and although she had no obvious connection to him, Casey Rushmore had seen her at the hotel, so she might already be of interest to the law.

Briefly, Gabriel considered leaving the canister in a left-luggage locker at one of the stations, but it was too impersonal – too much like leaving luggage. There was no choice. He had to get it to Unity. It was perilous, but less perilous than keeping it with him. And perhaps he could reduce the risk by getting someone else to take it to her – someone he could trust because she did.

At that moment, an unforgettable name popped into Gabriel's head. It was a name Unity had mentioned one time – and it was his only available contact with her.

Gabriel stood up and pushed his dripping hair from his face, then he crossed the road to a wine bar. He waved the barman over.

'Pardon me,' he said, in control now, working on a problem. 'Could I get a Beck's, a towel and the phone book?'

CHAPTER TWENTY-FOUR

PURSUED BY FEAR AND panic, Casey Rushmore fled to the only place in which he felt really secure – the grey concrete tower of Splendid Reach.

Tumbling from a cab on Hammersmith Bridge Road, he dashed through the pouring rain up the steps to the building and fumbled in his wallet for the swipe card that would open the smoked-glass doors. He dragged the card through the reader slot and waited for the electronic pip. Once inside, he'd be safe. The read-out flashed *Access Denied*, and Casey tried again, cursing. Again, the doors refused to open. Casey looked at the card, and yelped. Emblazoned upon it were the words 'Kensington WestPark'.

He glanced around guiltily. He could already see the stern face of some single-minded copper, leaning across the table in a featureless little room. 'So what are you doing with the key to the hotel room in which Mr Rabblestack's headless body was discovered, son? We've already got you for burglary and conspiracy to blackmail. We know you stayed over at Todd's house in Boston . . . Have you got a girlfriend, Johnny?'

Casey dithered on the steps of the building with the keycard in his hand, waving it pointlessly in front of him as he turned on the spot, looking for some way to be rid of it. He scanned the street, biting his bottom lip – and then stumbled down the steps to the kerb.

Cars were passing, slowing down as they approached the roundabout, tailing back now so that the end of the queue was level with him. Casey pretended to be waiting for a break in the traffic. Keeping his hands loosely at his sides, he surreptitiously flicked the card forward towards the grille of a drain at his feet. The card bounced on one corner and came to rest across two bars of the drain.

He let out a pained whine of frustration, and stepped off the kerb, still attempting to look like an ordinary pedestrian, peering down his nose at the card whilst keeping his head upright. He didn't want any public-spirited motorist to remember a man scrabbling in the gutter in the drizzle.

Thirty yards to his left, the lights went green and the line of cars moved off. Casey shuffled his feet sideways, hoping to push the card through a slot in the drain. He chanced a downward glance. The damn thing had simply slid across a gap or two. Lying flat, it was too wide to slip through. He swallowed, and gazed despairingly at the heavens. He'd have to bend down and poke it between the bars. He looked to his right to check oncoming traffic, and an approaching Renault slowed to a near halt and flashed its headlights at him, inviting him to cross.

'You sonofabitch,' Casey mumbled through a taut grin of thanks.

He trotted across to the central reservation, and the Renault accelerated towards the roundabout. As soon as it was out of sight, he turned to go back across the street, but now a steady stream of traffic was rumbling past him. The rain was getting heavier. Casey hopped from foot to foot, waiting for a gap.

On the other side of the road, a tramp in a huge, sodden mackintosh was plodding stolidly along the kerb, his eyes following the line of the gutter. Casey watched as he drew level with the drain, stopped and, slowly, carefully, bent down. He straightened up with the keycard in his grubby hand, and turned it over, examining it for value.

'Hey! You!' Casey yelled, but a juggernaut trundled past, drowning the words in roar and splash.

The tramp pocketed the keycard and resumed his plodding towards the tube station, head down and the collar of the raincoat turned up around his ears. Casey tracked him along the central reservation, walking sideways, almost skipping, with one eye on the traffic coming from behind, looking for a break in the flow. As the tramp reached the junction, the lights changed to red and Casey shot across the road.

'Give me that card,' he demanded, positioning himself in the old man's path. 'It's my property. Give it to me right away.'

The tramp regarded him quizzically, his head held to one side. He was fifty, sixty, a hundred or so, bearded and crusty.

'An' what card moight that be, young fella?' he asked. The accent was pure Northside, as Dublin as an empty Guinness glass. It was just about all Casey needed. He grabbed the man's lapels.

'Don't come that with me, you Paddy bastard. Give me the fucking card.'

The tramp bridled. 'Now don't you be after talkin' to me in that tone, mister, or you moight wake up with a crowd around yer.'

Casey released one lapel and drew his hand back in a fist. 'I'm warning you, Seamus,' he hissed, 'if you don't give me that card, I'll break your stupid Irish face.'

Suddenly a voice at Casey's back said, 'Is there some problem here?'

Terrific, Casey thought. We're attracting bystanders.

Without looking round, with his eyes fixed on the tramp, he growled, 'Butt out and mind your own fucking business.'

There was a moment's silence, filled only by the sound of the falling rain, and then the newcomer spoke again.

'This is a side of you I had not hitherto perceived, Casey.'

The speaker was Robert Spleen.

It had taken very little research for Spleen to discover the connection between Rabblestack, whose album sleeve featured the Nevada Cryonic Research Institute, and Dr Todd, whose face smiled out from the cover of the Sunday magazine. It was Spleen's habit, when intrigued by some new notion, to make some unobtrusive observations of the people involved and build up a file of background information. In his experience, such intelligence could only be to his advantage when the time came to make his interest known. Hence his presence at Willie Rabblestack's final concert.

When Willie collapsed, Spleen recognised Todd as the figure who rushed on stage, and he noted the scientist's expression as he knelt beside the singer. The newspaper article had hinted distantly at the relationship between the two men, and the concern Spleen saw on Todd's face corroborated the paper's coy allusions. It occurred to Spleen that, whatever became of Rabblestack, Dr Todd would be shaken and uncharacteristically vulnerable over the coming weeks.

He waited with the rest of the audience for fifteen or twenty minutes as the backing band banged out an extended country jam, and then the stage manager appeared to tell the house that Willie had been taken to hospital, and that there was no news yet.

Making his way to the exit, Spleen noticed, some fifty feet in front of him, a head of jet hair. He craned to see and, sure enough, it was the fascinating Ellen, turning to speak, looping her thick mane behind one ear with a hooked thumb. Spleen tried to push forward to catch up, but the crowd was too dense and slow-moving. As the audience spilled into the lobby, fanning out to the souvenir stalls, gathering in loose knots, he slalomed through the spaces to the doors, running his eyes over the people ahead of him.

He couldn't see her. He peered left towards the car park, beyond which was the flyover and the neon sign of the Splendid building bright above it. He swivelled right, scanning the column of people heading towards the tube. Registering surprise at his own impetuosity, he too headed in that direction, cutting through the throng, splashing into gutter puddles. If he could catch her at the station entrance, he would hail her with surprise, suggest a meal – his treat as a thank you for her hospitality the other night. They could talk; he could get to know her, find out what she wanted from life, maybe help her in some way. Then, at the evening's end, he would pay for a taxi to take her home.

But he didn't find her. He stood just inside the station for fifteen minutes as the rain increased to a torrent. People scurried in from the concert, clutching their Rabblestack posters beneath their coats, shaking the water from their hair – but there was no sign of Ellen. Eventually, chiding himself for his ridiculous adolescent impulsiveness, Spleen turned up the collar of his coat and walked back out onto the street. He crossed the roundabout and headed for the office, planning to spend the night in his apartment on the eighth floor.

By the traffic signals on the corner of Hammersmith Bridge Road, two men were squaring up, nose to nose. As he approached, Spleen recognised the taller of them. It was Casey Rushmore, his suit soaked through, demanding something of a down-and-out. Intrigued, Spleen strolled up on Casey's blind side. The exchange was evidently heated, and Casey's end of it was couched in expletive and racist language that Spleen would never have expected from so circumspect and deferential an employee. He intervened. Casey spun round, wild-eyed and shocked.

'Mr Spleen! God! You see, this man—'

'I'll take yer fokken head off, son,' the down-and-out promised angrily. 'Makin' me out a t'ief. Have you not heard of finders keepers?'

'Do you think you might wait for me in the foyer of the office, Casey?' Spleen asked quietly. He raised his hand as Casey attempted to explain further. 'I shall be no more than a minute.'

As Casey slouched away towards Splendid Reach, Spleen took out his wallet and turned to the vagrant. 'If you have found some item belonging to my associate, I shall be pleased to pay you a finder's fee.'

A few moments later, Spleen walked into the entrance hall of his company's headquarters to discover Casey Rushmore slouched, damp and unhappy, on the wall of the ornamental fountain that formed the centrepiece of the atrium. Spleen sat down beside him and handed him the card. Casey took it, and muttered a thank-you without looking up.

'You're welcome,' Spleen acknowledged pleasantly. 'Now would you like to tell me why I've just paid twenty pounds for the key to a room at the Kensington WestPark?'

'No – not really,' offered the defeated Rushmore.

Spleen turned and looked at his dripping employee.

'I think you know me well enough, Casey,' he said, 'to reconsider that answer.'

In the office apartment on the eighth floor, Casey told his boss of the attempted burglary in Cambridge, the reconnaissance of the suite in the WestPark and the horror to which it led. The tale began sluggishly, with an overture of justifications and pre-emptive defences, but then the revelations tumbled out like garbage from a split bag. The leitmotif was an echoing insistence that all Casey's efforts had been for the good of the company. Each new disclosure was chaperoned by a plea for vindication – *I had no choice, did I? What else could I do?*

Spleen said little throughout. He nodded when Casey looked up and met his eyes; he gave a cursory 'Of course' in reply to each anxious rhetorical question. By the time the story was over, Casey had brightened considerably. He evidently felt that his employer would straighten things out from here.

They took the film down to the darkroom on the first floor. Casey sat on a stool in the corner, leaning back against the wall with his eyes shut, snoozing, as Spleen developed the pictures. Most of the reel consisted of snaps of Todd's sinister equipment. Spleen was carrying out the procedure on autopilot by the time he reached the last exposure of the strip. He enlarged the negative without paying it much attention and dropped it into the chemical bath.

As the unconnected monochrome blobs and planes congealed into recognisable shapes, the flat surface of the photographic paper took on depth and structure in the clear liquid. The red light of the darkroom seemed melodramatically appropriate to the emerging gory image. Spleen recoiled slightly, unprepared for what he saw.

Without looking up from the photo that rocked gently to and fro in the solution, he murmured, 'Casey, would you come here a moment, please?'

Casey opened his eyes and blinked. Then he pushed himself forward off the stool and walked over to stand beside Spleen. He looked down into the tray.

'Jesus!' he exclaimed, slapping a hand to his mouth. 'I don't remember taking *that*.'

Spleen nodded approvingly. 'Tight composition, crystal-clear focus, gripping subject matter. All in all, a prize-winning shot – but for the thumb in the top left corner.'

CHAPTER TWENTY-FIVE

IT WAS WELL BEYOND midnight and Don was lying in bed reading an encyclopaedia. He was teaching himself the succession of British poets laureate. This was, he knew, an intellectual displacement activity, designed to stop him thinking about Ellen, Unity and the looming inevitability of choice. Don shrank from any situation that involved choice because it could only lead to upheaval. He preferred to drift where the flow took him. He had a season ticket for the line of least resistance.

The sound of rain on the window added to the feeling of warmth and solitude. Don pedalled his legs slowly beneath the duvet, enjoying the cool crispness of the fresh-on covers. He hitched up the pillow in its clean case so that it sat more squarely behind his shoulders and reached to the side table for his cup of tea.

'Davenant, Dryden, Shadwell, Tate,' he said aloud, sliding his hand down the page to reveal the list as he recited it. 'Rowe, Eusden ... um ...' He lifted his little finger. '*Cibber!* Stupid name. Cibber, Whitehead, Wharton.' Unity and Ellen.

The choice might not be his, of course. Unity was quite likely to dump him, and Ellen may well tell him to take a hike. But, whatever, the choice was still there, if only in the abstract.

'... Wharton. Who's after Wharton? Er ... Pye?'

He could probably talk Unity back – he'd managed it before. Leave it a couple of weeks, then apologise for being shirty about Dr Todd. Show a little enthusiasm for this head-freezing nonsense. Buy a Rabblestack album.

'Pye, Southey, Wordsworth.' Much easier once you got past the eighteenth century – he'd heard of these guys. 'Tennyson, Austin.'

Actually, during the statutory fortnight's radio silence, he could push things along with Ellen a bit. If it came off, fine. If not, he'd patch it up with Unity.

'Bridges, Masefield, Day Lewis.'

The choice, in other words, would make itself.

'Betjeman and Hughes,' he concluded, grinning. 'A doddle.'

He tore a corner from his cigarette pack and marked the page as a reminder to test himself in a few days' time. Then he walked his fingers back along the top of the book to where a bus ticket was sticking out, and flicked it open there.

Champagne. Closing his eyes he began, 'Bottle One, Magnum Two, Jeroboam . . .'

There was a ring at the front door. A short, tentative ring. Don frowned at the clock – a quarter to one. The doorbell sounded again, longer this time. He shrugged as he got out of bed and dragged a bathrobe over his naked body. Whichever one of them it was turning up at this hour, he was glad he'd changed the bed linen that evening. The bell went once more as he turned the hall light on and padded towards the door.

'Yeah, yeah, wait a sec. Keep your hair on.'

He opened the door to see a bedraggled, dark-eyed man dressed in jeans and a blue T-shirt, clasping a canister to his chest. Rain was running down his face, dripping from his beaky nose, beading on his eyelashes. He looked at Don and gave a weak but personable smile.

'Are you Don-not-Donny Osman-not-Osmond?' he asked. 'I'm Gabe Todd – Unity's friend?'

Don's eyes widened with surprise and then narrowed. 'What's happened to Unity?'

Todd took one hand from the canister to wipe the rain from his face. 'Nothing. Don't worry. I just need to ask you a favour.'

There was a brief hiatus whilst Don considered. Here he was then – the purveyor of Professor Marvo's Patent Life-Giving Elixir. A charlatan preying on the dreams of the fearful. A drawn, sodden figure who looked like he could do with a decent night's sleep. Don was undecided what to do.

At that moment, Gabriel looked upwards into the downpour, gave a facetious grin and said, 'Come on in – the water's fine.'

Despite himself, Don chuckled and stood back from the door. 'You wanna cup of tea?'

Having installed Gabriel in the kitchen and put the kettle on, Don went to the bedroom and pulled on some jeans and a jumper. He got a towel from the bedroom drawer and picked up the bathrobe from his bed.

'Here,' he said as he walked through the door, and tossed Gabriel the towel. The poor bastard was in a sorry state, no two ways. 'If you want to bung those clothes on the radiator, you can use my dressing gown. It's tolerably clean.'

'Thanks,' Gabriel said, 'but I can't hang around.'

He towelled his hair and face. Turning from the kettle, Don noticed that the boffin still clasped the canister in his lap with one hand. Having half dried his hair to a damp frizz, he wiped the canister carefully, patting it with the towel as if it were a baby.

Don put two cups of tea on the table, and nodded towards the flask.

'Is that a bomb, or what?'

The laugh was slightly forced. 'No. A culture. Part of a research project that Unity's taking over from me. It's vacuum-sealed to keep it fresh. Thing is, I was hoping you could store it until she can pick it up.'

'Why can't you? Do you take sugar?'

'No, thanks. See, I suddenly have to go up to Nottingham on the early train – change of itinerary – and I called at Unity's place but she's not home. I mean, I guess I could have left it at the hotel but, well, this is a pretty valuable item here.'

'Right. Yeah, well, I don't see why not. It's not dangerous, is it?'

Again the trying-hard laugh. 'Not really – but it'd be better not to open it.'

'Uhuh. You're shivering. Sure I can't get you a jumper or something? Would you like some toast?'

'No – it's real kind of you but I have to go.' Gabriel slurped his tea and stood up. 'Do you have a freezer? That's the best place to keep this.'

Don shook his head. 'Could probably make room in the fridge.' He turned and opened it, bending down to take out a solitary green-flecked lump of cheddar and a crusty jar of mayonnaise. 'It's completely accustomed to housing science projects.' He lobbed the cheese and mayo into the swing-top and then bent again to pull out the refrigerator's plastic shelves. 'There you go,' he said.

He stood back as Gabriel Todd crouched to place the canister in the fridge. He did it slowly, reverentially, with both hands. Then he straightened up and looked at it – just gazed for five or six seconds, his hands clasped together in front of him. The attitude reminded Don of his dad, one holiday twenty-odd years ago in Northern France, staring wordlessly across the quiet ordinariness of Juno beach, thinking of his own father.

'Well,' Gabriel said, suddenly animated, 'I'll take another slug of tea and I'll hit the road.'

He slurped from the mug, put it back on the table and made for the front door. Don followed him.

'I'll leave a message on Unity's machine,' he told Todd, 'and tell her to drop by.'

Gabriel stopped and turned round, a brilliantly carefree smile on his face. 'No need,' he insisted expansively. 'Absolutely no need. I left a message myself and also put a note through her door. She'll be in touch with you. Don't you go to any trouble.' He turned again and opened the door. The rain was still tipping down. 'Anyway, thanks for your help. Don't open the flask and, like I say, no need to call Unity. I'm real sorry to have got you out of bed at this hour.'

'Sokay,' Don replied. 'Listen, it's filthy out there. Do you want me to call you a cab?'

'Nope. I parked the rental car around the corner. Got it for the whole week. I'm even getting used to driving on the wrong side of the road.' He strode down to the pavement, and looked back. 'Thanks again. Tell Unity I'll be in touch. And, hey, look after my beloved project. So long.'

Gabriel half ran towards the end of the street.

Don closed the door and walked back to the kitchen. He grabbed his tea and pulled up a chair in front of the fridge. He swung the door open and looked at the flask. It was a tapered cylinder in a light metal – maybe aluminium – about the size of a party keg of beer. It contained – what? Microbes. Some kind of vegetable matter. Viruses. There were four flip catches around the lid and, presumably, a thread to screw the lid off. There was no padlock, or any place for a key to fit, so there was nothing to stop him opening it.

'Pandora's icebox,' he muttered.

He pushed the fridge door shut, and padded to the bedroom, turning off the kitchen light on the way. He undressed and got into bed.

As he drifted into dreams of a world threatened by killer yoghurt, he thought, 'Why does a man who's hired a car for a week take the early train to Nottingham?'

More rain and another shop doorway. Gabriel hunkered down and assessed the situation.

Unity's boyfriend was not dumb. He hadn't asked many questions, but he had real intelligent eyes. Gabriel had spent a lifetime encouraging curiosity in bright young people, telling them that the urgings of their inquisitiveness should propel them beyond mundane taboos – but for once he hoped that the social convention against snooping would prevail. If Don did decide to peek, Willie would be fine, as long as the flask wasn't left open too long, but Don might panic. Even so, it was unlikely that he'd go to the authorities without first contacting his girlfriend.

And right there was another problem. If the police were taking an interest in Unity, they might well monitor her calls. Gabriel wondered whether he'd oversold the don't-call-her-she'll-call-you angle. If she was tied up with the cops, it could be a while before she got in touch, which would be fine. But then, the cops might have her followed, in which case . . .

Squatting in the doorway of the Jobcentre on the Camberwell New Road, Gabriel Todd pounded his fist against his forehead.

Can't have been thinking straight, he scolded himself. There's just too much that can go wrong.

He decided he had to retrieve the canister. Then, whatever happened, Willie would be his direct responsibility, would be right there with him. They could go to earth somewhere, figure something out. He'd go back to Don's and—

'You all right, mate?'

Gabriel looked up. Two policemen were standing over him, peering into the gloomy doorway. One of them bent forward, his hands on his knees.

'Had a bit of a drink-up, have we?'

Gabriel pushed himself to his feet. 'No, I'm fine, thanks, officer.' He gave a little self-deprecating chuckle. 'I ate a plate of your British curry this evening and, er, I guess I'm not used to it. Had these terrible stomach cramps.'

The policemen exchanged amused glances.

'Better get a shift on then, mate, before the trots set in. Got far to go?'

Gabriel shook his head. 'Only two or three blocks.' He put a hand to his stomach and swallowed hard. 'Excuse me – I think I'd better be going.' He began to walk briskly away, calling 'Thanks, fellas,' over his shoulder. As he reached the first side street, he heard a burst of laughter from behind him.

He was heading away from Don's apartment. What if he'd had the canister with him? The cops would have been curious, less easily shaken off with some glib invention. That would have been the end. He'd have to stick with his first decision – trust Unity and her boyfriend with Willie's welfare while he disappeared, straightened his head out.

He reached into his back pocket for his billfold and flicked through the notes. Twenty-five pounds – about forty bucks. He'd need more.

At a main junction, he found a bank with a teller machine. He slid his TransEurope card into the slot and punched in the number. Accepted – so they hadn't put a stop on it yet, though he guessed they would. And they could trace his movements through such transactions, so he'd have to take out the maximum amount and move on.

Two minutes later, with five hundred pounds rolled into his hip pocket, he stood on the corner and looked up and down the main drag. The rain was petering out at last. Across the way, an orange light flashed above an open door, next to a sign that read ABC MiniCabs. He had to get off the street, but where would he go? A hotel would be risky – no passport, no luggage, a Yankee accent. Hardly inconspicuous. What was the last place the authorities would look for a fugitive homosexual American academic?

Gabriel glanced both ways along the deserted, glistening road and trotted across to the cab office. Once more, and with an exhausting, final effort, he forced his face into the winning grin that had so often smoothed his path. He strolled up to the booth, and the shirt-sleeved guy behind the desk looked at him through a cloud of cigarette smoke.

'Where to, mate?'

Gabriel leaned forward on the window shelf and twitched his eyebrows up and down.

'Wherever a guy goes for a good time in this town,' he leered happily.

CHAPTER TWENTY-SIX

WHEN IT BECAME OBVIOUS that the police had not found Gabriel in the WestPark suite, Unity left – quickly, before the staff thought to mention that she'd arrived with the American scientist and the country singer in the same long white limo.

She took a taxi home, slouching down in the seat, as if every policeman in London was scouring the city for her. She scurried up the stairs to her apartment, and once inside she double-locked the door. Without even taking off her jacket, she hurried to the bedroom and sat on the bed, pulling the duvet around her. She was shivering.

Willie was dead. Gabriel had vanished into the night. The police had a headless corpse to clear up. And she was the only one who knew what had happened. Although she didn't think she had done anything wrong, Unity could see how things would look to the law. If they found her, there would be questions – *an interrogation* – and she doubted that the interrogators would understand the pact between Willie and Gabriel. For her own part, she was terrified by the prospect of police stations, interview rooms. She whimpered and bit one corner of the duvet. God, they might keep her overnight – *in a police cell.* They'd beat her up. They'd leave no bruises.

She was close to tears now – which was enough to make the unforgiving adult in her snap at the terrified child.

'You will not cry,' she scolded out loud. 'It's pathetic. *Listen* to me.'

There was nothing to worry about. The police didn't know who she was. She'd been introduced to Willie's band only as Unity – no surname

– and that wouldn't be enough to identify her. So, the adult concluded, let's have no more of that pitiful whining.

She sniffed, wiped her nose on the quilt cover. Then, suddenly, the child howled, *Casey! What about Casey?*

Before the sobbing could get out of control, she grabbed her own left wrist with her right hand, like a mother snapping at a toddler. *Listen*. Listen! Whatever Casey was doing there, it can't have been anything he'd want to tell the police about. We can deal with Casey later. Now calm down . . .

Reassured, she stood up and went to get herself a drink of milk, turning off the answering machine as she passed it. It was all going to be all right. Casey wouldn't tell, and there was absolutely no other way that she could be connected to the concert or the WestPark. Eventually Gabriel would sort things out and make contact with her. There would be time to mourn Willie and then get on with the work. All she had to do was wait.

She was pouring a second glass of milk when there was a knock at the front door.

'Gabe!' she exclaimed. She ran along the hall and undid the double-lock, flinging the door open. Outside on the landing was a policeman, with a policewoman standing slightly back at the top of the stairs.

'Unity Siddorn?' the copper asked. 'We understand you went to a concert at the Sunrise this evening.'

Unity gaped, called up her adult, bristled slightly. 'What makes you think that?' she demanded.

The copper grinned, and pointed at her chest.

'You were on the list,' he said.

Unity looked down at herself. Clipped to the lapel of her denim jacket was a plasticised badge: 'Unity Siddorn – Willie Rabblestack/Access All Areas'.

The interview room was smaller than those she had seen on TV, but as featureless and blankly-lit as the cop shows had led her to expect. There was a Formica-topped table, bare but for an ashtray; a chair on either side, and a third to one side, occupied by a woman police officer. A double cassette recorder was set into the wall. Unity sat facing the door, taking deep breaths in an effort to stay calm, but each dragged lungful of air came in a shaky rush of fear.

As a student, she'd been on all the marches – Cruise, poll tax, the miners' strike – chanting the slogans, waving the banners; but she'd always avoided being arrested. When the bricks started flying, she tended to slip away. She didn't want to hurt anybody and she certainly didn't see any political mileage in getting hurt herself. The following day, in King's Bar, rumpled and bruised comrades would relate dark stories of kickings received in the back of police vans, or would chronicle the casual inhumanity of nights in the cells. Unity would be genuinely and openly appalled but, covertly, she also felt that this was a pointless martyrdom, more ritual passage than radical politics. There was no grim bravado to be found in her current situation, though. All she could do was hang on to the truth that she'd done nothing wrong.

The door opened to admit a slightly tubby, balding man of about Unity's age. His tie was loosely knotted and slightly askew, and his shirt was half untucked from his trousers.

'Hello,' he said brightly. 'Unity Siddorn, right? I'm David Jennings.' He glanced towards the policewoman. 'Hello, Mary. All right?' He sat in the vacant chair and hit the Record button on the cassette machine, then peered into the tape window. 'Is that going round? Yes – fine. This is a test. 'Twas brillig, and the slithy toves did gyre and gimble in the wabe.' He rewound both tapes and played them back. When his voice emerged from the speaker, he looked mildly astonished. 'Oh, extraordinary.' He pressed Record again. 'Right, it's November the second at . . . ummm . . .' He looked at Unity. 'You haven't got the time, have you?'

Unity lifted a finger and pointed tentatively at the clock on the wall. Again, bemusement flitted across the policeman's face.

'Of course – sorry. It's a quarter to three in the morning,' he told the cassette player, 'and frankly we should all be at home in bed. This is Sergeant Jennings – actually, it's *Acting Inspector* Jennings – interviewing Miss Unity Siddorn. Or possibly Ms. Do you prefer Ms?'

'Yes,' Unity said primly. In the presence of this laughably dishevelled copper, her terror had subsided somewhat.

'Fair enough.' He leaned back in the chair and it tipped alarmingly. 'Oops!' He sat upright again and drummed a little tattoo on the table with the palms of his hands. 'Right! Off we jolly well go then. So, Unity, you've had quite a night, eh?'

It was very easy to tell David Jennings the story. He asked few questions, merely interjecting the occasional 'Goodness, really?' and 'No, how awful for you!' Recalling her frantic drive towards Charing Cross Hospital, Unity mentioned that she'd run a red light on the roundabout. The policeman gave a sympathetic shake of the head. 'Heavens, I don't blame you. You must have been beside yourself with worry.'

Throughout, certain that she had committed no crime, Unity was completely honest. Her only evasion came at the end, when she carefully omitted to say that she had phoned Gabriel from the lobby of the hotel to warn him that the police were on their way up. When she'd finished, David Jennings put both hands to his mouth in an attitude of prayer, raised his eyebrows and breathed out through pursed lips.

'Well, quite an adventure,' he nodded. He interlaced his fingers and bounced his hands against his chin a few times. 'So, where do you think Dr Todd's got to, then?'

'I have no idea,' Unity said. 'But he must be in a terrible state.' She leaned forward onto the table. 'He hasn't done anything wrong, you know. He and Willie had a pact. They wear these envelopes on chains round their necks . . .'

'Uhuh – yeah. I read the one that was found on Mr Rabblestack. I'm not certain what the legal position is there, but the intention's pretty obvious. "As soon as I croak, chop my head off" is more or less the gist of the thing.'

Unity winced, but pressed her argument. 'So there you are. Willie wanted Gabriel to do what he did. It was a sacred trust. Gabriel needn't be running away.'

'Mmm,' the policeman mused, steepling his index fingers and pinching the end of his nose. 'Which makes me wonder why he *is* running away.'

Unity spread her hands. 'Because he's upset, obviously – grief-stricken. His lover died and he had to cut his head off, for Christ's sake.'

'Or vice versa.'

'What?'

David Jennings put his hands on either side of his face and gently tapped his cheeks. 'See, I have a slight worry here and it's this – I have no way of knowing that, at the moment Dr Todd cut his head off, Mr Rabblestack was actually dead.'

Unity gasped. 'That's a terrible thing to say! You must have a really sick, twisted mind to come up with that! Jesus, how do you sleep at night?'

Jennings rubbed his eyes, sighing.

'It's murder,' he admitted.

CHAPTER TWENTY-SEVEN

SUNDAY SAGS IN THE middle, like a wet towel thrown over a washing line. Slippered old ladies pad to the corner shop, phantom shopping bags dragging their shoulders down. They shuffle to the bread shelf, and ponder the choice of a solitary sliced brown or a pack of six tired, tripey crumpets. Desiccated students with hangover breath and sockless plimsolls wander in, wincing – *Sunday Sport*, *Observer* and some longlife orange juice. Oh, and ten Bensons. Really must quit soon.

The pub doors open reluctantly at noon. Fat lads haul in Saturday's headache, feed it a pint, cheer it up. At the end of the bar, an ageing professor – leather patches, another straight Scotch – billows Sabbath clouds from his trademark pipe and scans the cryptic liquor labels for a clue to nineteen down. Meanwhile, the no-chicken barmaid tops up her lippy, checks the luggage of her eyes, smoothes the flouncy collar of last night's apricot blouse.

Outside, in the exhausted sunshine, the Gardener's Arms Sunday lea-guers slouch heads down on the still-damp benches, Nike bags between their feet, waiting for the minibus, muttering low. What about Chelsea – total rubbish, atserlute crap. Christ, you look rough, mate – owdjoo get on last night? Beggin' for it, she was. You *didn't*!

Loony Lenny, still in his pale blue pyjamas, wanders over from the sheltered housing to ponce a cigarette. There you go, Len – nice out, innit? You *leave* it out then, son – hahaha! He's all right, old Len – 'armless.

The black ladies in prints of roses and marigolds, in petal hats and lilywhite shoes, blossom on the steps of the redbrick Resurrection chapel, as their silent, serious little boys – all grown up in their tiny suits – watch Daddy park the car. It'll be a long time till dinner.

The spuds are going on all over the Estate. Do plentya them, Sheryl – the joint's gotta stretch to seven. And you be nice to yer Nan – she can't help it – she's old. Wanna little sherry, Mum? Duntya? Woodja? Danny, look in the sideboard see if we got any gin f'yer Nan.

Along the Common, the windows of the Georgian terrace delight in sporting their colour-all-year-round window boxes that set off the shiny-black solid front doors, the we-live-here knockers, the looping, literate ceramic house numbers. Juanita feeds the children in the basement kitchen – she does a superb paella out of *prac*tically nothing – while the dear friends down from Edinburgh vie for the arts section, and smile and nod to 'Autumn', humming the counterpoint. There's something about Vivaldi – *isn't* there? – that's just so *Sunday lunch.*

Don woke around midday. He blinked and groaned as the light of noon speared through the tear in the Ikea blind, jabbing maliciously at the bedhead. He reached for a cigarette and his talisman Zippo, coiling his nose at the expected petrol stench, firing up the first little death of the day.

He retched at the initial drag and held it, slinging one arm behind his head and gazing at the ceiling. The damp patch was spreading. When it reached the doorframe he'd have something done about it.

It took him several seconds to figure why he was thinking about the fridge. *Gabriel Todd.* He groaned a cloud of smoke and decided against dealing with that intrigue until after breakfast. He sucked in another chestful of mortality and switched his attention to a more mundane and immediate quandary. He peeked under the duvet. Could he be bothered?

At twenty-five past twelve he left the house in yesterday's T-shirt and last week's jeans. His hair, he had noticed in the hall mirror, was flattened spikily to one side, fresh from the pillow – but you could go out like that when you were a grown-up. You could wear scuffed Doc Marten shoes with the laces undone. You could eat sugar-soaked cereals for breakfast, knowing they were crap. It's what adult Sundays were for.

'Morning, Farooq,' Don croaked as he went into the corner shop. 'Got any Coco-Pops?'

The radio was on in Mr Raja's shop, the music sufficiently audible to tease the attention but not loud enough to enjoy. As Don sloped over to the chill cabinet for bacon, the muffled high range of the melody tugged at the hem of his memory. Mid-seventies; one-hit wonder; what the hell was it? He could have asked Mr Raja to turn it up but that, to Don's mind, would have been cheating. You had to solve life's little posers as they were presented – that was the deal. The name of the band was on the tip of his tongue as he rummaged for rindless streaky. He might have heard the DJ back-announce it, but as the song came to its end, one of the darts players from the Gardener's came in.

'Wotcher, Ali,' he boomed. 'Twenty Roffman's anner *Newsa the Screws.*'

Don took his bacon, chocolate cereal and sliced white to the counter, picking a hefty Sunday off the pile and, as if it were an afterthought, adding a tabloid. The radio chimed its hook for the half-hour news bulletin.

'And a pack of Marlboro Lights,' Don said, as Mr Raja rang up the purchases.

'*Mumbly-mumbly,*' intoned the newscaster, '*mumbly West London death horror.*'

'Some matches for you?' asked Mr Raja.

'*Mumbly decapitated burble pop-star,*' the radio insisted.

'Er . . . sorry? No, thanks,' Don replied distractedly.

'Six pounds eighty-seven,' Mr Raja told him.

'*Sumblety Rabblestack burble-bub constant companion.*'

'Could you turn the radio up a sec?' Don asked.

Mr Raja twisted the knob. 'Six eighty-seven,' he repeated.

'. . . police wish to contact Dr Gabriel Todd who is believed still to be in the London area.'

'Bloody hell!' Don exclaimed.

'I know,' Mr Raja nodded. 'The price of bacon, eh? I never touch the stuff myself.'

Unity was not in and she hadn't turned her answering machine on. Don sat in the kitchen listening to the radio, waiting for the one o'clock news as he scoured the papers for details. There was nothing to be found, so whatever had happened must have been too late for the morning editions. Unity had been at the concert – he was sure she'd mentioned she was going – and Dr Todd must have been there too, which threw doubt on the excuse for last night's visitation.

Every so often, Don glanced at the fridge, but he hadn't summoned the nerve to open it. He'd picked up the word 'decapitated' and an uncomfortable suspicion was forming in his mind.

When the one o'clock news came on the radio, he stood and turned it up.

Willie Rabblestack, the celebrated country singer, had collapsed at the end of his performance. He had been driven away, unconscious, by his constant companion, the controversial scientist Dr Gabriel Todd. Later, police discovered Mr Rabblestack's headless body in his suite at an exclusive West London hotel. Inspector David Jennings, the officer in charge of the investigation, appealed this morning for—

Don turned the radio off and sat down at the table again, putting his face in his hands.

'Oh, God,' he groaned aloud. 'There's a head in the fridge.'

He tried to picture it. Then he tried not to picture it. He lit a cigarette, having rather lost interest in his bacon sandwich.

This was bloody Unity's fault, the cow, associating with that bedenimed

Frankenstein, signing on for some fantasy beam-me-up future. And now he was sitting here in his perfectly ordinary kitchen, trying to avoid the sight of his perfectly run-of-the-mill fridge which, *unfuckingdoubtedly*, was cooling the sliced loaf of the world's most celebrated C&W poof.

He picked up the phone and hit the recall button. He let it ring for the count of fifty, but Unity was still not there.

'Jesus!' he snapped.

Tapping the receiver against his forehead, he considered his options, then he dialled 99 . . .

Hi, Don Osman here. I believe the missing portion of Willie Rabblestack is currently occupying my Zanussi. A mad scientist dropped it off last night . . .

He put the receiver down.

'I'll kill her,' he murmured. 'I'll bloody swing for her.'

Suddenly the phone rang. He grabbed it, and barked, 'Unity? Unity, you cow!'

'No, sorry,' said Ellen's voice calmly. 'It's the other one.'

'Shit! No – I mean . . . Bad time. I wanted it to be . . . Sorry.'

'I don't want to know. I'm going up to Camden. Would you like to come?'

Don sighed. His talent for saying the wrong thing had reached an effortless apex with Ellen. 'I can't. I'm babysitting. Did you hear about Willie Rabblestack?'

'No!' Ellen replied, immediately curious. 'I went to his gig last night and he was taken ill. What happened? Is he dead?'

Don glanced at the fridge.

'I bloody well hope so.'

Gabriel woke up, sweating but rested, at half past one. For a moment, he couldn't imagine where he was. Then the inescapable sadness of the previous day crashed down on him like bad weather, and he let out a deep, tremulous sob.

He rolled onto his back and surveyed the room. Faded, flowered drapes. Clip-framed Athena black-and-whites. A dressing table of oils, perfumes, unguents. He shifted onto his side, and looked across the pink sheet, the frilled pillows. What was her name? Began with K. *Kerry.*

Easiest seventy-five pounds she'd ever earned, apparently. He'd picked her up in some tacky joint in Soho. She'd been the third he'd approached – he needed someone who worked from home because he had to be able to stay the night. They'd taken a cab. When they reached her place, they'd gone directly to the bedroom. He'd been effusively apologetic, acted the sheepish straight. This had never happened to him before – really. Maybe he was just too tired, or drunk, or guilty. Would it be okay if he grabbed some sleep? Then maybe in the morning he'd be able to . . .

She was so reasonable it bordered on the uninterested. *Whatever you say, darlin'. It's your money.*

Gabriel hugged the pillow – it smelt of woman, of childhood, of Christmas – and closed his eyes. He could feel his eyelashes wet on his cheek. Willie used to kiss his eyelashes in the morning, to wake him up. It tickled and irritated. He'd shift his head and groan. *Five more minutes, Willie. Please, let me be for five more minutes.* What was five more minutes when you had forever?

The door opened and Kerry came in, carrying a tray.

'Mornin', lover boy – breakfast. Eggs, bacon, mushrooms, fried slice. Potter tea. That'll put lead in yer pencil.'

Gabriel sat up and looked at her as she swept a pile of *Cosmopolitans* from the bedside table and put the tray down. She was thirty-some, skinny beneath the terry bathrobe, and short dark hair corkscrewed around her tan, pointy face. She grinned at him, like a nurse, and knelt on the bed. The bathrobe rode up, and Gabriel caught a glimpse of brown curls between her legs. He was taken aback by a jolt of disapproving primness that popped within his chest.

'You slept like the dead, didn't you?' Kerry remarked, leaning over to pour the tea. 'Mumbled a bit, but you were out like a light.'

Gabriel fought to get back in character. 'Yeah, well – listen, I'm really sorry. It's not that you aren't—'

'Don't worry about it, lover. You're not the first and you won't be the last. You'd be surprised how many blokes can't get it up when it atchally comes to it. Bloody good thing for me I don't charge by the inch, that's all.'

Gabriel wolfed breakfast as Kerry nibbled toast, painting her toenails bright red and glancing at him from time to time. As he put the tray to one side, and lay back with his mug of tea held on his chest, she said, 'You're queer, aren't yer?'

Gabriel gulped the tea he had in his mouth and thought about protesting, but denial was not in his nature. 'Yup,' he admitted, shrugging. 'That obvious, huh?'

'You haven't made enough excuses. And apart from that, I'm sitting here with me knees up and you didn't even pretend not to look. Y'not interested.'

Gabriel grinned. 'Honey, I'm a doctor.'

'A *queer* doctor,' Kerry nodded. 'And not bashful about it, either. So why'd yer pony up seventy-five quid to go with me?'

'I just needed a good night's sleep.'

She looked at him quizzically for a moment, and then got to her feet. 'You're right,' she said, picking up the tray. 'It's none of my soddin' business. It dun't matter to me.'

And she left the room.

Gabriel lay back and stared at the ceiling. He felt he'd offended the woman in some way – exploited her, maybe. Though he had little compunction about offending entire communities, or exploiting faceless corporations, he couldn't justify slighting individuals. He owed Kerry an explanation – though not necessarily the truth.

He shrugged on a robe that was hanging on the back of the door and padded along the unfamiliar corridor to the kitchen. Kerry was sitting at the breakfast bar, smoking a cigarette and reading the newspaper. He sat on a stool beside her.

'Uh . . . okay. I'm gay, and I had a big bust-up with my partner. I didn't want to go home, but I didn't want to sleep with some anonymous guy I just picked up. I don't know what I'm going to do, but I'm really sorry that I . . . well . . . *lied* to you, I guess.' He paused, and his shoulders slumped. 'I can tell you this though – I could really use a hug right now.'

Kerry turned to him, and thumbed her hair out of her eyes.

'I toldja,' she said pleasantly. 'It's none of my business. It dun't matter.'

Gabriel looked at her, and saw that this was a mundane truth. She was utterly indifferent. That had simply not occurred to him as a possibility.

The front door bell rang and Don answered it. As expected, it was Ellen.

In the kitchen, she lifted the canister out of the fridge and put it on the table. She leant over it, her hands flat on either side, gazing down. Don was thrilled to realise that he could see down the front of her T-shirt.

What am I like? he wondered disgustedly, turning away.

Ellen sat at the table and looked thoughtfully at the canister, her head tipped to one side. Don stayed in the doorway, lounging against the jamb in an attempt to appear calm. Almost idly, she flicked one of the flip catches on the lid. Don tensed, clenched his fists.

The second catch clicked open under Ellen's slim fingers, and Don shrank back, edging away into the hall. In the breathless silence, Ellen released the third catch and, after several seconds' pause, the fourth – by which time Don had left the room entirely, as if by capillary action. Like a small child waiting for the Daleks to make their entrance, he peeked round the doorframe to see Ellen flexing her fingers, safe-cracker style, in preparation for unscrewing the lid. She looked up, giving Don a caricature grimace of tense expectation, which broke into a little grin of excitement. Don smiled weakly back and waggled his fingers at her. He didn't trust himself to speak.

Ellen put one hand on the lid of the canister. 'For the next part of the trick,' she announced mischievously, 'I require a volunteer from the audience. How about you, sir?'

'No chance,' Don replied quaveringly, shaking his head. 'None.'

She shrugged and began to twist the lid. Don withdrew into the hall, holding his breath. He heard the soft *chink* as the top of the canister came free, and then the sound of it being put on the table. There was a pause, and then the scrape of chair legs on the floor as Ellen leaned forward.

'Oh, my God,' she breathed. 'The poor man.'

Out in the corridor, Don winced and closed his eyes. 'It's really him, then, is it?' he called, gulping.

'You were expecting maybe someone else? Come and take a look.'

'No – it's okay,' Don replied. 'I believe you.'

Ellen appeared in the doorway, holding out a hand towards him. 'Come and see. There's nothing to be frightened of.'

Don had always considered himself man enough to admit to being a complete coward, but Ellen's encouraging smile, her upturned palm, prevented him from backing away towards the front room. He took the few steps into the kitchen, and saw the canister on the table, vapour spilling in billows down its sides. He approached it with his chin lifted, peering down his nose, trying to stay as far away from it as possible. He leaned forward just enough to see inside, his eyes half shut – but there was too much vapour to make out the contents. To his relief, all he could see was a cloud of steam.

He glanced sideways at Ellen, and said, 'Yeah, well. Astonishing.' He was about to turn away when Ellen leaned forward and blew hard into the container.

For a brief moment the cloud parted, and there, in the mint-clear nitrogen, was Willie Rabblestack's head. It was tipped back a little, the eyes closed and the mouth slightly open, as if the singer had been caught in the act of hitting a soulful blue note in a melancholy spiritual. It looked like a wax model, a fake. Don moved a little closer, and blew away the vapour himself. He knew that he was looking at a dead person, but his mind couldn't cope with the incongruity of a human head in a keg, and so interpreted it as an effect, a camera trick. Ellen was right; it was nothing to be afraid of.

'Well, what do you think?' she asked. 'Shall we drink it right away, or let it breathe for a while?'

'Oh, for God's sake,' Don groaned. 'Close it up, eh?'

Ellen resealed the canister and put it back in the fridge, as Don tried Unity's number again. Still there was no reply. With a muttered curse, he took some shot glasses from the cupboard, and the two of them went into the front room where Don opened a bottle of vodka.

'A toast,' chuckled Ellen, lifting her glass. 'To present friends.'

'You're really enjoying this, aren't you?' Don chided irritably. 'This is a serious problem, you know. What am I going to do? The mad scientist's on the loose. Unity's incommunicado . . .'

Ellen downed the vodka in one. 'All right, all right,' she grinned. 'Don't get all cut up about it.'

CHAPTER TWENTY-EIGHT

ROBERT SPLEEN HAD A picture of his own torso – a smudgy, impressionist black-and-white taken by a top snapper in the field of internal portraiture. Against a washy grey background, his alimentary canal showed as a bright coiling path. An expert critic of the form had told Spleen that the picture was of no particular interest – *nothing special there, old man* – but to its subject, the image was a source of constant, reassuring fascination.

The value of this piece, like that of most art in which Spleen took an interest, was both incalculable and ephemeral. This image was soon to be replaced by another snap – one that, please God, would be identical.

Spleen laid the X-ray down on the desk, beside Casey's photo of Gabriel Todd cradling Willie's head in his arms. If Spleen had doubted the American's faith in cryonics, that photograph was proof of total sincerity. Spleen was touched by the horrible, transfixing nobility of the image – the tender, supportive curl of the fingers, the incredulous agony in the face and the unarguable, dark, splashy blood. It resembled some mediaeval painting of an obscure saint's passion.

Spleen closed his eyes and concentrated on his guts, trying to feel them, flex them, check them out. He envisaged the white-pink, wet coils of his bowels, travelled along them in his mind's eye, like a potholer, looking for what he hoped he wouldn't find. He stood beside his liver, regarding it as if it were a used car, scanning for giveaway leaks and breakthrough rust. He gave his kidneys the once over.

The cancer would be back, he knew it.

'Let me show you some statistics,' Robert, the quack had said reassuringly. He'd reeled off the starting prices, quoted the form book. 'You see? Doesn't that make you feel better?'

'You bet your life,' Spleen had suggested pointedly.

The Spleen family motto was 'Render Unto Caesar'. His grandmother had paraphrased it as 'The House Takes Five Points'.

'And, of course, Robbie, it's our house,' she said.

Whatever odds the actuarial tables offered, Spleen realised that for the first time in his life, he was just a punter playing the house. And, in the long run, the Big C Casino would scoop his stake. He reached forward and picked up the photo of Gabriel Todd. If you're losing on the wheel, you switch to *vingt-et-un*. It was time to put all his money on the calculated bet.

Dr Todd was at large and in trouble. He would need influential help to extricate himself, and Spleen could supply it. In exchange for this service, Spleen would ask only that the scientist come to work for Splendid and concentrate his energies on the problems of reanimation. If the American shunned such an offer, Spleen would point out that Casey's fortuitous snap carried exactly the kind of emotive clout that might swing a court case.

Spleen tapped the photograph on the edge of his desk. He knew his hand was weaker than he'd like. It would help if he could get to Gabriel before the police did. Once the man had been caught up in the official process of law, it would be difficult for Spleen, despite his influence, to sway events. Moreover, if he had Gabriel, he would also have Rabblestack's head – and he was certain that Gabriel would do almost anything to keep *that* from the authorities.

Spleen shouldered the phone and flicked through the antiquated card index on the table, then punched out a number.

'Ray Knowles, please. Ray? Robert Spleen. Yes, ages. Ray, I need some gossip. No – personal. The sort of thing you might very easily pick up and happen to mention over drinks with an old friend.'

There was a brief pause.

'*Everyone's* busy, Ray,' Spleen pointed out, sympathetically. 'Nobody – as I'm sure you remember from our Parisian adventures – is ever busier than I am.'

Jennings had been a copper for ten years, having joined the job as part of a drive to recruit graduates. That alone would have been enough to put the mockers on any chance of currying favour with the middle-ranked officers who controlled his early career, but other aspects of his personality made him a complete pariah.

He read the *Guardian*. He rarely swore and never made racist jokes. Every so often, after a few drinks, he would espouse his philosophy that the role of a copper was to be analytical but never judgemental. Judge not, he would say, unless you're a judge. Few colleagues understood why this always made him laugh – but then few colleagues were as familiar with the Scriptures as David Jennings.

After seven years of mild persecution and filthy assignments, Jennings came under the wing of an Inspector who recognised his potential. He got made up to Sergeant and went plainclothes. Now a nasty and widespread strain of Hong Kong flu had given him the chance to take charge of the Rabblestack case.

It was Sunday afternoon, and he was sitting with his feet on the desk, staring out of the window and absently chewing a cheap biro. He was working very hard – though he had in the past worked for superiors who'd found it impossible to believe that crimes could be solved by chewing biros and staring out of the window.

The self-possessed Ms Siddorn had been released at eight. She was obviously honest and sincere, and had therefore put absolutely no spin on the case at all. A post-mortem was being carried out on what was left of Mr Rabblestack. Jennings gave a silent chuckle. They were cutting up a headless corpse in order to establish the cause of death.

'Were there any suspicious circumstances?' one of the journalists had asked. 'Are you treating it as murder?'

It was a good question. If the singer had died of decapitation, then murder was indisputably what it should be treated as. If, on the other hand, Mr Rabblestack had given up the ghost before he was sawn up, Jennings was at a loss as to how Dr Todd might be charged. A corpse is considered the property of the next of kin. Given the relationship between the two men, Mr Rabblestack's next of kin appeared to be Dr Todd himself – and there's no law against carving up your own property. Even if it turned out that Mr Rabblestack had closer kin to claim the remains, the best Jennings could come up with against Dr Todd was a rap for criminal damage. The newspapers, lapping up the mixture of gore, homosexuality, celebrity and weird science, would have a field day with any copper who proposed a charge equivalent to that for flinging a brick through a pub window.

The media interest had made the brass jumpy. Chief Inspector Knowles had been down in the incident room this morning, insisting that he be kept abreast of any development, so that he could *monitor image hygiene.* Despite Jennings' assurances that he was on top of it, the CI had mused aloud about handing the case over to *someone with a broader feel for high-profile operations.* Progress needed to be seen to be made, apparently, and Jennings should be aware that there was a *time-window around his personal involvement.*

Get Todd, in other words.

The same central switchboard that had connected Robert Spleen to Ray Knowles put Kerry Lynham through to Acting Inspector David Jennings. When the phone rang, Jennings snapped to it. He leaned forward to pick up the receiver, and knocked over a cup of cold coffee.

'Rats! Hello, Acting Inspector David Jennings. Bother!' He picked up a plastic folder and held it over the litter bin as it dripped.

'Is that the policeman looking for Gabriel Todd?' came a whispered female voice.

'Yes, madam. How can I help?' Jennings tossed the file onto the floor and picked up a chewed biro.

'He's here,' came the hurried whisper. 'He's in the shower.'

Jennings pulled a pad towards him, slooshing a puddle of coffee into his lap as he did so. 'Jolly good,' he said, wincing as he glanced down at his cream cords. 'Just give me the address.'

'Flat B, 46 Elmshurst Mansions, W6.'

He began to scribble but the biro wouldn't write. 'Blast. Wait a minute.' He grabbed a pencil. 'Okay. Flat B, and then what?'

'46 Elmshurst Mansions, W6. My name's Kerry Lynham. Is it all right if I go out?'

'Oh, for Pete's sake,' Jennings groaned as the lead of his pencil snapped. '46 Elmshurst . . .'

'He's turned the shower off. Come quickly.'

The caller hung up and Jennings leapt to his feet and rushed over to a colleague's empty desk.

'Flat-B-46-Elmshurst-Mansions-West-Six, Flat-B-46-Elmshurst-Mansions-West-Six,' he chanted as he scrabbled for a pen. He jotted the address down, and then breathed out heavily. 'Thank you, Lord,' he muttered. Then he stuck his head into the corridor and yelled, 'Brian, kindly get the heavy mob in two cars and meet me out the front.'

Retreating into the office, he picked up the phone. 'Detective Chief Inspector Knowles, please,' he said, dabbing resignedly at his coffee-damp crotch with a blank search warrant. 'Hello, sir. We've got something. An address in Shepherd's Bush where Dr Todd might have gone to ground. We're on our way. Uh, yes, I have it here if you really think you need it.' He read from the scrap of paper on his desk. 'It's Flat B . . . Sorry? Yes, I'll hang on, sir.'

He grinned. It was good to know that the universal law which discourages biros from working simultaneously with telephones applied in the offices of jumped-up Sergeants and Chief Inspectors alike.

CHAPTER TWENTY-NINE

SPLEEN PICKED UP THE phone. The caller didn't announce himself – merely gave a brief message. Spleen memorised the address, and left his office.

Robert Spleen knew West London as well as any cab driver. He'd spent many summers wandering the streets of Squatville with Michael Moorcock. The writer had been looking for creative inspiration but, as he laconically pointed out, Spleen owned most of the mews already.

Elmshurst Mansions was a flaky Victorian block off the Goldhawk Road, too far west to have been baptised and reborn in the floodtide of money that washed up from Holland Park in the eighties. Spleen double-parked the Merc and strode up the path. There was no entryphone. He pushed the door open and strode into the dim hall. Flat B was on his left, and he rang the bell. It was answered in seconds by a slight, dark woman in jeans. She made a weak protest as Spleen swept past her into the flat.

As he walked into the sitting room, Gabriel Todd leapt to his feet from the sofa and adopted a crouched linebacker's stance, one hand resting on the coffee table. Spleen held up both hands and spoke quickly.

'Dr Todd, I am—'

'I know who you are,' Gabriel nodded, still wary.

'I'm flattered. In a very few minutes, the police will be here. I would suggest—'

Gabriel straightened up. 'Good enough for me,' he said. 'Let's go.' He walked past Spleen and made for the front door.

'What about the—' Spleen began.

'He's not here,' Gabriel told him. As he passed Kerry in the hall, he said, 'You called the police? What for? Breach of promise?'

Ten minutes later, a disgruntled David Jennings stomped down the path from Elmshurst Mansions and got into the passenger seat of the unmarked car. He'd just had a very disappointing conversation.

Gone? *Yeah, gone. Some bloke came and collected him.* What sort of bloke? *A posh bloke – I'm sure I know 'im from somewhere.* What, from around here? *No, not a local. And not a punter either. From the telly or something.* Well, if you remember who he is, please call me, Miss Lynham.

Disappointing and intriguing, Jennings thought, tapping his fingers on the dashboard.

Detective Constable Mullery ambled down the path and leaned into the open window of the car.

'Back to the shop, then?' he asked.

Jennings sighed. 'I suppose so.'

'Okay.' Mullery nodded over his shoulder towards the mansion block. 'Here, Sarge, do you want us to bring the slag in?'

Jennings turned in his seat, and fixed his subordinate with a firm and unblinking stare.

'I'm an Inspector,' he said quietly. 'And she is a human being.'

'Yessir,' Mullery agreed immediately, and turned to walk back up the path to collect his colleague. 'Yessir, you prat,' he muttered.

As he drove, Spleen watched Gabriel Todd out of the corner of his eye. The American was expressionless – staring, unfocused, at the dash. Spleen recognised the mien. Todd was processing information, figuring out the new situation.

As they pulled onto Shepherd's Bush roundabout, Todd turned to Spleen and said, brightly, 'Limited edition Mercedes, right? Custom interior. A gas-guzzler. Seventy-five, maybe seventy-six.'

'Spot on, Doctor,' Spleen replied, with a smile.

'Call me Gabe,' Todd replied. 'Doctor sounds like I'm about to inspect your prostate.'

Spleen winced, and looked sidelong at his passenger. There was nothing there but chumminess.

'Ever driven a sixties Pontiac?' Gabriel continued. 'They growl at you. Long bench seat in front. Why don't European cars ever have bench seats? Makes it real difficult to snuggle on up 'long that big, empty blacktop.'

Spleen heard an accent there – a tune in the phrasing that echoed the Deep South. It wasn't Todd's natural accent. It was a melody picked up along the way.

'The British don't snuggle, as a rule,' he offered.

'Don't know what you're missing,' Todd grinned.

'We're missing big, empty blacktops,' Spleen suggested.

They drove to Holland Park, and swung into a square off the avenue. They got out of the car and Spleen walked down a flight of steps to the front door of a garden flat. He unlocked the door and beckoned Todd to enter.

'Nice place,' Gabriel nodded, standing in the middle of the open-plan front room.

'I usually rent it out, but it's unoccupied at the moment,' Spleen explained, opening the fridge. 'It's yours for the duration.'

'Nice bars,' Todd added, nodding towards the security grille across the window. 'Do you hold all your hostages here?'

'You can come and go as you please, Dr Todd,' Spleen shrugged, reaching a corkscrew from the cupboard. 'Why would I imprison you?'

Todd crossed his arms and breathed out through his nose. 'Well, I figure it like this. You knew where I was holed up and that the police were coming for me, so I reckon that you must have a friend amongst London's finest.

If you were prepared to use that pull, you must have wanted to get to me pretty bad. That would imply that you have a use for me – so I can't see you letting me go too easily.' He dropped into an armchair, and crossed his legs at the ankle. 'Your eager puppy dog, young Rushmore, has been on my case for weeks, so it's better than evens that you want me to come work for you. Now I'm suddenly in deep trouble and you, with all your influence, must see an opportunity to put me in your debt. Cheers.'

'Cheers,' Spleen replied quietly, raising his glass. He was somewhat taken aback by Todd's forthrightness. He had been expecting an afternoon of cagey negotiation, implicit pressure. He'd planned to spend an hour or two getting to know his guest before he even broached the possibility of a trade-off.

'Not bad wine. Spanish?' Todd continued breezily. He took another slug of the Rioja. 'You're right, more or less. I won't run out on you, because I can see the validity of your logic. But whether I need your help enough to sign my soul over to the corporation . . . well, I don't see how you can tie me into that. You'll just have to rely on my instinct for fair play. Pretty British of me, huh?'

'I must offer you my condolences,' Spleen ventured, taking a seat himself.

For the first time, Todd's easy grin slipped, replaced by a look of taut grief. 'Yeah, there's that too,' he admitted. The grin resurfaced. 'A man in my advanced state of emotional fuck-up – why, he might sign anything.'

'Casey took a picture of you, in the hotel room. I'm quite sincere when I say that I was, er, moved by the depth of feeling that you must have had for your partner. *Still* have, I mean.'

Todd leaned forward. 'Let me see it,' he said calmly.

Spleen had intended to do just that – to use Casey's snap as the hole card that would clinch the pot. But now he found himself reluctant to be so callous. Somehow, Todd had shifted the game and taken control with a low hand. To pull out the ace now would leave him exposed, like a five-bit player overplaying a natural in a high-rolling school.

'It's not . . .' he began. 'It's a disturbing image. I don't feel it's necessary to subject you to—'

'Let me see it,' Todd repeated, in the same measured way.

Spleen looked at the American. His eyes were a riot of intelligence, but there was an imperturbable stillness there. Again, Spleen found a comparison in art. Gabriel Todd resembled a Vermeer – the unsplashy acceptance, the life expressed in a tilt of the head, the concentrated, smooth-brushed gaze. Something of the light in him made him ungainsayable.

Spleen reached into his inside pocket and retrieved an envelope. He slid out the picture, and glanced down at it. Then he leaned across, and offered it to Gabriel Todd.

Todd turned the sheet round and looked at it. He caught his breath and bit his bottom lip. Spleen waited for the outburst – the sudden tears. Or the desperate, ironic throwaway.

Gabriel Todd stared at the picture and shook his head.

'Oh, my,' he said, low and chesty. 'Oh, Willie. Oh, my.'

CHAPTER THIRTY

THE ABSURDLY PLEASANT POLICEMAN had concluded Unity's interrogation at about eight, and then taken her to breakfast at a greasy spoon around the corner from the station, suggesting that she must be ravenous.

As she sat there, eating a cheese toastie, he'd talked about his wife and his baby boy, Jacob. A solid, no-nonsense name, according to David Jennings. They'd chosen it – he and his wife Sue – for two reasons. Firstly, because it had the Old Testament connotation that they wanted, without being born-again precious. And secondly because, if you're called David and Sue, you really want to give your child a name that's not as common as your own – so that he won't be one of five Jacobs at the playgroup. Jennings chuckled at this reasoning.

'Turns out we've given him the second most popular name of the year. You call "Jake" on Clapham Common, and the next thing you know you're up to your knees in jammy-faced toddlers.'

Unity smiled tiredly. As Jennings rambled on, she pictured his sandy-haired little boy, his bespectacled and quietly indulgent wife, their refurbished South London terrace. That sounded like a life.

She took a cab home, showered and went to bed, where she slept like a rock.

Something woke her mid-afternoon. Something had stopped. The phone – it had stopped ringing. She lay quite still, confused. The clock said a quarter to four. Why was she awake so early? No – so *late*. It was the afternoon. It was Sunday . . .

On Sundays, Unity usually worked at home, firing up her little laptop before she even had breakfast, pleased to hear its businesslike three-note start-up sound as she Clovered a Ryvita. During the summer, she'd open the doors to the balcony and glance from time to time at the pelargoniums bobbing in the hanging baskets as she tapped away.

When she had first come to London, this routine had been a rare one, forced on her by project deadlines and imminent presentations. She had resented having to forego long boozy lunches with friends, or weekend trips to the country. But as the industrious Sundays became more regular, Unity began to pre-empt any suggested arrangement – 'Oh, I'll probably have to work. I know, it's shit, isn't it? Can you make next month?' – and soon the phone fell silent, the friends drifted into marriage, the thought of a whole wasted day seemed unjustifiable. Like some fascinating but invasive plant, work crept beyond the border beds in which it had been planted, and established itself in the cracks of the patio, entwined itself around the legs of the sun lounger, choked any frivolous, carefree blooms it encountered. Unity lived in a world devoid of occupational biodiversity.

She swung her legs out of the bed, sat up and reached for her glasses. She noticed a huge sunset bruise on her thigh. That must have been Casey, knocking her over in the hotel foyer. Creep.

In the kitchen, she lit the gas under the kettle and leaned against the sink as she waited for it to boil. On the draining board was a saucepan, filled with water to soak off the remains of caramelised carrot. She'd put it there before going out to meet Willie for dinner on . . . what? Friday. Less than forty-eight hours ago.

Forty-eight hours . . .

Friday night, you might be eating Mexican food, drinking margaritas, kissing in taxis. Your ears are full of music and your eyes full of colours. Your mouth is talking, laughing. It's a moist, warm thing, with its intricate and delicate lips, its agile, athletic tongue. The mouth, the lungs and heart are in constant motion; the whole body – articulate limbs and humming skin – sweetly tuned; a complex orchestration of balance and tension, rhythm and throb.

Suddenly, Sunday lunchtime, you're a sack of wet salt.

The kettle was boiling furiously, its lid chinking up and down and dribbling. Unity reached a mug from the shelf and dropped a tea bag into it as she lifted the kettle. It was surprisingly light – she'd forgotten to top it up – but it felt as though there was a cupful in there. With one hand round the tea mug, she tipped the kettle steeply. The lid fell off and boiling water poured over her right hand.

'Jesus!' she screamed, and frantically turned on the cold tap, running water over the scald.

As she stood there whimpering, turning her hand in the flow, the phone rang again. Cursing, Unity filled a plastic jug with cold water and plunged her hand into it. Then, carrying the jug in her other hand, she went out to the hall. Keeping the injured hand submerged, she lowered the jug onto the table beside the phone, and picked up the receiver.

'There you are, you cow!' came Don's voice. 'Where the fuck have you been?'

'Did you call earlier?'

'Ha! Once or twice, yeah.'

Unity experimentally lifted her hand from the water. It was white and puffy. Wincing, she dunked it again. 'What do you want?'

'I got a visit from your mad professor last night. He left me a present for you. I'll be round in an hour.'

'What? Don, what are you on about?'

'It's the perfect gift for the frosty nymphomaniac. A stiff Willie in a vacuum flask.'

All that afternoon, Don had slouched on the sofa watching the football, the hamburger telephone at his elbow. Every ten minutes or so he would hit Redial, and listen to Unity's phone ring. Ellen was reading the spines of the books along his shelves.

'You really do like games, don't you?' she remarked.

'Huh?'

'You have three copies of Hoyle.'

Don shrugged. 'Inefficiency. I bought the second one because I'd forgotten I had the first, and then I bought the third when I couldn't find the first two.' He indicated the room with a wave of his arm. 'As you've probably guessed, I'm not the most organised person in the world.'

Ellen glanced at the trestle table on which Don's PC stood amongst piles of loose paper and teetering towers of reference books. Coffee cups were lined up along the windowsill, and crumbs spilled from an empty packet of Digestives on the floor beside the chair.

'I like it,' she said. 'It indicates a busy mind.' She picked up a deck of cards from the bookshelf.

'Or a lazy body,' Don suggested. He zapped the TV off. 'Bit different to your front room, though, isn't it?' he ventured, remembering the weird, extraordinary flat in Eldritch Place. 'Now, that's really something . . .'

'Something Godawful,' Ellen tutted. She riffled the cards. 'It's my dad's idea of style. I love him to death, of course, but he has the design sense of a Dada magpie.'

'Ah,' Don nodded, nonplussed and a little let down. 'The bald flautist . . .'

'On the other hand, the old loony did teach me to do this . . .' Ellen squeezed the deck of cards between her palms, and they fountained into the air. As they fluttered to the ground, she showed Don the cards she was still holding – a fanned hand of four aces. 'You're not the only one who likes games,' she grinned. 'Mine's poker.'

Don blinked. The woman just got more and more intriguing.

As Ellen collected the deck from the floor, Don reached for the phone again. This time, there was an answer. After speaking to Unity, he snapped the hamburger shut and got to his feet. 'Right, she's in. I'd better be going.'

Ellen walked across the room and put the cards on top of the TV. 'Fine,' she said. 'We'll get your friend out of the fridge and drive over there.' She raised a silencing hand as Don began to protest. 'What are you going to do? Let a severed head roll around in the boot?'

Don considered for a moment. 'Suit yourself. Over to Unity's, drop the stiff off and then out for a meal, okay?' He pulled on his jacket. 'And with any luck, I shall see neither Willie Rabblestack's nor Unity Siddorn's face ever again.'

'You reckon so?' Ellen asked, following him to the kitchen. 'I think you're pretty fond of her, really.'

Don frowned. Maybe he had been a little too dismissive, but he didn't want Ellen taking that line. He shrugged. 'I figure I *deserve* better,' he drawled in mock-Californian as he opened the fridge.

Ellen leaned against the door jamb. 'And what could be better than a woman who acts out your most unspeakable celluloid fantasies and earns a small fortune?' she asked disarmingly.

Don handed the canister to her, and stood looking into her eyes. He dropped his voice to a half-embarrassed murmur. 'Ummm . . . well. You. For instance.'

To his surprise, Ellen shrieked with laughter. 'Oh, right! And now I'm supposed to clap my hands in girly glee and fall into your experienced arms, am I?'

Don bridled. 'No! I mean . . . Well, you could do worse. What's wrong with me?'

'Nothing!' Ellen exclaimed. 'As arrogant, patronising, self-satisfied thirtysomethings go, you're a really nice bloke.'

Don crossed his arms and looked incredulously around the kitchen. 'Well, shucks. Thanks,' he said ruefully. 'And when did I do all this?'

'It's just the way you are. Take that time with George. You went out of your way to make him look really small – and all to impress me.'

'Ah, he didn't notice. He's an idiot.'

'Just because he's inarticulate doesn't mean he's insensitive. Now *there's* patronising for you.'

'Jesus,' Don said sulkily. 'I'm sorry I brought it up. I withdraw my arrogant offer.'

Ellen cradled the canister in one arm and patted the side of Don's face. 'Put your bottom lip away, little boy. Let's just see how it goes, eh?'

As it was Sunday, Casey wore loafers to the office. He'd got in a little before ten, allowing himself this tardiness after the extraordinary events of the night before. He worked on his budget plan until mid-afternoon, immersing himself in projections and pie charts – keeping his mind busy. But by four, he was finding it impossible to concentrate.

He stood by the window and stared mournfully down into the car park. There was his Alfa, in its designated space – the one with a plaque above it, reading 'Reserved for C. Rushmore'. Next to it was Mr Spleen's bay. For a backhand fiver, Mr Spleen's chauffeur would often clean Casey's Alfa when he was doing the Chief Executive's Merc. The same chammy that buffed up Mr Spleen's windscreen was then rubbed squelchily over Casey's own bodywork. The very thought made the Senior Finance Controller misty with pride.

Casey Rushmore loved Splendid Corps. Or, more precisely, he loved Mr Spleen. He wore this love at all times, every moment of his life, like an heirloom ring. It was encrusted with flashing gems of fear and awe and respect, and these he tried to keep hidden, turning them into his palm. But he couldn't conceal the untarnished metal in which they were set – the gleaming and eternal longing for approval.

But Casey knew he'd failed. He'd screwed up, got scared and lost it. His stock had undoubtedly fallen with Mr Spleen, who must even now be considering whether Casey Rushmore might not benefit from a career challenge in a non-Splendid environment. Casey didn't blame him. A man of Mr Spleen's stature couldn't possibly countenance a Senior Finance Controller who burgled houses, broke into hotel rooms, planned blackmail scams and assaulted winos on the sidewalk. Casey was aware that he had become that most despised of corporate lepers – a suitable candidate for outplacement.

He was about to turn back to his work station when Mr Spleen's Mercedes swung off the Hammersmith Bridge Road and into the forecourt below. The barrier pole lifted and the car slid across the lot into its reserved space; the door opened and Mr Spleen himself got out.

Casey swallowed as he watched his boss walk towards the front of the building. There was nothing for it – he'd have to go and apologise. Admit he'd screwed up royally, and plead for another chance. He took his sports jacket from the back of his guest's chair, and shrugged it on, smoothing down the lapels and fastening the middle button. Then he walked out of his office and pressed for the elevator. After a few seconds, the bell ding-donged and the doors slid open. Standing in the lift was Robert Spleen.

'Casey. Just the man,' Spleen said – not in an unfriendly way but certainly in the tone of one with something on his mind. 'Come up to my office. Sorry if you were on your way home – this won't take long.'

Casey gave a weak smile and stepped into the lift. They stood there in silence, side by side, watching the numbers rise. As they made their way to Spleen's office, Casey was rehearsing expressions of self-immolation. Perhaps he could make himself so repulsively abject that Mr Spleen would be embarrassed into giving him another chance.

'Take a seat, Casey,' Spleen nodded, as he sat in his own unpretentious swivel chair. 'Well, it's been quite an eventful day or two, eh?'

'I'd just like to apologise, sir.'

'Hm? Oh, I shouldn't worry. Boiled sweet?'

'No, sir. I just want you to know that I failed you and the corporation, and I realise I can never pay that back.'

'I've just come from a meeting with your Dr Todd.'

'I'm so sorry. Terribly, terribly . . . Sorry?'

Without giving details of how he came upon Gabriel Todd – and Casey was too agog to think of asking – Spleen explained that the scientist was even now ensconced in a nearby house, and that he was quite aware of the advantages of accepting assistance. However, Gabriel had made it very clear to his new benefactor that he was not about to give away the whereabouts of Willie's head. As he put it, 'Once you got that, brother, you got me hog-tied. I guess Willie and I are safer apart right now.'

'So,' Spleen asked Casey, 'what on earth has he done with it? Where do you hide a severed head at a moment's notice in a foreign town?'

Casey had still not quite recovered himself. 'I've no idea, sir. Sorry,' he shrugged. 'I'm really sorry.'

'Think back over last night. There must be something we've missed.'

Casey furrowed his brow melodramatically, and stroked his chin. He'd rather not have thought about last night at all, given the choice.

'No, sir,' he sighed eventually. 'Nothing. Sorry.'

'Oh, well. If anything occurs to you . . .'

Going back down in the lift, Casey let out a whimper of relief. It appeared that he was still in the job and tomorrow he'd be in his office as usual. He'd say good morning to his secretary, just like any other Monday. He'd have his decaff brought in at eleven. He'd chair the R&D meeting at eleven thirty, as he always did. He'd have a row with Unity Siddorn and . . .

Unity! Oh, boy – Unity! He'd forgotten to tell Mr Spleen about his fleeting collision with her. Or maybe he'd deliberately omitted it. Whatever, that must be the answer. *Todd had given the head to Unity Siddorn.*

Casey frantically hit the button for the eighth floor, but the elevator continued its descent.

'Come on, come on,' he pleaded through gritted teeth.

This was the clincher. This would get him back on Mr Spleen's good side. Casey was hopping from foot to foot like a five-year-old too excited to leave the room.

When the elevator reached the ground floor, he immediately pushed 8 and made little coming-together motions with his hands, as if to hurry the doors up. But then, as the doors were nearly shut, he thrust his loafered foot between them. The doors buzzed in protest, and Casey ignored them.

If Mr Spleen would be grateful for the snippet about Unity's involvement, how much more impressed would he be if Casey were to turn up with the head itself? That would *really* get him out of the hole, wouldn't it? Might even leave him a little ahead of the game.

Casey pulled his foot from between the elevator doors, and pressed the button for his own floor. He could pick up Unity's address from the Human Resources database. Then he could drop by and pick up the head. Then he could come back here and pick up serious career points.

CHAPTER THIRTY-ONE

UNITY'S PHONE RANG, AND she picked it up with her left hand.

'Hello?'

'Don't speak. Would it be unrealistic of me to figure that one of these two phones may be tapped?'

'Gabe!' Unity exclaimed. 'Gabe, where are you? Are you all right?'

Gabriel sighed. 'Nice going, Mata Hari. Is Willie with you yet?'

'Sorry?'

'Obviously not. Seen your beau today?'

Gabriel confirmed what Don's phone call had implied concerning Willie's whereabouts. Unity explained that Don was on his way over, and should be there any minute. She also told him that the police were considering treating the case as murder. Gabriel tutted.

'Yeah,' he mused, 'they need a cause of death. We're going to have to come up with a system here, otherwise this is going to happen every time.'

'Where are you, Gabriel?'

'Out of the frying pan. Don't worry about it. Just keep Willie safe, and please say nothing to anyone.'

At that moment, the doorbell rang.

'That'll be Don,' Unity said. 'Hang on – I'll be back in a minute.'

She ran to the door and opened it. Casey Rushmore pushed past her into the flat.

'Where's the singer's head?' he demanded, striding along the corridor to the kitchen. He looked in the freezer and the fridge, slamming them each disgustedly when he failed to find the flask. 'Look. I'm in a hurry. Dr Todd is with Mr Spleen right now, and he wants me to bring him the head. What have you done with it?'

Her initial shock having subsided, Unity crossed her arms and stood by the phone as Casey came back up the hallway.

'It's not here, you jerk,' she sneered. 'And don't lie to me – it's pathetic.'

Casey clenched his fists at his sides in frustration. 'Look, it's true. Mr Spleen is hiding Todd – they're all good buddies now.'

As if in sorrow at the transparency of the deception, Unity shook her head and picked up the phone.

'Excuse me a moment,' she told Casey with a smile of icy pleasantness. 'Dr Todd? I have a Mr Rushmore here who claims that you are currently the guest of his employer, Mr Spleen.' She turned to look at Casey, her freeze-dried smirk still in place. 'Could you kindly confirm whether or not he's talking complete shit?' She paused for a moment, listening to the reply, and then her face sagged.

'Oh,' she said defeatedly. 'Hm.'

Casey pointed at the phone. 'That's him?' he squealed.

'But whatever you do, don't let him get Willie,' Gabriel was saying. 'Get him out of the apartment quick, before your boyfriend shows up.'

'Okay. Call me back in fifteen minutes.' She hung up, and turned to Casey again. 'Look, I was in a police station all last night, and I've been asleep all day. Willie's not here. So will you please go away and leave me be?'

As Casey considered this, there were footsteps on the stairs beyond the open front door, and then Don's head appeared round it, his face a picture of facetious chirpiness.

'Interfauna!' he announced.

'Oh, shit,' Unity muttered. And then she yelled at him, 'Go away, you idiot!'

Don tutted. 'No chance,' he said, stepping through the door. 'I want to get rid of this bloody thing.' He held the canister out towards her, and Casey lunged for it. Don whipped it out of his reach.

'Who's the straight?' he asked Unity. 'Don't hang about, do you?'

'Give me that fucken head,' Casey spat, his accent slipping slightly in the excitement.

Ellen appeared in the doorway. 'How unseemly,' she commented as Casey made another attempt to grab the canister. This time he swatted it with one hand, and it teetered in the crook of Don's elbow. Casey followed up fast and hooked an arm round it.

'Stop it! Stop it!' Unity screamed. 'You'll hurt him!'

Ellen looked sidelong at Unity and raised one eyebrow, then turned back to watch the struggle between Don and Casey, each of them with an arm wrapped round the prize. They were rocking back and forth, and in the confusion a stray foot caught the cable of the telephone and pulled it, unnoticed, from its socket.

In one movement, Ellen stepped forward and brought the ball of her hand up in a sharp blow to the bottom of the canister. It popped up between the combatants and as it juggled between their chests, Ellen lifted it free and stepped back.

'Calm down, boys,' she said. She nodded towards Casey. 'And who are you?'

Casey pushed back his hair and smoothed his jacket. Then he took a deep breath and spoke directly to Ellen. 'Listen. I represent Mr Robert Spleen of Splendid Corps. That item is the property of his personal friend Dr Gabriel Todd, and I have the authority—'

'Spleen's involved in this, is he?' Ellen nodded. 'Well, well.'

'Look,' Unity said, 'you're a friend of Don's, right? So maybe he's told you about my friendship with Gabriel Todd. I was just speaking to him on the phone and, believe me, he wants *me* to look after Willie's head. Honestly.'

Ellen looked from Unity to Casey, and back again. Then she sighed and shook her head. 'Well, if you can't share nicely,' she admonished, 'then neither of you shall have it.' She turned round and strolled to the door. 'Don, we'll reschedule dinner for tomorrow, shall we?'

Don glanced warily at Unity. 'Uh, okay.'

As she disappeared down the stairs, Ellen ordered, 'Mr Rushmore, tell Robert I'll have my people call.'

Casey gasped and started after her, but Don grabbed him by the shoulder. 'Don't tempt me,' he murmured.

Unity slumped into the phone chair. 'What's she going to do?' she asked, anguished.

Don stepped forward and pushed the door shut.

'Tempt me,' he murmured.

'What's that on your hand?' Don asked Unity after Casey had left, peeved.

'Latex laboratory glove. I scalded myself, and I'm trying to keep the air off and the skin intact.'

'Right,' Don nodded. 'I suppose a wrist job's out of the question, then?'

'You're repugnant,' she remarked, disinterestedly. She looked exhausted, monochrome.

Jesus, Don thought, she must have had a terrible time.

Whatever the current state of their relationship – and he sensed it wasn't on tip-top form – he couldn't bring himself simply to chuck her a 'Well, see you then' and walk out of the door. As far as he knew, he was about the closest friend she'd got.

As the thought occurred, he blinked in silent surprise. Swiftly scanning the past year, he realised that, in all the time they'd been going out, Unity hadn't introduced him to any of her friends. He'd never been paraded before any knowing confederacy of old school chums. There'd been no smug, cool ex-lovers met as part of cagey pub foursomes. She hadn't even demurred at his invitations with the excuse that she was having a night out with a couple of the girls. If ever she was occupied, it was with work or with catching up on her sleep.

She was slumped in the armchair, shivering slightly, her eyes closed. Don threw his jacket on the sofa.

'Repugnant I indubitably am,' he admitted brightly, 'but I can cook. You stay there, and I'll knock something together.'

He made some pasta which they ate in virtual silence, watching the TV. When she'd finished, Unity laid her tray on the carpet, and pushed her glasses up as she rubbed her eyes.

'Thanks,' she said.

'You couldn't be welcomer,' Don shrugged. He reached for his wine. 'I've been ringing you all day and night. I know it's none of my business, but where've you been?'

Unity shifted her shoulders against the back of the armchair and stretched her arms above her head, her fingers interlocked.

'I was at the police station all night, being questioned.'

'Blimey. Sounds heavy.' He sipped his wine. 'The whole thing sounds pretty disturbing, actually,' he remarked.

Just that hint of sympathy was enough. Unity's breath caught for a moment, and then her face crumpled and she burst into tears. Don froze, his wine glass tipped in mid-air, not knowing how to react.

'It's been *horrible*,' she sobbed. 'It's been a complete nightmare . . .'

Don's shoulders dropped, and he wrinkled his nose. He put down his glass and held his arms open. 'C'mere,' he said.

As he hugged her to his chest, she choked out broken phrases. 'The white limo . . . poor Willie . . . carrying him into the hotel . . . I've done a terrible thing . . . the police coming to the door . . .'

When the crying subsided, Don led her, like a child, to the bedroom. He removed her glasses and helped her off with her skirt and T-shirt, negotiating the sleeve carefully over her scalded hand; then he put her into bed. As she lay back on the pillow, eyes shut, jagged sobs still hiccuping in her chest, he realised that he'd never seen her without make-up before. It was like turning an unfamiliar street corner and seeing a landmark from a new vantage point – it rekindled fascinations that had become mundane.

As he pulled the duvet up to her chin, and kissed her on the forehead, she opened her eyes.

'Don't go, Don,' she murmured.

'I won't. I'll sleep on the couch.'

'No. Sleep here.'

Don thought about it, assessing how much of a bastard he was prepared to be. 'No,' he said eventually. 'I couldn't trust myself.'

Unity smeared tears from her cheek with the flat of her hand and pushed the duvet back, holding out an arm towards him.

'Good,' she nodded, with a diluted smile.

Gabriel phoned Unity back within fifteen minutes as promised, but there was no reply. He hung up, and put a hand to his mouth, wondering what could have happened.

He was unused to the pass in which he presently found himself – not in control; depending for his wellbeing upon the actions of others. He had to find something active to do. He had to feel he was making progress. He stood up and paced. Pacing always helped.

There was a British branch of the Second Lifers – he'd met some guy at a convention in Massachusetts. They had facilities someplace out in the boondocks. Gabriel tapped his forehead but couldn't remember what they were called. He sat down again and picked up the phone, checking his watch to see what time it would be in Nevada. When his call was picked up, he spoke to a friend at the Icebox, and asked him to dig out the name of the Limey organisation, and their phone number.

When the answer came, Gabriel laughed aloud as he wrote it down. He read the name and number back to his colleague.

'Isn't that typical of the British?' he chuckled, shaking his head. 'I love 'em. "Double or Quits".'

CHAPTER THIRTY-TWO

'FRANKLY,' SAID DETECTIVE CHIEF Inspector Knowles, 'and I pride myself on being frank, I'm a little disappointed in your results, David, performancewise.'

Jennings clasped his hands together in his lap. It was Monday morning, and he'd been dreading this interview for twenty-four hours.

'Someone got there first,' he explained. 'These things are in the lap of the gods.'

'The one question you must ask yourself, David,' Knowles continued, 'is, could I have done better? Could I have moved faster?'

Yes, Jennings admitted wordlessly. If I hadn't stopped to ring you, I would have been there seven minutes earlier.

'But let's not dwell on our failures at the present time,' the Chief Inspector went on. 'Have we at least tied up the formalities?'

Jennings ruffled his hair and pulled the lobe of his ear. The Chief Inspector's allusion was to the formal identification of the body – which, as Knowles was aware, could not be completed without the next of kin. He'd raised the subject merely to force Jennings into another admission of failure, so that the score against could be demonstrably racked up.

'Mr Rabblestack's immigration papers name his mother as the second point of contact after Dr Todd,' Jennings said, keeping the tone neutral. 'She has been contacted, and is currently in transit.'

'So no formal identification, then, as per yet,' Knowles summarised, nodding.

'No, sir.' You so-and-so. You crafty old—

'Let me put *this* to you, David. And I ask this as a colleague and a friend. How do you see your career developing from here on out?'

David Jennings left the DCI's office furious. He sat at his desk and crunched a Bic between his teeth, biting right down to the plastic tube.

In an attempt to identify the mysterious 'posh man', Jennings had contacted Dr Todd's publisher and a couple of academics working in his field. They had not seen the fugitive. He'd also been in touch with an organisation of harmless loonies called Double or Quits, but turned up nothing of use. He considered calling Ms Siddorn in again, but dismissed the notion as pointless.

The door opened and the office typist came in. She was a cottage-loaf woman called Mrs Greaves who, rumour had it, had started out drafting letters for Robert Peel. She laid some mail on the desk and said, 'You look like you've got the cares of the world on your shoulders, dear.'

Jennings flicked the end of the biro off his front teeth. 'I feel like Douglas Bader,' he sighed.

'Beg yours?' Mrs Greaves inquired.

Jennings drummed his fingers on his temples. 'I'm stumped.'

Robert Spleen listened, aghast, to Casey's account of the encounter at Unity's apartment.

'What the bloody hell did you think you were playing at?' he demanded, gazing at the ceiling in frustration. 'Why on earth didn't you come to me with this information, rather than barging in there like a, like a . . .' He looked at his hapless employee. Casey was biting his bottom lip and quivering, like an under-gardener who'd pulled up the petunias thinking they were weeds.

'Oh, for Heaven's sake,' Spleen tutted, shaking his head.

'You see, sir, I thought—'

'No. You *didn't*,' Spleen told him. 'Now, wait a minute while *I* think.'

Casey had described a black-haired young woman with neon-green eyes. It sounded like the captivating Ellen. The description of the tousled young man called Don – Unity's boyfriend, if you please – appeared to clinch it.

Spleen consulted the Human Resources database for Unity's number and then picked up the phone.

'Look,' Don explained to Unity as he pulled on his jacket. 'Casey will go back to Spleen and then Spleen will contact you. He'll want to get to me, and through me to Ellen. I don't need that, and neither do you.'

Unity was sitting on the bed, lacing her knee-high boots. 'But what's your . . .' She wondered how to refer to Ellen. There was an argument in the offing, and she wasn't up to it. 'What's your colleague going to do with Willie?'

'No idea – but I trust her more than your Machiavellian boss. I'm going home and you're welcome to come with me.'

'But what if Gabriel needs me?'

'For what? Spleen's got him, right? And now Spleen's after the . . . He's after Willie. If you want to help Gabriel, you have to keep away from Spleen.' He walked into the hall and looked towards the door. 'I'm out of here. You coming?'

Unity dropped her head and sighed. 'I don't know . . .'

'Suit yourself.' He noticed that the phone connection was pulled out of its socket and bent to replace it. 'But, believe me, this phone is going to ring at any second.'

At that instant, the phone rang.

'Spooky,' Don remarked, and picked up the receiver. 'Yeah?' He listened for a moment, and then held the phone out to Unity. 'It's a Mr Spleen for you. You in?'

After a brief pause, and without looking up, Unity shook her head. Don put the phone back to his ear.

'Trying to connect you,' he singsonged, and hung up.

CHAPTER THIRTY-THREE

AT SEVEN THIRTY THAT evening, Robert Spleen and Dr Gabriel Todd were led to a reserved table for two at Tête-à-Tête, a formal French restaurant on the Fulham Road. During the afternoon, Spleen had received a cheerful but efficient phone call from Ellen telling him of the reservation, which had been made in his name.

'Nice diner,' Gabriel commented, as the waiter flourished a napkin into his lap. He ran a finger round his spacious shirt collar. 'Last time I wore a necktie was at my graduation. I'm not doing it justice.' In deference to the dress code of the restaurant, Spleen had lent him a business suit, which fitted perfectly down, but less so across. 'I'm just not as skilfully cut as the get-up, I guess.'

Spleen ordered wine without looking at the list, and took a bread roll from the basket. 'Are you sure the reservation wasn't for a party of three?' he asked the waiter. He was assured that it was not.

'So, tell me about this woman,' Gabriel said, as he devoured salmon pâté. 'What's her angle?'

Spleen thumbed a breadcrumb from the corner of his mouth, and reached for his wine. He'd been watching Todd closely since telling him that Rabblestack's head had been hijacked – and he'd been impressed by the American's apparent equanimity. But he'd quickly perceived that the breeziness Dr Todd displayed was generated by the agitation he truly felt. In the cab to Fulham, Todd had chattered incessantly – about London architecture, English culture, academic politics – but he had not once looked directly at Spleen. In fact, his darting eyes hadn't rested for a moment, and Spleen suspected that this kangarooing monologue betrayed an equally anxious and restless mood.

It was an impressive show – like skiing on an alligator swamp.

'Yes, Ellen,' Spleen mused. 'I've only met her once. She's certainly bright, good-looking. I barely gave her a second thought. But she seems well-balanced – as far as one can tell.' He chose his words precisely, not wishing to agitate Todd. On the other hand, he wanted him to feel sufficiently insecure to agree to any arrangement that might seem workable. 'She has very green eyes,' he added, as if it were darkly relevant.

'Have you seen that movie *The Girl with Green Eyes*?' Todd offered. 'Rita Tushingham – the only woman I ever got hot for.' And he was off on another cheerful anecdote.

As Todd chattered and the waiter cleared the starters, Spleen wondered about Ellen. At first, he had assumed that she would want money, but on reflection he felt that the idea didn't sit. She certainly hadn't the smell of fiscal greed about her. Perhaps it would be some favour – an opportunity, a break. Spleen would have no problem with that. Indeed, it wouldn't be the first time in his life that he had bargained with something that he'd have been happy to give gratis. This was, in the end, a business negotiation. He had to keep in mind what he wanted to achieve – to gain custody of the head. In order to have some sway over Gabriel Todd. So that he could direct the scientist's research. And live forever.

He felt the familiar nicotine tug and reached for a breadstick to assuage it.

'Tut-tut, let's not spoil our dinner,' came a voice from behind him.

Spleen turned to see Ellen, who pulled a spare chair across from a nearby table and sat down. 'I'll take a glass of the wine, if you'd be so kind,' she told Spleen.

The CEO of Splendid Corps raised himself from his seat slightly as Ellen settled in. 'Good afternoon,' he nodded, determined not to appear disconcerted. As he poured white wine into a red wine glass, he said, 'May I introduce Dr Gabriel Todd?'

'Howdy,' Todd nodded.

'Nice to meet you,' Ellen assured him. She held out a hand. 'Ellen Faustinelli.' She accepted the wine from Spleen and sipped it. 'Not bad.' She put the glass on the table in front of her, and took a breadstick, holding it between her fingers like a cigarette. 'To business,' she said, biting off the end of it. 'I find myself at an impasse, gentlemen. I have conflicting reports as to what is for the best. Dr Todd?'

Todd was momentarily nonplussed. Then he took a deep breath.

'I want Willie back,' he said simply. 'He has been my friend and lover for thirty years. Nobody has the right to separate me from him.' He leaned forward on his elbows. 'There's no argument here.'

Ellen nodded, lips pursed. 'Sounds pretty unassailable,' she suggested, turning to Spleen. 'What do you think?'

Looking across at Ellen, Spleen struggled to contain a baffling mixture of emotions – admiration, irritation, attraction. He felt wrong-footed and slow, and he wasn't used to it.

'Look,' he demanded, 'who *are* you exactly?'

Ellen gave a reassuring, nursery-nanny smile. 'Just think of me as the head waiter,' she advised. 'Now, what do you have to say for yourself?'

Spleen closed his eyes and massaged the bridge of his nose for a few seconds as he thought things through.

'Let's be clear,' he said eventually, looking up. 'I have no intention of separating Dr Todd and Mr Rabblestack. I merely wish to have Dr Todd work exclusively in the field of cryonics, under my auspices. In return for that, I will use all my influence, both legitimate and covert, to keep him out of prison. I want Mr Rabblestack to be placed in my care only as a goodwill gesture – a token of trust on both sides.'

'Not as a hostage,' Ellen confirmed, again with that drink-your-cocoa smile.

'No.'

Gabriel banged a fist on the table. 'Goddamn! All this gaol stuff is horse feathers! They're not gonna lock me up, for Christ's sake. I haven't done anything.'

Ellen laughed and shook her head. 'Have you been in our country long?'

With a groan, Gabriel slumped back in his chair. Then he gathered himself and leaned forwards again, addressing Ellen but looking at Spleen. 'Willie and I can look after ourselves, okay? But if I sold my soul to the corporation – well, it's not our way. He'd never forgive me.'

Spleen nodded. 'This is the same Willie Rabblestack who signed to Sony for two and a half million, I believe.'

For a moment it looked as if Gabriel might lunge across the table and grab Spleen by the throat, but Ellen spread her out-turned palms between them. 'Now, now,' she admonished. She took another sip of wine, and gazed into the distance for a few seconds. Then she finished the glass in one long slug and put it back on the table.

'So,' she said, looking from one man to the other and interlacing her fingers, 'to summarise. In the blue corner we have the inalienable right of the individual to control his own destiny and that of his loved ones, even if the exercise of that right leads to rank injustice and the criminal waste of God-given talent; and, in the red corner, the fine altruistic principle that the advancement of the commonwealth is more important than any solipsistic concept of self-determination, even unto the negation of personal freedom of choice.' She picked up the salt cellar and rolled it reflectively between her palms. 'Well . . .'

Spleen and Todd both gazed at her tensely.

'Hmmm,' she mused. 'I don't suppose you'd consider settling this by playing paper-scissors-rock?'

Todd's shoulders dropped and he gave a weary, resigned little chuckle. Spleen, unmoving, muttered, 'Oh, God.'

Ellen put down the salt cellar, and got to her feet. 'A game of some kind. It's the only fair way. You'll each need a playing partner. We'll play tomorrow – at your offices, Robert, if you'd be so kind. I'll call with the details.'

She turned to go, and then paused and looked back. 'I recommend the American meatloaf,' she suggested. 'It's very good here.'

As Ellen weaved away from them through the restaurant tables, Spleen thought quickly, looking for an edge.

A game. A game with a partner – but who might one bring in?

The only candidate appeared to be Casey Rushmore – but he was no games player. A less strategically adept personality it would be hard to imagine. Spleen riffled through a mental card index of acquaintances with whom he shared the occasional poker night or casino session – and dismissed them all. There would be no way to explain the circumstances that had led to this.

Suddenly, he leapt from the table and scooted towards the entrance, buffeting waiters as he ran. He caught up with Ellen at the door, and laid a hand on her shoulder.

'The young man,' he insisted, 'the one who was with you at that place Movers and Shakers.'

'Don,' Ellen replied calmly, turning.

'Yes. I want *him*. I'll only do it if I can have him.'

Ellen smiled.

'Join the queue,' she said.

CHAPTER THIRTY-FOUR

AFTER FIFTEEN YEARS AS a customs officer, it gets so you can tell a wrong 'un, even before they come round the corner into the channel. It's the sound of the footsteps – a picking up of pace or, just as often, a slowing down. 'A subconscious reluctance to be scrutinised,' was how Ray England referred to it when training the newbies.

He'd been on since six in the morning, and his moustache had been twitching in overdrive. He'd picked up two yuppies returning from Amsterdam with plastic bags of cannabis folded within their laptops; a middle-aged woman with a perfectly legal but embarrassing souvenir of the Reeperbahn; and a retired colonel concealing an excess litre of Courvoisier inside his plastic leg.

It was a little after eight, and Ray England was considering knocking off for breakfast, when a slender, diminutive figure appeared at the top of the green channel. She was dressed in loose blue jeans, a leather biker's jacket and mirror shades. Her hair was waist-length and pure white, and she was hugging a vast carpetbag in both arms. She must have been sixty-five if she was a day.

Ray's moustache waggled like a puppy dog's tail as he stepped in front of her.

'May I ask where you're travelling from, madam?' he asked.

The little old woman looked up at him over the top of her carpetbag, and Ray could see himself reflected in the lenses of the sunglasses.

'Vegas via Chicago O'Hare,' she replied with a Southern twang. There was a smoker's croak in her voice, and an edgy urgency.

Ray got her to come across to the table and asked her to open her bag. He checked her passport. Judith Rabblestack. Date of birth: 16th December 1928. The passport was stiff with stamps and visas. This little old lady had evidently been around.

'Ain't nothin' in there but mah drawers 'n' hose,' she told Ray as he rummaged through her things. She kept glancing towards the exit, evidently anxious to get away.

Ray pulled out a pack of two hundred Lucky Strikes. And then another. And another.

'And a few smokes,' Judith Rabblestack admitted, with a winsome smile.

From the depths of the vast bag he retrieved a bottle of Jack Daniels. Two bottles. Three.

'Helps the circulation,' Ma Rabblestack explained.

'Are you aware of this country's statutory limits on . . .'

The little old woman pulled her shades down her nose, and peeked at Ray England over the top of them. Her eyes were pale blue, like sun-faded denim, and red-rimmed from exhaustion or tears. From the front pocket of her jeans, she produced a roll of English currency.

'Save it, son,' she advised. 'What's the raise?'

Ray obligingly totted it up, and Ma Rabblestack peeled off the correct amount. As he was filling out the receipt, Ray inquired, 'What's the purpose of your visit, if I may ask?'

'Family business,' she replied, piling her things back into the bag. 'I've come for mah boy.'

And she gave a cackle that was completely empty of mirth.

Unity spent Monday night at Don's and left around ten on Tuesday, while he was still sleeping. She arrived home and pressed the button on the answering machine.

'Unity, it's Gabe. Monday night, around eight. I sure hope you hear this.' His voice was strained, shaky. 'I need you to meet me at Splendid Reach at noon tomorrow. This is real important. You can reach me anytime tonight – anytime – on the following number . . .'

There were four more calls, spaced throughout the night, and the tone of desperation in Gabriel's voice was more obvious in each.

'Unity, it's seven in the morning. Please get in touch. I need a partner. You're the only one who can help. I'll give you the number again . . .'

She called, but got no reply. It was a little after eleven. She showered and changed, then tried once more – but there was still no answer.

She left the house, sick with apprehension, and trotted along the Fulham Palace Road towards Hammersmith.

David Jennings took a call at ten forty-five.

'Zat Jennings?' came a croaky drawl. 'I guess you bin expectin' me. Judy Rabblestack – Willie's ma.'

Jennings had not been looking forward to this call. He would have to get Mr Rabblestack's old mother to formally identify the body – a procedure which, in the circumstances, would be both difficult and unpleasant.

'Where are you phoning from?' he asked, tapping a biro against his teeth. 'Right. No, you stay there. I'll come to you. What's the room number? Fine. I'll be twenty minutes. And can I just offer my deepest . . . hello? Hello?'

He scribbled a note of his whereabouts, gave it to Mrs Greaves, and walked out to his Renault. This frail little blue-rinsed old dear, he felt, should be spared the sight of uniforms and squad cars. The day was going to be disturbing enough for her, without all that.

Tears pricked suddenly as Unity walked briskly past the Sunrise. Willie's picture was still on the hoardings outside, his head framed in the round silver plate of a National steel guitar. He was wearing that look of amused knowingness that was all in the eyes rather than the mouth.

She walked beneath the flyover, and broke into a jog to beat the lights at the top of Hammersmith Bridge Road. Lounging on the low wall outside Splendid Reach sat Don, smoking a cigarette, and gazing at his shoes. He looked up as she approached.

'Wotcher,' he said. 'I thought you might show up.'

'What are you doing here?'

'Mulling.'

He'd been woken that morning, soon after she'd left, by a phone call from Ellen. A proposition had been made – a very strange proposition. Ellen reckoned he should go for it, but Don wasn't so sure. He'd been thinking about it all the way over in the Merc that had been sent to pick him up.

There was going to be a game. Some kind of partner game.

Unity gasped. 'Gabriel said something about that. He wants *me* to be his partner.' She paused. 'So . . . whose partner would you be?'

Don lit another cigarette from the stub of the previous one. 'Spleen's,' he murmured. 'They're going to play for Rabblestack's head.'

'No!' Unity sat down shakily on the wall beside Don. She fiddled with the tight cuff of the latex glove that still protected her scalded hand. 'Well – Christ – you're not going to *do* it, are you? Obviously.'

As soon as she said it, Don snapped his head round to glare at her. '*Obviously?* What the fuck does that mean? I'll do what I bloody well like.'

Unity fought to be reasonable. 'But you hate Spleen. You've always said that.'

'So what? I'm not crazy about *Todd* either. Though if Spleen wins, incidentally, Todd gets to do his mad work – and I guess you will too. On the other hand, if *your* man wins, there's a good chance of him going to jail. That's what *you'll* be playing for.'

Unity lowered her head, and rested her brow in her rubber-gloved palm. She could not believe he was considering this betrayal. 'I promise you,' she said quietly, without looking up, 'if you do this, that's it. We're over for good.' She turned to him. 'I really mean it.'

Don had a vision of her, last night, her curved back below him, her buttocks pressed against his thighs. She had shrieked and panted. Later, she'd clung to him in her sleep, scared and out of it. He understood precisely what he was for.

'You always mean it,' he muttered. The sentence was trite and melodramatic, and it had precisely the effect he expected. She bit.

'What the fuck do you mean by that?' she yelled.

Don shrugged dismissively. 'You dump me on a regular basis,' he explained, 'and come crawling back the minute you need an ear, shoulder and cock.'

She stood up, hit him hard across the face, called him an arrogant bastard and stalked off towards the doors of the office block.

He rubbed his stinging cheek, satisfied. He'd engineered a justification. Now he could tell himself he was cruising into Splendid Reach on a righteous wave of principle.

But he'd known what he was going to do from the moment Ellen phoned him. The game was raised – and he just couldn't resist a game.

Gabriel walked across the atrium and greeted Unity with a weak smile and cursory kiss on the cheek. 'Boy, I'm sure glad you showed.' He looked terrible – drawn, pale, watery. At the sight of him, Unity's fury at Don evaporated.

'You okay?' she asked. 'What's going on?'

He led her to a sofa beside the reception desk, and they sat down. Gabriel was hunched forward, his elbows on his knees and his hands clasped. He was staring at his feet.

'How the fuck have I got myself into this position, Unity?' he asked, without looking up. 'I got it wrong somewhere. I can't figure it out.'

'There's going to be some kind of game . . .' Unity ventured.

'Ha – right! A game. Thirty years of love and planning and endeavour – and it's all comes down to Snakes and Ladders.' He put the balls of his hands to his eyes and rubbed hard. 'I need some sleep. I didn't sleep at all last night.' Dragging his palms down his cheeks, he took a deep, jerky breath. 'Y'know, I really miss him.' His face crumpled and his voice cracked. 'I never understood how much I'd miss him . . .'

Unity put an arm round Gabriel's convulsing shoulders as he wept. 'It'll be all right. It'll all turn out all right,' she assured him, close to tears herself.

Gabriel swallowed the sobs and opened his eyes. 'See, this was all supposed to be simple if Willie went first. Like one of those months where he was recording in Nashville. Understand? Like he'd be back for Thanksgiving.' He slumped back onto the sofa and stared up into the greenery that spanned the vault of the atrium. He blinked away tears and sniffed. '*Christ*, I can be stupid,' he said, viciously. 'I didn't think any of it through – not the practicalities, or the mechanics.' He ran a hand through his hair. 'Or the Godawful loneliness.'

'Oh, Gabe,' Unity whispered, squeezing his shoulder.

'Ever since I can remember,' Gabriel continued hoarsely, 'I've been a genius. Everybody told me so – my foster parents, my teachers. Gabriel, you're a gold-plated freakin' phenomenon. But until I met Willie, there was no joy in me except the joy I found in books. Suddenly, at the age of twenty, I became a whole person. I've always believed that. I've congratulated myself on it. Intellectually brilliant and emotionally together – what specimen of a man is Dr Gabriel Todd.' He bit his lip. 'But not brilliant enough or together enough to have figured this one, huh? Just another smug, conceited academic putz.'

Unity leaned across and looked directly into Gabriel's face.

'Gabriel,' she declared urgently, 'you have to snap out of this. There's no time for self-pity. We've got to go upstairs and do whatever it takes to get Willie back. You love him. You're in the right. Are you listening?

We have to get Willie back for you, and that's all that matters at the moment.'

Gabriel nodded, still staring at the ceiling. 'Uhuh. Sure we've got to get him back – no question at all.' He turned to Unity. 'But I've been thinking about this . . .' He put one hand on his heart and the tears welled in his eyes again. '. . . and – tell ya true – I'm really not sure a dumb jerk like me deserves him.'

Casey Rushmore, to his chagrin, had been ordered by Mr Spleen to sit at the secretary's desk outside the Chief Executive's office. His task was to prevent the entry of unauthorised visitors. He'd watched as Mr Spleen had ushered through the beautiful, green-eyed girl, carrying the canister. Then Unity Siddorn had shown up with Gabriel Todd, and neither had even acknowledged him as Spleen had re-emerged from the office to greet them.

After a few minutes, the scruffy smart aleck from Unity's flat loped in from the corridor.

'Morning, Miss Goodbody,' he said cheerfully to Casey, nodding at the nameplate on the desk. 'I think I'm expected.'

Casey clenched his fists in his lap as Spleen reappeared from the inner office.

'Don! I'm so glad you could come,' Spleen said, reaching out to shake hands.

'Flattered to be asked,' Don offered. He winked at Casey. 'I must say, Bob, I fancy your secretary something rotten.'

As soon as the door closed behind them, Casey, plum-coloured and steaming, leapt to his feet and kicked deafening hell out of the filing cabinet.

A round table and four chairs had been arranged in the middle of Spleen's large, neat office. On a smaller table, by the door to the emergency stairs, stood the canister which contained the head of the once and future Willie Rabblestack. It gleamed in the cold light of the early winter sun.

Ellen invited each of the players to take a seat. Gabriel, with his back to the canister, sat looking towards the door that led to Spleen's apartment. Unity sat opposite. Don was in the chair facing the window and Spleen was across from him, his back to the light. Ellen walked round the table and then stopped to Gabriel's left and surveyed the set-up. The others watched her expectantly.

'Good morning,' she said. 'I believe you all know each other – but you don't all know me. My name's Ellen Faustinelli and I've taken on the role of arbitrator in this extraordinary affair. Of course, I've absolutely no right to assume that role, unless Dr Todd and Mr Spleen agree to my taking it.' She looked at each of them in turn.

Gabriel crossed his arms. 'Why would I agree to that?' he asked. 'What's to stop me picking up Willie and walking out of here right now?' He turned to Spleen. 'What you gonna do? Use your fists?'

'No,' Spleen admitted. 'The phone.'

Gabriel stared at him impassively for a few moments. Then he looked back at Ellen and waved a hand. 'Okay, go ahead.'

Ellen glanced at Spleen, who nodded.

'Thank you. We are to play a game,' she explained. 'A simple game but one that demands skill, strategy and good fortune.' She smiled. 'Life stuff, in other words.'

Unity gave an incredulous gasp. 'Do you realise how *important* this is?' she demanded.

Ellen regarded her sidelong. 'No – okay. You're right. Perhaps it would be better if Mr Spleen and Dr Todd went down to the car park and beat each other senseless. Last one capable of walking can carry Willie's head away.' She paused and looked at Gabriel. He held up a quietening hand to Unity, who sighed resignedly and sat back in her seat, shaking her head.

'The game,' Ellen continued, 'is Happy Families. The objective is to collect sets of cards representing the families depicted. The deck will be dealt and, at your turn, you will ask another player for a card that you need. If the player you address is holding that card, it will be given to you, and you may have another go. Otherwise the turn passes to the left.'

'This is sick,' Unity muttered. 'It's frivolous and sick.'

Ignoring the aside, Ellen reached into a patchwork bag slung over her shoulder, and produced a pack of cards. They were unusually large – like a Tarot deck. 'There are twelve families in the pack. We will play two complete games. Each of you will play as an individual, but the scores of each team will be aggregated over both games to decide the winner. I shall deal.'

She slipped the cards from their box, and glanced at her watch. 'We agreed that we would start at noon, which gives us ten minutes yet.' She glanced at Unity, and then at the canister on the table in the corner. 'Perhaps we should all like to spend that time considering the frivolity of the situation.'

She turned to the window and looked out across Hammersmith Bridge Road towards the church clock by the roundabout.

It said twenty-five past five.

CHAPTER THIRTY-FIVE

DAVID JENNINGS PRESSED HIS forehead against the bathroom mirror in Room 325 of the Holiday Inn, Marble Arch, and gazed into his own eyes.

'Absolutely marvellous,' he murmured, not for the first time.

He'd reached the door of Mrs Rabblestack's room at a little after eleven, and knocked in what he hoped was a sympathetic fashion. He'd expected Mrs Rabblestack to be a rosy-cheeked little thing in a shawl and wire-frame spectacles, dabbing away maternal tears with a lace-trimmed hankie. He was somewhat taken aback when the door was opened by a sexagenarian biker babe holding a glass of bourbon and a filterless cigarette.

'Jennings, right?' she asked, standing aside to let him in. 'Fixya some kinda drink? Jack Daniels?'

Jennings accepted a mineral water from the minibar, and sat in an armchair. Ma Rabblestack perched on the corner of the bed, and placed an ashtray beside her.

'Mrs Rabblestack—'

'Never married, son,' she interjected firmly. 'Came into the world a Rabblestack and that's how I plan to leave it. Most everyone calls me Ma.'

Jennings, discomfited, scratched his head with both hands. 'Umm . . . I don't think I can do that, really.'

'Lord, the English,' Ma Rabblestack chuckled. 'You do whatever makes y'comfortable, son. That's the only way in this life, I reckon.'

'Thank you,' Jennings nodded. He was twisting his wedding ring round his finger as he spoke. 'Mrs Rabblestack, I'm aware that this is a desperately trying time for you . . .'

Ma Rabblestack lit another Lucky Strike. 'You don't know, son. You jest don't know. Got kids y'self?'

It was understandable, Jennings felt, that the old lady wanted to avoid the matter in hand. He was prepared to take as long as it took.

'We've got a little boy – Jacob,' he replied, with a fond smile. 'He'll be four in January.'

The old lady nodded. 'When Willie was four, we's livin' in a room over a general store on Jackson Square in Del Harta, Texas. I was waitin' tables eight till six and dancin' at the Silver Rig nine till two.' She wagged a crooked finger at Jennings. 'But I was always there to sing him to sleep, and he never woke up in the mornin' without his mamma was lyin' right there beside him.'

'I'm sure,' Jennings agreed.

'I did okay by that boy – cain't ask more.'

'You certainly can't.'

'You fellas found Gabe Todd?' the old lady asked suddenly.

'Uh, not yet,' Jennings admitted.

'Now, listen up. I know how cops think – I've dated one or two – but there's no way that Gabe harmed Willie. They were real close, bin buddies fer a coon's age.'

Jennings raised his eyebrows, but the old lady continued.

'I guess they had some high ol' times in that little frat house back East. Drinkin', womanizin', goin' out to the game. That's a sacred thing, that kinda friendship.'

Jennings' eyebrows leapt another notch. Was it possible that Willie's mother was unaware of the nature of her son's relationship with Dr Todd? It would be a sterling feat of parental self-deception.

'Gabe,' she went on, 'he's got a fine, smart head on his shoulders.

278

Filled with crazy notions, no denyin' it, but there's not a peck o'bad in him.'

This was an entirely accurate diagnosis, in Jennings' opinion, but it was not yet the official or proven line. 'We still need to contact him in relation to our inquiries,' he intoned dully.

'Well, you be sure to let me see him when you do, boy,' Ma Rabblestack insisted, wagging the finger again.

'I'm not sure I can promise that,' he told her. 'Circumstances may—'

'Hear this, son,' the old lady cut in. 'I got a right to Willie's mortal remains. I aim to take him back to Texas for his final rest.' She paused, and her body sagged a little. 'All of him,' she murmured, jaggedly.

Suddenly Jennings understood. 'Oh, I see,' he said quietly. He clasped his hands together and bumped them on his knees. 'You don't want . . .'

Ma Rabblestack had lowered her head, her white hair flat across her face, falling into her lap. Her voice was low and throaty. 'I won't have Willie frozen in some vault like a . . .' She looked up at Jennings, and tears were rolling down her wrinkled face. She was every day of her sixty-six years. 'Like a goddamn TV dinner!' she choked, shaking her head. She wiped her nose on her sleeve and took a deep breath. 'Jest ain't *right*, Lord. Jest ain't right.'

They sat in silence for a few moments. Jennings was casting around for some way of resuming the conversation when the phone rang on the bedside table. Still sniffing, Ma Rabblestack leaned over and picked it up.

'Rabblestack. Uh-uh. He's right here.'

She offered the phone to Jennings and, as he took it, she walked round the bed and into the bathroom. Jennings could see her through the open door, washing her face.

It was Constable Mullery on the line.

'Got a call from that, er, woman who Todd was holed up with,' he said. 'She's identified the bloke who came to pick him up. Saw his picture in the paper. Get this, guvnor – it was Robert Spleen.'

'Wow – really?' Jennings said excitedly. 'What would Robert Spleen want with Todd, I wonder.'

'Fuck knows. So, what do you want? Get a couple of squad cars over to his office? Maybe chuck in some dogs?'

Jennings sighed. What was it with these coppers that they felt the job consisted exclusively of bombing around town at sixty miles an hour with sirens blazing?

He glanced into the bathroom again. The old lady was brushing her hair, an incongruously intimate thing to witness. He looked away.

'Mullery, this is not the hot pursuit of a desperate psychopath. I'll tootle over to Splendid Reach myself, and talk to Mr Spleen like a civilised human being. Stay by the phone, okay?'

There was an disgruntled snort. 'You're the guv'nor.'

'As of even date,' Jennings agreed. 'I'll see you.' He put down the phone and turned to the bathroom again. The old lady had disappeared.

'Mrs Rabblestack?' Jennings called. Her head appeared round the door. 'Ah, there you are. Look—'

'Son, could you help me here with this darned thing?' she asked irritably.

'Umm, certainly,' he replied, a little wary. He wasn't certain what the form was with old ladies' zippers and hooks.

As he stepped into the bathroom, she ducked under his arm and pulled the door shut behind her. There was a click of the key turning in the lock, and a triumphant little cackle.

'Mrs Rabblestack!' Jennings cried, reaching for the handle. He rattled it up and down. 'Mrs Rabblestack, this really isn't going to help, you know.'

He heard the door of the hotel room slam, and then silence. He turned and leaned slackly against the door, pursing his lips.

'Absolutely marvellous,' he breathed.

He looked across at the toilet, and saw his career going down it.

*   *   *

'Where's the smart money, you reckon?' Don asked Ellen in a low voice. They were standing looking out of the window, West London overcast and fuggy before them. Behind them, Unity and Gabriel were huddled in a corner, muttering conspiratorially, and Spleen could be seen through the doorway, talking to Casey.

Ellen shrugged. 'Does it matter? They're all as bonkers as each other. Fascinating, but bonkers. Why? You think you and Spleen are going in favourites?'

Don lipped a cigarette. 'I rarely take part in a game I don't think I can win. It's not ego, it's just . . . well, okay. It's ego.'

Ellen smiled. 'You don't think you're fighting a cause then?'

'Jesus, no. I've got no time for Spleen particularly. Though he has a well-stocked bar, which tends to endear a bloke to me.' He swigged his beer. 'And Todd? Well, sincere but misguided, like all fanatics.'

Ellen reached out and took Don's cigarette, and inhaled from it – a gesture so relaxedly intimate that Don took a swift over-the-shoulder look at Unity, to see whether she'd caught it. Ellen handed the Marlboro back to him, shaking her head.

'We shouldn't be flip,' she said. 'This isn't just a social game of rummy to them, you know. As far as they are concerned, lives depend on it. Certainly from Gabriel's point of view and – somehow – from Spleen's. I can smell a kind of fear on him. The outcome of this is desperately serious to these people. Don't underestimate what's at stake here.'

Don tutted. 'Oh, for Christ's sake, in real life, *nothing* depends on it. Willie's dead. This is a sort of displacement activity, to divert them all from that hard, boring fact.'

Ellen raised her eyebrows, questioningly.

'No, okay,' Don amended. 'That's a bit harsh. But, really, in the end, it's just a game.'

Ellen took the cigarette again, sucked in and then blew out two long plumes of smoke through her nostrils. 'Tell me,' she said. 'To you, what isn't?'

'Cricket,' Don came back immediately. 'But, I mean, this must just be a game to *you*. It's not like you have a real interest, any more than I do. This is a gag to you, isn't it?'

Ellen pursed her lips, and looked sideways out of the window for a moment. 'It's pretty funny, yeah.'

'See?' Don smiled, nodding. 'You're just mischievous. I knew it. I knew all that stuff about it being serious was so much bull.'

'Don,' Ellen said, and she turned and fixed him with her tropic-green gaze, 'the world is full of cretins who think that "funny" and "serious" are mutually exclusive. Don't be one of them.'

Spleen came back into the room, and closed the door behind him. 'Two minutes to,' he announced, looking at Ellen. 'Can we get on with it?'

'Of course,' she replied, turning back into the room. 'Will you all take your seats round the table, please?'

At that moment, a minicab drew up outside Splendid Reach. The driver turned to ask for the fare and a banded bundle of two hundred pounds sterling bounced off the bridge of his nose. The car door was swinging open, and a small leather-jacketed figure was scurrying up the steps to the entrance of the tower block, white hair streaming out behind like cartoon whizz lines.

As he flew backwards through the door of Mr Spleen's office, Casey Rushmore marvelled at the momentum that may be generated by a determined little old lady moving at high speed. The security guard in the lobby had been similarly amazed as he'd ricocheted off the reception desk.

'Ma!' Gabriel yelled, getting up from the table as Judy Rabblestack stepped over the sprawling Rushmore and surveyed the room through her mirror shades. Ignoring the disconcerted company, she put her hands on her hips and addressed Gabriel.

'I've come to take Willie home, Gabe,' she said grimly, 'and I don't plan to sit still for no fancy Yankee argufyin' 'fore I do it.'

Casey was scrambling to his feet. 'Mr Spleen, I'm really sorry. She just came out of nowhere. I'm really, really . . .'

Without taking his eyes from Ma Rabblestack, Spleen murmured, 'Get out, Casey.'

'She just barrelled through the office, you see . . .'

Spleen turned his gaze on the yammering Rushmore.

'*Get OUT, Casey!*' he roared.

The Senior Finance Controller blinked forlornly and his bottom lip quivered. As he backed sheepishly from the room, Spleen leaned across the table and took a cigarette from Don's pack. 'Christ All-fucking-mighty,' he muttered, lighting it.

Gabriel hurried round the table, glancing agitatedly at his watch. 'Ma, we need to talk,' he said. 'But this is really not the right time.'

Ma Rabblestack peered over the top of her shades. 'You 'spect me to wait outside in the buggy,' she suggested, indicating the table and the undealt cards, 'whilst you get a little action here, Gabe? Told ya, I'm takin' Willie home. Ain't nuthin' more to say about it. Now, iff'n you wanna—'

'Oh, come *on*, Ma!' Gabriel interrupted angrily. 'Where's Willie's home been for the last thirty years? Texas? Florida? Vegas, for Chrissake?'

'Willie's a Southern boy, Gabe,' the old woman insisted, jabbing a finger. 'He ain't some kinda scientific experiment fer you to—'

'I can *save* him, Ma!' Gabriel almost sobbed. He held up both hands, pacifyingly, swallowing hard. 'Listen, listen. You can have . . . You can take home Willie's body. Okay? I'd be pleased for you to take care of it, really . . .'

Ma Rabblestack stamped her foot in frustration. 'It ain't *enough*!'

Ellen stepped forward before Gabriel could retort.

'Excuse me,' she said. 'Could I please have a word with Mrs Rabblestack? We'll step into the outer office.'

Gabriel turned to Spleen, looking for an opinion. Spleen shrugged, and took a deep drag on his cigarette. 'This is developing into a most singular event,' he observed.

As she opened the door for Ma Rabblestack and followed her through it, Ellen was saying, 'Ma, my dad often speaks of that World Series showdown with Memphis McCluskey where you hit a third queen on Fourth Street. I was brought up on those stories . . .'

The door closed and there was a moment's silence. Don got up from the table and went to the executive fridge, from which he took a can of Bud.

'So that's the mother-in-law then, Gabriel, is it?' he inquired, pulling the tab. 'Rather you than me, mate.'

'Shut up, Don,' Unity advised, as Gabriel sat down again.

'Sorry,' he said, giving her a contrite smile. 'Just making conversation.'

He wandered over to the window, and looked out at Hammersmith roundabout. He was already feeling ashamed of the way he'd spoken to Unity earlier, but this seemed to be the pattern of his relationship with her. He'd push it; she'd bite; he'd lash out and then feel remorseful. If he was honest, he was as likely as she was, after such a spat, to be the crawler-back. In the wake of a row, he'd sit at his desk at work, looking at the phone, knowing that just a few apologetic words, an undignified but painless act of self-abasement, would lead to another few sessions snuffling around those enthralling stocking tops. Even now, so soon after winding her up to the point of violence, he was looking for a chance to get back on her good side.

The truth was, he realised, he liked it that way. Okay, the green-eyed Ellen was complex and unplumbable, an intriguing other. But with Unity, the *relationship* was complex, the *dynamic* was unplumbable. Being with Ellen was like tennis – your volley, her return. Your brilliant serve, her inspired lob. While the thing with Unity was a contact sport – Sumo – an apparent stasis composed of constant shifts in weight, aggression and balance. Two competitors locked in a single teetering mass. Sure, he was amazed by Ellen's backhand shots, and admiringly applauded them. But you can't applaud when you've got a couple of handfuls of buttock. You really don't need to.

Don pressed his forehead against the window, and chuckled. 'Then again, can't beat a little white tennis skirt,' he murmured under his breath.

The door opened, and Ellen ushered Ma Rabblestack into the room. The old lady was flexing her fingers, like someone about to administer a massage.

'People,' Ellen declared, 'we have a late entry. Ma Rabblestack has agreed to participate in our game. I think that you'll agree that she has as much right at this table as anyone. Due to a lack of alternative applicants, I shall be her partner.'

Gabriel Todd threw up his hands. 'This is totally absurd. She's a professional card player, for God's sake.'

'Gotta tell yer, Gabe,' Ma Rabblestack interjected, 'Happy Families ain't frequently dealer's choice in the games along Fremont Street.'

CHAPTER THIRTY-SIX

SPLEEN LIT ANOTHER CIGARETTE and glanced around the table.

Don, his partner, was opposite him, lounging insouciantly in his chair, a smoke lodged in the corner of his mouth. He was watching the cards skid across the table, eyes narrowed.

To Spleen's left sat Ellen, dealing the pack. She caught Spleen's gaze and smiled. Beyond her was Gabriel Todd, leaning forward on his elbows, picking up each card as it arrived in front of him. His eyes ran back and forth over them, and his fingers kept plucking them out of the fanned hand, arranging and rearranging.

On Spleen's immediate right, Unity was chewing her nails and staring at the cards skimming towards her as if they were knives. She fidgeted intermittently with her glasses, pushing them up her nose, adjusting the way they sat over her ears. Beside Unity was Ma Rabblestack, expressionless and sinister in her reflecting shades and leather jacket. She was completely still, except for her mouth, which she would twist to one side occasionally, in order to blow tobacco smoke over her shoulder.

Until Ma had arrived, Spleen had not taken the game entirely seriously. He hadn't believed that the outcome would be truly definitive. If he won – fine. Todd would almost certainly acquiesce. But Spleen was certain that, if he lost, he could busk some further fudge or compromise by pointing out that Todd still needed support in his dealings with the authorities, and protection from the processes of law and journalism. Now, however, there was the possibility that both men would come out of the game empty-handed. And Spleen could see no edge he could use to influence Ma. The head would be taken back to the States, and that would be that.

Suddenly, and with an emotional force that surprised him, Spleen realised that the issue would be settled, once and for all, by the result of this surreal nursery game. He was playing the house – no angle, no cut – and he *had* to win.

Ellen dealt the last of the cards and looked around, hooking her hair back with a thumb. 'As there are three teams, we'll play three complete games,' she said. 'Mr Spleen will begin the first game. When you're ready, Robert.'

Spleen picked up his cards and fanned them. The figures depicted were grotesque – there was something of Tenniel about the style. And they were hand-drawn, in coloured inks that were barely dry.

'Careful,' Ellen warned, as Spleen rubbed a thumb lightly across the face of a card. 'I was up all night making those.'

Spleen looked at the cards more closely and chuckled. The top card in his hand was Miss Betty Bunsen the Boffin's Daughter. It was a sharp-faced, pig-tailed lampoon of Unity Siddorn, prim in a white lab coat and sellotaped spectacles. Spleen slid it aside to see the next card – Mrs Mary Million the Magnate's Wife. She was dressed in a wide-shouldered pinstripe suit, of which the skirt was indecently short. An unflattering caricature of Spleen's own face peered out from under a heavy blonde fringe, the eyes glancing sidelong at an enormous pile of gold bars.

'Oh, that's not entirely fair,' Don remarked, looking up from his own hand and regarding Ellen with a pained grimace.

She twitched her eyebrows and gave an amused pout.

Spleen arranged his cards. He had another member of the Magnate family – Mr Montague Million, a cold-eyed, cigar-sucking depiction of avarice. Again the Middletort-Spleen features were satirised. Were it an heirloom, the Spleen family might have hidden such a portrait in the attic.

Spleen glanced at Ellen. She was sitting quietly, legs crossed, face impassive. Her artwork revealed in her a mischievous malice that Spleen found rather compelling.

She turned her jade eyes towards him. 'When you're ready, Robert,' she said.

Spleen nodded. 'Right. Umm ... Mrs Rabblestack, do you have the daughter of the Magnate family?'

Before Ma could reply, Ellen laid her cards face down on the table, and sucked in air. 'No, no, no,' she tutted. 'The traditional address is 'May I see Master Million the Magnate's Son?' Any other construct will lead to the forfeit of a turn. Please try it again.'

Spleen was unused to being reprimanded, but he swallowed and nodded and asked once more, using the appropriate terms. Ma Rabblestack, her eyes invisible behind the mirrors of her dark glasses, shifted her head slightly.

'Nope,' she said, deadpan.

'To me then,' Ellen said. 'Unity, may I see Mrs Egghead the Eternalist's Wife?'

Unity scanned her cards. 'Yes,' she admitted, and tossed a card across the table.

Ellen picked it up and slotted it into her hand. 'Thank you. And, still with Unity, may I see Mr Egghead the Eternalist?'

Again Unity studied her cards. 'No, you can't,' she told Ellen, with obvious relief. 'I haven't got it.'

Ellen shrugged, not displeased. 'Promising start, though. It's to you, Dr Todd.'

Gabriel concentrated on his hand for a few seconds and then gazed around the table. 'Ma,' he said, with a tremor of strain in his voice, 'may I see Mr Melody the Minstrel?'

Ma Rabblestack's cards were folded face down on the table in front of her. Without hesitation or expression, she said, 'Nope.'

Gabriel gave an exasperated sigh and slid down in his seat, still with his eyes focused on the cards in his hand.

Don was slumped almost horizontal in the chair to Gabriel's left. He raised his eyes towards Ellen.

'My go, right?'

She nodded. Don hiked himself out of his slouch and leaned forward on the table. 'Right. Ellen, may I see Mrs Egghead the Eternalist's Wife?'

Ellen tossed the card across the table with a resigned grimace.

'Thanks,' Don said. 'And now, Ellen again, may I see Mr Egghead the Eternalist?'

Ellen skimmed another card towards Don.

'Fine,' Don remarked, scooping it up. He kept his eyes on Ellen. 'And may I see Miss Egghead the Eternalist's Daughter?'

Ellen tutted and flicked a third card across. Don plucked it almost out of the air and then laid the complete Eternalist family face up on the table. There were four caricatures of Gabriel Todd, each wearing white gowns and golden wings. Don sucked on his cigarette, blew out a jet of smoke and clicked his tongue off his teeth.

'Bob,' he told Spleen with a smug grin, 'we're laughing.'

The game progressed, and Spleen became increasingly convinced that his choice of Don as a partner was inspired. Certainly, Ma Rabblestack had the nerve, the blank face of a gambler, but this was not her game. And anyway, she – like Gabriel – appeared shaken by the thought of the prize. Both the Americans were making errors of logic as they framed their inquiries to the other players.

Unity, too, was flustered. Her disappointments and triumphs were nakedly expressed in groans and squeals. She apologised to Dr Todd for every failed speculative punt. Ellen, on the other hand, was dangerous and incisive – but she seemed as interested in the players as the cards. It occurred to Spleen that this may be the reason she was here – she was studying the people. He remembered a time when he had been that fascinated by his fellow human beings.

Don, though, was focused on nothing but the game. He affected nonchalance, all drooping cigarette and hand-held Bud, but his restless, flicking eyes were picking up clues, paths, possibilities, odds. He was a natural competitor.

Having drawn a blank on his own turn, Spleen looked at the cards on the table. Unity and Gabriel between them had collected three sets. Ellen and Ma Rabblestack had two. Don had five families ranged in front of him, and he himself had none. There were very few cards left, and it was Ellen's turn. She wouldn't need much luck to haul in the two remaining sets. As he watched her compile the last families, Robert Spleen reached inside his jacket and fingered the folded note from his secretary that he'd slipped into his pocket the previous evening.

Pls ring Dr Hunter urgently re X-rays.

He didn't want to make the call, and he didn't need to. He knew what it was about. He could feel it in his gut.

'Robert?' Ellen was saying. 'Hello?'

Spleen looked over at her. 'I'm sorry. What did you say?'

'I said, may I see Mr Titus Tock the Timekeeper?'

Spleen glanced at the sole card in his hand. It showed a skeleton in a sports blazer, holding a clipboard and a stopwatch.

'You're welcome to him,' he muttered, handing the card across.

'The scores after the first round,' Ellen announced, writing them on a whiteboard behind the executive desk, 'are Spleen five, Rabblestack four, Todd three. We'll take a ten-minute break before Round Two.'

Don stood up and helped himself to another beer from the fridge, then wandered through to the outer office. Casey was gone, so he slumped into the secretary's swivel chair and put his feet up on the desk. Spleen came in, closing the connecting door behind him. He was carrying a bottle of mineral water and smoking one of Ma Rabblestack's Lucky Strikes. He coughed on it as he lowered himself into the leather couch and undid the buttons of his waistcoat.

'A very good start,' he said to Don. 'You're a natural games player.'

Don swigged from the can of Bud and tapped a Marlboro out of the pack. 'We were lucky early on. People were giving their hands away. It was getting tougher towards the end as everyone constructed strategies.'

'Hmm. I think the old lady's a little shaky. About halfway through the game, she asked me for a card that, as it turned out, she already had.'

'Mrs Allah-Kazam the Almighty's Wife,' Don nodded. He screwed up one eye against the smoke that was curling from the cigarette in his mouth. 'At that point it was deducible that only you or she could have had it. Ellen was holding at least two of the others in that set. Ma asked for the card so that Ellen would know you hadn't got it. She picked it up from Ma on her next go.'

'Ah,' Spleen nodded, deflated. 'I must admit I didn't see that.'

'You're playing too much as an individual. You have to remember that we're a team here.'

Spleen hunched forward in his seat. 'Perhaps we could come up with some kind of simple method by which to communicate. Subtle hand signals, or a verbal code . . .'

Don laughed and swung his feet off the desk.

'Now that,' he said, taking the cigarette from his mouth and pointing at Spleen, 'sounds like cheating. There's no fun in winning if you cheat.' He stood up and stretched, flexing his shoulders and rolling his head from side to side. 'It's only a game, Bob,' he continued, picking his beer off the desk. 'It's not life and death.'

Don did some quick mental arithmetic as he took his seat again. Three games – a total of thirty-six tricks. Winning eighteen would clinch it, but fifteen would probably do. Don mentally set himself a target of six tricks in this round, giving a running total of eleven. Dumb luck would bring three or four in, so all he had to do was actively win two.

Making this calculation, Don barely considered Spleen's contribution. Despite having scolded his partner about teamwork, Don was not naturally a team man. In the end, he would rather the responsibility, the congratulation and the blame were his alone. He had no patience with players who were not up to his standards, and he hated to be carried by those better than him. So – he focused his sights on fifteen tricks, and single-mindedly set about winning them.

He got lucky at the start of Round Two – he was dealt all four members of the Hedonist family, each of whom wore his own face. Mr Harry Hangett the Hedonist was depicted as a dissipated, dishevelled rake, his arms slung round the shoulders of two women who bore a striking resemblance to Unity and Ellen. He made Don feel quite unsavoury.

For maximum psychological impact, Don declared his set before the others had even arranged their hands. He was pleased to note Unity's unconcealed dismay at this, and made a note to take a card – any card – off her at the first opportunity, simply to disconcert her further. On a personal level, he felt slightly uneasy about this, but the game was the game. It would be dishonest not to press the advantage.

Within ten minutes, there were only three sets unclaimed. Don had a pretty good idea where all the cards were. If he could bring in one set with his first request, a simple process of elimination would secure the other two straightaway, giving his team a score of eleven going into the last round.

He glanced at his hand. He was holding Mr Mordecai Melody the Minstrel and his daughter Maybelline – Willie's twinkling smile in stereo – and Miss Millie Million the Magnate's Daughter. The other two Minstrels were shared between Unity and Spleen – but who had which?

Don's eyes flicked between Unity and Spleen. He grimaced and bit his bottom lip.

'Okay,' he said, finally. 'Unity, may I see Mrs Melody the Minstrel's Wife?'

Unity yelped with delight. 'No!' she squealed. 'No, you bloody can't!'

Spleen, groaning, put a hand to his face and shook his head. Ma cleaned up the Magnates and Unity took the last two sets.

'Spleen eight, Rabblestack seven, Todd nine,' Ellen called, writing the scores on the board. 'Take a break, people. We'll resume on the hour – you've got thirteen minutes.'

In a tone that brooked no argument, the church clock by the roundabout struck six.

Gabriel picked up his orange juice and walked over to the window. He patted the canister on the table by the emergency exit, and then looked away, closing his eyes. Unity came up beside him and put an arm round his waist.

'We're in the lead, Gabe,' she said softly, encouragingly. 'We're going to win.'

He laid a hand on her shoulder. 'We'd better,' he croaked.

She looked up sideways at his face, and saw tears collecting on his dark lashes.

'Pride,' he murmured. 'That's always been my problem. If I'd just given in to Spleen, Willie would have been safe and I'da been able to work. I should have just said, sure, it's a workable arrangement, let's do it. But now Ma's here, I can't even do that.'

Unity hugged her arm tight round him. 'The odds are still in our favour, Gabe.'

'Yeah,' he said tonelessly.

As they stood in silence, staring down into the street, a large white van turned off the Hammersmith Bridge Road into the car park of Splendid Reach. Gabriel leaned forward and craned to watch it pull into a space. Two men got out and looked up at the building.

'Yes!' Gabriel breathed. He turned to Unity, putting his hands on her shoulders, and glanced at the others in the room. 'I'm going downstairs for a coupla minutes.' He checked his watch. 'There's plenty of time.'

Unity, puzzled, peered down at the car park. 'Who are those men?'

Gabriel spoke quickly. 'They're from an organisation called Double or Quits. They've got a truck full of kit down there to keep Willie safe until we can get him to their installation in the West Country. I won't be long.' He strode towards the door. 'Just gonna get some air,' he told the others.

Ellen got up from her seat. 'Good idea,' she said. 'I'll come with you.'

Unity turned back to the window, idly pinging the cuff of her latex glove. She saw Gabriel stroll across the car park and shake hands with the men from Double or Quits. Ellen wandered over to sit on a low wall and lit a cigarette. After shaking hands, Gabriel gestured towards the van, and the driver unlocked the back doors, inviting Gabriel to take a look. He ducked inside, followed by both the men, and the doors were pulled shut.

Unity was sure that if she and Gabriel won the game, everything would turn out right. There would be no question of prison. Even the detective, David Jennings, didn't really seem to believe that that was a possibility. And he, in the end, was a cop, albeit an unusually reasonable one.

'I want three vans of thugs,' Jennings yelled, 'a squadron of cars with bells and sirens, and all the big, nasty dogs the kennels can offer.'

He had a career to think of.

Banging on the walls of the hotel bathroom had got him nowhere, so Jennings had put the plug in the bath, turned on all the taps and waited for the overflow. Eventually the people downstairs had complained.

He squelched furiously across the forecourt of the police station in his sodden Hush Puppies, and climbed into the passenger seat of a souped-up unmarked Sierra. He turned to Mullery, who was looking innocently delighted in the driver's seat.

'Get going then,' he ordered, waving an irritated hand at the windscreen. 'Preferably without due care and attention.'

CHAPTER THIRTY-SEVEN

UNITY HEARD THE SIRENS far off in the distance, and thought nothing of it. Suddenly a fleet of police cars appeared around the Fulham side of the roundabout and screeched into Hammersmith Bridge Road. They pulled up on the far side of the dual carriageway, and dozens of policeman tumbled out, holding up hands to stop the traffic as they leapt the central reservation and made towards Splendid Reach. Acting Detective Inspector Jennings was in the middle of the wash of blue that swept across the forecourt and narrowed on the door of the building.

Looking down to her left, Unity saw Gabriel's head appear briefly from the back doors of the van, and then withdraw.

'What the fuck's going on?' came a voice from behind her. It was Don, and then the others, crowding to peer out of the window at the street below.

'Perfect,' Robert Spleen muttered, turning from the window. The phone on his desk rang, and he picked it up. 'Yes,' he said in reply to a gabbled squeak emerging from the handset. 'Thank you. I'd noticed.' He slammed the phone down and looked around the room, planning. He'd been caught up in police raids before, and he knew that clarity of thought was vital. 'Right. Dr Todd's on his own. Nothing we can do to help. But the head needs to be hidden.'

As he stepped towards the table on which the canister stood, Unity realised that the moment he picked it up, it would be his. She lunged forward and grabbed it, hugging it to her chest.

Spleen stopped mid-stride. 'Unity, we have very little time,' he said calmly. 'If the police get Willie, all our differences of opinion will be academic.'

Unity looked at him, his hand extended towards her. She turned towards Ma Rabblestack, who reached out her arms and peered over the top of her shades.

'Gimme mah boy, honey,' the old lady said quietly.

Unity backed away, gripping the canister to her chest, until the small of her back was touching the bar on the fire door. She looked pleadingly at Don, who was staring straight back at her, his head lowered slightly, his expression thoughtful.

Don's mind ticked rapidly as he held her gaze for a moment, taking in the anguished indecision on her face. He glanced sideways, first at Spleen to his left, and then at Ma Rabblestack to his right. Unity was asking him for a pointer – she wanted to know how to choose. Jesus, he was the *last* person to ask.

His eyes flicked from side to side again, as if he could weigh the justice of the claims being made. But it wasn't fair – not all the claimants were present. It was a bum deal, and it should be re-thrown. New game. Don raised his eyebrows, exhaled and clucked his tongue against his teeth.

'If you want my advice . . .' he said in a measured tone – and suddenly, in a burst, he leapt forward, his leg outstretched. His foot smacked against the crash bar on the emergency door behind Unity, and it banged open into the stairwell.

'RUN!' Don yelled, shoving her through the doorway.

Unity staggered out onto the dim landing, as Don pulled the door shut behind her. She could hear scuffling from the office she'd left. Don was buying her time.

She started down the stairs, still hugging the container to her stomach, and wincing as she steadied herself on the banister with her scalded, latex-covered hand. She had reached the first half-landing when she heard heavy running footsteps coming towards her from deep below in the stairwell.

'Shit!' she gasped, and turned back. She scurried past the door to Spleen's office, and kept going up. She was on the ninth floor. To her right was the door to the computer room which she knew was locked. To her left was the last flight of stairs that led to the roof. She ran up. Thudding against the crash bar, almost tumbling, she dashed out onto the roof of Splendid Reach. Behind her, raised on scaffolding, was the blue neon Splendid logo.

She put her rubber-gloved hand to her mouth and looked around in panic. There was nowhere to go.

'You *stupid* fucking cow!' she screamed. She turned back to the door, and could hear the echoing thuds of coppers' feet bounding up the stairs towards her. She trotted forward to the low wall that ran round the edge of the roof. Directly below her, at the door to the building, stood a little blue cluster of policemen. She moved round the wall, so that she was looking into the car park, and there was Gabriel, crouched behind the van, out of sight of the police, peering up.

Unity leaned over the side.

'Gabriel!' she yelled. 'GABE! GABE! LOOK!'

He raised his head and saw her, and then peered around the fender of the van towards the policemen. He waved at her.

Unity held out the canister. 'LOOK!'

Gabe nodded, and held his thumbs up.

Unity shook her head. She pointed over her shoulder. 'THE POLICE! THE POLICE ARE COMING!'

Gabriel simply stared up for a moment and then raised a hand, telling her to wait. He ran in a crouch to the driver's door of the van.

Unity turned round and looked at the door that led to the stairs. She put the canister down and, panting with fear, ran over and pushed it shut. Once the policemen got to Spleen's office, it might take them a minute to work out where she'd gone. She scurried back to the wall. The white van was nosing towards the street, and Gabriel had moved further along the car park, out of sight of the main door. He indicated that she should come along the wall level with him.

Unity picked up the canister and jogged to her left. Gabriel raised both hands, in a gesture that meant 'relax'. Then he mimed the unscrewing of the canister. Unity gasped. Again, Gabriel twisted his outstretched fingers above his other clenched fist. Unity let out a squeak of disbelief, and unclipped the lid of the canister. Pulling it into her chest with one elbow, she turned the lid until it came free. A cloud of white billowed out from under the lid as she lifted it, and laid it on the wall.

She looked down at Gabriel, terrified that he might suggest what she suddenly realised was the obvious solution. He did. He mimed a scooping motion, and then drew back his arm and flung an invisible football up at her.

'NO!' she screamed. 'I CAN'T! PLEASE, GABE! I CAN'T!'

He nodded, completely certain that she could. He mimed the throw again, like he had on the patch of park by the Thames the day Willie had died. *Pull your arm back, way back. Push through the ball. Look where you want it to go . . .*

Unity shook her head hopelessly. 'I can't,' she gulped.

Gabriel was making beckoning motions, very calm. He was shaking his legs, loosening them, ready to run.

'I can't, I can't,' Unity sobbed, as she plunged her latex-gloved hand into the canister. Her fingers curled round the solid lump inside and she tipped the canister away from her. Liquid nitrogen hissed onto the wall in a cloud of steam, evaporating into nothing. Willie's head rolled forward into Unity's right hand. Without actually looking at the horror she was holding, she steadied it with the fingers of her left hand, and felt the skin of her fingertips harden and crack, painless in the unimaginable cold.

Suddenly, the door behind her burst open and Unity turned to see David Jennings run out onto the roof.

'Unity!' he yelled as he ran towards her – and then he pulled up short and his shoulders dropped.

'Sweet Heaven,' he breathed, 'what are you doing?'

Unity turned away from him, and pulled her arm back.

'GABRIEL!' she screamed – and with every horrified iota of strength in her body she launched Willie Rabblestack's brittle head into the air.

It was an inexpert and terrible throw, sliced wildly towards the street. Gabriel started forward as he saw Unity shape up for the pitch, but adjusted mid-stride as he assessed the trajectory. He ran sideways, his eyes on the spinning head, sprinting towards the Hammersmith Bridge Road. He glanced to his left, and saw that he was about to collide with a parked car. He shot forward round it, taking himself too close to the building. Willie's head – Willie's precious, beautiful, porcelain head – was dropping behind him, and way to the left. Gabriel back-pedalled, almost level with the corner of Splendid Reach now. As he leapt the low wall that ran along the sidewalk, and twisted to sprint away from the building, a policeman spotted him.

'Hey, there he is!'

Two or three cops had started in his direction.

Linebackers, Gabriel thought instinctively. And he realised, in a click of insight, that that was the way to think. It was the last minute of the fourth quarter, and he was going for the final touchdown. He'd done it a hundred times – it was easy. He pushed his feet hard into the sidewalk and accelerated to meet the path of the ball. Cheerleaders were spelling his name in a chant, and the boys from the frat house were on their feet in the bleachers.

'Go Bills!' Gabriel silently urged himself, single-minded, oblivious, diving full length towards the falling head. 'Go Bills!' he yelled, his eye on the ball, both arms straining towards the ol' pigskin.

He stretched and grasped, and Willie's head bobbed on his fingertips.

It balanced for a moment as Gabriel tried to grasp it, and then bounced up into the air again. Gabriel hit the ground face down, his hands empty. He was sobbing even before he hit the concrete. He pressed his face into the paving stones, clasping his hands to his ears, not wanting to hear it – the shattering of the unreclaimable.

'Oh, sweet boy,' he wept, 'I'm so sorry.'

He felt the paving stones cold against his cheek – and he slammed his forehead hard against concrete, as it seemed he always had. Clasping his arms round the back of his neck, he howled into the pavement.

It was all gone.

A foot nudged his ribs, and he looked up. It was Ellen, holding out her jumper, cradling something there.

'Can you take this, please?' she asked reasonably. 'It can't be good for the cashmere.'

Gabriel blinked at her through his tears.

'Plus,' she added, nodding towards the building, 'large policemen are imminent.'

Gabriel scrambled to his feet and lifted his lover's frozen head from her sweater. Ten yards ahead of him, the white van was pulling away in low gear, the back doors open and the man from Double or Quits yelling at him to get a bloody move on. The skin on Gabriel's hands bubbled with cold burns as he leapt into the van, and it revved away.

'Thank you,' he yelled from the doorway. 'Thank you! Thank you!'

Ellen waved, and turned to the panting policemen who were lumbering up to her. She fixed them with her bright green eyes, and pushed her jet hair from her forehead.

'I simply cannot wait to find out what you're going to charge me with,' she told them.

Don watched Ellen walk back to the building, apparently leading the bemused coppers. He shook his head, smiling, amazed at her. He turned back into the room to see Spleen and Ma Rabblestack leaving through the outer office.

Pulling a fresh pack of cigarettes from the pocket of his denim jacket, he sat on the windowsill. He looked at the card table, the Happy Families deck neatly stacked in its centre, waiting to be dealt for the final round. Pushing himself up from the sill, he walked to the table and flipped the top card. It was Miss Betty Bunsen the Boffin's Daughter – Unity's quizzical, intense face on the body of a little girl.

He pictured Unity, up on the roof with the plainclothes detective, and knew that she must be in a hell of a state. He could see her crouched and sobbing. She'd been pursued, probably arrested, and she'd just flung her career off the top of an office block. She was going to need looking after.

We're all connected to those around us, Donald. It was his father's voice. *And we have a duty to each other, bourgeois as you may consider that notion.*

Don pulled out a cigarette and, without thinking, tapped it against the packet. He recognised the gesture immediately. The cigarette should have been a Senior Service and the tapping hand should have been cuffed by the sleeve of a honey cardigan, but the gesture was his dad's.

. . . you might think differently one day.

Someone had to get her through this – just through the next couple of weeks maybe – and he was the only one who could do it. He sighed. A couple of weeks, a month tops. And there would be the payoff – the sex would be tremendous. He snapped his Zippo, lit the cigarette, and walked towards the emergency door.

Handle today, he thought, and sort the big stuff out tomorrow.

'Where do you think you're going?' demanded the copper who was blocking the door to the stairs.

'Good question, mate,' Don told him wearily, 'but one I try to avoid.'

'You what?'

Don pointed at the ceiling. 'I want to go up and sort out my girlfriend,' he said.

'No chance, son,' the policeman replied, crossing his arms.

'Suit yourself,' Don shrugged, turning. 'I'll take the lift.'

He walked through the door that led to the outer office, and was just passing the desk when the phone rang. He paused, looked at it for a moment, and then picked it up.

'Miss Goodbody speaking,' he trilled. 'How can I help you?'

'I hope you know how to post bail,' Ellen said, 'otherwise we might have to postpone dinner.'

'Jesus!' Don exclaimed. 'Have you been nicked?'

'No, it's okay. But I'm not to leave town, so eloping's out of the question. Come down to the foyer. I'm feeling a bit flaky to tell you the truth, and I really need to go for a beer.'

She hung up.

Don put down the phone, leaving his hand resting on it. He lowered his head and screwed his eyes tight shut.

'Great,' he muttered under his breath. 'Now what?'

He took a drag from his cigarette and walked out to the corridor, his head hung low, his eyes fixed on the carpet a few paces ahead of him. As he arrived at the elevator, the bell pinged and the door slid open. Don loped in, expressionless with contemplation.

The doors closed and Don looked at the panel of buttons. He reached towards them, one finger extended. The finger hovered and drifted.

'Oh, God,' Don muttered, dropping his hand to his side. He sucked on his cigarette. 'Where to then, bub?' he asked himself aloud. 'Up or down? Down or up?' He leant against the side wall of the elevator and, tipping his head back, blew a jet of smoke against the ceiling.

'It's a tough one,' he admitted. He turned his head to one side and looked long and hard at the floor buttons, biting his bottom lip.

'That really is a tough one,' he said again. 'How long have I got?'

ENDPIECE

HAVING TOLD HIS COLLEAGUES he was going for lunch, Ray England walked down the stairs to Departures, heading towards the Harrods concession, where he was to pick up Mrs Davenport who worked on Parfumerie.

In the two years since his divorce, Ray's life had been devoid of romantic interest, but his friendship with Irene Davenport, though in no way improper, was showing signs of blossoming. She was a delicate creature, Irene, the English rose type, all blush and flutter, as a woman should be. She didn't know much about the seamier side, having spent all her life in scents, so she was impressed and delightedly horrified by Ray's stories of encounters with currency smugglers, drug couriers and other assorted scum. She made Ray feel like a bastion of British decency, stemming the tide of insidious foreign filth.

She waved and picked up her handbag as he appeared on the concourse in front of the store.

'You're looking lovely today, Irene,' he told her as she teetered towards him.

'Flatterer,' she laughed, and smacked him gently on the lapel of his uniform.

As they were walking back across the concourse, heading for Garfunkel's by Gate 16, Ray's attention was caught by a commotion around the X-ray machines that let out onto the flight side. A tall, aquiline man in denim and longish hair was arguing with the security guards, apparently refusing to put his luggage through the scanners.

Ray had very little time for the security people, with their invented liveries and their spurious authority. There was always the very real danger that an average traveller might mistake one of them for a customs officer – a mere bouncer confused with a servant of Her Majesty.

'Just better sort this out,' he told Irene. 'Duty calls. Won't be a tick.'

With an air of one who has been in the business more than a week, he strolled over to the conveyor belt, and was pleased to note that Irene followed him, a pace behind.

'What seems to be the trouble here?' he asked. 'Nothing we can't sort out, I'm sure.' He could feel Irene at his shoulder, practically pressing against his serge.

The traveller turned, and gave a cocky smile. 'Are you in charge around here, officer?' he asked.

Ray recognised the face – it was his job to remember faces. This was the bloke who, a couple of weeks before, had tried to get smart with the syringes and saws and all that disgusting equipment. The queer one.

'Leave this to me, lads,' Ray told the brownshirts. He glanced back at Irene, who was looking on with fascinated, wide eyes.

'May I see your passport, sir?' he asked the American.

It was handed over with a shrug and Ray flicked through it. Gabriel Paul Todd. Date of Birth: 22nd July 1948 – the same year as Ray himself. Old enough to know better, in other words.

'And what seems to be the problem?' he inquired, handing the passport back.

Dr Todd indicated the silver canister on the table beside him. 'This is not going through the X-ray machine. I have special documentation.' He offered a sheet of paper bearing the crest of the Metropolitan Police. Ray took it and scanned it.

'Had a brush with the law, sir, have we, whilst we've been in the country?'

The American grinned his clever-clogs grin again. 'We had a slight misunderstanding, but it worked itself out.'

Ray re-read the chitty from the Commissioner of the Met. It gave incontrovertible dispensation for the man's carry-on to circumvent the rules. Ray's moustache tick-tocked, and he turned his head far enough to see Irene, hard by his side, glancing between him and the Yank.

'And may I ask,' Ray suggested firmly, 'what is contained within this receptacle?'

The man laughed. 'Sure,' he allowed. 'But I'm not going to tell you.'

Ray's moustache stiffened. The bloke was pushing his luck.

'Right,' Ray demanded. 'Open it.'

Dr Todd gave a look of exaggerated boredom, his head dropping to one side. 'Aww, you don't really want me to do that.'

Ray checked Irene again. She was alongside him now, desperately curious and alight with admiration.

'Yes, *sir*,' Ray said, with just a touch of authoritative sarcasm. 'I really do want you to do that.'

A resigned expression came over the American's face, but he still had that superior smile on. Ray knew that he could wipe it off. He could keep the bloke here all day, if necessary. He was going to show this smart aleck that it didn't pay to play silly buggers with HM Customs and Excise. While the American unclipped the lid of the canister, Ray turned his head again to Irene. She gave him an encouraging furrow of the brow, and he returned it with a wink.

Steam erupted from beneath the lifted lid of the canister and billowed across the table. Both Ray and Irene craned forward to look inside, but they could see only mist.

Dr Gabriel Todd leaned over the cloud of white and looked up at the customs officer and his lady friend.

'Gaze deep,' he told them, smiling like death. He puckered his lips, and blew.

There was a brief hiatus – and then a shocked, feminine shriek and the thud of an English rose hitting linoleum.

Gabriel Todd made his flight. Ray England never remarried.

MITCHELL SYMONS

All In

Steve Ross has had enough. Of gambling. Of losing. Of feeling bad about losing. Of worrying about what he's going to do when he's lost it all (the money, that is, followed by the wife and kids).

So naturally enough he makes a bet with himself. If his gambling account is in the black at the end of the year, he'll carry on. If it isn't, he'll top himself and leave Maggie to cop the insurance. That way, at least the kids are looked after, and he can escape the hell his life is fast becoming.

With Steve's luck it could go either way. But one thing's a dead cert. For the next twelve months he's going to experience the thrill of the ultimate high-stakes games . . .

Set in the twilight world of all-night poker games, betting shop coups and spread-betting mania, Mitchell Symons' debut novel is the darkly funny diary of one man dicing with death.

0 7472 7316 2

review